The Scarred Wrists

by

V M Steele

First published 1935 by Stanley Paul & Co. Ltd. London

V. M. Steele was one of the pseudonyms used by V M Firth, more commonly known as Dion Fortune.

Library and Archives Canada Cataloguing in Publication

Steele, V. M., author
    The scarred wrists / V. M. Steele.

Previously published: 1935.
ISBN 978-1-896238-20-3 (softcover)

    1. Title

PR6011.I72S33 2017   823'.912   C2017-902917-7

TWIN EAGLES PUBLISHING
Box 2031
Sechelt BC
V0N 3A0
pblakey@telus.net
twineaglespublishing.com
2017

Foreword

The Teller of Tales

You, gentle reader, hold in your hands an invitation to an unusual, twofold adventure.

This novel, *The Scarred Wrists*, is an adventure story, and even a fairy tale, one in which the lowly are raised up, the mighty rebuked, and the evil get what they deserve. But the fact that you are able to read it is also an adventure, since the book itself has been for so long itself ignored, disavowed, and rejected.

Now, through the kind offices of the British Library, and the work of Twin Eagles Publishing, the V. M. Steele novels are becoming available to a wider audience than they have ever known.

It is very likely that, if you are looking at this book, you are interested in it because of the author, so it's probably useful first to talk about this novel in the context of her other works.

The Scarred Wrists is the first of a set of four novels published by Violet Mary Firth (1890-1946) under the name V. M. Steele. Unlike the novels she published under her most famous pen-name, Dion Fortune, these are not, overtly, "occult".

The Scarred Wrists was published in 1935, in the same year as *The Winged Bull*, the first of Dion Fortune's series of initiatory novels: novels deliberately constructed to provide not only the emotional reorientation but also some of the information that might be transmitted in an initiation. Two articles, describing her aims and methods in the initiatory novels, were published in her Society of the Inner Light house magazine. These have recently been republished in *Dion Fortune's Rites of Isis and of Pan* (edited by Gareth Knight, 2013). They are well worth reading.

Those articles do not mention her V. M. Steele books at all. However, when the novels are read in the light of the articles, and set next to the Dion Fortune novels published at the same time, it is hard to avoid feeling that the same project was at work in both sequences of books. In other words, the V.M. Steele novels are also intended, through imaginative identification with a central character, to trigger in the reader an initiatory awakening.

There are clear similarities in certain bits of stage machinery between The Winged Bull and The Scarred Wrists: both involve a slum-based "secret hideout" that is far nicer inside than out; both involve characters caught between the spiritual destructiveness of an oppressive, self-satisfied respectability and vengeful, underworld criminality; both involve a romance between a man and woman who are of very different classes and backgrounds, but who are brought together by other qualities.

A major difference, however, is that The Scarred Wrists has no initiating adept: it is less The Tempest than it is "Beauty and the Beast." If there is a stage-managing Prospero, it is the voice of the story-teller, which calls forth the whole extravagant drama—and finishes it off with a casual gesture.

The novel takes place in a Britain well after the First World War: internal evidence suggests it occurs after 1920, when the post-War gun control legislation took effect. This is not the stereotypical Britain of subtlety and sophisticated restraint, but the Britain of riverside gangs, blackmailers, and detectives (and police) who work very close to, and across, the borders of legality. The male protagonist suffers from poor health, and from what is now called post-traumatic stress—not as a result of the War, but as a result of serving hard time in prison, preceded by a difficult childhood. The female protagonist has had a similar experience of familial rejection; for this and other reasons, the two characters are immediately drawn to each other when they meet through a plot device no doubt borrowed from a Sherlock Holmes Story.

The story that unfolds is something of a pell-mell combination of madcap comedy and film noir, and comedy it ultimately is. Despite the generally unapologetic violence, the casual cruelty, and neurotic self-destructiveness, there is underneath and within it all a sense of glee, and the coming into its own of a kind of savage innocence that makes a place for its new life in the decaying ruins of the old.

* * *

It has been said that the difference between an expert in a field and a scholar of the field is that an expert knows everything worth knowing about a subject, and a scholar knows everything. Things are not so clear-cut: even mere experts have to know more than what's worth knowing in order to be sure they haven't missed anything.

I make no claim to being a scholar, or even an expert, but I am vastly curious. Violet Firth—Dion Fortune—is a very interesting figure for anyone curious about the overlap between the daylight world of psychology and psychotherapy, and the night, or twilight, world of occultism and magic. And for the curious, there are few things as intriguing as those one is warned away from, or solemnly told are not worth knowing, or are better not known. This is especially true for someone with even a little of the old-fashioned psychoanalytic suspiciousness that finds bored dismissal almost as much of a red flag as passionate rejection.

When I had a little extra time, then, in London, I made a special point of looking up these novels. I was fully prepared to find them as trivial as they were said to be—but I wanted to see for myself. I set myself a program of reading at both the British Library and at the Wellcome Library up the street (which holds books and papers by significant early practitioners of psychotherapy and medical psychology). I did spend some time at the Wellcome, looking into its collection of materials on and by Dr. Lillias Hamilton, who was Warden of Studley Agricultural College when Violet Firth was there. But, finally, I was unable to tear myself away from the V.M. Steele novels. I had to get through them: even if it cut into my time at the Wellcome, I thought the time well spent. I still do.

I have come to see these novels as energetic expressions of the same project that shaped the later occult novels: not the work of someone in decline or in retreat, not simply the work of a compulsive story teller, but the work of someone for whom psychoeducational intervention and initiatory drama had become two aspects of one pursuit.

But this is now your book, awaiting your response. For you, dear reader, the curtain is about to rise. See what you shall see; hear what you shall hear, and enjoy the tale.

Richard Brzustowicz, April, 2017

THE SCARRED WRISTS

By

V. M. STEELE

"The Pharmakos was a purification of this sort of old. If a calamity overtook the city they led forth as a sacrifice the most unsightly of them all as a purification and remedy for the suffering city. Him they called the Pharmakos. And they gave food into his hands, and smote him seven times with the boughs of wild figs and other wild plants. Finally they burnt him with fire of the wood of fruitless trees and scattered the ashes into the sea and to the winds for a purification of the suffering city."

Tzetzes.

CHAPTER I

IT is a terrible thing to be born with red hair into the midst of a mouse-coloured family. For one thing, people with red hair are usually also a skin short; and people who might politely be described as near-black in their looks often have a few extra skins to compensate them. Strained relations are apt to ensue, to the infinite discomfort of both parties. Mr. Stone used to declare that it was nothing to do with him when Patricia's temperament came up for discussion, pursing up his lips into a bitter line and looking out of the window as he declared it. Mrs. Stone would flush an angry magenta and reply: "I deny that." Helen, the eldest, would flush a painful pink and say: "Need we discuss this before the children?" and the children, who had been paying no attention, would prick up their ears.

When Patricia left school at eighteen, Mrs. Stone thought that he ought to help Helen with the younger children. Helen thought so, too. Consequently Patricia helped Helen. But it is not a good thing to employ as general trot-about, whipping post, lady's maid, and universal what-not, a person with red hair. Mr. Stone came home from harassing days on the Stock Exchange to be met with tales of woe. Neither is it a good thing to meet with tales of woe a gentleman who has paid cash for commodities that are going down, and has bought "on tick" commodities that are going up. Mr. Stone said the equivalent of "a plague on both your houses," and when the friction culminated in Patricia flinging an entire tea-tray on the floor at her mother's feet, he decided that the young person of whom he always spoke to his wife as "your child," had better be trained for wage-earning, this being especially desirable in view of the fact that the commodities in which he dealt were dipping and soaring like swallows in a manner that bore no relation whatever to his calculations.

Helen and Mrs. Stone set to work, and they sought out a secretarial training-school in the near neighbourhood which had two advantages; firstly, it was for one sex only, the female sex, thus avoiding any possibility of Patricia being led into temptation. Mrs. Stone always seemed to be convinced that Patricia would prove much more vulnerable in the face of temptation than Helen. Secondly, being within a penny bus-run, Patricia would not be exposed to the risks and expenses of a daily journey into the vastnesses of the city of London, which they visited as seldom as if they had lived in Cornwall or Cumberland.

It is not an ideal plan to put a person with red hair to learn shorthand and typewriting and office routine, but Patricia was truly thankful to escape from the role of rag-doll between two puppies for which she was cast when her mother and Helen decided she should make herself useful in the home, and she buckled down to her shorthand and her typing and her ledgers, and threw the whole of her fiery red-headed soul into the task of making herself independent of a family that loved her not and permitted her no rest for the sole of her foot.

From her earliest days, when the family was being introduced to strangers, Patricia was accustomed to hear them say: "And who is the other little girl?" For the Stones were stony in more than name; they were narrow-hipped, narrow-shouldered city weeds, with faces like slices of cake. Whereas Patricia was cast in a more generous if less fashionable mould.

Young thing though she was, she was deep-bosomed; her neck rose like a column from her strong young shoulders; her arms were rounded, with dimples where the rest of the little Stones had sinews. Her eyes were set wide apart, and of the amazing blue that sometimes goes with red hair, and her skin was of the creamy magnolia white that by a great effort sometimes acquires two, or at most three freckles, to the horror of its owner, though others may not regard them with the same distaste.

And she was alive, so very much alive. Every golden-red hair was alive with a life of its own. The sallow, narrow Stones were no match for her save by weight of numbers.

But one can not carry on an unequal fight indefinitely, even if one has hair that stands out like a fiery aureole round one's head, looking as if, were one to get even a little angrier, it would stand straight on end. One gets tired-one gets very tired of it all. Of the endless pecking and nagging and steady pressure and lack of friendliness and goodwill; for red heads are friendly and sociable things, never very happy when driven to seek safety in solitude. The cat that walked by itself was not a sandy cat. Pat would have been sweet-natured, given a chance; but she was not given a chance in the bosom of the Stones. Consequently, she grew into a most redoubtable and rebellious little fighter, who would listen to reason from no one and go no way but her own, which everybody agrees is disastrous in one so young. Though perhaps it is better, on the whole, to survive as oneself, though battered, than to become extinct through trying to be a Stone.

Matters were not improved when the course at the secretarial college came to an end, for the college accepted for training a great many more pupils than there was any prospect of placing in situations during the period of trade depression that was playing Old Harry with Mr. Stone's finances. Consequently, he found that he had spent good money on Pat's training, and yet she was not bringing home any salary to go into the family exchequer. He found it very hard, good Christian that he was, to forgive Pat for that trade depression.

The secretarial school had an agreeable habit of sending half-a-dozen candidates out in a party for a prospective employer to select from (a most embarrassing and bad-bloodmaking performance from the point of view of the candidates), and no one ever selected poor Pat. Who wants golden-red aureoles and sea-blue eyes and milk and roses in an office? They only make trouble for all concerned. Had she gone to the stage-door of a theatre it would have been a different story; but Stones do not go to the theatre, by either stage-door or foyer, for they have souls to save, and they know that the theatre is the devil's den and playing cards his picturebooks.

Consequently, each time the raiding-party returned emptyhanded, Pat's rebellious soul grew fiercer, and the sea-blue eyes grew stormier, and the warm, red lips were compressed in a narrower line, entirely contrary to their nature. Poor, badgered child, all sorts of grudges were being worked off at her expense.

And it was not only domestic friction that was bothering her. Another and more acute form of trouble had made its appearance during the last few months. One of Helen's most desirable admirers had transferred his attentions to Pat, and Pat had done a very foolish thing-she had encouraged him, not because she wanted him, but because she wanted to annoy Helen.

Things had finally come to a head within the family, at any rate, when Leonard Matthews presented Pat with a gold bangle. Mr. Stone took her aside and told her that although she had better not cause a fuss by returning it now that she had accepted it, she was never to wear it, and must clearly understand that her position in the family was different to Helen's, and that she must not prejudice his daughter's chances. If any eligible young men directed their attentions to her before Helen was safely disposed of, they were to be discouraged. Mr. Stone did not say what was to be done with the ineligible ones.

Pat, however, though she privately considered Leonard Matthews an exceedingly poor fish, responded by holding her arm at an awkward angle and declaring that the bangle could not be got off, and persisted in flashing it before the eyes of the agitated Helen. She also started a correspondence with Leonard via the tobacconist's shop at the end of the road, employing a small brother as go-between; the small brother, being a Stone, naturally betrayed her, as Pat intended he should, thus exacerbating an already intolerable situation.

Altogether, with each passing month of her rapidly maturing young life, Pat was making the house too hot to hold her. Mrs. Stone was acutely conscious of that one step aside into romance that had produced Pat, and hated the child as one always hates the sight of one's own *faux pas*. Mr. Stone not unnaturally grudged the expense of rearing a cuckoo in his nest.

The wound was never allowed to heal; and as Pat grew older and the alien blood in her showed more clearly, it became inflamed and festered. Mr. Stone was only waiting till Pat was twenty-one to disclaim all further responsibility for her.

So what with one thing and another, the long-smouldering friction was getting nearer and nearer bursting into flames, and Mrs. Stone would get the tea-tray at her head instead of her feet next time there was any more trouble.

It was in this frame of mind that Pat betook herself to the reading-room of the local free library and began to study the advertisements in the newspaper sheets put up on the wall for the convenience of the unemployed. She was sick at heart from going out with batch after batch of candidates and seeing her comrades absorbed one by one and their place taken by fresh aspirants from a junior class, and herself returned empty as ever. She thought she might possibly have a better chance if she went out on her own, without so much competition. Surely there must be some employer who had fallen low enough to be willing to engage Pat Stone?

She had gone through the advertisements for typists and secretaries, and was idly glancing at the agony column, trying to guess what the cryptic messages meant, and killing time till the luncheon hour should demand her return to her home, when her eye was caught by an advertisement headed "Red Hair." She glanced at it out of idle curiosity. Was it a preparation to render the hair of the red less red? Or to give red hair to the non-red? It is curious how the human soul, whatever the station in life may be to which it hath pleased God to call it, always wants to make of it a junction and change there for somewhere else.

But the advertisement was for none of these things, and as her eyes took in the next sentence she suddenly stiffened to attention.

"Secretary with red hair required immediately. Not over thirty. Salary £2 10s. per week. Apply J. Pharmakos, 92 Crispin House, Strand, between 3 and 4 p.m. to-day."

Pat's red head went round and round. She could certainly fill the bill as far as red hair was concerned. She also thought she could fill it as far as secretarial attainments were concerned, for she was no fool, and a worker. But what would her people say? It was a queer advertisement. Moreover she knew nothing whatever about J. Pharmakos, and had no means of finding out anything about him. His name was obviously foreign, probably Greek, she guessed; it had a Greek sound about it, and the Greeks-well—*Timeo Danaos.*

The secretarial school had impressed upon her mother and Helen, when arrangements were being made for her that should spare her all unnecessary temptation, that they always made a point of knowing all about any post to which they sent a girl. It was rather a risk to put in for a job with a foreigner about whom one knew nothing.

All the same, Pat determined to take that risk. Life as lived amid Stones was simply unendurable. Her red-haired soul was raw. She realised, however, that she would be unwise to invite her parents to share that risk unless she wished to become even more raw. She, who had hitherto never thought of deceiving anyone in even the least of these things, made up her mind that she would have to make a start in the art of deception if she were to survive, and assume protective colouring to match her environment, like many another hard-pressed creature.

So when she came in for lunch she informed the assembled family that she had to go out again immediately to present herself at a post that the secretarial college had instructed her to apply for, and demanded the necessary money for fares, for Mrs. Stone did not believe in pocket-money, but rather in supplying legitimate needs after a good deal of argument, she to decide in what legitimacy consisted. Pat got her money after the usual wrangle; and being red-headed, also succeeded in extracting sixpence for her tea and a penny for the waitress; a thing a mouse-coloured Stone would never have succeeded in doing.

The journey from suburb to City seemed a great adventure, taken thus alone and in secret, as it were; very different from the weary *via dolorosa* with half-a-dozen other anxious candidates, all powdering their noses simultaneously. Crispin

House was a large new block of office buildings, the back of which looked out over the river, as Pat ascertained by walking round it while waiting for the appointed hour of three.

When she entered, however, it appeared she was not the first arrival, for the lift-man began to grin as she nervously arranged a red lock with the aid of the glass at the back of the lift. When she disembarked at the appointed landing, she saw why he had grinned, for there were red-haired females, some of whom might have been under thirty, in every possible direction. Sitting on the stairs, on the radiators, anywhere, and obviously overflowing out of a small office the door of which opened just opposite the lift-gates.

Pat joined the party and her heart sank. This was even worse than going out on patrol with the detachment from the training school, which was always strictly limited to six. She had never realised before what a variety of shades could pass for red with their respective owners when there was a job in prospect. Anything from eyebrowless sandy to hennaed grey.

It was a devastating assembly; and knowing the kind of temper that goes with red hair from her own bitter experience, she hoped and prayed that a riot would not break out among the competing red-heads, for she was sure that if this happened, none of them would be left alive to tell the tale.

As three o'clock struck on innumerable City clocks, she heard a laugh, a man's laugh, of a very peculiar quality. Everyone stiffened to attention. It reminded Pat of the time she had been to see *Faust* along with the high-school (there had been a terrible row about it, too, when she got home), and Mephistopheles had laughed just like that when he had come for the soul of Faust. For a long time, Mephistopheles had been her girlish ideal, and he still haunted her dreams occasionally, not as a devil, but as a lover. She was thrilled to the marrow by that laugh. She was sure it was a wicked laugh, for several of the hennaed seniors had looked down their noses at the sound and one or two were even edging towards the stairs.

But before they could make good their escape, the laugher, still laughing, came out of the office door, and surveyed them.

He was a very tall, very thin man, with a sallow complexion, and even in the dim light of the passage it was obvious that he, too, had red hair. Very dark red hair, cut very short and growing in a kind of peak over his forehead. He was truly Mephistophelian if anybody ever was, and Pat's rebellious heart was ravished by him. She had never wanted any of the other jobs before, save as a means of escape from her soul destroying home, but to work for this man, she felt, would be a romance, a thrill of the first water. She demanded that job, she willed that job, with all the fiery ardour of her redheaded soul. The man turned round and looked straight at her.

"Dear ladies," he said, and his voice was full of mockery, "There are so many of you that I really must take a look round before I start interviewing. I had never dreamt of this *embarras de richesse.*"

The lift came up and disgorged four more red-heads. Two more arrived panting by the stairs.

The red-headed man looked slowly round.

"I will choose three of you to interview," he said. "The rest I regret to disappoint, but I cannot very well do otherwise."

The ranks fluttered, sidled, came to attention, each according to her disposition. The red-haired man looked straight at Pat again, and then, Oh, agony, Oh, misery, Oh, bottomless pit of devastation-turned away his eyes!

"You, madam?" he said, pointing to a matronly soul, carrying a heavy coating of henna. "And you?" pointing to a sandy flapper with obvious adenoids. He looked up. He looked down. He turned round and surveyed the females roosting on the radiators. Finally his eye lit on Pat once more. "And I think we may as well have a look at you," he said. He held open the door of his room and the chosen three filed in; Pat, at any rate believing herself to be almost swooning with excitement. But that is always the way of the red-headed, and they never seem to take any harm from it. A chestnut filly of fiery mien sprang at the closing door and thrust a packet of testimonials through it.

"Just one moment, Mr. Pharmakos," she gasped.

"No thank you, madame," he said, and shut the door in her face. It was noteworthy that no one attempted to knock on that door thereafter.

Mr. Pharmakos turned and surveyed the chosen three. "Chairs, ladies?" he said. "I think there is a chair for each of you if you will be good enough to sit down." Pat, who was very intuitive, felt that there was an undercurrent of amusement in his voice.

"Now whom shall I begin with?" he said. "I think it would only be courteous to take the eldest first," and he beckoned to the sandy flapper, who scampered after him into the inner office. Pat was left alone with the lady of the henna, who was very angry.

"What a perfectly appalling man!" she exclaimed." I think that a young girl like you would be very unwise to take a post with him. I should make your escape while his back is turned, if I were you."

Pat shook her head solemnly. "I need the work," she said. Mrs. Henna snorted, and began to powder her nose, knocking off nearly as much powder as she put on, for she had not stinted her make-up in any department.

In a very short space of time the sandy flapper re-appeared. Mr. Pharmakos bowed her out, politely opening the door for her. "I will let you know," he said. Then he beckoned Mrs. Henna, who swept after him, casting a look of triumph and hate at Pat.

Pat sat alone, and looked around the office. Its windows gave upon the river, and she had an excellent view of the broken line of tumble-down factories and warehouses on the opposite bank. The river itself she could not see from where she sat, for the office was at the top of the building. She looked round the room, taking in its details, which were few, and striving to deduce from them what manner of man her prospective employer might be, and what manner of business he was engaged in. She noted the red and blue Turkey carpet, the roll-topped desk in fumed oak, the leather-covered table in the window, and a shelf full of files over the fire-place. There was nothing else. There must have been thousands of just such offices within a hundred yards of where she sat. It told her absolutely nothing. In a very few seconds out came Mrs. Henna, her chestnut eyes flashing dangerously as she gave Pat an awful look as if she could have annihilated her. Pat was unable to withdraw her eyes from that look until Mrs. Henna's skirts vanished through the door with an angry swish, and she glanced up to see Mr. Pharmakos watching her from the doorway leading to the inner office, with a smile of amusement on his face.

"Will you come in ?" he said.

Pat followed him into the inner office, which was as totally devoid of personality as the outer, being, in fact, its exact replica plus a couple of easy chairs. Mr. Pharmakos sat down in a swivel-chair before the open desk, and waved her to a straight-backed one beside it, tilted himself back in the swivel chair till she thought he would go over, and looked at her without speaking, still apparently very much amused.

"Did you know," he said, "That there were so many red headed people in the world?" and he passed his hand over his close-cropped red hair. Pat did not know what to reply.

She had been well drilled in office manners at the secretarial school, where the teachers always insisted on the pupils treating them as if they were irascible employers, this being part of the training. Her wits were distracted for the moment because she had observed that, although Mr. Pharmakos had the voice and bearing of a gentleman, the hand with which he had smoothed his convict crop was the hand of a navvy. What manner of man was this? Would it really be all right to take a job with him?

"Well, now, let us get to business," he said. "What experience have you had?"

Poor Pat had to admit that she had no experience save that of the commercial school. He nodded, and she was relieved to observe that he did not seem put out by this.

"May I see your certificates?" he said.

She handed them to him. She was on firmer ground here, for her certificates were good. He nodded again.

Then he looked at her, hesitated, "Would you mind taking off your hat?" he asked.

Pat took off the wide-brimmed hat that half hid her face, and the red-gold aureole shot out as if on springs and stood up all round her head.

"Heavens!" exclaimed the man, "What a baby it is!"

"I'm nineteen, nearly twenty," gulped poor Pat, almost in tears.

The man tapped his teeth with a gold pencil-case and hesitated. "My dear child," he said at length, "I hadn't bargained for anything quite as immature as you."

"I'm not immature!" red-headed Pat rapped out tartly. "I'm just on twenty, and I've done nothing but fight all my life. That ages you pretty quickly."

"Who have you fought?" asked the man, greatly amused.

"Everyone I came across," said Pat.

"That would be no recommendation to the average employer," said Mr. Pharmakos, smiling.

Pat's face fell. "No," she said, looking very crestfallen, "I suppose it wouldn't be," and tried to remember the opening gambits practised at the training school when rehearsing interviews with prospective employers.

"I, however, am not an average employer," said Mr. Pharmakos, "And I am not sure that rather a fightable secretary might not be useful to me. But you are such a child, 1 haven't got the heart to take you and use you for a job like mine," and he tapped his strong white teeth again, and stared at her thoughtfully. Pat guessed that he would like to have her, but had scruples.

"I don't know what you want me for," she said," but it can't possibly be worse than what I am doing now."

"What are you doing now?"

"Living at home, where they don't like me."

"Have they all got red heads like yours?"

"No, all the rest are mousey. I am the only red-head amongst them, and they don't like me."

"Perhaps, Miss Coppernob, to judge from the sample of your spirit that you have already shown me, there is something to be said on their side."

"I know there is," said poor Pat, "But I think I should be very different if I weren't being nagged all the time."

"So you don't think I'll nag you, then?"

"Well, not like they do," said Pat. "And besides, there's only one of you. I could stand up to one."

The man shouted with laughter.

"I've got the devil's own temper," he said.

"So have I," said Pat. "And so, you see, I'll understand yours, having a red head myself."

"I really think we shall have to give each other a trial," said Mr. Pharmakos, amid his laughter. "What do you say to an experimental week? We aren't likely to kill each other in that time."

Pat flashed him a beaming smile, too overcome for words.

He smiled back. "Put your hat on, you infant," he said. She obeyed.

"That's better," said the man. "You are a most disconcerting child without your hat on. You will have to put your head in a bag if you want to work for me. You can start at once, I presume.?" he continued.

Pat nodded. Her voice was not quite under control. It meant so much, this job; to get away from her home and all the nagging Stones and work for this man whom she liked so much, and who was so nice with her, so different in his manner to the other employers she had interviewed in company with the miserable six.

"No time like the present," said Mr. Pharmakos. "Here is a ten-shilling note. Would you be good enough to go out and rootle about, and get some China tea, and a lemon, and sugar, and crockery, and a tray, and all the et ceteras; you know what. There is a Woolworth down the street, and Lyonses galore for the tea. Covent Garden is handy for the lemon. I hope you take your tea without milk, or, at any rate, can learn to. It is much better with lemon if freshly made, believe me. There is a gas-ring in the outer office, and some sort of a glory-hole to the left down the passage where you can get water and dispose of the garbage. Now run along, my child, and as soon as you get back, make me some tea, and incidentally, make yourself some also."

"Do you want anything to eat?" said Pat shyly .

"Eat? Good God, no. I never eat anything. But get yourself a currant bun, or a cream horn, or whatever it is you fancy."

Away went Pat, with the precious ten-shilling note safe in

her tightly-clutched hand, and had a heavenly time at Woolworth's. It almost seemed to her as if she and Mr. Pharmakos were a newly-married couple setting up housekeeping. She got some crockery that she thought was really charming, and Woolworth even produced tea and a lemon.

She returned on winged feet and brewed Mr. Pharmakos his tea. She arranged everything on the pretty tray and took it in to him. .

"My word, this is really stylish," he said, "Do you mean to say that Woolworth's produced all this?"

He took up the lemon. "A knife, my child?"

Poor Pat's face fell. She had forgotten to purchase a knife.

Mr. Pharmakos felt through all his pockets, and produced some loose silver. Pat felt through her bag, and produced a nail-file.

He shook his head. "This is the most hopeful," he said, and commenced to operate on the lemon with the edge of a halfcrown.

Pat watched his big navvy's hands, fascinated. They were very well kept, in fact obviously manicured by a professional; all the same, they were coarse, powerful hands, the hands of a man accustomed to handling pick and shovel.

She looked at his face, seeing it in a good light for the first time, for during the interview he had had his back to the window, and it was not easy to see his expression or the details of his features. She saw that it was a rather Red Indian countenance, with high cheek-bones and a peremptory, Wellingtonian nose. The skin was very sallow and seemed to be drawn tight over the cheek-bones. The mouth was large, the jaw aggressive. He was certainly not pretty, and he looked as though he were in bad health. He was much younger than she had at first thought him to be, however. She had put him down as somewhere in the neighbourhood of fifty; but now she saw that he was probably nearer forty. Across the back of each wrist, as he wrestled with the lemon, she noticed a jagged, white scar.

He gave the lemon up as a bad job. "Take this down to the porter, will you?" he said, "and ask him to cut the damn thing in half."

Away went Pat on her errand, and was lucky enough to find the lift at the top landing, and made her request to the lift-man.

"I haven't got a knife up here, missy," he said, eyeing her curiously, "But if you will come down with me, my missus will cut it for you."

She got into the lift and descended with him to the basement.

"You got a job with Mr. Pharmakos?" he asked as they travelled downwards.

"Yes," said Pat.

"Know who he is?"

"No."

"Neither do I."

There was an awkward pause. The lift stopped in the darkness of the basement, but the lift-man did not open the gate.

"I'll tell you something, though, if you want to know it, missy. When a chap 'as the tongue of a gentleman and the 'ands of a navvy, and the nerves of a hactress, you don't need to look far to see what 'e's done. 'E's done time."

"Done time?" asked the mystified Pat, thinking of clock-making.

"Yes, done time. Been in quod. That's an old lag, that is, what you've taken up with. See them marks on 'is wrists? That's what you get when you kick up a shindy in hand-cuffs."

Pat proffered the lemon miserably. Her little world, so

sunny a moment before in the light of Mr. Pharmakos' approval, had crashed about her ears.

The lift-man took the lemon .

"You watch your step, young lady," he said, "I should get your Pa to have a look at Mr. Pharmakos, if I was you."

CHAPTER II

PAT was on the verge of tears as the lift-man took her back to the top landing. So this was the end of her venture that had started so bravely. Her new employer, whom she liked so much, had turned out to be an ex-convict. Now she understood what he had meant when he had said, "I haven't the heart to take you and use you for a job like mine." What crimes was he planning? Burglaries? Murders?
Every detective story she had ever read flashed through her mind. And yet she liked him so much. There was something awfully nice about him. She did not know where she was. Ought she to tell him she had found out about him and couldn't work for him? Ought she to work for him, knowing what he was? She stood debating on the threshold with the lemon in her hand when the door opened, and Pharmakos looked out at her.

"What's the matter?" he asked, and took her by the arm and pulled her into the room. He put her into a chair, with the lemon still in her hand, and took his stand with his back to the door.

"Come on, now. Out with it. What has happened?" he demanded harshly.

He was facing the window now, and she could see every line of his sallow, hollow-cheeked face. She stood up to him pluckily .

"I don't quite know what to do," she said.

"Don't you? What about?"

"I have just heard about what—what your work is."

"And what have you been told my work is?"

Pat squeezed the lemon nervously, and the juice ran out on to her frock. Pharmakos took the lemon from her and put it on a plate.

"Now, my child," he said more gently, "Someone has been talking to you, and I want you to tell me what has been said, and who has said it, because it may be important to me to know."

Pat stared up at him miserably. He was so awfully nice, how could she tell him that the porter had said he was a criminal?

"You are perfectly useless as a liar, my child. Truth will out with you. Come along. You may as well tell me. Do you want to help me, or don't you?"

"I'd like to help you," said poor Pat, almost in tears, "But—but it's awfully rude and unkind, and I don't believe it."

"Well, what is it? Let's get it over."

"The—the porter said you had been in prison."

Pharmakos said nothing. There was a long silence while she stared at him and he looked out of the window. She thought she had been mistaken in thinking him younger than he had appeared to be at first sight.

Finally he spoke. "The remark is, as you say, rude; very rude. Possibly unkind also, if one allows oneself to consider such things. But you had better believe it because it happens to be true."

He withdrew his gaze from the distance and looked her straight in the eyes. "I came out of prison two years ago. I have run straight ever since and I intend to continue to do so. What about it, Coppernob? Do you care to work for me under the circumstances?"

"Yes," said Pat, decisively.

"You believe what I tell you about running straight?"

An equally decisive "yes" rewarded him.

He smiled faintly. "What makes you believe me?"

"I don't know. I do, anyway. And I should like awfully to work for you. I like you."

"That is more than most people do, my child, quite apart from my record."

"It's the same with me," said Pat, "Everyone dislikes me, and my record is something awful. I threw a tea-tray at my mother once."

Pharmakos smiled. "I am afraid I did a worse thing than throw a tea-tray. Some day I may tell you. I don't know. We shall see. We have got a week on trial, haven't we, anyway? But now, come along, I want to get to the bottom of this. It is no joke for me to have this rumour following me round. Tell me, Coppernob, have you any idea how the porter knew ?"

"He knew by your hands?" said Pat.

Pharmakos thrust the offending hands deep into his trouser pockets and walked over to the window, avoiding her eyes. He stood staring out into the spring sunshine for a while. Then he opened the window and leant out with his elbows on the sill, presenting her with a view of a pair of very wide but very angular shoulders. Finally he sat down on a chair beside the window, resting his elbow on the sill, and his chin on his hand, still staring into space, completely oblivious of her presence. It was so obvious that he had forgotten all about her and believed himself alone that Pat wondered whether she ought to say something to recall him to himself, for it is a shameful thing to see a man with his mask off. Almost as bad as seeing him with no clothes at all, thought Pat, horribly embarrassed. But Pharmakos was away in another world, and as that terrible silence lengthened out moment by moment, it became more and more difficult to break it. Finally Pharmakos folded his arms on the sill and dropped his head on them.

It had ceased by now to be in Pat's power to move. He was so quiet, yet it was terrible to watch him. Her eyes began to fill with tears, and the room disappeared in a misty blur. Her handkerchief was in her bag and her bag was out of her reach. Should she try to make her escape on tip-toe, or would he hear her, and be more upset if he came to himself and found her trying to make her escape after she had witnessed his self-betrayal than if she stood her ground and faced it with him frankly? She felt intuitively that the latter was the better way, and much less likely to leave a nasty taste behind it.

Finally Pharmakos straightened himself and rose slowly from his chair as if he had difficulty in moving. But when he saw Pat, he jumped as if he had touched something hot, and flushed crimson to his temples. It was an exquisitely painful moment for both of them, but that silence had got to be broken somehow, and broken in the right way if it were to be possible for them to work together; otherwise he might hate the sight of her and get rid of her forthwith to spare himself embarrassment.

"I'm frightfully sorry," said Pat in a strangled voice which she struggled desperately to control, her tears enraging her by suddenly overflowing on to her cheeks, "I think it's a beastly shame. But I'll stick by you. I'll stick by you through anything. I'll never let you down."

Still Pharmakos did not speak. But as he leant against the table she saw that the rigidity had gone out of him and he looked her in the face without embarrassment. She felt that the worst was over.

At length he spoke. "What are you crying about, Coppernob?"

"Nothing," said Pat crossly. She reached for her bag and rummaged it. Felt in her sleeves; dived down the front of her dress; searched every possible place that a female can secrete a handkerchief, but without result. Pharmakos' drawn face relaxed into a smile.

"Here you are, take mine," he said, and drew a beautiful bandana from his breast pocket and handed it to her. As she buried her nose in the soft silk she smelt all the perfumes of Araby. It must be wonderful to be rich, and able to afford handkerchiefs like that. Crime must be profitable.

She returned the handkerchief to Pharmakos and watched him twist it into a tight ball and grip it in the palm of his hand.

"I fancy I'll feel better," he said, "If I go and have a word with our friend the porter," and he turned on his heel and left the room.

Pat began to breathe again. She felt that Pharmakos had accepted the invitation, and in some measure given her his confidence. He would not sack her now because she had seen too much. Metaphorically speaking, she gathered him under her wings and clucked threateningly at anyone and everyone who came near him. The ex-convict would be better served by his new secretary than the ninety and nine just men who have never gone astray.

The door had hardly closed behind Pharmakos when there was a knock on it and Pat opened it to find a large man standing there, obviously a policeman in plain clothes. Her heart leapt to her throat. Had he come to drag Pharmakos off to prison again? Pat ruffled up her feathers like a broody hen that sees a dog approaching.

"Mr. Pharmakos in, miss?" enquired the newcomer.

It was useless to deny any knowledge of Mr. Pharmakos because his name was painted on the door.

"No," said Pat, "not at the moment."

"Will he be back soon?"

"I couldn't say."

"Well, as his hat's on the peg, I don't suppose he's gone far, so I'll just step in and wait," and he planted his large bulk in the nearest chair.

Pat retreated to the inner office and closed the communicating door. She had observed that it also had a door leading into the passage. Out of this door she let herself noiselessly and stood half-way between the lift and the stairs. She would warn Pharmakos of her suspicions concerning his visitor. She was no longer on the side of the law and righteousness. Pharmakos should not go back to prison again, whatever he had done.

She had not many moments to wait before she heard the sound of the ascending lift, and Pharmakos stepped out of it. In one corner there was something that looked like a piece of chewed twine clad in a porter's uniform, which slammed the gates and vanished into the depths almost before Pharmakos was clear of the lift.

Pat lifted a warning finger for silence, and Pharmakos paused in mid-stride and looked at her enquiringly.

"There's a man come to see you," whispered Pat, "who looks like a policeman in plain clothes."

"A red-faced chap with a big black moustache, just beginning to go bald?"

"Yes, that's him."

"There's nothing to worry about there. He's a friend of mine." He looked down at the agitated Pat and smiled. "So you thought you'd tip me the wink and let me do a getaway, did you?"

"Yes," said Pat, "I told you I would not let you down."

"That was rather sweet of you, Coppernob. I appreciate it, even if it wasn't necessary. I am on good terms with Scotland Yard these days, so there is nothing to worry about if large men looking like policemen in plain clothes call on me. Ask them in and treat them as friends of the family."

He entered the office with Pat at his heels. The plain-clothes man rose.

"Good afternoon, sir," he said, "I happened to be passing so I thought I'd just drop in and have a word with you."

"Very good of you, I'm sure, Inspector. And what's the word?"

The plain-clothes man glanced doubtfully at Pat.

"Go ahead," said Pharmakos, "This is my sister who is acting as confidential secretary. She knows all there is to know."

"Pleased to meet you, miss," said the large man, "And I'm very glad to see Mr. Pharmakos has got someone belonging to him to look after him."

"So you think I need looking after, do you, Inspector?"

"Yes, sir, I do. No one as has been through what you have ought to live alone the way you do. It's bad for you. You'll never get right as long as you go on doing it."

"But what about Skilly? He'd be frightfully hurt if he heard what you have just said."

"Skilly's no company for the likes of you. I'm real glad to see the young lady has joined up with you. There were times when I was real anxious about you."

"Well, come on, Inspector. You have not dropped in to kill time, if I know you. What's up?"

"Well, sir, the thing that's up, not to say uppish, is your blooming porter, begging your pardon, Miss Pharmakos."

"And what's the matter with our porter?"

"He was a warder at Wormwood Scrubs before he retired on his pension, and he knows the hall-mark, so to say, and he isn't half talking. I should put your solicitor on to him, if I was you."

"So I have just discovered. He talked to my sister, and struck a snag, didn't he, Coppernob? She sent him off with a flea in his ear. It appears I wear the brand of Cain for all the world to see."

"Oh, no, sir, I shouldn't say that," said the plain-clothes man uncomfortably. .

"Well, wouldn't you have spotted me for an old lag? Come now, Inspector, be honest."

"Well, I might have, because it's my trade, and I know what to look for. But most people wouldn't. You needn't worry about that."

"And what do you look for, Inspector?"

"I know what the marks on your wrists mean; I should use a bit of grease paint on 'em if I was you."

"No use; tried it. It only comes off on my shirt."

The plain-clothes man looked at Pharmakos' hands, and he immediately put them behind him.

"You must have cut some magnificent didoes to get marks like that, sir."

"I did, I hold the record for solitary. I packed more of it into seven years than anyone who ever went to Portland."

"That's a bad thing, that," said the policeman, shaking his head. "Too much solitary is no use to anyone. That's probably what's the matter with you. I've seen lifers less broken up than you, and you only a young feller, too. How old were you when you went in?"

"Twenty-two."

"Gawd!" said the policeman, "they cracked you up properly!"

Pat did some hasty arithmetic. If he were twenty-two when he went to prison, and had served a seven years sentence, and had been out for two years, that would only make him thirty-one. And she had taken him at first sight for fifty!

"If you handle that porter feller properly, like you know how, you can probably get him to pack up his traps and clear out."

"I don't want to do that, Inspector. Where's the poor devil

to go in these hard times? He's got his home here and all. It is much easier for me to hunt a fresh office than it is for him to hunt a fresh billet. Besides, he's probably told every charwoman in the place already."

"That's very generous of you, sir, I must say. I wouldn't feel inclined to let a chap down so light that had blowed the gaff on me if I was in your shoes. I'll have a word with him as I go out. We don't like that sort of thing. If a chap wants to run straight, we won't have him interfered with. You can rest assured of that."

"I've had a word with him already, Inspector. Several, in fact. You will have to prop him up before you can hit him."

The Inspector bowed himself out politely, and Pharmakos shut the door behind him. Then he came back and looked at Pat.

"Young woman, do you know what I suggest you should do?"

Pat braced herself to storm Scotland Yard if he demanded it.

"I should brew some fresh tea, if I were you. That won't be fit to drink, and I think we could both do with a little refreshment."

CHAPTER III

JUDGED by conventional standards, Pharmakos was as ugly as sin, and the close-cropped hair exaggerated the effect, making him still look like a convict even two years after his release. Pat wondered why in the world he wore it like that, not realising what health can do to the hair, and that there was no other way in which hair like his could be worn.

He resembled nothing so much as an Egyptian mummy; or a well-pickled corpse on a dissecting-room slab. He could not even be called a finely-built man, in spite of his size, because he was nothing but a walking skeleton. He was like a building that has been gutted by fire, of which only the walls are standing.

One thing, and one thing only his imprisonment had left to him, and that was an extraordinary grace of movement. For all his gauntness, the man was as graceful as a stag. As the plain-clothes man had said, many men were less broken by a life sentence than Pharmakos by his seven years' penal servitude. Red-headed people do not submit to prison life well; as previously noted, they are born with a skin short, and prison discipline is planned with a view to making an impression on recalcitrant rhinoceroses.

But with all his drawbacks of looks, of record, of apparent, if not actual age, no film star of the first magnitude could hold a candle to him in the eyes of his new secretary. Pat went in with his tea as if she were serving communion.

"Hullo? Only one cup, Coppernob? Where's the other? Bring it along. I am not so enamoured of my own company as to suggest that you should drink tea in one room, while I drink it in another, with the door carefully shut between us. And remember, in the eyes of the law, you are now my sister. Old Saunders swallowed that yarn, and will have trotted back to Scotland Yard by now with it, and added it to my dossier."

"Why did you say I was your sister?" demanded Pat.

"Well, that's rather a long story. I had not meant to tell it to you just yet, but to get to know you a bit first, and let you get to know me. That was why I suggested a week on trial.

"As a matter of actual fact, I have turned my prison experience to account by setting up as a private detective. I do not want this generally known, because it would destroy a good deal of my usefulness in certain quarters if it leaked out. A good many people think I am a bookie, and that is very useful cover for me. What I was really after, when I inserted that ridiculous red-headed advertisement, was a girl whom I could train to help me in my work as well as do letters, and such like. I especially wanted a good shorthand writer, because she would sometimes have to be stowed away behind a screen taking down everything people say to be used as evidence against them. The reason I advertised for a coppernob was in order that she could pass as my sister if we had to go away out of London together. The only other thing she could pass as, and avoid social complications, would be my wife, and that might lead to all sorts of difficulties. I did not see myself carting about a female who could pass as my mother. I had naturally meant to ask your permission before I introduced you to society as Miss Pharmakos, my kid sister, but old Saunders took me by surprise, and I could not very well start you off as a hireling and then promote you to be a relation. You see, my child, everyone would have thought the very worst of us both if I had done that, and my reputation is not one that will stand any additional strain. I have to be as careful as Caesar's wife, with my record.

"So I advertised for a red-headed secretary in order that we could pass as relations. It did not matter so much about resemblance of feature, because I have obviously been ill; but I thought good, rich, ripe, mahogany-coloured hair would serve to carry off the deception, and you see it did. Even such a suspicious person as our plain-clothes friend accepted you at your face value, though I hope to goodness, for your sake, there is no family resemblance beyond the colour of our hair.

"I advertised for a female secretary because I had to have a woman for certain jobs that neither Skilly nor I could do, being mere males. And I advertised for one under thirty because I wanted her to be reasonably seductive, for that sort get what they want more easily than homy-faced daughters of toil on the wrong side of forty. I give you fair warning, however, that I have absolutely no use for women, horny-faced or seductive. I have been far too badly bitten, my child, ever to trust your sex again, in any shape or form. Use you? Yes; but trust you? No. Put that in your pipe and smoke it at the outset.

"What I should ask you to do, if you work for me, will never be on the wrong side of the law. You saw the terms I am on with Inspector Saunders. I work in pretty close touch with Scotland Yard, and we play into each other's hands. There is always the risk of personal unpleasantness in work like mine, but I should never let you do anything that involved serious danger. I never carry any more formidable weapons myself than a stout stick and a packet of pepper. The yarns you hear about detectives armed with revolvers are all my eye. You daren't shoot, and everybody knows it. And anyway, with my record, I couldn't get a gun licence. Skilly uses brass knuckle-dusters because he's an ex-bruiser and feels at home with them. But I used to be a bit of a fencer, and it takes a good man to get under my guard when armed with a broomstick. If you work for me, you will have to trust to a packet of pepper and a good pair of lungs if you land into any unpleasantness. I can't have you flourishing round with lethal weapons. My reputation wouldn't stand it.

"Now then, my child, are there any questions you would like to ask me? It's only fair that I should put the cards on the table, my position being what it is, before you make up your mind. I won't ask you for a final decision at the moment. That must wait till the end of the week on both sides. But you will want to do a little thinking, in the circumstances, before you make up your mind whether you turn up here tomorrow morning at ten o'clock, or not. Now then, fire away, what do you want to ask?"

Pat hesitated. There was one thing she very much wanted to ask, and on the answer to that question would depend a great deal of their future relations. But dared she put that question? It was rather a terrible one. She hesitated. Then looked Pharmakos straight in the face and said, "I would like to know what you went to prison for."

Pharmakos' face twitched, and he did not answer at once, but looked out of the window.

"I thought you might want to know that," he said. "I am glad you asked. I respect you for asking. I killed a man in a fit of temper. If 1 had had my rights I should have been, hanged, but a merciful judge talked about manslaughter to the jury, and a merciful jury brought it in as that. I got seven years, and lucky to get them, and I served every day of them. I have one of the worst records of any man in Portland. I had several jolly good tries at killing warders. Whether I would ever kill anybody again, now that I am out I do not know, but I give you fair warning I have often been tempted to kill myself. Perhaps having you running around will put a check on that, however. I have got the temper of a fiend, as I've already told you. I have always had that, having red hair and being well ragged in the days of my youth. But since I have been in prison my nerves have gone all to pieces, and there are times when I am none too sane. It just depends how you handle me at those times, what I do. If you rub my fur the wrong way, I am liable to fly off the handle, and you will get it in the neck. You must bear all these things in mind before you decide to take me on."

"Do you know," said Pat, " I think I can understand all that very well. You see, I've got red hair myself, and I know just what one gets like after one has been ragged and nagged long enough. I threw a tray full of crockery at my mother, and I'm certain I would have killed her if I had had anything to kill her with."

"Luckily for me, I did not have anything except my two hands to kill with," said Pharmakos, "or there would have been no chance of a verdict of ,anything but murder. But I hammered a man's brains out against a marble mantelpiece, though the doctor refused to say whether he thought he'd had one blow or several. Several? Good God, he'd had half a hundred. I pounded his head to a jelly."

Pharmakos stopped, his face an unpleasant clay-colour. He opened his left hand and took out the bandana, crushed to the size of a walnut, shook out its creases, and wiped his forehead with it.

"Do you know, Coppernob, you are the first person I have ever spoken to about that? They say confession is good for the soul. Perhaps you have broken the spell of my evil enchantment and I shall stop dreaming about it. I always dream about it when the moon is full. By the way, you will have to look out for trouble with me when the moon is full. I become highly explosive on those occasions. Now, is there anything else you want to ask? Fire away. I would like to have everything clear and above board with you and no *arrieres pensees.*"

"There is only one other thing," said Pat, "Pharmakos is not your real name, is it?"

"No, it is not. My real name is an honourable name, and I have disgraced it pretty thoroughly; therefore I do not feel entitled to use it. My Christian name is my real one, however. I was christened Julian after my old aunt Julia, who was a decent sort. I should probably never have killed anybody if she had had the bringing up of me. You don't need to know my real name, do you, Coppernob? I would sooner you didn't. It can serve no useful purpose."

"No," said Pat, "There is no need to tell me anything you don't want to. But I would awfully like to know why you called yourself Pharmakos, and what it means? It means a drug, doesn't it? I learnt a little Greek at school."

"Inquisitive puss, aren't you?" said the man, smiling, and Pat was relieved to see that his attention had been successfully diverted from his memories.

"No, Pharmakos does not mean a drug. That is Pharmakon. It means quite a different thing. It means a scapegoat. In old Greece it was a custom if pestilence or any other act of God came upon a city, to lead out the worst specimen of a human being they could find within the city limits, and make a living sacrifice of him outside the gates. They called this chap a Pharmakos. Probably the same sort of idea as a Pharmakon, or drug, because he was supposed to heal, or make pure the city by being sacrificed for it. It seemed to me, when I wanted to re-Christen myself, that his name would suit me very nicely. I don't want to excuse myself; nothing could excuse what I did; but I honestly think that it was not altogether my own sins I suffered for. Now, you young minx, have you finished cross-examining me yet?"

"Yes," said Pat, "I shall never ask you anything else. I know just where I stand. And I can tell you this, you can rely on me. I shan't let you down."

Phannakos made no reply for a moment, but looked at her in silence.

"Thanks," he said at length; and then, after a pause, "I suggest you clear away the tray, my child."

When she returned from her washing-up, she was relieved to see that he looked comparatively normal.

"Come here, Coppernob," he called to her, through the half-open door between the two rooms, "I haven't finished with you yet. It's my turn now."

She went in to him.

"Sit down," he said, pointing to one of the arm-chairs, and dropping into the other himself. This was not at all according to Cocker as interpreted by the secretarial training college. It had been repeatedly impressed on her that any departure from impersonal formality on the part of an employer should be regarded as an insult and resented as such, and that any secretary who found herself treated as a human being should immediately put her name down on the employment register of the college, who would move heaven and earth to secure the insulted one another job. But Pat felt perfectly safe with Pharmakos, murderer and gaol-bird though he was.

"I hope you don't mind having to pass as my sister?" said her employer. "I am afraid we are committed to it now."

"Rather not," said Pat, "I'd love to be your sister. I think you are an enormous improvement on my original family."

Pharmakos laughed, and for a fleeting second looked his real age. Pat had made up her mind that the orthodox secretarial manner was not acceptable to Pharmakos. He loved being amused, and he was craving for companionship. The perspicacious policeman had been right when he said it was not good for him to be alone after all he had been through.

"You realise," said her employer, "that as my sister you

are hardly likely to address me respectfully as Mr. Pharmakos?"

"Yes," said Pat, blushing.

"Then," said the man, "you had better practise in private addressing me as Julian, because if you blush as pink as that when you call me Julian in public, the least nosey will smell a rat."

Poor Pat flamed to the roots of her hair.

"And what is your Christian name?" continued the man. "It is obvious I can't call you Miss Stone if you are my sister. And it is equally obvious that you were not christened Coppernob. I need to know your Christian name, my child, and no offence intended."

"My name is Patricia, and I am generally called Pat for short."

"Patricia—Pat. Yes, all right. I will call you Pat till you get used to it, but I shall always think of you as Coppernob."

Pat snorted.

"Yes, you have got red hair, haven't you?" said Pharmakos, chuckling at her wrath.

"Now, my dear," he continued, "Since we are engaged in this general gaol-delivery of embarrassments, I may as well tell you that there may be occasions when convention requires me to plant a chaste kiss on your maiden cheek and to venture on mild endearments, but I promise you that they shall be very mild. Are you used to being kissed?"

"No, I am not," blazed Pat, "And I haven't the slightest intention of getting used to it, either."

"My dear little turkey-cock, there is no occasion to burst a blood-vessel. It will only be done in the way of business. I have already told you I have no use for women. I can kiss you as chastely as if you were a marble washstand."

"Can you?" snapped Pat, "Well, you won't get a chance to try. You will get a jolly good smack in the face if you even look like it."

Pharmakos hooted with joy. "I've got a jolly good mind to try now, just to see what happens."

"I'll walk out if you do," said Pat, "I mean it."

"All right, my dear, all right, I won't. I'll confine myself to verbal endearments when occasion requires it. Keep your hair on."

All the City clocks began to boom in a disjointed chorus.

"Good Lord," said Pharmakos, "It's seven o'clock. Off you go, my child. Your family will think you have been kidnapped."

He watched her gather up her bag and her humble cotton gloves and depart.

"Heigh-ho," he said to himself, stretching his long limbs to his full height, "What has that child done to me? I have not felt like this for years. Good-bye to Portland and all that. I haven't even thought of it for the last hour. I think she must have bewitched me."

CHAPTER IV

PAT arrived home shortly after eight to be greeted by an indignant family, who, as Pharmakos had rightly surmised, had made up their minds that she had come to a bad end, and being made irritable by their anxiety, vented their annoyance on its cause. She ought to have phoned if she were going to be kept late, they said, and Pat could not deny that there was no reason, save thoughtlessness, why she had not done so. To teach her to be more thoughtful and affectionate in future she was sent to bed without her supper, and as she had only had a cream-horn since midday, she had a broken and uncomfortable night.

The next morning, as she walked to the train with her father, she was subjected to a rigorous cross-examination as to who and what Mr. Pharmakos was. Was he a foreigner? Foreigners were especially suspect among such as the Stones, who had never been nearer the Continent than Brighton pier.

Pat agreed that he might possibly be a foreigner, for he was a very funny-looking man with a very yellow skin. Possibly a half-caste Chinaman? No, she thought not. She thought he might be of foreign extraction, but brought up in England, because he had no foreign accent. That explanation was grudgingly allowed to pass muster.

What was his business? Pat didn't know. (A private detective who passed as a bookie was hardly likely to find favour in the eyes of Mr. Stone.) But how had she come to spend half a day working for him and fail to find out something about his business? What had she been set to do? She had had to hang about showing people in and out, and run out on errands, and keep on making tea and washing it up. There had not been anything else. She had not taken down any letters nor had she been able to overhear any conversations. Then, said her father, she had better have a look through the files the first time she was left alone, and report to him what she found, and he would make enquiries. Pat dutifully agreed. Moreover, said her father, she was to tell this Pharmakos that if he kept her after six, he must pay her overtime. Pat said, "Yes, Father," and as the train came in, they parted company, as he always travelled first, even if times were bad.

At London Bridge they met again and walked over the bridge together. Mr. Stone informed his putative daughter that he had thought matters over carefully, and he thought it would be advisable for him to see this Pharmakos for himself in view of the fact that he was probably a foreigner, so she could tell him that he would look in, in the course of the day.

Pat panicked. She was perfectly certain that her father would not approve of her employer, and thought it doubtful if her employer would approve of her father. Moreover, supposing the porter told him that Pharmakos was an exconvict? The most likely thing was for her father to make enquiries of the porter, who would be sure to know as much as anybody about the tenants of the offices.

"I—I would much sooner you did not do that until I have got settled down. I am only engaged for a week on trial. Mr. Pharmakos might not like it."

"He will not object if he has nothing to be ashamed of," said Mr. Stone drily. "He will appreciate that it is the natural and proper thing for a father to make enquiries concerning the conditions under which his daughter is employed, especially if he has daughters of his own. What age is this Mr.

Pharmakos ?" he added suspiciously.

"He looks about fifty," said Pat.

They parted on the Embankment, Mr. Stone going north to the Stock Exchange; and Pat turning west towards the Strand. The porter looked at her sourly as he took her up in the lift, and neither gave even the customary "good morning" to the other. She suspected that he would be delighted to make mischief if given half a chance.

Pat was in good time, but Pharmakos was even earlier, as she saw by his hat as she entered the outer office.

"Hullo, Coppernob I" he said, coming out of the inner office as he heard her step. "You look as if you had been having a night on the tiles. Family haven't turned rusty, have they?"

"No more than usual," said Pat. "My father said he wanted to come and see you. But he is no more than usually rusty. I am so awfully sorry you are being bothered. I told him not to, but he means to do it."

"I expect I can cope with your father all right," said Pharmakos.

"What about the porter?" said Pat.

"The porter won't give any trouble. He's had his money's worth. If he does any more talking, he will be beaten up by Skilly, and he knows it."

There was a portable typewriter on the table, with whose breed Pat was fortunately acquainted; and she got out her notebook and settled down to take dictation. The letters were practically all to solicitors, save for two long reports to Scotland Yard itself, and they dealt almost exclusively with the personal habits of assorted blackmailers.

"Do you see what my line is, Coppernob?" said Pharmakos. "I blackmail blackmailers. Or to be precise, if someone is being blackmailed, and daren't go into court, I take on the negotiations and put the fear of God into the blackmailer by finding out all about his sticky past and batting him over the head with it. Skilly bats him over the head with knuckledusters occasionally, too, but that is an extra, and we don't tell Inspector Saunders about it because he says he would rather not know."

Pat soon saw that Pharmakos had an exceedingly extensive knowledge of the underworld, and gathered that he drew his information from Saunders on the one side and Skilly, whoever that gentleman might be, on the other. She was so absorbed in her work that a caller, evidently having failed to make himself heard at the outer door, opened the inner one, and there stood her father, looking exceedingly prim and proper, with a tightly rolled umbrella in his hand, although they were in the throes of a miniature spring heat-wave. Pat was truly thankful that he had caught her at legitimate secretarial business, instead of drinking tea with Pharmakos.

Pharmakos, whose nerves left much to be desired on the score of steadiness, being startled by the unexpected intrusion, barked, "What do you want?" so loudly and suddenly that Mr. Stone dropped his umbrella and had to grovel under the table to recover it, arising very hot and red and angry. The interview could not possibly have had a worse start.

"My name is Stone, and as my daughter has been engaged by you as secretary, I consider it desirable that I should make your acquaintance."

"Well, I don't," snapped Pharmakos. "When I engage a secretary I don't expect the entire family to come calling in business hours. I don't want your acquaintance, and I'm busy. I'd be glad if you would go out and shut the door behind you."

Mr. Stone turned to Pat. "Put on your hat and come with me," he said. "My daughter will not accept the post, Mr. Pharmakos, if that is your name."

Pharmakos jerked back his head like a startled horse.

"She can give a week's notice if she wants to, but she can't go off like that and leave me in the lurch. Or at any rate, she will have to pay a week's wages in lieu of notice if she does."

"We'll see about that," said Mr. Stone; but at any rate, he withdrew and closed the door behind him as bidden.

"That's tom it," said Pharmakos as the door closed behind the unwelcome visitor. "I'm frightfully sorry I barked at him, Pat, but he startled me, and I am apt to bark when I'm startled."

"It wouldn't have made any difference, whatever you had said," replied Pat, "He came here to make trouble in any case."

"What is all the fuss about, child? Why should he wish to make trouble for you?"

"Well, you see, I'm not really his child, and he hates me. He forgave mother and did not divorce her, but we've never heard the end of it."

"And your mother?"

"She hates me too, because of all the pickle she got let in for on account of me, and because I give father such a handle against her, and because I don't fit in with the rest of the family."

"Well, Coppernob, supposing your father delivers an ultimatum, as he looks like doing, what about it?"

"I shall go into digs."

"You are under age, my child, there may be difficulties."

"Then what am I to do?" Pat's eyes were filling with tears, and Pharmakos turned away to the window.

"I don't know, my dear. We must think it over. I have got to see Sir Charles Otway, of Otway and Harvey, this afternoon, and I will ask him how things stand legally. But apart from legality, Pat, are you wise to quarrel with your family over me? You know my position."

"I don't care," said Pat, her mouth set in a mutinous line. "I'd far rather stick to you than to them if you will have me."

"I'll have you all right, my child, but what about you? Your future, I mean? I've seen more of the world than you have, and I can't let you make ducks and drakes of your prospects just to suit my convenience."

"I haven't any prospects," said Pat, struggling to keep back her tears, "They all hate me. I've never met anyone I really liked, except you. I'd far rather stick to you than to them."

"And I'd like to have you, but there are all sorts of complications that perhaps you don't realise. I must think things out very carefully. I think I'll go out now. I have some appointments. We'll finish the letters this afternoon."

He took his hat and departed precipitately. He did not want to see Pat weep. His imprisonment had left him far too emotional for comfort.

He left the building by the Embankment exit, and turned into the gardens and took a chair as far from the band as possible. He wanted to think, if think he could, but his mind was playing him annoying tricks. There were times when concentration was almost impossible for him, and this was one of them. He could only think of Pat, and how much he wanted to hang on to her. It suddenly occurred to him that he could marry her if there was no other way out of the difficulty. There was no reason why he shouldn't; he was a bachelor and she was a spinster. But he repudiated that idea immediately. He was absolutely smashed up, in mind, body and estate. He could not give her what a man should give a woman. He wasn't capable of being a husband to any woman. Too completely burnt out. Pat amused him and distracted his mind in a way nothing else had ever done. She prevented him from thinking, and brooding, and going over things in a never-ending circle, with Portland as an eternal drop-scene behind him wherever he was and the voices of the warders and the clang of the cell doors as a perpetual obligato; for the minute Pat appeared, the ceaseless, senseless reiteration stopped, faded clean out, and his mind was normal for the time being. He did not want her as a woman; he had spoken the literal truth when he had said that he had no use for women. He wanted her as a drug.

It was a devilish situation in which to put a young and inexperienced girl, and especially a warm-hearted, impulsive child like Pat. If he kept her constantly with him, as every overstrained nerve urged him to do, and did not marry her, he was doing her a great wrong; but if he married her and could not be a husband to her, he was doing her a greater. If he packed her back to her family, which was much the wisest thing to do, he would drop back into the bottomless pit of melancholia, from which he now saw hopes of escape.

The very idea of letting the girl go set his head whirling. He had important letters to do, and he could not concentrate on them. He had important interviews that afternoon, and if he took anything to eat or drink between now and then, in the state he was in; he would probably vomit; and if he didn't, he would probably keel over in a faint in the middle of an interview.

It was at that moment that a shadow fell across his chair and a cheerful voice said, "Well, sir, and what are you doing, taking time off during working hours?" and he looked up with a nervous start to find Inspector Saunders standing over him.

Now Inspector Saunders had had a long experience of prisoners and captives, and he knew only too well the mental confusion and sudden, uncontrollable outbursts of hysteria to which they are liable, and he saw that Pharmakos was blowing up for storm.

"I think the best thing I can do for you," he said affably, "Is to take you home to your sister."

"Leave me alone, damn you!" snarled Pharmakos.

" Come on, stand up," said Saunders.

Pharmakos had listened to the voice of authority for seven long years, and he responded automatically in his confused state, as Saunders had known he would. He stood up and came to a limp kind of attention. Saunders did not take hold of him, but just touched elbows with him, and he fell into step alongside the detective, moving like a man sleepwalking. Saunders marched him back to Crispin House by the simple expedient of keeping step with him.

Pat looked up from her typing to see a dazed-looking Pharmakos, who did not seem to see her, being pushed into the room by Inspector Saunders.

"He's got one of his turns, miss," said Saunders, dropping him into an arm-chair as if he had been a rag-doll. Then he beckoned Pat to follow him into the outer office.

"Ever seen him like this before, miss?"

"No, never. But then I've only just joined up with him. I've only just left school."

"Then you've got your hands full. You had better send for Skilly. He knows how to manage him. Now look, miss, I'll give you a word or two. I've seen chaps like this before. You talk to him. He mayn't take any notice of you but he hears more than you think. You make him pay attention and wake him up. Then you give him a nice cup of tea, see? He mayn't be able to take much when he's like this, because fellers like him generally come out of quod with indigestion; but make him take something. If he gets noisy and making a fuss, you speak to him loud and firm, and chuck some water at him. It's just hysterics, same as housemaids get. I wish I could stop with you till he settles down, but I can't. You get hold of Skilly on the phone, miss."

He opened the door between the two rooms and looked in. Pharmakos was sitting with his elbows on his knees and his head in his hands. It is the attitude of a man who gets what ease he can in a backless seat.

"Look at him," whispered Saunders, "He thinks he's back in chokie, sitting on a three-legged stool. Go on in and keep an eye on him. I must run." And he pushed Pat into the room and shut the door behind her.

CHAPTER V

PAT looked at the immobile figure, sitting in the crouching attitude of Rodin's *Pensur*, and just as still. She felt rather scared, now that the kindly detective had taken his departure. Despite his reiterated advice to get hold of Skilly, he had omitted to tell her where Skilly was to be found. Any form of mental abnormality is an alarming thing to those who are not used to it. They know of no half-way house between sanity and homicidal mania.

She had had her instructions, however, and from a man who she felt knew what he was talking about. She was to speak to Pharmakos, attract his attention, make him come back from the past, where he had wandered off and got lost in dark places. The smallest of the Stone tribe, the only one she cared anything about, was subject to night terrors, and used to sit up in his cot and howl till Pat came to him. No one else could do anything with him. It seemed to her that if she dealt with Pharmakos in the way she had found effectual with the small Eric, she might be able to get some sense out of him. She did not like Saunders' suggestion that she should throw cold water over that passive figure. Scolding and punishing were no use with Eric; and sympathy was worse than useless, it would only make him howl the louder.

She had learnt with Eric that the sound of his own name had a curious power over him, to command his attention, even when he was absorbed with his bogeys. She would try the same trick on Pharmakos. But what should she call him? Pharmakos was an assumed name. It would mean nothing to him in his present state. Julian was his own name, however; she would have to call him Julian. Pat blushed at the very idea. She had been very strictly brought up and had had no experience of boy and girl flirtations, and in consequence was very shy at heart with the male of the species, though her fiery, red-headed spirit enabled her to carry off her embarrassment without revealing it.

However, there was nothing else for it. She had got to make a start. Pharmakos could not sit there for ever. She cleared her throat. "Julian," she said. The man took no notice. "Julian," she said again. Still no response. This was worse than the howling Eric; one knew he was alive, anyway. However, she had broken the ice, and she began to warm up to her work. In dealing with Eric, she laid hold of him, and either patted him on the back or shook him according to the quality of his howls; but she shrank from touching Pharmakos. Like many impulsive, warm-hearted people, there was something deeply virginal in Pat that had never been broken down by the casual familiarity of flirtation. It was bad enough to have to call her employer by his Christian name; touch him she wouldn't.

She sat on her heels in front of Pharmakos, thus bringing her head on a level with his. She was close to him, within hand-touch of him, and yet he seemed a long way off. Something of the obsession that was upon him was beginning to creep over her. It began to seem to her as if he actually were sitting in a cell in the drab convict garb, and his cropped head bore out the illusion. This would never do. She would be as bad as he was if she did not keep herself in hand. That motionless, bowed figure was a painful sight. She could have wept over him, but that would have been a fatal thing to do. She must keep her head. She remembered that Saunders had said that she was to talk to him, and that he would hear much more than he appeared to do.

"Julian," she began again. She must say something, anything, to break the spell and touch his wandering mind. "Julian, it's me, it's Pat talking to you. You have got to wake up and come back. Come back and we'll have tea together. This is just a bad dream, you must wake up and come back."

It was so exactly the way she talked to Eric that she almost expected to see Pharmakos double his fists into his eyes and raise a howl. She wished she dared pat him on the back. She was sure it would have done him all the good in the world; but she daren't.

So she went on, calling him by his name over and over again and telling him to come back and have tea with her. Finally he stirred, and lifted his head from his hands and looked at her with misty, half-blind eyes, like a man rousing with difficulty from a drugged sleep.

"Why, it's Pat," he said. "What are you doing there? What's this I hear about tea? Are you going to make me some? That would be a splendid idea."

"It's the best and brightest idea I ever had," said Pat, talking desperately for the sake of talking as she watched Pharmakos struggling to pull himself together. "And while you've been out I've been practising in front of the mirror calling you by your Christian name, and I don't blush anything like I did."

Pharmakos began to smile. "Let me hear you do it," he said.

"No," said Pat wriggling, "I can't do it in cold blood. I'll make you some tea instead."

When she returned with the tray Pharmakos was lying back in the chair with his long legs stretched out, relaxed. He looked very tired, and every line in his sallow, dry-skinned face was exaggerated, but his eyes were normal.

She had hardly put the tray down when the telephone bell rang. Pharmakos jumped half out of his chair. She hated to see those nervous starts of his because she knew he hated her to see them. She answered the phone, and to her amazement found it was her father.

Pharmakos saw by her face and voice that the message was for her. He had not yet recovered full mastery of himself, and in his unstrung state leapt to the conclusion that she was being told to go home and that she would abandon him and go. He sat crouched in his chair, watching every change of expression on her face, his eyes like those of a hunted animal.

He heard her say, "Yes. Yes. I understand. Yes, I understand perfectly. Yes, I fully realise. That's my lookout. Can I have my things? Very good," with long pauses between each sentence that sent him half crazy with anxiety. Finally she hung up the receiver and turned towards him, and saw his face.

"Pat, what are you going to do?" he demanded urgently.

Pat was so startled by his ghastly appearance that she could not speak for a moment. He looked like a skull dug up from a graveyard. The effect was horrible. He saw he had frightened her, he had got enough wits left for that, and he turned round and buried his offending face in the cushions.

"All right," he said in a muffled voice, " Go."

Pat wished to goodness she knew where to lay hands on Skilly. What had upset him now? Something that had happened while he was out, she presumed. Well, there was nothing for it but to go on talking and trust to luck that he would come to his senses in the near future. She knew he had appointments that afternoon, and he was in no state to keep them. It was also urgently necessary that she should have a serious talk with him before six o'clock arrived. The communication she had just received on the telephone demanded consideration, to put it mildly. Pat was of the opinion that in a case like this, one nail might drive out another. It had done so on one occasion with Eric when his Golliwog got its hair in the candle. If she let the latest loose on him, and gave him something fresh to worry about, he might pull himself together. It was frightfully bad for him to be going on like this.

"Now look here, Julian," she said, "You've jolly well got to wake up and give me a little attention. I'm in the dickens of a hole." It was not the opening gambit taught for use with employers by the commercial college, but it served. Pharmakos lifted his head and looked at her.

"What's the matter?" he said.

"That was my father on the phone."

"Yes, I thought it was."

" Well, he's chucked me out. Cut me off without even the proverbial shilling."

"My dear child, what do you mean?"

"You remember he told me this morning to put on my hat and come with him, and I wouldn't?"

"Yes?"

"Well, he said he had been through to mother on the phone, and they were both agreed that as I was now on my own, I could jolly well be on my own. I had made my bed, and I must lie on it. That was how he put it. And they don't want me back."

"What do you mean, child? Do you mean that you can't go home to-night?"

"Yes. That was what he said, and I know he means it. You see, I don't really belong to him, and he is only too glad of the opportunity to park me somewhere. I asked him if I could have my things, and he said no, he was giving them to the children. I've got nothing but what I stand up in. I am afraid I shall have to ask you for an advance on my salary, Mr. Pharmakos."

"My dear child!" Pharmakos sat up very straight now, all

his nerve-storms forgotten. "This is a bit of a bomb-shell, we must think it out."

But he did not need any thinking out as far as he was concerned. He was only talking to cover his tracks. A dope fiend with a hypodermic syringe in his hand was the only thing to which he could be compared, but it would not do to appear too eager and so scare Pat off.

"I have nearly finished the letters," said Pat. "Perhaps you wouldn't mind if I went off while you are out this afternoon, and looked for digs. I don't want to leave it until too late as I have got no luggage, and I must get some things for the night."

"No, my child. My little Coppernob does not run around on her own looking for digs on two pound ten a week. I think we may be able to do something better for you than that. Since your father has parked you on me, it's up to me to look after you. This is a judgement on me for telling lies to Inspector Saunders; I said I was your elder brother, and I've jolly well got to be."

Pat was so amazed with her unbelievable good fortune that she could only stare at him speechlessly. He was her film star, her employer, and her sick child in one. She was rid of the unbearable Stones for ever. She was to be Pat Pharmakos, his sister, in good earnest. Never again would she answer to the hated name of Stone. She would erase from her memory all trace of the loathly existence of such creatures.

"Pat, my child, what is all this talk of tea with which you mislead me? As soon as ever you make a pot of tea, it practically explodes on our hands. You must never do it again. We must stick to vodka, or vitriol, or something that is innocuous by comparison with what you seem to brew in a tea-pot."

"Oh dear," said Pat, "I always was a Jonah. What shall I do? Shall I make some fresh tea?"

"No, my dear. I've had quite enough of your brews for the moment. I may see a wife and ten children coming out of the tea-pot next. We will go out to lunch. It may be rather early, but I feel I could do with a little refreshment after the shocks you give me. 'Go and put your bonnet on, Patsy!' "

Pat was amazed to hear his whistling the tune of the old song as she furbished her face in front of a little looking-glass in the outer office. Was this the same man that had been brought home by Inspector Saunders less than an hour ago?

He took her to an old-fashioned City eating-house in the basement of a tavern, where the ancient waiter who paddled up on fiat feet seemed to know him, and to have unlimited respect for him.

"Good morning, John," he said, as this worthy put an enormous menu in front of him and stared at Pat. "I will have my usual, but I expect my sister will want something different. What have you got that will amuse her?"

"I am afraid we have not got very much that young ladies like, sir," said the waiter.

"She will like anything, John, she is just home from school, where they fed her on the bread and water of affliction. What will you have, Pat? Salmon and green peas?"

"Lovely," said Pat, her eyes sparkling, for she was very young in spite of her gallant attempts at maturity.

"And what will you have to drink?"

"May I have a lemon squash?"

"Right you are. Large lemon squash and two straws, please, John. A lemon squash is nothing unless you drink it through straws, is it, Pat?"

The waiter returned with a plate of white soup for Pharmakos, and an enormous helping of salmon and green peas for Pat. Pharmakos sipped at his soup very slowly, and with many pauses, as if it went down with difficulty, but Pat's salmon vanished like a conjuring trick. She was ravenously hungry. She had had no supper the previous evening, and had been so excited in the morning over her new job, and so agitated by the rumpus her father was making about her mysterious employer, that she had hardly eaten any breakfast.

"I perceive that you are not going to cause me any anxiety about your diet, Coppernob," said Pharmakos, watching her with amusement.

"I'm simply ravenous," said Pat, "Do you know, I've had nothing since your cream horn yesterday."

"My dear kid, why didn't you tell me? Why have you had no food? What have your family been up to?"

"There was a row when I got back because I was late, and as supper was finished, I didn't get any. And there was another row this morning over you, and I couldn't, or didn't, eat any breakfast."

Any lingering qualms of conscience Pharmakos might have had about his adoption of Pat were removed by this piece of information.

Pat having polished off her salmon, and Pharmakos having got through about half of his soup, the waiter again produced the enormous bill of fare.

"Now, my child, what about apple tart and cream?"

"I'd love it," said Pat.

"Apple tart and cream for one, please, John."

"But aren't you going to have any? " asked Pat, as the waiter padded off.

"It would take a return ticket if I did," said Pharmakos. "I don't know what His Majesty's guests get when they dine at Buckingham Palace, but at some of the other places where he entertains, the menu leaves much to be desired. I've got no inside left, Pat, after being his guest for seven years."

He looked round to see if there was anyone within earshot, but it was early, and they had the big dingy room almost to themselves.

"Pat, do you mind my talking to you about my prison experiences? Does it bother you?"

"No, it doesn't bother me a bit," said Pat. "And it is a jolly good thing for you to talk and get it off your chest."

"It's a wise child," said Pharmakos. "Where did you learn all this wisdom in your short life? Who taught you how to handle gaol-birds when they are cutting their capers? I cannot imagine your revered parent associating with the criminal classes."

"I tell you where I learnt," said Pat, nodding at him serenely. She saw that he was referring indirectly to the incidents of the morning, and answered the question he shrank from asking. "I have a small brother who gets nightmares. That's how I learnt."

Pharmakos sat silently stirring his coffee for some time. Pat had got to understand his silences now, and the sudden change of subject that followed on them; therefore she could not for a moment think what he was referring to when at length he spoke.

"You have said an extraordinarily true thing, Patsy. It is exactly like a nightmare. And while I am having it I am under seven. You bear that in mind when you deal with me and you will be able to manage me all right."

He fished a lump of sugar out of his coffee, and watched it slowly dissolving in his spoon.

"Patsy," he said at length, "are you a witch?"

"Not to my knowledge," said Pat.

"Then what is it you do to me? I have never talked to anybody in my life as I talk to you, you callow throstling. Skilly never asks me anything; he knows better. Saunders asks things sometimes, and it is like pulling teeth. But if you give me the slightest encouragement, I simply gush."

Pat did not know what to answer. But apparently he did not require any answer. He was filled with an accumulation of conversation, and out it had to come.

"You know what I told you yesterday about the fellow I killed? Smashing his head on the mantelpiece, I mean? Well, I have thought of it as I dropped off to sleep every night of my life ever since. But last night, for the first time, I went to sleep without thinking of it; and to-day I can talk to you about it as calmly as if it hadn't been me at all that did it. Do you know what I am going to do, Pat? I am going to use you as a kind of kitchen sink, and gradually pour my horrid past down you. You are going to earn your salary, my child, I expect you will be asking for a rise before long."

Pat nodded. "Yes," she said in a very matter of fact voice, "I think that would be a very good plan. It would do you an awful lot of good. I shall never ask you any questions, and I shall never even refer to anything you say. A kitchen sink is the right idea, Julian."

He glanced up at her use of his name; it came out so naturally, and without any self-consciousness or embarrassment. He smiled to himself. What was it that he was proposing to take home with him? Was it an unborn child? Or a very *rusé* woman? Or, as he had originally opined, a witch? Perhaps a little bit of all three.

He gathered up his hat and stick. "Pat," he said, "There is one thing that I especially like about you, and that is that you never offer condolences."

"I am with you there," said Pat. "There is only one thing worse than receiving condolences, and that is receiving apologies."

So she had been right not to sympathise. Pharmakos was exactly like Eric. Sympathy would only have made him howl the louder.

CHAPTER VI

PHARMAKOS and Pat walked up Ludgate Hill together as far as St. Paul's Churchyard. The food had done him good and the lines of his face had relaxed; and with his hat on, hiding the hideous convict crop of the hair he affected, he was almost nice-looking, thought Pat, not merely interesting-looking. But even at his best he was no winner in a beauty contest. However, that did not matter to her, for she had got a thorough crush on him. When they parted company in the shadow of the Cathedral, he handed Pat two pound notes .

"Get yourself a nighty and a toothbrush, my child, and whatever you need for the moment. We can sort things out at our leisure afterwards. I suppose you will want a complete trousseau since papa has given everything you possess to the children; and I am sure I hope nothing fits them."

"I am afraid I am going to be an awful expense to you," said Pat .

"A fellow must be prepared to back his fancy, Pat. And perhaps you can help me economise in other ways. Stop Skilly from putting the butter on his hair instead of the toast, for instance."

Pat was within measurable distance of falling prostrate before him. So she was actually going to live with him and the mysterious Skilly? Never in her wildest dreams had such avenues of bliss opened up.

She procured herself a cheap little cotton nightgown, and a skimpy cotton kimono. She was not used to elaboration in her toilette; Mrs. Stone had seen to that. Her favourite

Woolworth provided the rest of her toilette articles, and she returned to the office with the second pound still intact, and plenty of change from the first. Pharmakos would not have his money wasted by this new secretary.

He had not said what time he would be back, but nothing would have induced her to have her tea without him, and finally he turned up at half-past five looking lined and tired, but very cheerful.

"Tea, Patsy, tea!" he cried as he came in at the door. "My tongue is literally hanging out of my mouth."

Everything was ready, and tea was produced almost before he had hung up his hat. Pat took it for granted that she joined him in the inner office; no need to send for her formally on each occasion, he noticed. She was quick in the uptake, like most red-heads, thank goodness. He had already come to realise that she divined his moods with an uncanny accuracy, which was a blessed mercy, for he was quite inarticulate and powerless to explain himself when his moods were on him.

Pat was indulging in a bath bun, but beside his cup was a plate full of little plain crisp biscuits of various shapes. Well done, Pat; this was the sort of thing he could manage to eat. What a sensible child it was. He nibbled a crisp, sharp-flavoured biscuit, and a palate long inured to slops responded gratefully. There was certainly something magical about Pat's power over him. The soup had gone to its appointed place and stayed there without a murmur, which was a good deal more than he had expected, for after one of his nerve-storms he generally had at least nausea, if not more severe symptoms, for a couple of days. The biscuits, too, were being gratefully accepted by his usually ungrateful stomach, and did not taste like sewage in the mouth and feel like fish-hooks inside him. If, under Pat's ministrations, he could get food down, and manage to keep it down, it was going to make all the difference in the world to him. The thing that was chiefly the matter with him was semi-starvation from sheer inability to take food, a not uncommon complaint among prisoners and captives.

"Now, Pat, my child," he said at the conclusion of the little meal, giving her a cigarette, and observing from the way she went to work with it that Mr. Stone had not allowed smoking.

"We have got to have a little business talk together."

Pat, who would have been willing to discuss the higher mathematics with him so long as she enjoyed the pleasure of his company, acquiesced.

Pharmakos paused. It was a little difficult to know at which end to begin. But what did it matter with Pat? She was such an understanding little soul she would not misjudge him, however he put it, but see through to his meaning.

"Do you think you could endure life in an empty warehouse, very dilapidated, which is liable to fall down and hit you on the head at any minute, and where the rats sit up and wash their whiskers and stare at you while you are having a bath?"

"Yes," said Pat, "I am sure I could, as long as there weren't too many rats."

"Well, I am putting the worst complexion on it, so that you will not subsequently be disillusioned. It is not quite as bad as all that. The rats only did that once. The part of the warehouse that I inhabit has been repaired, and there are various devices by which the rats can be excluded from the actual living apartments, though to eliminate them from the place as a whole is a hopeless undertaking.

"Now, in addition to rats, there are other drawbacks to the place as a habitation for a maiden lady of tender years. Skilly and me, for instance. I need no introduction to you, as the announcers say; but Skilly needs a good deal of introducing. Perhaps if I tell you something about him, you will understand him better. Persons can only be seen in perspective against their backgrounds, don't you think?"

"Yes," said Pat, tremendously thrilled, for it all sounded so intensely romantic. Pharmakos noted her sparkling eyes, and a qualm of self-contempt seized him. It was a rotten thing that he was doing to the child. He ought to have taken her to the G.F.S. hostel. But will the dope-taker lay down the syringe that he holds in his hand? He will not.

Pharmakos continued. "Skilly started life as a bargee. He continued it as a bruiser, and he was busy ending it as a burglar when I took him in hand and persuaded him that honesty was the best policy, which is the only kind of honesty that a person like Skilly comprehends. But he is a decent creature, Pat, awfully decent in his way; and if it hadn't been for Skilly there wouldn't be any Pharmakos. He was my next-door neighbour at Portland, and used to knock on the wall to me when I started cutting capers. Chaps in prison talk to each other by tapping on the cell walls, you know; or perhaps you don't know, never having done time yourself. At any rate, I owe what little sanity I have to Skilly. I should have gone clean off my head and stayed there if it hadn't been for him. When I came out, he met me. No one else did, Pat. That was when I made up my mind to change my name.

"I hadn't a bean, but old Skilly took me to the sort of dive where a person like myself would be welcome, and he introduced me to an individual of the name of Jurgens; at any rate, that was what he said his name was, same as mine is Pharmakos. Skilly had taken on a job with Jurgens. He isn't quite as young as he was, and he had contracted rheumatics while he was stopping with King George. Catburgling is a thing for the young and slim, like mannequin parades; and Skilly had lost the figure for it during his last stretch. Prison diet agreed with him better than it did with me. So he took on a job with Jurgens as being more restful than his previous occupation. Jurgens wanted Skilly as a professional bully and beater-up, which suited Skilly down to the ground, what with his bruiser's experience and bargee's vocabulary.

"He had talked to Jurgens about me, which was kindly meant, and when I came out of Portland there was a job awaiting me with the firm. Well, to make a long story short, Skilly took me to interview Jurgens in a posh house out on Hampstead Heath; Jurgens received me in what was ostensibly an office and had probably been a billiard room, because it was built out at the back into the garden, and had only a skylight and no windows. Well, Jurgens unfolded the tale, with Skilly sitting by and looking on and admiring his brains; which was a jolly good job, or once again I shouldn't be here to tell the tale, but should have swung in good earnest that time. And Jurgens' tale was this, that he had applied scientific organisation and modern methods to the development of blackmail, and was carrying on business on a large scale and wanted me as one of the sub-contractors.

"Well, Pat, it was owing to blackmail that I landed in my trouble; and when I realised what he was driving at, and what he was (and he didn't mince matters), I saw red; and I went for Mr. Jurgens, and I got him by the throat and commenced to swing him about, and if it hadn't been that Skilly pulled me off him, and laid my head open in the process," —he raised his hand to a scar plainly visible through the close-cropped, rusty red hair— "I should certainly have killed him in just the same way as I killed the other fellow.

"Well, we laid him gently down on the hearthrug, and uncommon dead he looked; but Skilly, who is an authority upon how dead an apparent corpse may be, said he was only pretty thoroughly concussed. Then the question arose as to what Skilly and I were to do, for Skilly was now out of a job, and I had obviously failed to obtain the engagement, and neither of us had private means. So we took up a collection from Mr. Jurgens. It was Skilly who put the idea into my head, I'll say that for myself, Pat, but he just wanted to go through his pockets and get the ornaments off the mantelpiece, because that was the best he knew. But Jurgens had been right when he thought I could apply scientific methods to crime, and I made Skilly leave the chandelier on his shirtfront alone; and we took the fire-irons, and opened up his desk and got his papers. We got his keys off him, too, and opened his safe; a whacking great safe, Pat, like a young strong-room; and we cleared that out also. We pulled a *portiere* off the door, and shoved the loot into it, and I gave Skilly a leg up, and out we went through the skylight, and down through the bushes, and over the garden wall, loot and all.

"Skilly knew of a friendly taxicab proprietor in that neighbourhood who had not got a soul above such things, and went to look him up, leaving me in the bushes on Hampstead Heath, bleeding like a stuck pig. There was a good deal of light from a lamp in the road, and I squatted down in it and took a preliminary look through the loot. It was a mad thing to do, of course, but you know what my nerves are like, Pat, and I was only just out, and I simply couldn't have kept quiet in the dark and waited. I'd have yelled. I had to have light, and I had to have something to do. I was a dashed sight less scared of the police than I was of the dark. That's the sort of imbecile I am, Pat.

"Well, by the time Skilly and his motoring friend arrived round with the taxi, I had been through a good many of those papers, and had seen the kind of stuff we had got. Pat, I could have blackmailed the whole of Debrett!

"Well, to abbreviate my story once more; we went off in that taxi to God knows where. The first thing to do was to find a suitable doctor who would ask no questions and put some stitches in my head, where Skilly had koshed me in his laudable endeavour to prevent a breach of the peace. We also wanted to put as much distance as possible between ourselves and the scene of our crime; that is a basic criminal instinct, Pat, and if you ever commit a crime, you will know why. So we tootled off right across London, the taximeter ticking up tuppences that nobody meant to pay, and finally we landed ourselves in Lambeth where Skilly had other friends, and I got a tuck run in my scalp by a pretty competent artist—when he is sober, that is.

"But we still had a curtainful of highly incriminating loot on our hands, and if we had taken it back to the dive where we were lodging, the whole place would have wanted to come in on the deal. So we couldn't go there. We tootled through the back streets of Lambeth at a foot-pace, trying to put in some effective brain-work. Then I had another inspiration.

"It was only six o'clock in the evening, though it was pitch dark, and I caught sight of a house agent's that was just engaged in putting up the shutters. So we pulled up the taxi, and I popped in. My clothes were pretty good, being the ones I had gone into clink with, which had had a complete rest for seven years, and I put on my best haw-haw manner and the estate agent took me at my face value. Anyway, I don't fancy they are frightfully particular about anything except the rent in that district.

"I told him I wanted a small warehouse; I did not ask for an office or anything like that, because that would probably have been one among many; but a warehouse usually stands on its own feet, as it were, and is at least semi-detached, and the one thing we wanted was privacy. I also explained that I wanted to have a look round then and there, dark as it was, as I had got to have somewhere to dump stuff that was paying demurrage—sitting at the railway station, and paying the rent of its trucks, that is—which is an expensive job, so he would understand why I was in a hurry. I also asked him if he would be good enough to take me round to look at some warehouses forthwith. Wasn't I wily, Pat? It was the last thing I wanted him to do, for the very look of Skilly and that bulging *portiere* would have been enough to have sent any honest man to the police with the information. But I knew that if I showed signs of wanting to be alone with the keys, he would smell a rat. But I knew also that he would be wanting to go home to his tea, as he was putting the shutters up, and I reckoned that if I inspired him with a reasonable amount of confidence, he would trust me with the keys, especially as they weren't his keys.

"And I was right; he not only gave me handfuls of keys and positively pushed me out of the shop, but he also lent me a very serviceable electric torch. What it is to look honest, Pat!

"Well, we went to the nearest address of those he had given me. Any port in a storm was good enough for us to unload that darned curtain into. We were terrified of being stopped by a bobby who might want to have a look inside the taxi, for we had beastly guilty consciences, not having made any preparations for a crime of this nature. I was sweating like a frightened horse because I was so scared, and I knew if I had another go of pneumonia it was all up with me, as I was barely convalescent from the last one. I wasn't going back into prison on any terms, and I hadn't got the means of suicide on me because I hadn't expected to get into trouble; and altogether, what with one thing and another, and my cut head, I was just about all in. So we went to the nearest, and our luck held.

"It's the sort of place that might have come out of Dickens, Pat. I've christened it Quilp Cottage. It's right on the edge of the water, and it's got a dear little private dock of its own, full of dead cats and other corpses, that smells like Margate sands at low tide. It suited me absolutely down to the ground and I've been there ever since.

"You see, Pat, I can't stick low rooms and small windows, having had rather more than my fair share of them. I feel as if I were going to choke and smother; and if I can't get air quickly, I get a kind of asthma attack, and start choking in good earnest .. It's all nerves of course, and I don't suppose there is the slightest likelihood of my really choking, but it is rather unpleasant while it lasts.

"Well, this little warehouse has got four magnificent windows twenty feet high apiece, overlooking the river. So there was all the air and space that the most fastidious gaolbird could desire. I have made it into a bed-sitting room and it's positively palatial. We haven't done up the outside of the building; that retains all its original grime and dilapidation; but the inside is O.K.

"Skilly camps out in a kind of door-keeper's shanty at the far end of the yard, by the big gates that lead into the street, so when he gets tight and waxes musical it doesn't bother me. Now it is in my mind, Pat, that if we can make it rat-proof, you could camp out in the caretaker's quarters, which are immediately underneath my palatial abode. How does the idea appeal to you?"

"Oo-oo-oo-ooh!" said Pat, entirely past speech.

"Your remarks are not very lucid," said Pharmakos. "But I gather from the way your mouth is watering that my suggestion is acceptable. Very well, Pat, you can furnish at Woolworth's according to your own ideas of taste and good form, and send the bill in to me."

CHAPTER VII

"I THINK we will treat ourselves to a taxi, I'm rather tired," said Pharmakos as they alighted from the lift on their way out, after shutting up the office. "Taxi, please, porter." The porter did not answer, and moved off sullenly to fetch the taxi.

"Yes, Warder Mills" said Pharmakos to his oblivious back. "You will fetch a taxi for me, Number One-three-nought, and you won't get a tanner for doing it, either, my lad."

"Waterloo Station," he said to the driver as he put Pat into the taxi, and the porter, who was lingering within earshot, turned away in disgust. Waterloo station is a very non-committal address.

"I have no intention of taking you away by train, my child," said Pharmakos, "But Waterloo station is handy for my little place, and this is a regular taxi-cabby on our rank, and probably a pal of the porter's, so I did not wish to confide in him the address of Quilp Cottage."

"You are very quiet, my dear," said Pharmakos, when they found themselves alone in the intimacy of the taxi. "What are you thinking about. Have you got the wind up at the prospect that opens out before you? I can take you to a girls' club, Pat, if you would prefer it."

"It isn't that," said Pat; and turning round in the confined space of the taxi, she faced him, to find him looking down at her with a very intent gaze, and his mouth twitching.

"I want to ask you something."

"What is it, Pat?"

"Did you—did you blackmail all those people with the papers you had got hold of?"

"No, Pat, I did not. I sorted them into two piles; those who were making use of solicitors to deal with Jurgens and those who were not. Wherever a solicitor was mentioned, I went straight to him and handed him the papers and said, "These papers have come into my possession. You mustn't ask me how. I have just come out of gaol after doing a stretch of seven years for manslaughtering a blackmailer. I haven't got a bean. I look to you to do the decent thing by me if these papers are of any value to you. And, by Jove, Pat, they practically all of 'em funded up handsome."

"Oh, Julian, I'm so glad," said Pat. "I would have hated you to have done anything dishonest."

Pharmakos looked down at her eager little face, flushed under its big hat. "Would you, dear?" he said ... Well, I have always wanted to run straight. I haven't got criminal inclinations, Pat, in spite of my record. And now I have got you to look after, I shall have to run extra straight, shan't I?"

The taxi pulled up in Waterloo station, and they got out and made their way through dense crowds of holiday makers.

"Now, my child," said Pharmakos, "I am going to show you a side of London which I don't suppose you have ever seen before. The salubrious spot we are now in rejoices in the name of Lower Marsh, and it is well named. You will go a long way before you find anything lower or more marshy. This opening which looms before us is the mouth of Hell, and we will go home that way, for we fear the light because our deeds are evil."

He led Pat, who could hardly repress a shudder, into a vast underground road that appeared to stretch away into echoing infinity. There was not a soul in sight. The place was fairly brightly lit, and the white-tiled walls were clean, but the effect of the sudden passing from bright sunlight into this subterranean way was eerie in the extreme. The impression was not improved when an appalling din smote upon their ears, coming from the shadowy distance, and growing gradually louder as it approached till it was simply deafening. By the time Pat had made up her mind that her last hour had come, a lorry full of empty milk-churns came around the corner.

"We are underneath Waterloo station," said Pharmakos, "and these tunnels represent old rights of way, which it would have required an Act of Parliament to extinguish. They are useful short cuts when you know them and perfectly harmless, being thoroughly well policed. You need never hesitate to make use of them, Pat, no one will cut your throat, though I admit they are unprepossessing at first sight."

They came out into the bright sunshine again, and made their way over ankle-twisting cobbles, Pharmakos covering them with his long strides, and Pat stepping daintily from one to another, like a cat. Sundry slatternly women stood at the doors of country cottages and stared at Pat. Pharmakos seemed to cause them no excitement. He was evidently a familiar figure in this part of the world.

"Good evening, Mrs. Mullins," he said, nodding to one of the better specimens. "My sister is coming to keep house for me. Can you give her an hour or two if she wants a bit of cleaning done?"

Mrs. Mullins was all smiles and assurances that Miss Pharmakos should be well done for, she having been in good service in a fried fish shop in the days of her youth.

"Now you are duly ticketed, Pat, and no questions will be asked, and no one will stare at you in this district, except to see what your latest hat is like. My record, Patrick, is as good as a Norman pedigree on this side of the river."

Pat's heart was beating painfully as she hurried to keep

pace with his long strides. She had got an attack of cold feet, red though her head was. Her Stone training rose up and smote her; the impress of a person like Mr. Stone is not readily thrown off, however much one may dislike him, Pat was by no means ignorant of the seamy side of life, for Mr. Stone believed in being plain-spoken on the subject of sin; in fact, an uncharitable person might almost have said that he dwelt on it with gusto. Was it possible, she wondered, that Pharmakos was kidnapping her for the White Slave Traffic? It did not tend to reassure her when they turned into a narrow, dingy street, walled in by windowless warehouses like cliffs. The street was a blind alley, and its end consisted of a dark archway in the fortress-like façade entirely filled in by a pair of enormous solid wooden gates, paintless, but nevertheless in an excellent state of repair, and allowing neither foothold nor peephole to the curious or evilly disposed. In the left-hand gate was a small door, which opened to a Yale key inserted by Pharmakos.

"We're home, Pat," he said, as he held the low, narrow door open for her to enter, and she stepped over a high sill into a paved yard, to be greeted immediately by the smell of the river. This was certainly the kind of place from which girls could be shipped to Buenos Aires, the great gates rendering all thought of escape impossible. Ahead of her was a twenty-foot drop to swirling brown water, and on either hand rose the windowless walls of warehouses. It was as private, and about as prepossessing, as the yard of a slaughterhouse.

"Come along, child, and remember to keep well into the wall on a dark night; if you fell into my private dock, you would have to stop there, for there is no way of climbing out. I had to fish Skilly out once when he came home tight, and I have no wish to have to perform the same service for you."

Pat saw that the centre of the yard was composed of emptiness bounded by nothing more substantial than a piece of stout cord looped between bollards. From the depths of the emptiness rose a smell as of sea-beaches. They had to proceed in single file, for the way between the edge of the wharf and the wall was too narrow to permit of two persons walking abreast in comfort. That was where they disposed of the bodies of the girls they could not bend to their will, thought Pat, and shuddered as she- gazed into the depths, and saw, twenty feet below, what looked like the dregs of a vast cup of cocoa slowly stirring upon themselves.

Pharmakos pushed open a battered door in the cliff-like wall. "We don't trouble to lock up in here," he said. "The place is as strong as a fort." A remark which did not add to Pat's peace of mind. He was telling her plainly that resistance was useless.

They found themselves standing on a spiral stone staircase, that led both up and down. There was nothing by way of an entrance hall, and anyone entering precipitately would have taken a header down the awkwardly placed, curving stairs. They looked as if they had not been swept for years, and as far as could be seen in the dim light, the whitewash of the walls had not been renewed since it had suffered during Noah's flood.

"You are never to touch these stairs, Pat, they are part of my stock in trade. You must keep your housewifely hands from picking and stealing where the entrance to the premises is concerned. It doesn't do to be too clean in this district. Only excites suspicion."

Pat, in a state of cold terror, followed him up those dreadful stairs, and heard things scuffle and squeak in the depths that opened up like a well below them. It was impossible to see what lay ahead, for the staircase was apparently built in the thickness of the wall. They climbed to a considerable height, so it seemed to Pat, and then Pharmakos inserted a Yale key in another battered, heavily-constructed door, almost bereft of paint. It opened, and she followed him into a room lit only by such light as filtered through a partition of frosted glass. It was a dingy kind of office, such as might be used by a warehouse foreman. In the outer door was a little pigeon-hole closed by a shutter, through which it was possible to speak to whoever might be outside without having to open the door. The only furniture was a battered roll-top desk of the cheapest make, a deal table, and two or three wooden kitchen chairs. A bare electric bulb hung by its flex from an enormously high ceiling. The floor was carpetless and filthy dirty.

"How do you like it, Pat?" asked Pharmakos, turning round with a laugh. Then he saw her face. "Child, what's the matter?" he said, "Have I scared you with my beastly abode? I thought I had warned you. What's the matter, kiddy?" He came back and stood close to her, but he did not touch her.

"It's all right, Pat, there is nothing to be scared of. You are my little kid sister, you know. You are not frightened of your big brother, are you? I have to keep my outer premises like this, because it's what callers in this district like and expect. It's only camouflage, dear, it does not represent my personal tastes. Now come along and see something more cheerful."

He opened a door in the partition, and immediately a golden-red ray of the setting sun shone into the dusty atmosphere, and Pat found herself looking into an enormous room, almost big enough to be a concert hall, furnished with a beauty and a gorgeousness such as her insular eyes had never beheld since they opened to the suburban light.

"O-oh!" she exclaimed, "How perfectly lovely!" All her fears were forgotten at the sight of the marvellous room before her.

"Like it, Pat?" said Pharmakos, laughing with relief at

her sudden recovery from her panic at the sight of his treasure house, and the natural delight of a flattered man who sees that he has really made an impression in the quarter where he most desires it.

"O-oh," said Pat, "I've never seen anything like it. Isn't it simply too lovely for words!"

The parquetry floor was polished till it shone like a lake where the pools of light fell on it from the setting sun that poured in through the enormous, curtainless windows.

"Mind how you walk, Pat," said Pharmakos, "It's darn slippery. This floor is the pride of Lamprey's life. You will sit down with a bang if you don't walk warily."

Strewn about on the great expanse of highly polished wood were superb blue Chinese rugs. Carpets, to be precise, but they looked no more than rugs in its huge acreage. At one end was a big anthracite stove, and at the other, the far end, a wide brick hearth, such as might have graced the hall of a baronial castle.

"Come and see the view, Pat," said Pharmakos, and led her across to the windows. It was quite a long walk from the door to the windows. Pharmakos had certainly got all, that the most exacting ex-convict could desire by way of contrast with his cell.

Pharmakos tried to open a window, but failed.

"Damn!" he exclaimed, angrily, "Skilly has screwed them up again!" He seized hold of a pair of stout cords that hung at either side, and the upper half of the window slid down on well-oiled runners. It would take a very active man to fling himself out of a window of that size, the lower half of which had been rendered immovable.

The contretemps seemed to ruffle Pharmakos. He glanced at Pat to see if she had realised the significance of those screwed-up windows, but she had not, and was gazing enraptured at the view that opened before her.

The river, a golden glory in the setting sun, rolled in a great curve to Westminster. Just below the windows a tug was panting along with a string of barges, keeping well into the bank to avoid the current. The only drawback to the enjoyment of the view was the fact that the windows had not been cleaned on the outside for years.

"Sorry to have to keep the windows like this, Patsy, but to have a clean window in this part of the world would be just about the equivalent of chalking a cross on it and writing, 'Lord have mercy on us' underneath. Now come and sit down, if you've done admiring the view. It's rather nice, isn't it?"

He led her off on another long walk to the fire-place, and put her into an enormous arm-chair; a chair so enormous that when she settled herself back in the cushions, her feet stuck out in front of her like a child's. He himself dropped into another such chair on the opposite side of the hearth, and put his feet on a pouffe. She saw that he wore exceedingly well-made dark brown suede shoes and silk socks of a slightly lighter shade; but his ankle-bones destroyed the illusion of elegance by sticking out like door-handles on either side of the long, narrow foot, and the bones of his knee-cap showed through the thin cloth of his elegant summer suiting. He was like an inadequately draped skeleton, for all his Saville Row tailoring.

"It's good to be home," he said, heaving a sigh of relief, "By Jove, Pat, I'm tired." He looked about nine feet long, stretched out like that, with his extreme thinness.

"I suppose I ought to rise up and do the polite and offer you cocktails, but really, old thing, I'm going to ask you to excuse me. I am too tired to put one foot before the other. There are the makings of innumerable cocktails in that cupboard, if you fancy one. Do you take cocktails, Pat?"

"No," said Pat, "Ice-cream sodas are my beverage."

Pharmakos waved his hand towards the magnificent room.

"Prowl around and amuse yourself, my child. There is plenty to amuse you if you have got a cultivated taste. I am going to have forty winks. I'm dead to the wide. Then I shall be able to talk to you more intelligently than I am capable of doing at the present moment. Have a look all round the establishment. Explore the park. I am sorry there is no one to show you around. It's the butler's afternoon out. In other words, Skilly is engaged in trailing a gentleman of easy virtue who may or may not be departing for the Continent."

CHAPTER VIII

PAT watched him lay his head back on the cushions and look not merely dead, but decomposed. What a terrible face he had, yet how fascinating, she thought. The only person she had ever seen that he resembled in the very least, was the ancient Egyptian curled up stark naked on his side in an imitation grave in the mummy room at the British Museum. There was really a very strong resemblance between them, even to the hair. The principal difference lay in the fact that the mummy had met with a misfortune about the nose, while Pharmakos had a magnificent eagle beak. Their complexions, however, were practically identical.

Pat scrambled cautiously out of her chair and began to explore the room as bidden. She saw that what had appeared from the far side to be a gimcrack wooden partition filled with frosted glass, from this side turned out to be a lovely piece of carving that was evidently taken from the choir-stalls of an old church. The door itself probably came from the same source. The partition was far from gimcrack. It would, in fact, have resisted anything except pickaxes, and being double, made eavesdropping impossible.

There were wide, cushioned window-seats under the windows, and Pat perched on one and watched a river steamer duck its funnel as it went under Blackfriars Bridge. The river was simply fascinating. She could have watched it for hours. But curiosity was still unsatisfied, and Pat resumed her prowlings again.

Between the windows hung enormous curtains of midnight blue velvet. A superb velvet, none of your common cotton velour, such as they had in the dining-room at home. They were not meant to be drawn, however, and the immense windows evidently stood bare and open, day and night. Pat remembered what Pharmakos had hinted about his reactions to the narrow confines of a prison cell.

Dotted here and there about the room were beautiful pieces of furniture, each a museum specimen. On several of them stood great lamps with gorgeous shades. How wonderful they must look when they were all alight, thought Pat, and how brightly the room would be lit when they were all going.

In the corner between the fire and the windows, immediately under one window, in fact, was a gigantic divan, exactly square, covered with a very dark plum-coloured velvet spread that toned like the petals of an exotic fuchsia with the blue of the curtains that hung beside those enormous windows. Everything in the room was of gargantuan size, she thought with amusement. She supposed that everything in a prison cell was correspondingly small and cramped. The window beside this divan was made to open at the bottom, however, but there was a kind of wire window-box on the sill that would have made it almost impossible for anyone to do more than stick their heads out of it.

A long refectory table, superbly carved and supported by bulbous legs, stood in the middle of the room. At each end were arm-chairs with very high backs covered with embossed velvet of wine-dark crimson, thus continuing the midnight fuchsia effect. On either side of the table were backless benches with elaborate legs; on these lay long pads of the same velvet, with heavy, dull gold fringes.

There were innumerable coffers, chests, cabinets, and God knows what, ranged at intervals along the far wall, a blank windowless wall of such immense height that Pat could not see where it joined the ceiling, for the sun had sunk behind the buildings across the river, and dusk was creeping into the huge room through all its four vast windows.

She returned to the fire-place end of the room. There was a blue carpet on the floor into which she felt that she literally sank to her ankles. There was also a gargantuan chesterfield facing the fire-place, and two or three low tabourets and pouffes scattered between the chesterfield and the edge of the wide brick plinth that served as a hearth. The place had obviously been equipped regardless of cost, and by someone who knew what comfort was, as well as beauty.

Pharmakos lay motionless in his chair, apparently asleep. But somehow Pat doubted if he really were asleep; he seemed rather to be deliberately resting by means of relaxation of all his limbs. She did not wish to disturb him, so she slipped quietly back into her chair, and curled up in it like a kitten, which was the only comfortable attitude for a person of Pat's size, for the chair was apparently designed for the use of Lifeguardsmen.

"Seen all you want to see, Pat?" said Pharmakos, without opening his eyes.

"No," said Pat, "I haven't. It's simply marvellous. It would take me days to see all there is to see."

The death-mask opposite her wrinkled its dry skin into a smile. He dearly loved Pat's admiration and artless flattery.

"I am wondering what to do about your supper, Patsy. You see, we weren't expecting visitors, and I don't suppose Skilly has laid in any supplies. You had better burgle about in the kitchen and see if you can find his breakfast, and eat that."

"Where is the kitchen?" asked Pat.

"It is the door behind me," said Pharmakos. "The one behind you is the bathroom. We shall have to share a bathroom, my dear; though we need not necessarily indulge in mixed bathing. I look my best when draped."

Pat looked round to see where the doors might be, for she had not observed them during her exploration of the room, and she saw that set in the bookcases that flanked the fireplace were two plum-coloured velvet curtains, similar to the one spread on the enormous divan, which she presumed was Pharmakos' bed. He had probably taken a dislike to narrow beds while in prison.

She thrust back the curtain behind his chair, and opened the door hidden by it, and found herself in a white enamelled kitchen, small and elaborately equipped, like a ship's galley. Everything was beautifully neat and as clean as a new pin.

There were no signs of a larder or a meat-safe, but she suddenly realised that the large white-enamelled object that clicked faintly at intervals, was an electric refrigerator. She opened it and discovered a great pile of rashers of bacon on a plate, and any quantity of eggs in a basin. SkiIly would have to have an appetite on the same scale as the rest of Pharmakos' furniture if he were going to eat all that for his breakfast.

But even so, she could not give Pharmakos fried bacon for his supper; he would never be able to digest it. She penetrated farther into the ice-safe, and found a large bottle of milk. She possessed herself of this, and while her bacon was frying, warmed some milk, beat up an egg in it, and then added meat extract. This she bore in to Pharmakos.

"Your bacon smells good, Pat," he said, as the aroma wafted after her through the open door. "Wish I dared have some, but I daren't. It would explode inside me."

"You will be able to manage this all right, though," said Pat, proffering the small tray she held in her hand.

He glanced at it, saw the long glass of pale-coloured liquid, and his soul revolted within him.

"I don't want anything," he said peevishly. "I never take anything at this time of night. I can't sleep after it."

"Come along," said Pat, "This won't hurt you. You will sleep all right after this."

"I don't want it, I tell you, Pat." He rolled over in his deep chair and turned his back on the offending slops in exactly the same way that Eric did when urged to take something he did not like. Really, he ought to have been wearing a Wolf-cub's outfit instead of his smart lounge suit.

"Oh, Julian, and I made it specially for you and I thought you'd like it!" said Pat plaintively. This was a gambit that worked well with Eric; she would see if it would serve her with Pharmakos; and it did. He turned right side up at once.

"Pat, you're a tyrant," he said, "Why did I ever bring you here to plague me? I'll push you in the river first thing tomorrow morning." But he took the glass in his hand, sniffed at it resentfully, took a sip, and then settled down to sip it steadily with evident relish. She thought he might have expressed his appreciation and returned thanks; she did not know that the effect of a lot of solitary confinement is to leave men very emotional, and that it took very little to reduce Pharmakos to a state when he could not trust his voice. Her innocent mothering of him completely bowled him over and reduced him to the verge of tears.

To his relief, Pat went off to attend to her bacon, and he got a chance to avail himself of his handkerchief without being observed. When she returned she found a cheerful and self possessed Pharmakos sitting straight up in his chair, and apparently endeavouring to lick out the glass.

"Pat, this is a noble mixture," he said. "I have lived on the foulest, most mawkish scoff for such ages that I have forgotten what decent food tastes like. I'll take this sort of stuff indefinitely; eat it out of your hand, in fact."

Pat was delighted. She put down her own tray on one of

the low tabourets, perched herself on a pouffe, and fell to. Pharmakos lay back and watched her happily. What a child it was! Ready to tuck into anything at any hour. And what an appetite! Probably Mr. Stone believed in mortifying the flesh. He looked that sort.

Pat's mixture had done him a most amazing amount of good. He wondered if there were any alcohol in it, concealed under the flavour of the meat extract. He must tell Pat not to give him any alcohol; it wasn't safe in his unstable nervous condition. God only knew what he might do if he so much as had a smell at the cork.

"Pat," he said, "What is the recipe for this noble mixture?"

"Warm milk, raw egg, and meat extract," said Pat promptly.

"Is that all?"

"Yes."

"It acts like a stimulant."

"It is a stimulant. That's the raw egg. It digests so quickly."

"Well, it's marvellous stuff," said the rejuvenated Pharmakos. By Jove, if Pat fed him on this sort of thing he would be pushing buses over before he was much older. It was food he needed. If he could take food, his nerves would soon quiet down.

"Dump the garbage in the kitchen, Pat," said Pharmakos, when the meal was concluded. "Don't bother to wash up. A gentleman of the name of Lamprey comes in the morning and does that. Lampreys are the things of which King John died of a surfeit, and when you see him you will know why. He is a retired ship's steward, compulsorily retired, I believe, and he is a most efficient housemaid but not a very good cook. He also was an acquaintance that I made while I was stopping with George. But you will find him perfectly honest, Pat. You can leave your pearls about with impunity. One of the great advantages of employing ex-convicts is that you never have to lock anything up, for they never pilfer.

"Lamprey spends his evenings, I believe, snigging suitcases from stations. That is why this job suits him for the mornings. It's so handy for Waterloo."

Pat threw back her head and chuckled. "You're just like father," she said. "He never would employ a maid unless she'd had a baby."

Pharmakos roared with laughter. He wondered whether Pat had divined the inwardness of this manoeuvre on Mr. Stone's part.

"Now, come along," he said. "I am trying to talk business to you and you mustn't distract me. I have got an awful lot to tell you, and to instruct you about, and generally to bedevil you. You have left life's broad highway, and are cutting cross-country now, and I must put you wise to the lie of the land.

"Now you were asking me in the taxi about the use I made of those documents I got from Jurgens. Well, they were the basis of my present business. After I had dealt with all the available solicitors, as shown by the documents, and had been suitably rewarded—and I may say, Pat, that I did most of the furnishing of this room on the rewards, which were, in many cases, most suitable—I started to work my way through the great majority of Jurgens'—well—clients, who hadn't consulted solicitors, poor devils.

"I called on them personally also. I had no *arriere pensée*, Pat. I simply wanted some amusement, having just come out of quod. It was an awfully quaint experience. And most illuminating. I heard some stories, I can tell you. And to each one I gave the same advice, 'Why don't you round on the fellow, and tell him that if he gives you away, you'll give him away? The Dutch police want him for forgery, and want him badly. He will go down for a long stretch if they can lay their hands on him.' That was a titbit supplied by Skilly, quite innocently, as being something in Jurgens' favour.

"Well, they lapped up my advice as a kitten laps milk, but none of them had the guts to put it into practice, Finally, one venerable old boy, a parson in public, but with queer tastes in private, poor old devil, and as decent a chap as ever breathed apart from his little weaknesses, which really hurt no one but himself—asked me if I'd act for him in the matter, and he'd pay me handsomely. Said it would suit him a darn sight better to give me what Jurgens was asking because he knew I wouldn't try to get paid twice over. So I acted for him, and put the fear of God into Jurgens, and the old boy slept easy in his bed of nights, and swore he'd turn over a new leaf, and I believe he has.

"Then another of the victims asked me to do the same thing; and I acted for her, and reduced Jurgens to pulp. And so it went on. I twisted Jurgens' tail till it pretty nearly came off in my hand, and everyone of my clients paid me as if I'd been an operating surgeon.

"But they came to an end after a while, however, and I was out of a job, though in the meantime I had been able to equip this little place, and equip it handsomely, as I think you will agree. And I wondered where I'd turn next for occupation, amusement, and my daily bread, likewise Skilly's, for we'd stuck together, and if I'd turned him loose to fend for himself, he'd have gone straight back to quod. And I bethought me of the various solicitors whose esteem I'd' won, or so they said, in the course of the earlier negotiations, and I went to see one of the most eminent, and I told him what I had been doing recently, and how my access to the underworld had put me in a position to speak their own language to blackmailers and turn the tables on them, and I suggested to him that if he had got any clients who were being blackmailed and daren't go into court, I might be able to handle their cases more effectually than he could, who had a character to lose. And he jumped at the idea, and turned over to me three noble lords and a well-known actress forthwith, and *they* all rewarded me suitably.

"Then the fun became fast and furious, and I am in great demand among solicitors, Patsy, for all sorts of queer jobs; but the backbone of my business is disentangling the blackmailed, for whom a fellow-feeling makes me wondrous kind.

"Skilly was a ticket-of-leave man while all this was going on, and the local police soon got their eye on us and got very worried about me, for they found out that I was an ex-gaol bird, too, and thought I was much too prosperous to be respectable, but they could not catch me out. How could they? I banked at one of the Big Five and was always paid by solicitor's cheque. Finally, they decided to investigate me, for they had made up their minds I must be a fence.

"Well, old Saunders was put on to do the investigating, and it was a case of love at first sight on both sides. I must say the police have been awfully decent as soon as their minds were at rest about me. They have helped me a lot with my work, too, especially Saunders. And in return I put them on to anything I get that may be of use to them. Nothing desperate, you know, Pat, but endless lists of little items of mutual interest. That is the way they keep tab of the underworld and build up their cases. I don't get anything out of it in the way of cash, only the thanks of an ungrateful country, and pay your own bus-fares when you visit Scotland Yard, but it means that if anyone tries to frame a case against me, I'm all right.

"It was tried once, Pat. I had no evidence it was Jurgens, but I am pretty sure it was; but as good luck would have it, the offence was supposed to have taken place in Westminster, and I was hauled off to Cannon Row police station. I referred them to Saunders, and they got him at once from the Yard, which is just across the way. I think they were just as pleased to see him as I was; for as soon as I found myself in a cell again, I started going out through the roof; and as the roof was of concrete, my efforts did not meet with success, and did not do either me or the cell much good."

Pharmakos sat up and clutched the arms of his chair and stared into space with terrified eyes as the memory of that experience resurrected. Then he pulled himself together and continued in the half-jocular manner that he used as a defence against emotion.

"I think they thought they were going to have one dead prisoner or one wrecked police station on their hands, and they got me out of that cell and into the open air quick. They are used to that sort of thing in convict prisons, but not at police stations, and it put the wind up them properly. They laid me on the ground and six of them sat on me, and I bit the seats out of their trousers until Saunders came and collected me, and brought me back here, and stuck sticking plaster on me where I'd skinned myself, and sat with me all night. And I imagine the Cannon Row police did the same with their cell—stuck sticking-plaster on it and sat up with it all night." He gave a nervous laugh. " Saunders is a real old brick, Pat; if ever I let you in for difficulties, you go to him."

CHAPTER IX

THE last of the light had faded while this recitation was going on.

" Patsy, my angel," said Pharmakos, "will you think me a lazy lout if I employ you as lamplighter? I am much too comfortable to turn out of this chair, and you are so young and active, my sweet Patsy—"

He really wanted to get rid of her while he thought things out. Where was Pat to sleep that night? He could not very well put her in with Skilly, much as Skilly would no doubt have appreciated it. Neither bathroom nor kitchen was big enough to get one of his large sofas into, and none of the rest of the building was rat-proof. Supposing he gave Pat his bed, and took the large sofa at the far end of the room, and put the big Japanese lacquer screens across the corner, would Pat be satisfied? God knows, she was as safe with him as with a graven image, but would she think so? He remembered how panicky she had been when he brought her in with him. She would have to be handled tactfully. The best way with Pat, he thought, from what he had seen of her, was the direct approach. Put the cards on the table. She was a plucky and sensible little thing. No affectation or false modesty about her, and yet a kind of limpid virginity that was as hard as a diamond. God help the fellow who trespassed on it! No one else could after Pat had done with him!

He watched her flitting about the great room with her light, almost dancing step, switching on one after another of the gorgeous lamps till the place looked like a set for the

Russian Ballet. Presently she returned, and curled up in his big chair like a kitten. Poor child, her legs didn't reach the ground. What a child it was! What an absolute infant in arms. And yet so potent. So all-important to his mental balance .

"Now, Patsy," he said. "Listen to the words of wisdom of your elder brother, who looks about ninety and feels about a thousand."

Pat gave him her attention and prepared to listen.

"Where do you propose to sleep to-night?"

Pat looked at him, startled. "I don't know," she said, "I left that to you."

"And I am fully aware of my responsibilities, but I can't hang you on a peg. Accommodation is ample in this building, but so are the supplies of rats, and you must have a rat-proof sleeping apartment, whatever else may be lacking.

"Now look, Patsy, seriously. Would you object to taking my bed while I have a shakedown at the far end of the room, duly barricaded by screens? It is about ten minutes' walk away, but it has not, I fear, got a sound-proof partition. I cannot think of any other arrangement. I wish I could. It is rather like the old riddle of the wolf and the sheep and the truss of hay, isn't it? If you and I remain within the same four walls, Mrs. Grundy will expect us to eat each other; and if either of us adjourn outside, the rats will get him."

Pat looked him straight in the face. "Julian," she said, "I came here as your sister, and that's how I think of you, and that's how I think you think of me. I don't see any reason, as we both feel like that about it, why we should not fit in as you suggest. If I must be eaten I would sooner be eaten by you than by rats."

"Pat," said Pharmakos, "I am very grateful to you for trusting me, and you shall never have any cause to regret it."

***

When Pharmakos awoke the next morning to find the sun high in the heavens he could not think what in the world had happened to him. He remembered tucking the blankets in around himself as best he could on the sofa, and he remembered nothing more. The blankets were still tucked in, therefore he could not have turned over, or they certainly would not have been. He had evidently fallen asleep the moment his head touched the pillow, and slept till after eight, according to his wrist-watch. Such a thing had never happened to him since that first sleepless night at the police station after his arrest, save when warders, in despair, had fetched the prison doctor to drug him into oblivion and let the whole wing get some sleep.

He rolled out of bed, and wished he had not been such a fool as to forget his dressing-gown. He had no wish to appear before Pat in his pyjamas, and possibly scandalize her. He solved the problem by swathing himself in the purple spread off the divan that had served him as an extra cover, and when Pat opened her eyes at the sound of movements, she found an amazing figure standing over her, looking like a later Roman emperor in one of his worse moods. She could not for a moment imagine where she was or what this apparition might be. Her father had always impressed upon her from her earliest years that if she were not good the Devil would come for her one night, and that sort of teaching makes an impression if it is given firmly to the very young. She sat up, too terrified to make a sound.

How tiny she looked in his big bed, thought Pharmakos, clutching her skimpy little nighty about her, with her golden-red hair in her eyes, like a Yorkshire terrier. She did not look a day more than four, and she aroused no emotion in him save affection and amusement.

"It's all right, Patsy, I'm not the bogey man," she heard

him say, and recollection returned to her. She tossed her hair out of her eyes and laughed.

" Now I had made sure you were," she said. "Father always said he would come for me if I wasn't good, and I was always as bad as bad could be."

How completely unselfconscious the child was, thought Pharmakos. She could not have been less embarrassed with him if they had really grown up together in the same nursery.

But he could not stand and stare at her all morning. He was particularly anxious that they should both be up and dressed before Skilly came barging in.

"Pat," he said, "are you a quick dresser? Then skip like a rabbit into the bathroom while I go to the kitchen and heat my shaving-water, because I am one of those persons who cannot bustle about before breakfast. If I do, I am a wreck for the day."

He retired to the kitchen, and heard a patter of bare feet across the parquetry and the slam of the bathroom door. In an incredibly short space of time Pat reappeared to ask if she might borrow one of his hair-brushes, as she had forgotten to include that item in her purchases.

"You can have anything that's mine, Pat, except my braces and toothbrush. How quick you have been, child, I don't believe you have washed behind your ears."

"You learn to be quick," said Pat, "when you are one of seven."

While he was in the bathroom, Pat set to work on the breakfast. A lightly poached egg and dry toast, she thought, should suit Pharmakos' fidgety inside. While thus engaged, she heard a husky but booming voice exclaim:

" 'Ullo, Governor!"

Evidently the mysterious Skilly had returned from his task of shadowing gentlemen of easy virtue, and now Pharmakos had to explain her presence in the warehouse, or Quilp Cottage, as he called it. She burst into a repressed fit of the giggles. She wondered if Skilly were narrow-minded, and doubted it.

She heard Pharmakos come out of the bathroom and make a long oration in low tones, and at the end of it the husky one boomed: "All right, Governor, if you say she's to be your sister, that's good enough for me," and Pharmakos replied angrily: "Well, even if you don't believe it, you can damn well hold your tongue."

Evidently the redoubtable Skilly was not as credulous as Inspector Saunders.

Pat issued forth from the kitchen. She was dying to see Skilly, about whom she had heard so much. She wanted to see what a professional criminal was like. She did not fancy that Pharmakos was a typical gaol-bird. She saw before her a short, thick-set man, with abnormally long arms that gave him something of the appearance of a gorilla, which was borne out by his heavy animal jowl and low bulging forehead, shadowed almost to his eyes by a thatch of fiery carrots. He was absolutely the criminal of the films. Nature had even exceeded art when she had designed Skilly. No producer could have put on anything so caricaturishly criminal, save in a comic. He was grinning widely out of a gap-toothed mouth at an angry Pharmakos, who, clad only in his shirt and trousers, stood over him as if about to strike him.

He turned at the sound of Pat's step, and his grin grew even wider, with one coal-black snaggle-tooth sticking out of it perfectly horizontally.

" 'Ullo, lidy?" he said, " Pleased to meet yer. My nime's Skilly. Wot might yours be?"

"I keep on telling you she's my sister," foamed Pharmakos.

"Yus," said the snaggled one, "'We're all bruvvers an' sisters, we are. Gawd bless Moscow. But what'll I call yer, lidy, since we're to 'ave the pleasure of yer company?"

Pharmakos looked so angry and excited that Pat thought she had better take the situation in hand. She knew it was essential that she and Skilly should contrive to keep the peace, as he was an important cog in Pharmakos' machine. Well, since she had thrown in her lot with rogues and vagabonds, she had better accept the situation and settle down to it.

"You had better call me Coppernob," she said, "But do I know you well enough to call you Skilly? Hadn't I better call you Mr. Skilly?" She hoped he would take the hint, and he did. Instinctively she felt that there was something decent about Skilly, in spite of his truly awful appearance.

"Right yer are, Miss Coppernob, but there 'aint no misters for me. Yer can call me Comrade Skilly if yer like."

He winked massively at Pat, cocked an eye at Pharmakos, who was livid with rage, and decided that discretion was the better part of valour. He had been knocked about before now by Pharmakos in his rages, and knew that his strength, though quickly exhausted owing to his bad health, was formidable while it lasted; for his muscles were hardened by labour on breakwaters, and even the professional bruiser was no match for him for the first five minutes, during which time anyone as utterly reckless of consequences as Pharmakos in a tantrum could do a lot of damage.

Safely inside the kitchen, from which there was another exit that Pat had not yet discovered, he burst into song.

> *"Dear little Rowsy-Powsy,*
> *Who, could it be but yew?*
> *Yew are the only, only, only,*
> *Girl I could e-ever*
> *Woo-oo-oo, oo-oo-oo!*
> *Sy you will tike my nime?*

Ti-ike me wiv it too.
Then you'll be Rowsie somebody else,
But who? Who? Who?"

The last three whos were three distinct hoots, exactly like a sports car, driven by an impatient driver, asking for the road from a lorry.

Pharmakos, looking like a devil, came striding across the great room towards the kitchen, but before he could do any damage to the insubordinate Skilly, Pat put him completely out of court by hooting back with exactly the same note.

She was rewarded by a squall of laughter from the kitchen. Pharmakos pulled up short and burst out laughing too.

"Pat, you owl!" he said, and departed into the bathroom to complete his toilette.

Pat judged there must be another door to the kitchen, because Skilly made his departure without returning through the big room. She did not dare to venture into the kitchen while he was there, because she had divined that he was an exceedingly rough customer, and although she had made a propitious start with him by taking him in the way he liked to be taken, she was not sure whether he could be relied on to take her in the way that she liked to be taken.

Hearing silence at length from the kitchen, she ventured in, and found the spotless table strewn with bacon-rind and eggshells, and the remains of a burst and burnt egg in the frying pan, which she had to clean before she could use. She was rather annoyed. Skilly certainly was not going to be an unmixed blessing.

"Do you take tea or coffee?" she called to Pharmakos through the bathroom door.

"Tea for me, child," he replied, coming out in his shirtsleeves. "What have you done with my hair-brushes, you imp of mischief?"

Pat had taken them to the kitchen to do her hair, and being excluded from the bathroonm during his ablutions, had been unable to return them. He followed her into the kitchen to get them, and saw the chaos on the table, and his eyes flashed angrily.

"It is too bad you have this mess to cope with, Pat," he said, "I'm frightfully sorry. I'll speak to Skilly about it."

"I shouldn't if I were you," said Pat, " Skilly and I have got to shake down together somehow. You let me do any speaking that is necessary. I haven't had four brothers for nothing."

Phannakos heaved a sigh of relief. Pat was a marvel. He dreaded having a row with Skilly, because what with his own imperfect self-control, and Skilly's sheer brutishness, there was no saying where it would end.

They sat down to breakfast together. Pat was relieved to see that Skilly did not expect to join them.

"Comrade Skilly insisted on sitting down to table with me, in his shirt-sleeves for choice, when we first joined up," explained Pharmakos, "I dared not say anything, he is such a box of tricks. But fortunately my way of eating irritated him just as much as his nauseated me, so we each go our own way nowadays. But what is this you have put in front of me, child? I never take anything except a cup of tea at this hour of the day."

"It's only a lightly poached egg and dry toast," said Pat, "I am sure you can take that."

"I can take it all right, Pat, it looks lovely; but what will it do when it gets inside me? I've got a day's work before me, you know, and I can't afford to be laid out."

"You will do your work all the better if you've something inside you," said Pat with authority. She had already suspected that Pharmakos' dyspepsia was nervous in origin. She had seen Eric throw up so often when he was excited that she was familiar with the symptoms. Give Pharmakos something light and easily digested, and keep him amused and quiet while he digested it, and everything would be all right. She thought that he was probably so scared of the consequences of indiscreet eating that he just wasn't getting enough to eat.

With his Wellingtonian nose and pugnacious jaw, Pharmakos ought to have had a domineering disposition; and so he had when he was roused; but when a man is broken before he is mature, curious things happen to his temperament, and the one thing that Pharmakos liked above all others in Pat was that she took him firmly in hand and would stand no nonsense from him, and he was in process of delivering his soul into her hands utterly and completely, and finding relief from his intolerable nerve-strain in the process. He was like nothing so much as a Sealyham puppy lying flat on its back with its legs in the air, and asking to be carried. Very pleasant, no doubt, for the Sealyham, but what about the person who has to carry it, as it gets bigger and heavier?

CHAPTER X

"**HERE** is the key to the fortress for you, Patsy, darling," said Pharmakos, sending a flat, narrow key sliding towards her over the polished wood of the little gate-legged table at which they sat at breakfast in one of the great windows.

"Now listen, Sister Ann, and make a note of my instructions, and obey them carefully.

"You are never to let anyone into Quilp Cottage under any pretext whatever unless you know them. You will gradually get to know the people I have dealings with, and if anyone comes in whom you don't know, even if he swears he's my long-lost brother, you are not to admit him. It is better to be safe than sorry."

"Dear me," said Pat, "Are we in a state of siege?"

"Practically, my child. You see, my old friend Jurgens is about again, and has done me the honour to pay me one or two little attentions. The evening at the Cannon Row police station, which was so unsuccessful, was one of them; and I never quite know where he is going to break out next. Therefore, Patsy, admit no one except personal friends."

"But how am I to know who is who until I have opened the door?"

"Ah, that is where we are well provided for in this establishment. I would love to know who built this little place, Patsy, and what his business was. Come with me, and I'll show you where Sister Ann can watch for the cloud of dust that heralds my return of nights."

He led her through the kitchen, and opened a door so cunningly concealed among the fitments that she had never suspected its existence. What a fascinatingly exciting place Quilp Cottage was! It was just like a story in the vividly illustrated periodicals her brothers used to smuggle into the house, carefully concealed from Mr. Stone's eagle eye, who preferred S.P.C.K. productions—for them, at any rate.

They went down a long, dingy passage, that seemed as if it must lead all the way to Waterloo station. At the end of it was a little room, empty save for a coil of light rope in one corner. Its window looked on to the road immediately to one side of the great gates of the yard, and at a considerable height above them.

"You see, Patsy," said Pharmakos, "our little place is tucked away behind someone else's big place, and if you did not know the anatomy of this district pretty thoroughly, you would not know we existed. Hawkins' Repository extends right over our gate, and any stranger would think it was his gate. This passage runs along the side of his main warehouse. Underneath us, down these stairs, is Skilly's bachelor abode. Now have you got the geography clear? This is an L-shaped property, with me at one end and Skilly at the other, with the slender connecting-link of this passage between us, and this jolly little look-out-house beside the front gate. It couldn't have suited me better if I had designed it myself.

"If anyone rings the front-door bell, and Skilly and I are both out, you come along here, and stick your head out of this window, and take a look at him; and if you don't like the look of him, lie low and say nuffin, like Brer Rabbit till he goes away."

"And supposing he doesn't go away?"

"Then you can chuck dishwash at him, my child. And if that is no use, you must phone the police. I will take you along with me one day to the police station and introduce you to the Super, who is a very good friend of mine; sometimes he comes along and has a smoke and a chat with me. Decent chaps, some of these senior policemen, and no fools, either. And you know, Pat," he continued, "I think he really turns up to have a smoke with me because he likes me, and not in order to keep an eye on me."

He turned away from the window and led the way down a corkscrew stone stair, and came out into the bachelor flat inhabited by Skilly. That gentleman had already gone out, but traces of his occupancy were everywhere, though the bed was quite neatly made.

Pharmakos looked at the bed and smiled. "He doesn't use that bed much," he said, and Pat wondered why Skilly sat up of nights.

In one corner of the room was a bright yellow button boot with very pointed toes and plaited leather uppers. In the opposite corner was its fellow. A suit of genuine chessboard checks was draped piece by piece over various bits of furniture, bright blue socks hanging out of the ends of the trousers, making them look like a limp suicide.

Pharmakos waved his hand towards all this vividness.

"When you have spent a lot of your time wearing drab-coloured garments, Pat, you enjoy a bit of colour when you have the choice."

They went out of a door that led into the yard of the premises. The tide was high this morning, and the water lapped at the edge of the stones bounding the miniature dock and rippled in the sunshine.

"All right for bathing when the tide is high, so long as you can forget what is at the bottom of it," said Pharmakos.

They went down the narrow path along the side of the water.

"Got to come home sober here," said Pharmakos, "If you want to come home safely."

He led her to the corner of the wharf, and the river, brimming its banks, swirled before them, sparkling in the sun. A seagull, and then another, swooped towards them.

"By Jove, I've forgotten your bacon-rinds!" said Pharmakos.

He vanished through the low door in the wall, leaving Pat alone on the river-brink, the chocolate-coloured water lipping at her feet. The sea-gulls withdrew with the disappearance of Pharmakos; apparently she did not interest them as much as he did. In a moment, however, he reappeared, and back they came at the sight of him, and he commenced to throw pieces of bacon-rind up in the air. Not a single piece ever reached the water. More gulls came, and more and more, till the place was a flying cloud of them. Finally all the bacon-rinds were gone, and the gulls departed, squawking their thanks.

"Always keep anything tasty for them, Pat," said Pharmakos. "They are particular friends of mine. Now come and see your future abode. At least, I would like it to be your abode, if it finds favour with you."

He led her through the low doorway which she had entered the previous evening with such fear and trembling, and turned to the left. Another battered and evil-looking door confronted them.

"I am afraid I dare not have the front door done up for you, Pat, but we can make things nice inside," said Pharmakos.

They entered what had apparently been a living-room, with a kind of semi-kitchen stove in it.

"I will have that pulled out," said Pharmakos, "and give you a decent grate."

They passed through a door into another room, equally empty and dirty, and passed beyond it into a third, of less than half the size, which contained a battered sink.

"I thought that this could be made into a bathroom for you, Pat, there must be a drain somewhere, since there is a sink."

The early morning sun was coming in through the windows, and the ceilings were dappled with the light reflected from the surface of the water in the miniature dock, for the windows looked into the yard. Pat saw at once that the little flat had possibilities, dirty and dingy as it was.

"Julian, I'll just love it!" she said.

The man smiled down at her. It gave him a thrill to hear her use his name, and she was using it quite freely now. It seemed as if she actually thought of him as her brother.

"The next thing will be to get this place cleaned up and decorated, and made rat-proof, but what I want to know is where are you going to sleep meanwhile, for it cannot be done in a day."

"Well," said Pat, "I have got to have a bed, haven't I? So suppose we got it at once, and put it at the far end of your big room, and put screens round it; and then you could have your own bed back again, and be comfy. It couldn't have been very comfy on that sofa."

"Right you are, my child," said Pharmakos, and added to himself under his breath, "Oh, you little child, how much have you seen of life? Thank God it is me, who am a dead man, that you are treating like this"

Finally Pharmakos took his hat and stick and prepared to depart to his day's work. He seemed reluctant to go. He kept on giving Pat instructions as he took his departure, so that she had to accompany him down the stairs, and walk beside him along the narrow path beside the water, at the imminent peril of her life, until they finally came to the gate.

Pharmakos opened it and looked out, but the street was empty. He turned back to Pat again, and gave her a few more instructions. Then—"Good-bye, my sweet," he said abruptly, and slammed the gate behind him.

When Pat returned to the big room upstairs she found there the original of Tenniel's illustration of the Mock Turtle in *Alice in Wonderland*.

It touched its forehead politely, with all the obsequiousness of a steward looking for tips.

"Miss Pharmakos, madam?" it said ingratiatingly.

"Yes," said Pat.

"I have already seen Mr. Skilly, madam, and he has explained the situation to me."

Pat wondered what version of the affair Skilly had given to the Mock Turtle, whom she guessed must be Lamprey, of a surfeit of which King John had died. She was not surprised. It would not take much of Lamprey to make one surfeited with him, he was so very smarmy and obsequious.

"I shall be very pleased to have your instructions, Miss-madam."

"I suppose you are Lamprey," said Pat.

"Yes, Miss-madam," said Lamprey, wriggling like a mongrel pup that wishes to ingratiate itself. Pat felt she could hardly bear him. This creature must be handled in an entirely different way from the redoubtable Skilly. She could see that they were both utterly criminal types, but Skilly was the bold and reckless type, given to deeds of physical violence, whereas the miserable Lamprey was obviously a sneak-thief, stealing milk-bottles from areas and anything else he could lay his light-fingered hands on. It was a marvel how such a cringing creature ever worked up the pluck to break the law. She was thankful to have Pharmakos' assurance that he was perfectly honest while engaged at Quilp Cottage; for she would never have thought it to look at him.

Acting on Pharmakos' instructions, she took him down and showed him the little caretaker's fiat that was to be hers. She speedily found that the Mock Turtle had a head on its shoulders. He took the whole matter in hand, and went out and came back with a: bag of cement and some sheets of tin in one hand, and an indignant Mrs. Mullins literally in the other, for she had not wished to leave her washing, but had been commandeered in the holy name of Pharmakos, who was apparently a power in the district.

The two of them set to work. Lamprey making the place rat-proof with the tin and cement, and Mrs. Mullins washing the paint according to his instructions. After they had broken the back of the work, Skilly appeared, and leaning against the doorpost and smoking, began to give orders. To Pat's great amusement, Lamprey took them obsequiously, saying, "Yes, Mr. Skilly," every time he paused for breath. But not so Mrs. Mullins.

"Some folk get too big even for their yaller boots," she said with a sniff, and Skilly suddenly remembered an engagement elsewhere. Pat was even more amused to see how easily the redoubtable Skilly could be routed by a determined female who meant to stand no nonsense.

In the early afternoon there was a ring at the front door bell, and Pat, obeying instructions, sped along the passage to Sister Ann's look-out, and saw a Maple's van outside, with a divan bed being decanted from it, as Pharmakos had told her to expect, for he had forbidden her to try and obtain a bed at Woolworth's, though no doubt she could have done so at the rate of sixpence a slat.

She ran down the winding stair and through Skilly's dishevelled abode, and opened the big gates with a good deal of difficulty to let the bed come in, for it was obviously impossible to get it through the little door.

As she did so, a lounger of the dock-rat type, with a faintly nautical flavour derived from a greasy blue serge suit and a peaked cap, appeared from nowhere and offered to lend a hand.

The van-man was disposed to accept, for it was difficult for him to get the divan bed along the narrow path between wall and water single-handed, and the tide now being low, there was an ominous drop to deter the weak-headed. But Pat would have none of it, being mindful of her instructions.

"No, thank you," she said firmly, "I have got a man here, I will call him.".

"Ain't a feller to earn an honest penny, lidy?" protested the dock-rat, beginning to sidle forward.

"Don't let him come in," said Pat to the vanman. "I won't have him."

"Now then, mate," said the vanman, " 'op it. The lady don't want yer."

"I ain't a-goin' ter 'op it," said the dock-rat viciously.

Pat saw that three similar dock-rats had come up quietly behind him.

"Gawd!" said the vanman, looking over Pat's shoulder at something that had come up behind her. She turned round hastily and saw Lamprey, his long yellow horse's teeth bared in a horrible snarling grin and a huge sailor's knife in his hand.

The dock-rats saw him too, and vanished as quietly as they had come. They did not go, they just were not.

The vanman thrust his book into Pat's hand to sign, and departed with his van without even waiting for a tip, and the measly, skinny Lamprey hoisted the bed on to his shoulder with one swing, and walked steadily along the very curb of the narrow path overhanging a twenty-foot drop to the eddying water without blinking an eyelid.

Pat, following him, heard the telephone bell ringing upstairs, and ran up to answer to it.

"Is that my sweetheart?" said Pharmakos' voice at the other end.

"No, damn you, it isn't," said Pat. "It's your sister. That's the way brothers and sisters talk to each other in my family."

She could hear Pharmakos laughing. "All right, you imp of Hell," he said. "I shall be back to tea at half-past four. Getting on all right?"

"First rate," said Pat. "I say, Lamprey is a wonder. He carried in my bed with one hand and chased bandits with a knife in the other."

"What's that, Pat?" Pharmakos' voice was so sharp and startled that she wished to goodness she hadn't referred to the matter; never had she met such a bundle of nerves!

"It's all right, I was only joking. It was a lounger who wanted a job carrying in the bed. He got uppish, and then some of his friends appeared as well, and it might have been unpleasant if Lamprey hadn't turned up, pulling the most awful faces and waving an enormous carving-knife."

"Pat, you are not to leave the house, or open the door to anyone. And tell Lamprey he is not to leave until I get back."

"It's all right, Julian, there's nothing to worry about," cried Pat, vexed with herself for having disturbed him, but she knew by the total absence of all sound in the receiver that she spoke to a dead line.

In less than ten minutes she heard a quick step on the stair that certainly belonged to neither Skilly nor to the Mock Turtle. She rose up, startled, for the adventure of the dock rats had alarmed her more than she was prepared to admit, even to herself; for we cling desperately to the normal and the commonplace in defence of our peace of mind. She thought she could make good her escape by way of the hidden door in the kitchen that led to the passage to Sister Ann's look-out if necessary, and she slipped behind the plum coloured curtain and peeped round the edge.

The heavy church door at the far end of the room flew open and in came Pharmakos, looking positively distraught.

"Pat, Pat, where are you?" he cried, staring round the apparently empty room frantically.

"Good Lord," thought Pat, "What's the matter with the man now?"

"Here I am," she said aloud, coming from behind the curtain.

Pharmakos literally ran across the big room and caught her by the arm, and then found himself unable to speak. It was horribly distressing. His face was working like that of a child that is about to burst into tears. She must do something and make him pull himself together if she were not to have a scene with him.

CHAPTER XI

"**WHATEVER** brings you back at this hour of the day?" said Pat, while Pharmakos hung on to her arm as if to keep himself up. "Are you going to have tea with me? How jolly! I wonder what I can give you to eat."

"Yes, I'll have tea with you, Pat," muttered Pharmakos. "I'll go and have a wash." And he let go of her and plunged into the bathroom and slammed the door.

Once safe from Pat's eyes, he let himself go. So Jurgens was raiding his Pat, his little child? God, why wouldn't they let him have a revolver? He would see that imbecile Super again. He had got to have a revolver if they were after Pat.

He took the bath-sponge in his big navvy's hands and tore it to bits. That calmed him, when he saw the mess he had made. What an imbecile he was. It would stop up the drain. And Pat would see the bits and think she had a lunatic to deal with. Then she would be scared and clear out. All the emotion that the bath-sponge had steadied, surged up again at the idea of Pat clearing out. He dropped the pieces that he had so laboriously gathered up. Had she gone already? He plunged towards the door. He must go and see. No, good God, he must not. She must never see him like this.

He turned on the taps in the basin, and began to splash the water over his face; then he dipped his head right in as the basin filled. He made a horrible mess, and got his collar soaking wet; but this would steady him if anything would.

But the shock of the cold water proved too much for him, and his heart began to miss beats; he sat down on the edge of the bath and prayed he wasn't going to keel over in a faint and scare Pat worse than ever. He could not remember whether or not he had locked the door. He had better not have it locked, for, if he fainted, Pat would not be able to get to him. No, good Lord, it was best locked, and then she couldn't come in and see him in this mess. Oh, God, where was his self-control? Should he go to Pat? She could help him. She could pull him together. No, good God, no, a thousand times no. She must never see him in this state.

Then everything began to get quiet and far away. These three-legged stools were damned uncomfortable things. It wouldn't have killed the Government to provide them with backs. And it wouldn't kill the prison authorities to let him have his own bed during the day. What difference did it make to them if he sat or lay down?

In solitary again? He wondered what the row had been about this time. He hadn't the faintest idea. Oh, well, nothing to do except grin and bear it. His seven years would come to an end eventually.

God, there was no air in this beastly cell! If he did not have air he would go utterly and completely mad. Why couldn't they realise he had asthma and must have air? He would sooner have the cat again than be deprived of air. It was no use kicking up a row in solitary, they took no notice of that. He could kick up all the row he liked, and they would only leave him to get on with it.

No, they mightn't. If he made sufficient shindy, someone would come sooner or later, even if it were only to put him in irons.

He staggered to his feet and lurched across to the door. Miracle! It opened at his touch, and there, outside, stood Pat, looking up at him with a scared face.

She took him by the hand and led him across to his bed and laid him down on it. She opened the window and let the draught play on his face. She took off his sopping wet collar and loosened his shirt at the neck. Portland faded away like a bad dream when one wakes up. God, what an angel Pat was! And what sense she had. And what a nerve she had. He must have been an alarming spectacle for the kid. She had looked pretty scared when she saw him come barging out of the bathroom, imagining it was a cell. Poor child, he must never let her in for this again. He must keep out of her way when he felt himself getting windy.

But then Pat, simply by looking at him, was able to pull him out of his nose-dive. The wisest thing to do was to make for Pat the minute he felt himself beginning to wobble.

God, what a fool he was, had he got no self-respect? And now he was starting off again. Then he heard Pat's voice speaking to him. Her hand was on his head. Was she stroking it? No, by God, she wasn't! She was smacking it! Well done Pat! That's the stuff to give the troops.

"Now look here, my lad," she was saying. "You pull up your socks. I've had just about enough of this sort of thing."

He sat up. "Oh, Lor', Pat, aren't I a fool? What's the use of smacking my head? Get the poker and brain me."

"I will in a minute," said Pat.

"Do you know I've destroyed a perfectly good bathsponge in my enthusiasm?"

"More fool you," said Pat, "You'll have to buy another." She moved towards the kitchen. "I'm going to get you some refreshments," she said.

"No, Pat, don't do that," he called after her. "I couldn't take anything. I couldn't really, I'd only 'vom' it up. Give me a glass of water, there's a good lass. I'm as dry as a lime-kiln."

She brought him a glass of water, ice-cold from the refrigerator. He lay back on the soft cushions, luxuriously sipping it; enjoying the fresh air from the river blowing on his face. God, this was good! What a change from Portland—Portland and solitary! And Pat with him for company. How perfectly sweet Pat was. And what a head-piece the child had on her. He could depend on her utterly. She would pull him through anything. He had only to go to Pat—But his Sealyham soliloquy ended abruptly, for the ice-cold water smote his sensitive stomach with sudden spasms, and he rolled over in the agonies of abdominal cramp.

"Heat!" he managed to gasp. "Hot-water bottle!"

Pat flew to the kitchen, seized a vast hot-water bottle, filled it from the electric hot-water heater, and dashed back with it, rolled Pharmakos right side up, straightened him out sufficiently to enable herself to get it on to his stomach, and then held it there forcibly till his writhings ceased and he lay quiet.

"Oh, what an afternoon!" thought Pat, as Pharmakos lay on the bed gasping like a fish on the bank. "Are we going to have this sort of performance regularly? It will take years off my life if we are." Pharmakos had scared her too thoroughly for her to feel in the least sentimental over him. It was all very well to cope with these rumpuses in the case of the small Eric, whom she could pick up and tuck under one arm, but it was a very different matter in the case of six foot four of bony Pharmakos.

The thought of Eric steadied her, for she was not far off hysteria herself. It is an infectious thing. They were so much alike, the two of them. They were both so outrageous when they let themselves go, and both so amenable when properly handled. She could handle Pharmakos all right as long as she kept her head. Properly managed and properly fed, he would probably get completely over these attacks. And he really was an awful dear.

A long bony hand came out and groped waveringly towards her. She took it, and it gave her hand a squeeze, as if of thanks and then dropped it. Pharmakos turned over on his side away from her and shivered. She got the huge eiderdown out from the back of the divan and wrapped him in it. He neither moved nor spoke, nor opened his eyes.

The kitchen door opened and in came Skilly. He looked at the heap on the bed, raised his eyebrows, and beckoned Pat to follow him into the kitchen.

"What's up?" he demanded. "Governer bin 'avin' one of 'is turns?"

"Yes," said Pat.

"You manage 'im all right? Wot you do? Tie a wet rag round 'is 'ead and plank a 'ot water bottle on 'is turn? That's the gime with 'im when 'e turns queer, and mind 'e don't 'it yer."

So this was an added horror! Pharmakos might attack her? Good God, where was it all going to end? She even began to long for Mr. Stone; one knew where one was with him.

"I ain't 'alf glad to 'ave you to lend a 'and wiv 'im," continued Skilly. "Gawd, it fair wore me out, 'im and 'is didoes. And me single-'anded. They never tackled 'im less than three deep in Portland. The rows I've 'eard in our block-yer wouldn't believe it if I told yer. 'Im yelling the place down night after night, and not a wink of sleep fer anybody. Gaw' blimy, Bill, I've 'ad my money's worth I."

"What does one do with him?" asked poor Pat desperately.

"What can yer do wiv' 'im. Only wait till 'e's finished and see 'e doesn't 'urt 'isself. And see 'e doesn't 'urt you either when 'e gets lashin' abart. I seen some good ole smashes in our little corner in Block B. 'E'd chuck 'em abart, 'arf a dozen of 'em, like a terrier when the rats set on 'im. I seen plenty o' rows in clink and out of it, in my time, but I don't want to see no more like them. Come on, we'd better not leave 'im alone. Let's 'ave a look at 'im."

He opened the kitchen door cautiously. Pharmakos had not stirred.

"Look 'ere, if you can 'andle 'im like you seem able, you better do it, and I'll act reserve, see? The only thing I can do with him when 'e gets going is knock 'im out, and that ain't good for 'im, too much of it. If you kin simmer 'im dahn like this, wivout knockin' 'im out, well-praise the Lord, sez I. Look, there's a bell beside 'is chair, see? Well, you give a toot on that if you want any think, and I'll be along in two tweaks. It's better for 'im not to see me when 'e's like this. 'E might take a fancy for 'itting me, but 'e won't 'it you. Gawd, I'm darn glad yer turned up when yer did, Coppernob, I'd fair got to the end of me tether wiv 'im."

Skilly slid silently away through the concealed door and Pat returned to watch beside Pharmakos, who never stirred as the hours went by and the sun gradually got round to the western windows.

Pat began to get ravenously hungry. She had missed her tea, thanks to Pharmakos and his didoes, and now she was missing her supper. Flesh and blood could stand no more, and she slid quietly out of the big chair and made for the kitchen.

Pharmakos raised his head. She saw that his eyes were very bloodshot, but they looked much more natural.

"Hullo, Pat?" he said. "I am afraid I have been giving you a lot of trouble. I'm frightfully sorry, old thing."

Pat was so relieved to find him thus unexpectedly restored to his right mind that her eyes filled with tears and her lip began to tremble. Pharmakos saw it and cursed himself.

"How many meals have we missed, my child?"

"Four," said Pat, pulling herself together with an effort," Two apiece."

"Then," said Pharmakos, "I suggest you retire to the

kitchen and prepare brunch, or tunch, or whatever is the appropriate meal at the moment, and I will change into some fresh clothes. These look as if I had slept out under hedges for a week. Then I will send round the Fiery Cross and we will have a board meeting of the Forty Thieves Ltd., and hear your report re bandits."

"Oh, Julian," cried Pat, "They weren't really bandits. I was only joking."

"They were people whom Lamprey thought worthy of his steel, anyway, Pat, and when Lamprey climbs the ratlines with his clasp-knife in his teeth—well—things are happening. Now hop it, child, unless you want to assist at my levee."

Pat retired modestly to the kitchen and heard Pharmakos having a bath. What a quick pick-up he had. She had thought him good for a week in bed, at least.

Pharmakos' food was a problem. She had not been able to go out and do any shopping. She wondered if an omelette would be all right for him. If she could only get him to eat, it would make such a difference to him.

When she arrived with the omelette she found Pharmakos looking very trim in a double-breasted brown suit with Saville Row written all over it. He did not look so sallow in this as in his navy blue. Was it possible that this was the man who had been writhing and groaning on the bed a few short hours ago?

"So you are going to try me with the solids, are you, Pat?" he asked, poking suspiciously at the omelette with his fork. "I can't usually take solids for a day or two after one of my upheaves, but I suppose I must try not to be a back-seat driver, and you have been so successful with me hitherto that I am beginning to have faith in you. Now, if this refrains from walking about inside and biting me, I shall be all right."

CHAPTER XII

A RING on the bell produced Skilly, who winked at Pat when he saw the rejuvenated Pharmakos sitting at table, evidently having enjoyed a meal. He was despatched in search of Lamprey, who at that hour of the day would probably be meeting trains at Waterloo. Pat had hardly cleared away the meal when the two gaol-birds entered, Skilly resplendent in his beautiful bookie's checks and yellow boots, for he was all ready to go out and break hearts in the Borough when Pharmakos rang for him, and Lamprey neat and tidy in a blue serge suit that looked as if it had been a cast-off from Pharmakos, cut down by the simple expedient of shortening the trouser legs and cuffs. At any rate, the seat of the trousers was somewhere in the neighbourhood of his knees, and the effect from behind was more like the Mock Turtle than ever. He looked the typical gentleman's gentleman, and it was quite easy to understand how he would be allowed to pick up luggage unquestioned as it came out of the van of a boat-train.

Skilly plumped himself down in the big chair opposite Pharmakos that Pat had begun to look upon as hers, without waiting to be asked. But Lamprey twiddled his billycock hat in his hands and stood meekly drooping before his employer till bidden to seat himself, and then did so on the extreme edge of a chair and continued to twiddle his hat.

"Now, boys," said Pharmakos—though it was difficult to conceive of Lamprey answering to the designation—There is something up, and we must get to the bottom of it. I hear you had a spot of trouble this morning, Lamprey?"

"Yes, sir, yes m'lord," said Lamprey. Pharmakos frowned at him. Pat gurgled with internal amusement. This was the equivalent of the Miss-madam with which he addressed her. The Miss a concession to her alleged status as Pharmakos' sister, and the Madam a tribute to Skilly's account of her position in the *ménage*.

"Well, what happened?" said Pharmakos.

"There was a person at the gate, sir; trying to come in, sir whom I have seen before."

"Well, and where have you seen him?"

The Mock Turtle cleared its throat nervously and the hat spun like a top. "I travelled with him once, sir, for a short distance."

"On board ship?"

"No, sir, in a hautomobile, sir."

"Come on, Lamprey, cough it up. Don't spend all night over the job."

The Mock Turtle coughed nervously as if taking Pharmakos' instructions literally.

"I travelled with him, sir, on one occasion, between Pentonville and Bow Street."

"Oh, did you?"

"Yes, sir, he's a gangster, sir."

"Well?"

"It is a horganised thing, in my opinion, sir. There was three other men what came up so neat. It must have been a horganised thing, sir, or they wouldn't 'ave come up as slick as that."

"Did you know any of the others?"

"No, sir, they was strangers to me, sir. But I should know them again if I saw them, sir."

"Would they know you?"

Lamprey grinned, and changed suddenly from a Mock

Turtle into a wolf. "I think they would," he said.

"What do you make of it, Skilly?"

"Dunno anything abart it, Governor, save what old Lamp 'ere told me, but I don't like the look of it. I think we better keep our eyes skinned."

"And if I might make a suggestion, sir," said Lamprey meekly, "I do not think the young lady ought to be left here alone."

"Neither do I," said Pharmakos, "We will stand watch and watch, boys."

"Right you are," said Skilly.

"Yes, sir. Certainly, sir," said Lamprey. "And might I make another suggestion, too, sir?"

"Speak on, Lamprey," said Pharmakos, reaching for a cigarette from a beautiful pale jade box that stood open on a tabouret. Skilly also helped himself from the box. Pharmakos passed the box across to Pat, but she declined. She would not risk smoking and choking herself in front of Pharmakos' extraordinary retainers. He passed the box to Lamprey.

"No, sir, thank you kindly all the same, sir. I know my place," and he lifted his nose loftily. Skilly spat in the fireplace.

The billycock hat gave a twiddle that threatened to part its brim from its crown.

"Well, Lamprey, what is your suggestion?"

"It is this, sir. This is evidently a horganised thing, sir, and the local gangs won't like it. If I spoke a word to Joe Hannan, sir, I think it would do the trick."

"And have your friends beaten up?"

"Oh, no, sir. Not beaten up, sir. Can-openers and the bottoms of tumblers, sir."

"All right, Lamprey, speak a word in season to Joe Hannan, whom I fancy I have already met."

"Yes, sir, you met him over case 49, sir. And he thinks

most highly of you, sir."

Pharmakos rose to his feet to indicate that the interview was over. Lamprey bowed and scraped and twiddled his way out. Skilly said, "So long, Governor," and swaggered across the room. Pat noticed that he made no attempt to dispute Pharmakos' ascendency, but went as if dismissed by royalty.

"Which of these men is the more formidable, Pat?" said Pharmakos, as the door closed behind Lamprey's wriggling back.

"Lamprey," said Pat, without any hesitation.

"How do you know, child?"

"Because he has both brains and guts."

"And what about Skilly?"

"Precious few of either. You should have seen Mrs. Mullins shoo him off the premises like a stray cat."

Pharmakos shouted with laughter. "Do you know I am afraid Skilly's days of peace are numbered now that I have introduced female womenfolk into Quilp Cottage."

"Isn't it funny that everyone in Quilp Cottage except Lamprey, who is ash-blond, has red hair. Why is it?" asked Pat.

"Everyone in Quilp Cottage is blessed with a temper, my dear, and that is the only reason they keep the peace with each other. If I had not got the hell of a temper, Skilly would become unbearable. If Skilly had not got ditto and likewise, he would not be able to put up with me. And you, too, child. You are a Chinese cracker, my Coppernob. The arrangement is the same as that which prevails in asylums in one of which I was for a time; you didn't know that, did you, Pat? They are only one degree better than prison in that they have open wards and there is ample ventilation, not to say draughts, but the company is not so agreeable. Well, as I was saying when I turned aside to reminisce, in asylums they put all the homicidal maniacs together in one ward because they never slog each other. Not twice, anyway. I know, because I was in that ward. So there you are, my dear, with another fragment of my horrid past to fit into the great jig-saw puzzle entitled, 'Find the Pharmakos'."

He looked at her anxiously to see how she would take this revelation.

"Will you ever slog me when you get upheaved?" asked Pat, as cool as a cucumber. He heaved a sigh of relief. What a brick the child was. The Sealyham puppy rejoiced in its owner.

"No, my child, I shall never slog you because you know exactly how to handle me. But if I were handled the wrong way when I happen to be upheaved, there is no saying what I mightn't do, and I should know nothing about it afterwards."

They smoked for a while in silence, Pat having accepted a cigarette after the departure of the retainers, for she wished to acquire the art, though at present it could hardly be numbered among life's pleasures. Over in the far corner of the room, showing faintly white in the gathering dusk, stood Pat's bed. So this child proposed to bear him company at night for the best part of a week? thought Pharmakos. It would take fully that time to get her quarters in order, because paint has to dry between each coat, and it would certainly take three coats to make a job of it down there. One could not put Pat to sleep in the midst of wet paint. Well, he had no objection to offer. Far from it. The nights were his bad time. It would be delightful to have Pat's company, even if she were sound asleep. As for his own reactions, he just hadn't got any; his mainspring was broken. He was spared moral problems at any rate, whatever other wild beasts he might have to wrestle with.

"I vote we turn in early, Pat, we've had a strenuous day."

Pat agreed. She could hardly keep her eyes open. She

would sleep soundly enough, even if she were sleeping with a homicidal maniac. How funny it all was. Pharmakos was three parts lunatic, and homicidal at that; suicidal too, perhaps. And she felt as safe with him as if he had been her big brother; and she turned to him with the most perfect consciousness of care and protection. She had never felt so serene and secure in all her rather troubled short life.

They walked across the big room to the bed and examined it. Pharmakos produced a pocket knife and helped her to get the packing off it. Then they opened the bale of blankets and parcel of sheets, and he on one side and she on the other, they made that bed. Pharmakos watched her take the pillow in her strong white teeth and wriggle it into its case. Then he arranged the great lacquer screens covered with gorgeous birds so that she was completely enclosed, and wished her good night. He heard her scuffling about for a bit, and then all was quiet.

"Are you in bed, Pat? Shall I switch off the lights?"

"Half a second," said Pat, "I haven't got my hankey."

"Is the bed comfy?"

"Oh-ooh, it's awful comfy!" and he heard her bouncing up and down on the springs to test them. He laughed and walked about the room switching off the gorgeous great stand-lamps one by one, and then went to bed himself.

CHAPTER XIII

PHARMAKOS found himself sliding off into dreamland along a path that seemed to pass through Pat's new flat instead of Portland, and contained nothing more startling than Skilly being shooed by Mrs. Mullins, at which he found himself grinning even in his sleep. He was just catching up with Pat, who moved before him in her gay green kimono, when he was suddenly recalled to full consciousness by a sound. He was awake in a second listening. Was it just Pat fidgetting? But no, no sound came from behind the screens save a little grunt as she sank into deeper sleep, too faint to have aroused him. But something must have roused him. He lay with his ears cocked, listening.

Then it came again, the faint squeak of oars in rowlocks that were either muffled, or being used very carefully. He did not like that faint sound. A bargee going home would have been heard all over the river. He knelt up in bed, and tried to see out of the window. There was nothing to be seen on the broad expanse of dark water, and lights were compulsory on all law-abiding water-farers, so the boat from which the sound came must be either nefarious or close in under the wall, possibly both. He tried to put his head out of the window, but Skilly's anti-suicide device baffled him. He got up, fumbled for a pair of soft Russia leather slippers that were concealed under the bed, took a heavy stick from behind the curtain, and made his way across the dark polished floor as quietly as possible.

But luck was against him, and he tripped over a tabouret.

He heard the springs of Pat's bed creak as she sat up.

"It's all right, Patsy," he said in a low voice. "It's only me, going for a midnight prowl to see that the premises are locked up."

She grunted sleepily and he heard the springs creak again as she turned over and settled down. What trust the child had in him, bless her. He let himself out by the church door which moved noiselessly on its well-oiled hinges, and went silently down the dirty stone stairs in his heelless shoes, as soft as gloves, and opened the heavy door at the bottom a few inches and looked out.

The moon was in its second quarter, but the sky was overcast and there was not much light. There was enough, however, with the gleam of the water, to enable him to see a black bulk turning from the river into his little dock. He flashed the beam of a powerful electric torch on to it, and revealed a row-boat containing several occupants.

As the beam struck it, the row-boat panicked. Its four oars all began to wave simultaneously in different directions. Evidently its occupants were not experienced watermen. But the man at the tiller was, and his muttered directions soon straightened them out. They backed water, and the boat began to sidle out of the dock, catching the corner with a bump as the current took it.

"Sorry, governor, we took the wrong turnin'," cried a gruff voice. Pharmakos did not answer, but kept the beam of the torch steadily on them, blinding them. He heard another bump, and swearings. If there were not someone experienced in charge of that boat, his problems might solve themselves spontaneously, for the Thames below Westminster is no place for amateurs to go boating when the tide is on the turn.

They would not come back against the current, that was quite certain, so he closed the door, and after hunting around among the litter swept into a corner when Pat's flat was being cleaned out, found a piece of wood that would serve as a wedge, and jammed the door with it, for the key was missing. They had never troubled to lock the doors inside Quilp Cottage, for it seemed impregnable to all save aeroplanes when once the great gates were shut. He had had the steps removed from the wharf, and it had seemed as if a landing from the water were impossible. But recent changes in the management of the locks upstream had caused the water to mount very high in the lower reaches at times, and it was a simple matter for any active man to land from a boat on to the edge of the dock during one of these high tides, as Pharmakos now realised, and was considerably worried thereby, especially in view of the fact that Pat would be sleeping on the ground floor as soon as her new abode was ready.

He returned upstairs and went back to bed, but not to sleep. He was very wide awake now. There was no sound from Pat, however. What it was to have a constitution like hers; she would have eaten and slept on the day of the Last Judgment. He got out of bed and fetched his cigarettes. Perhaps a cigarette would quiet his mind and help him to go to sleep. He struck a match cautiously, so as not to disturb Pat.

But Pat was wide awake. She had been aroused by the rough voice of the midnight marauder, anxious to explain himself. She heard Pharmakos return to bed, and then she heard the scrape of a match, and smelt tobacco smoke, and knew that he was not sleeping. She hoped he was all right. She had taken him under her wing so completely that she was on the verge of getting up to tuck him in as she did with Eric, but then she realised that it would not be quite proper, as they were not really related. She lay quiet and listened, therefore, to see whether he were settling down, and being healthy and of a clear conscience, promptly fell asleep again.

But Pharmakos did not go to sleep so readily as Pat, his conscience not being equally clear. He smoked another cigarette, and then another, and then got up to go into the kitchen to see if he could find a drink of milk, in the hopes that food might succeed in quieting his racing brain where smoke had failed. He had got the refrigerator open, and was pouring milk from a bottle into a glass, when he heard a sound behind him and turned with a start that sent a shower of milk all over the kitchen, and there was Pat, swathed in her scanty little kimono, that was about as concealing as a bathing dress when she dragged it tightly round her as she was doing now, her red hair looking like a pen-wiper, for she never wore a slumber-cap. There certainly was no coquetry about Pat when she slept with him.

"You mustn't drink that milk cold," she said, "it will give you the tummy-ache again."

She took the bottle from him and got out a saucepan.

"Go back to bed and keep warm," she said.

"I'm quite warm, Patsy. It's a muggy night. I'd much sooner stop here and enjoy the pleasure of your company."

He turned a pair of Skilly's fancy boots off a chair and sat down. Pat looked at him as he sat there in his thin tussore silk pyjamas and red russia leather slippers, and thought that he looked like an illustration to a fairy tale by Rackham; one of those elongated creatures, half-goblin, half-tree, that he delights in drawing.

Pat took the glass of warmed milk in one hand, and hauled vigorously on her kimono with the other, tucking it modestly round her and securing the corner under her elbow; then she took up a plate of biscuits.

"Turn the light off," she commanded, and with Pharmakos meekly trailing behind her, she marched on her sturdy bare feet across the wide polished floor, popped him into bed, and tucked him up very firmly, as if she had no intention whatever of his getting up again till morning. Pharmakos had an idea that kids in prams wore a kind of harness which prevented them from falling out, and wondered whether Pat had any ideas in this respect in regard to him.

He leant back against his pillows and sipped the warm, comforting milk. Pat sat cross-legged like a tailor on the foot of the bed and ate the biscuits.

"I can't manage all this milk," he said, " Like to finish it up, old thing?"

"Sure you can't?" said Pat, stretching out her hand for the glass, and the milk disappeared after the biscuits into her insatiable maw.

"Now turn over and go to sleep," said Pat, switching off the bedside lamp, so that he had no option. "And don't let me hear you gallivanting about any more to-night. Go on, turn over; you will have nightmare if you go to sleep on your back."

Pharmakos turned over. He watched her patter off across the huge room and disappear behind her modest screens, and shook with silent laughter. Pat was a treat! Had there ever been anything like her? How scandalously Mrs. Grundy would say they were behaving, and yet how utterly innocent it all was. Either the warm milk or Pat's commands took effect, and the next thing he knew was a booming voice bawling: "Show a leg, show a leg!" and there was Skilly standing over him grinning broadly.

Pharmakos sat up; he was mad with himself for not being up and dressed before Skilly barged in. It was utterly repellant to him that Skilly should catch him sleeping with Pat, literally if not metaphorically, but he need not have troubled.

There was Pat, looking perfectly sweet in a sleeveless cotton overall that she had bought for two and nine in the New Cut as shown by the petty cash book. Pharmakos got out of bed and strolled into the bathroom. It never occurred to him to suggest that Pat should not be present at his levee this morning.

* * *

"Now listen, my child," he said to her as they sat at breakfast half an hour later, watching a tug struggling up stream with too many barges. "A workman and possibly his mate will be coming to knock a hole in the wall of the next apartment, and make a window in it so that we can use it as a genuine office. I am giving up my quarters in Crispin House. I maintained them as a front line of defence; partly so that people who were un-friends of mine might not get to know of the existence of Quilp Cottage, and partly so that clients should not be put off by appearances. But it is apparent from certain signs and symptoms that my un-friends know pretty well all that there is to know about this place, and I am sufficiently well known now as an unofficial sleuth, not to have to bother about cutting a dash. I can be as grubby as an old-fashioned firm of solicitors, and they will think all the better of me.

"So there is no point in keeping on those rather expensive quarters at Crispin House. I can always hire a sitting-room at an hotel for the afternoon if necessary. I just wanted to be sure that I could come and go without Warder Mills daring to spit in my eye, because I wasn't going to be hounded out by him, the blighter, and I can, Pat. I owe that to you, my dear. Fancy me, Number One Three Nought, standing up on my hind legs and yapping at a real live prison warder.! Can you believe it, Pat? I can't."

Pat insisted that he should rest for half an hour after his meal before starting forth to his day's work, and he lay on his back on the divan and chaffed her. She had a long list of articles she needed to purchase for herself and her flat, together with estimated expenditure. Every article marked W. she explained, could be obtained at Woolworth's. Four out of five were marked W.

Pharmarkos had a pang of compunction when he realised that the entire cost of equipping her little home would not be as much as that of one of his big sofas. He thought for a moment of taking her with him to famous shops and buying lovely things for her, for he was by no means a poor man nowadays, but he saw at once that she was far happier hunting for bargains in the New Cut, and left her to get on with her nest-making in her own way, promising himself that he would have the fun of adding all sorts of odds and ends and gadgets as the fancy took him, and enjoying Pat's squeaks of delight.

Finally she accompanied him down the long, dusty, dark passage, and saw him off, hanging out of Sister Ann's window to wave to him as he turned the corner into the main road. It was truly matrimonial, the way she saw her employer off, thought Pat, and she wondered what the commercial college would have thought of it. Anyway, he loved it, and that was the main thing. How he did love a bit of fussing, that man! She supposed the warders had not done much in that line during his seven years.

There were no more alarums and excursions for the moment. Pat did not know it, but there were four casualties in Guy's Hospital, horribly gashed about the face in a fight between rival gangs, which might possibly account for the peacefulness of the neighbourhood. All the same, Pharmakos was unremitting in his precautions, and Pat was never allowed to go out shopping unless chaperoned either by the wriggling, shuffling, shivering Mock Turtle, or the swaggering Skilly in his dreadful suit, who delighted in giving the neighbourhood to understand that this was his new donah.

Pat was immensely amused to watch the reactions of the workmen, who were decorating the new office, when they came in contact with Lamprey. They treated him like dirt, ordered him about, sent him on errands; and all the time there stuck out under his coat at the back something like a terrier's tail, which Pat knew to be a knife capable of disembowelling elephants, and was certain he would use it if he thought fit.

Pat had completely revised her original opinion of the relative fighting weight of Skilly and Lamprey. Skilly was a gentleman whose hooter was out of all proportion to his horsepower; Lamprey, on the other hand, for all his nervous mannerisms, was an exceedingly dangerous brute, she felt instinctively. She marvelled at the power of Pharmakos to bend two such men to his purposes by sheer force of character, and to make them love him into the bargain, for it was obvious that the pair of them worshipped the ground he trod on. And for the matter of that, thought Pat, so did she. Pharmakos was no ordinary person. She wondered what he would have been if prison had not broken his young manhood. He had the bearing of a man whose place in the world is assured, who is accustomed to deference. That Wellingtonian profile was vaguely familiar, she had seen a photo of him somewhere, or of someone very much like him, she felt certain.

As soon as the alterations to the outer room were finished, and a large window looking onto the river flooded it with light, Pharmakos fetched over all the furniture from Crispin House and fitted it up as an office for Pat in which she, with her files, typewriter and telephone, could keep track of his work. She was exceedingly efficient, and he marvelled how he had ever existed without her. She took his work in hand, just as she had taken his health in hand, and organised and card indexed it till he was able to handle double the bulk with half the labour.

Quite apart from her interest in him, Pat found the work fascinating as the panorama of human frailty and ingenuity unrolled itself before her in the files. She was particularly interested to see the way in which Pharmakos and Saunders played into each other's hands.

"I am what Saunders, in his professional terminology, would call a 'nose,' and what my pal Jurgens, in his euphonious dialect, would call a copper's nark, and that is why Jurgens has to keep his distance," Pharmakos informed Pat.

"What's a nose?" said Pat.

"It is a thing of which every detective officer has several, in addition to the one Nature provided him with. In fact he collects them sedulously and feeds them on half-crowns and flattery. A nose, Patsy, is a kind of amateur sleuth whom a detective has succeeded in attaching to himself as a source of information. He is not quite the same thing as a copper's nark, to be strictly accurate—a copper's nark is a criminal who splits on his pals: a nose is not usually an active criminal; most commonly he is a retired one who is glad to have his past forgotten at the price of making himself useful and agreeable to the police; but I've known noses who worked, and worked hard too, for the sheer fun of the thing. There's an extraordinary fascination about hunting your fellow-humans, Patsy, and if people once get a taste for it, they never drop it. I could no more help sleuthing than I could help breathing; and Saunders is just the same, I believe he'd like to come in with me on this job when he has to retire under the age limit, which won't be long now. So you see, he's a jolly good form of fire insurance for me, for he isn't going to have his best nose interfered with, not if he knows it; and he isn't going to let Jurgens do him out of a job in his old age by jugging me for back numbers either.

"I must say the police are extraordinarily good about not raking up back numbers if a chap is running straight. Of course they have to take notice of any definite charge that is brought, especially if there is a solicitor shoving it; for instance, if Jurgens laid an information against me, they couldn't ignore it, but they wouldn't go out of their way in the matter. Old Saunders knows the whole story. I blurted it out the time he brought me home after the fracas at the Cannon Row police station, and he spent the night either holding my hand or sitting on my head, I can't remember which, but he's never moved in the matter. When I'd simmered down sufficiently to realize how I'd given myself away, and asked him what he meant to do, he gave me a huge wink, and said he couldn't make any use of the information I'd given him as he hadn't cautioned me, and that's the last I heard of it; save that he always mentions in a casual and chatty manner any bits of news there may be to hand with regard to our mutual friend. That's my reward for being a nose.

"That's how the police work of this country gets done, Patsy; and it's a damn sight more effective than it would be if it were purely official-and a damn sight cheaper. The Exchequer starves Scotland Yard of men and materials, and the fellows get keen on their job and run it their own way on a back-scratching basis. I am steadily feeding Saunders with information about Jurgens' blackmailing methods, and one of these days he'll slip up and they'll land him; in return for this, Saunders keeps his mouth shut about a little matter of the robbery with violence wherein Jurgens got his head stove in. I don't say he'd have kept his mouth shut if Jurgens had pegged out, but the assault and battery, especially of a beggar like Jurgens, is a card of a smaller value than organised and systematic blackmail, and Scotland Yard is always willing to allow its men to give a sprat to catch a mackerel. So you see now, Pat, why I look on old Saunders as a friend of the family, and don't run for my life at the sight of him."

CHAPTER XIV

NOW Skilly, far from resenting the intrusion of the alleged Miss Pharmakos into Quilp Cottage, had been frankly delighted, and was at no pains to hide his delight, which he fondly believed to be flattering to all concerned. This bringing home of a woman humanised his employer in a manner as satisfactory as it was unexpected. Skilly hoped that his own tastes would meet with more consideration and sympathy in the future than they had in the past. He had never made any secret of his tastes or his adventures, being as sunnily amoral as a barndoor rooster, and Pharmakos was daily called upon to condole, advise or congratulate upon the previous night's adventures as occasion required.

It was a different matter, however, when it appeared that the young person whom Lamprey called Miss-madam was settling down for keeps and obtaining a degree of influence over the redoubtable Pharmakos which in Skilly's opinion no female ought ever to be permitted. Skilly was a primitive creature, and the result was a bad attack of jealousy that even Pat's tact and his fear of Pharmakos were unable to ward off.

He did not show his resentment very openly, for he feared his employer as he feared neither God, devil, nor police, but he showed it in a hundred ways of petty insult and spite which Pat found very hard to bear. But bear it she would, for Pharmakos was getting on so well, and improving almost hourly in health (she had actually dared to give him minced chicken), that she was prepared to pay almost any price of petty annoyance to save him from being upset before his health became re-established.

But all the same, whatever their good resolutions may be, it is an ill thing to bait the red-headed, and one morning, Pharmakos, singing in his bath, heard a sound of voices raised even above his vociferations. He leapt from the bath and went to the door and listened.

He heard a husky booming to the effect that, "If you think yer can teach me manners, yer damn well find yer can't." It was only the fact that he was stark naked and dripping wet that prevented him from rushing to the rescue of his beloved Pat then and there and committing a crime on Skilly.

Then he heard a yell of utter anguish; the cry of a lost soul in its last extremity of pain and despair; but it was not from a female throat that the cry issued, and Pharmakos paused to listen, a smile curling the corner of his lips. He remembered Pat's account of Skilly's encounter with Mrs. Mullins. Perhaps he was meeting yet another determined female who did not take him at his own valuation.

Then came another voice, which he presumed must be Pat's, though it was utterly unlike anything he had heard from her lips before.

"You shut your filthy mouth and behave yourself. Do you think I'm going to stand any more nonsense from you, you miserable, sneaking cur? I damn well won't. Take that!"

"That," whatever it might be, clashed like all the tin-cans in creation. Another howl, even worse than the last, went up to heaven.

"Lidy, lidy, I tike it back. I tike back everyfink I ever said. For Gawd's sake, don't throw the kettle, lidy!"

Pharmakos shut the bathroom door and picked up a towel and began to dry himself with an easy heart. Skilly had met his match for once.

It was Skilly who bore in the breakfast tray that morning.

Pat merely carried the teapot. Pharmakos observed that he had a nasty burn, blistering up nicely, on the bridge of his nose. Pat having returned to the kitchen to dish up, he said to his retainer, in a stern voice, "What is this trouble between you and Miss Pharmakos, Skilly?"

Skilly stood on one leg and scratched it with the other.

"There ain't no trouble, sir," he said.

Never had Pharmakos been called "sir" by that ardent Bolshie before.

"No trouble?" said Pharmakos harshly, following up his advantage at the double. "Then what was all that noise I heard?"

"Oh, that was nothink, sir, just a little friendly argiment, as you might say. We understand each other puffickly. Never met a nicer young lidy, sir, in all me puff." He scratched himself again, and smiled coyly over his shoulder at the re-entering Pat. So Pharmakos had to leave it at that. Pat looked serenely cheerful. It was difficult to realise that it was her voice that had been reviling Skilly in such good round terms only a few minutes before.

As soon as they were alone, he said to Pat: "What's all this shindy in the kitchen, Pat?"

"Well," said Pat, "If you must know, we had a bit of a set-to, and I got him in a corner and threw a hot frying-pan at him, and it's done him all the good in the world."

Pharmakos folded up in soundless laughter. It would not do for his retainer to hear loud laughter that morning if he still happened to be within ear-shot, as, knowing Skilly, he thought quite probable. .

Now Pat had got her new abode in order, and she instructed Skilly and Lamprey to carry down the bed from the corner behind the screens where it had stood for over a week. Consequently, when Pharmakos returned that evening he saw the great screens restored to their usual position and the corner, where Pat had slept standing empty. He picked at his lip with a nervous gesture, and that evening, for the first time for a week, he had pain after food.

He accompanied Pat down to inspect her finished abode with a cheerful countenance, however, and duly admired all the wonders she had found at Woolworth's, and the treasures she had picked up in the New Cut and even less salubrious neighbourhoods. She had certainly secured some most amazing bargains, for stall-holders seeing her accompanied by such famous local characters as Skilly and Lamprey, concluded she was queen of the gangs, and gave her things at knock-out prices as a kind of tribute to the banditti.

He finally inspected the little bathroom that had been contrived for her out of the third room.

"Phew, Pat, I don't like this!" he said.

"Why, what's the, matter with it?" said Pat, greatly disappointed, for she had thought it charming.

He raised his hands and pressed the flat palms against the ceiling. He stretched out his arms as if crucified and touched either wall with the finger-tips. He backed into the corner and took three paces the length of the little room.

"I thought so," he said, "It's just six inches short of the size of a cell in solitary. Come on, Pat. Out of this, quick!"

He seized her by the arm and hauled her up the stairs three steps at a time and into his big airy room. He picked up a newspaper and fanned himself. "That's better," he said.

"I shan't come calling on you very often, I am afraid. You will have to come and see me. I don't like small rooms."

Just then the telephone bell rang, and Pharmakos signed to Pat to answer it.

"Take the message, will you, Pat?"

He heard her say, "Yes ... Yes ... Yes ...." Then she hung up the receiver.

"It was Inspector Saunders," she said, coming back to

him where he sat in the window-seat, watching the brilliant moonlight on the water. "He asked me to tell you that the Dutch police have asked them for Jurgens, but they have had to refuse on a technicality."

Pharmakos was always pretty pallid, but he turned, if anything, three degrees sallower at this information. He said nothing, however, but continued to stare out at the moonlit water that lap-lapped at the piles supporting the old warehouse as the tide rose.

"What about bed?" said Pat.

"Yes, old thing, what about it?" said Pharmakos. "Brilliant idea," and he rose wearily.

That night was the first time for a week that Pat had not tucked him up and he had not drowsed off listening to her funny little grunts as she settled herself.

He did not attempt to sleep. He sat up, his knees making a tent of the bedclothes, and smoked cigarette after cigarette, which Pat would never have allowed and tried to estimate the significance to him of the few words spoken over the phone by Inspector Saunders. That Saunders thought them important was shown by the fact that he had come through at that hour of the night.

Pharmakos smoked, and the moon rose higher, sailing clear in a cloudless heaven, and the reflection from the water danced upon the ceiling and threw across it the shadows of the window-panes, and Pharmakos, looking at them, thought they were like the barred windows of some gargantuan cell, and his nerves began to tighten painfully.

It would never do for him to get the wind up now, when so much had to be thought out and decided, for this news of Saunders re Jurgens had put an entirely different complexion on all his affairs.

As long as Jurgens was wanted by the Dutch police, he dared not round on Pharmakos to any great extent; but if the Dutch police had been definitely told that they could not have him, then that check on Jurgens' activities was removed, and whole fields of enterprise opened up to him that had been closed before. Pharmakos, on his side, could never invoke the help of the police against Jurgens, whatever he might do, for Jurgens would then charge him with the burglary. However bad a man may be, he must not be burgled. Once a definite charge was brought, Saunders would not be able to help him out any further.

The prospect was not a pretty one, and Pharmakos, left alone by his Pat, did not take the brightest view of it. The black, wavering bars of shadow on the ceiling seemed prophetic to the wretched man, sitting up in bed, alone in the huge room, hugging his knees and staring into the darkness, wondering if his wits would hold together sufficiently to enable him to extricate himself from Jurgens' clutches.

But the things that worried him far more than the prospect of trouble with Jurgens were those wavering black shadows on the ceiling, so like prison bars. He could cope with actualities. Pharmakos had plenty of "nerve" though he had no nerves worth mentioning; the things that bowled him over were always things of the imagination, or resurrecting memories. It was the wavering bars on the ceiling, not the danger that threatened from Jurgens, that really made Pharmakos get out of bed and go to Pat, though he was firmly convinced, or at least told himself so, that as it was essential he should have a clear head, it was inadvisable to run any risk of a nerve-storm, and that he would probably stave off the threatened storm and get some sleep if he went and talked things over with Pat and told her all about the anxiety which Saunders' telephone message was occasioning him; for he had found that to talk about one of his bogeys with Pat was to lay it for good. He did not even wait to find his slippers, but went off bare-foot across the cold parquetry and down the filthy stairs to Pat's quarters. Then he had a sudden panic as to whether he would scare or offend her by this midnight call. But he did not think he would; Pat was such an understanding little soul, and if she did not realise by now that she could never be anything but his little sister to him, tenderly loved, but as a sister—well, the child was slower in the uptake than he gave her credit for being.

He knocked on the door of Pat's flat, but got no answer, and a panic rose in him again. Then he remembered that Pat had made the middle of the three rooms her bedroom, and naturally could not hear him when he knocked on the outer door. What a fool he was, always flying off the handle over nothing! He opened the door and entered quietly. He wanted to rouse Pat, but he did not want to rouse her suddenly and startle her. It was a beastly shame to waken the kid and spoil her night's rest. He was just on the point of going back upstairs again with his tail between his legs when he remembered those dark barred shadows wavering on the ceiling, and went on into Pat's bedroom. So it was that Pat woke up to find him standing over her and speaking to her.

She was not in the least startled. She had got quite used to his antics by now. It was no more to her that Pharmakos should walk into her bedroom in his pyjamas in the small hours of the morning than that Eric should trail in howling and clutching his golliwog.

"Hullo," she said, "What brings you here at this time of night?"

"Pat, I'm frightfully sorry to bother you, but can I come and talk to you?" He sat down on the end of the bed without waiting for a reply.

" You can come and talk to me and welcome" said Pat. "But you can't sit on my feet. Ouch! Get out!" And she dug her toes into his latter end till he shifted. Even in his perturbed, confused condition, he could not help wondering with amusement what Mrs. Grundy would say to this performance, and how absolutely off the mark she would be.

CHAPTER XV

"**WHAT'S** the trouble, old thing?" demanded Pat, as he seemed disposed to sink into meditation with his elbows on his knees in a manner that she knew meant threelegged stools.

"Trouble, Pat?" asked Pharmakos, looking at her with dazed eyes. Now that he was with Pat and away from those diabolical bars he could not remember for a moment that he was in any trouble.

Pat did not like the look of him at all. She would far rather see him upset than dazed. She suddenly remembered a remark he had once made about always being queer when the moon was full. She remembered that the very word "lunatic" is derived from the Latin for moon. Well, she had seen him quite queer enough when the moon was new; if he was going to be any queerer than he had already been, she would have her work cut out with him. But it never occurred to her to back out, or in any way to shrink from him. She had a vision of the soul of Julian Pharmakos wrestling with its damaged mind like a man getting a limping car home after a smash. Damaged steering-gear might cause it to swerve all over the road, but that was not the fault of the man who was trying to drive it, and who had no choice but to tool his cripple along as best he might, having no other means of transport.

She feared Pharmakos was sliding off into his old bad memories again, and dreading the upshot of that, she reached out and took him by the hand. It was cold and limp and unresponsive as the tail of a fish on a dish.

"Oh, Julian, come back to me. Don't go sliding away like this. It's me, it's Pat talking to you. Don't go off like this, my dear, it's so bad for you." The Sealyham was really beginning to get very heavy to carry. Pat's young shoulders were bowed under the burden.

Pharmakos pulled himself together. "Pat, I'm darned worried," he said.

"What about, old thing?" said Pat.

"About that telephone message from Saunders this evening. You remember who Jurgens is, don't you? The fellow Skilly and I beat up and burgled. Well, as long as the Dutch police wanted him, he daren't rat on me, because if he had I'd have blown the gaff on him; but now he hasn't got that hanging over his head, he can give me in charge for that burglary if he wants to; and he'll quite likely want to, considering the extent to which I've been twisting his tail. And Pat, if I'm shoved in a cell again, I'll go absolutely stark, staring, raving mad. And I can't face it, Pat."

Pat had no longer any need to worry about the limpness of his hand. Her problem was to extricate her own hand from the convulsive grip that was crushing her fingers. She could not see his face, because his back was to the window, and the window was curtained against the brilliant moonlight. It was, perhaps, just as well; Pharmakos had a queer enough face at the best of times, and when he got worked up, it looked like nothing human.

What could she say or do, poor child? What comfort could words be to a man in his position—a claustrophobic—a man with a morbid dread of enclosed spaces—faced with incarceration in a prison cell?

"But even if he charges you, will they convict you?"

"Probably. There is the evidence of the butler and a couple of footmen, who both had a good look at me, and I've got a face—well, the less said about my face the better."

"Would you get a long sentence?"

"Two years possibly. Certainly not less. You see, Pat, I'm not a first offender. But it isn't the length of the sentence, it's being locked up at all. You remember what I told you about the fuss at Cannon Row police station? Well, I didn't tell you the half of that. I was choking, Pat, choking and clean loony. I must have air. I can't stand being shut in. I felt as if the building were going to fall on me. Two years? Two hours would be too much for me. I'm finished, Pat. Finished and broken." He slid to the floor in a heap and buried his face in the bedclothes. Pat could not speak. She could only lay her hand on his head. The hair was rough and harsh to the touch like coconut matting.

Suddenly he leapt to his feet. "My God," he cried, "I must have air I" and springing across the room in one bound, he seized the window-curtains one in each hand and flung them back, bringing pole and everything down with a run. The brilliant moonlight shone full into the room through the wide-open window, which being on the ground level, was as heavily barred as any cell's.

Pat heard a kind of sobbing gasp, and saw Pharmakos grip the bars with both hands and start shaking them. Then he began to scream. It was not the shouting of a man, nor so high-pitched as a woman's screams; it was more like the cries of an injured horse. Pat cowered against the wall horror-stricken and terrified. So this was what had made the Cannon Row police send post-haste for Saunders; this was what the rough and tough Skilly had no mind to hear again.

Pat wondered whether anyone would hear the awful clamour and come to the rescue and require explanations. She hardly knew which was worse, to be alone with the screaming Pharmakos, or to have to give explanations to startled and scandalised neighbours. But nobody heard. Nobody could hear in that carefully concealed place, so obviously designed for nefarious doings. If Pharmakos turned on her, as Skilly had warned her he might, there would be no rescue.

At length the awful outcry began to weaken. Pharmakos' throat gave out. Pat did not know which was the most dreadful, his screams at their loudest, or his screams as he became exhausted.

Finally he staggered back from the window and came reeling across the room towards her like a very drunken man. She leapt from the bed and dodged behind him. He never saw her. Then an unlucky thing happened. The loose pyjama jacket, flying open, caught on the handle of a cupboard. The moment Pharmakos found himself restrained he took on a fresh fit of insane fury. The jacket, pulled off his shoulders by the drag of the cupboard handle, caught and held him behind the elbows. He started to fight with it. Muscles like cricket balls stood up on either arm, unpadded by any layer of flesh. His ribs were like park railings, thought Pat, as she stared at him in wide-eyed horror. The most amazing and unexpected muscles rose up like ropes in every direction on that half-naked and entirely fleshless body. He was like the anatomy diagrams in the first aid book. Would another page turn over in a moment and reveal his viscera? She believed it possible. Anything seemed possible in that nightmarish, moonlit room.

The pyjamas were the best that Burlington Arcade could produce, but even they could not restrain a madman indefinitely, and the heavy silk finally ripped, freeing Pharmakos, who stood up, naked to the waist. Pat thought of a picture of the battle of Trafalgar at the High School, to which her father had taken exception, and concerning which he had written to the governors of the school. That was how they served the guns in Nelson's day. Things were becoming dreamlike to Pat. She could not conceive that this extraordinary exhibition was real. It must be something at the pictures, or her own superheated imagination.

Pharmakos swayed uncertainly for a moment, and then pitched head foremost, full length on Pat's bed, and lay still, face downwards. Pat was truly thankful she had skipped when she did. Had she been pinned under the dead weight of Pharmakos, she did not know what she would have done. The moonlight shone into the room in a silver glory, revealing every detail as clear as noonday. The shadows of the bars striped Pharmakos from heel to head like the stripes of a tiger reversed. And then Pat saw that there were other stripes on him as well as those of the bars-white stripes that ran between shoulder and shoulder in an irregular lattice-work, showing up plainly, even in the moonlight, against the sallow discoloration of the skin. Pat stared at them, wondering what disease could have made such scars; and then she realised with a shock of horror that these must be the marks left by that dreaded instrument, the cat.

But surely, surely they could have realised that Pharmakos was not responsible for what he was doing? Fancy flogging a man in his condition! The crazy lack of imagination was the most amazing thing. How could anyone fail to realise that Pharmakos had no control over his outbreaks?

Pat seated herself on the bed beside him and gathered him into her arms. He was not a pleasant object to touch because he was dripping with sweat; but she cared nothing for that; clammy as he was, she gathered him up, and sat there with him in the moonlight, crooning over him; dry-eyed but weeping inwardly as she stared out of the barred window into the shadows, picturing in her imagination what must go on behind the high granite walls of prisons when men of the type of Warder Mills have the handling of men like Pharmakos.

Pat stooped down and picked up what was left of the pyjama jacket and used it as a towel to dry the sweat that was running in rivulets down Pharmakos' back. She had no idea one could perspire like that; it was a most amazing performance. It couldn't be healthy. It was just like the perspiration when a fever breaks. In a few moments the pyjama jacket was a sodden rag, and Pat saw that the only thing that could cope with such sweat was a bath-towel.

She started to slide herself gently from under Pharmakos' weight to go and get one, but at her first movement she felt herself held in a convulsive grip. Pharmakos was not nearly as unconscious as he looked.

What was going to be the upshot of all this? An unconscious man was one thing, and a conscious man whom one could reason with was another, but what was Pharmakos? What dream-state was he living in? Should she phone for a doctor? No, her instinct was emphatically against fetching a doctor to him. It would only distress him, and there would be so much to explain, and the doctor might not understand, and say that all he wanted was a tonic. Or, horrible thought, want to certify him insane. Pat's grip on the shoulders resting in her lap tightened convulsively. He shouldn't be certified insane! He probably was, but he shouldn't be certified.

There came to her the sudden realisation that her whole life centred about the battered wreck lying in her lap. Homicidal lunatic; convicted criminal; probably going to be convicted again in the near future, unless he succeeded in committing suicide first. A man much older than herself, grotesquely ugly with his extreme emaciation and discoloured skin; sick and bad-tempered-it mattered nothing to Pat. She just sat and clutched him, clammy as he was, and tucked the eiderdown round him and did not care how cold she got in her thin cotton nightgown.

She thought he was beginning to quieten down a little. The perspiration had stopped and he had remained dry since the last mopping she had given him; which was just as well, as she had used up everything within reach upon him, and he would not let her move to get a bath-towel. He was still as rigid as a board, however. One could have put his nose on one chair and his toes another, and he wouldn't have sagged, thought Pat. She had seen an exhibition like that once at the local music-hall, to whose gallery she sometimes went in company with her brothers when they were supposed to be attending the children's prayer circle. A hypnotist had done that with his subject, and sat on his tummy into the bargain. They had tried it when they got home, but no one had been able to manage it except Eric, and the effect on him was so disastrous, that they had held his head under the cold tap and stifled his squeals with a sponge, and then put him to bed and told their mother that he had received conviction of sin in the prayer meeting.

Pat's instinct was against trying to rouse Pharmakos just yet. If he were like Eric, he would be so exhausted after his outburst that he would go straight to sleep when the fit passed and wake up very chastened and give no trouble to anybody—till next time. There was nothing to do but wait. But it was beastly cold waiting. She wondered whether she could get Pharmakos under the blankets, and take the eiderdown herself. But she saw that it was impossible without disturbing him. The blankets were all rucked up under him and he would have to be lifted before he could be shifted, and that she could not do. She tucked the corner of the eiderdown as far round her back as it would go, and settled down to her vigil. To rouse him now would be fatal. All the trouble would probably start over again. The moon gradually passed to its setting, and the room was in complete darkness. A little cold wind blew in at the window, and Pat endured the cold and the cramp as best she might. The board-like rigidity had now gone out of Pharmakos, but at regular intervals a spasmodic shudder went through him. Pat thought that she could have set her watch by those shudders. Five times to the quarter of an hour they went, according to the distant chimes of Big Ben.

Her hand rested on his bare back under the eiderdown as she held him, and she could feel the ridges of his scars under her fingers, and it seemed to her that she would give her body to be burned if it would save him further suffering. It suddenly occurred to Pat to ask herself if she were in love with him. Was this the ideal of her dreams? Old, ugly and cranky, who had told her to make up her mind at the outset that there would never be anything doing in the way of romance between them? This was rather a staggering question. Pat's day-dreams included marriage and a home. She forgot how cold she was as she sat up and faced it. It had got to be faced. She saw that. What was the position going to be between herself and Pharmakos? Whither were they drifting? Pat was no fool, and Mr. Stone had always been explicit on the subject of sin; and although he had denied his daughters all practical experience in the conduct of life, this being, in his opinion, the best way of maintaining virtue, he had given them a sound grounding in the theory of it as it appeared to a Jehovistic Evangelical with more faith in Hell-fire than heavenly love as a means of grace.

What did she actually feel for Pharmakos? Pat asked herself, sitting in the dark with her hand on his scarred back, waiting for the next shudder. The fascination he had had for her at first sight had been more like the adoration of a Boy Scout for a popular patrol-leader than the love of a maid for a man. Pat could have imagined herself getting engaged to someone else and showing him with pride to Pharmakos to receive his blessing, and it never entered her head that Pharmakos might be jealous and grudge the blessing. That would have been too, too flattering, thought Pat. The imagination of the little typist, well drilled in the ethics of the commercial school, could hardly scale such heights in relation to her employer. Employers seduced their typists, but they never married them. A typist, therefore, must be careful never to get into any emotional relationship with her employer lest she be seduced, as marriage was not to be expected. That was the faith in which Pat's professional upbringing had taken place, and she accepted it, for it seemed to her common sense.

She could see that Pharmakos belonged to a different world from Mr. Stone, even if he had been to prison and associated solely with the criminal classes and the police.

He had told her at the very outset of their acquaintance that he had no use for women, having been too badly bitten by them ever to trust them again. He had also spoken of a wife and ten children coming out of the teapot. Pat's memory had registered every chance reference he had ever made to his emotional status. The latter reference she had judged was merely a joke, but the former, she thought, represented the truth because of the bitterness with which he had spoken.
She doubted if he were married if he had gone to prison when he was only twenty-two, so that disposed of one problem, anyway; there was no wife from whom he was separated to turn up when she was least wanted and make herself unpleasant. Pat's guess was that Pharmakos had been engaged to some girl who had not stood by him in his trouble. Or, alternatively, that when his trouble came upon him, he had not felt it right to hang on to her. Did he still care for her, or did he hate her, and all women because of her? Pat rather favoured the latter hypothesis, for he had spoken bitterly.

But however bitterly a man may speak of women in general, and one woman in particular, he is apt to fling himself at her feet if that woman so much as crooks her little finger at him. How would she feel, Pat asked herself, if the woman reappeared and claimed Pharmakos? She would be only too glad for him to have the thing that would make him happy.

If she could not give him what he needed, she was glad for him to find it elsewhere, so long as he was happy. There is no greater love than that, and it is very, very rare, but like faith, it can move mountains.

CHAPTER XVI

PHARMAKOS had missed his last shiver. It would soon be a quarter of an hour since he had shuddered last. Big Ben announced three in the morning, and Pharmakos sighed and turned over on to his side. Sleep at last, thought Pat, and wondered how long he would sleep before he roused. Would Skilly, or worse still, Lamprey, come through the yard and look in at that uncurtained window and see the tableau on the bed and draw the only possible conclusion?

Well, it was no use worrying, thought Pat. Quilp Cottage was not given to early rising, and the morning sun would probably shine in on Pharmakos and wake him long before Skilly was abroad. So she returned to her cogitations, and they helped her to forget how cold and cramped she was.

Pharmakos had evidently foreseen the possibility of her waxing sentimental over him; he had probably had the same trouble with other typists, for there was a peculiar fascination about him, ugly as he was; and he had told her very plainly that there could never be anything doing in that direction, and that he would never feel towards her other than as if she were his little sister, or, alternatively, as if she were a wash-stand. Pat remembered that phrase distinctly. There could be nothing colder or more unresponsive than a wash-stand. He had rubbed this fact into her at regular intervals until she felt as if it were the pivotal point in their relationship which she must accept if any co-operation between them were to be possible. She half believed it, and she half didn't. Pat tested statements by the flavour on the ear, as it were, rather than by logic and evidence. The impression this reiterated statement of Pharmakos left upon her was that it was the truth, but not the whole truth; but what supplementing it might need to make it complete, she was too inexperienced to know. She knew that Pharmakos was sincere when he made it, and that to the best of his knowledge and belief it was true; but nevertheless the feeling remained with her that when it came to be put to the test it might in some way prove to be built on sand, and there would be a landslide which would surprise no one more than Pharmakos. She could not rely upon that reiterated statement of his as representing the actual and ultimate state of affairs, and yet she could not get away from it. She sighed, and filed it for reference, retaining an open mind on the subject. Pharmakos' behaviour bore it out, for he never made the slightest attempt at familiarity with her; his attitude was literally that of a big brother, and she sensed that it was genuine. But on the other hand he indulged in an amount of verbal endearment that would not have been out of place between a newly married couple. The dears and darlings flew like sparks from an anvil, and she did not feel that they were merely small change, as in the theatrical world, where they are applied indiscriminately as a substitute of Hi, or any loud cry. She believed he was genuinely fond of her, and yet in another way, he did not care tuppence about her. Pat heaved another sigh, deeper than the last, and gave it up as a bad job.

 She wished to goodness that Pharmakos' skull was not so hard, and that it rested on her lap instead of her hip-bone. Likewise that his collar-bone had not made contact with her kneecap. It ought all to have been so very romantic, whereas it was merely extremely painful. He should have laid his head over her heart, but instead he had managed to plump it in the region of her dinner. Or rather the spot where her dinner had once been, and where her breakfast would be in the far-away future, for Pat was getting hungry. He was an awful dear, but there were also times when he was a sore trial. Goodness, how knobbly he was! Never had she felt such bones. She would take jolly good care concerning the anatomical lie of the land if she ever had occasion to cuddle him again.

One thing she saw clearly, however, as she sat patiently in the darkness, enduring the cold and the pressure rather than rouse him; whatever might be the state of his feelings towards her, there could be no question whatever as, to his need of her. That, she felt, was even greater than he knew. She literally stood between him and the Bottomless Pit. There was going to be a bad time ahead of him with this wretched business of Jurgens hanging over his head. It looked ugly, Pat thought; but then she had only heard Pharmakos' version of it, and he was in no state to assess it dispassionately. But even so, if the facts were as stated, which she believed, he was in an exceedingly tight corner. Inspector Saunders had evidently thought so too, for she felt that his message had been one of warning, to give Pharmakos a chance to do a bunk if he were so minded. She knew Pharmakos had Saunders' sympathy. Saunders probably knew his full story. It stood Pharmakos in good stead in Pat's eyes that he should thus be held in esteem by the man from Scotland Yard, who was exceedingly unlikely to be sentimental on the subject of crime. Pat believed that Saunders was the best friend that Pharmakos had; at any rate, he was the person Pharmakos had told her to go to if she were in trouble.

She could tell by Pharmakos' breathing that he was now asleep, and his sleep was being disturbed by dreams, and the dreams were not pleasant, she could tell that by the way he was twitching and muttering. A cold dread clutched at her heart lest there should be another outburst. He called out his prison number as if answering to a roll-call. Various names caught her ear in the indistinct mutterings. She guessed that he was busy in his imagination with his various cases, and was thankful; anything was better than prison memories, which might have precipitated every imaginable outburst. She heard the name of Skilly and Saunders occur at intervals as if he were speaking to them; and then he called out "Pat, Pat!" so loudly and clearly that she thought he must have wakened up, and answered, "Yes, dear, what is it?"

But he did not hear her. He was away among his dreams and memories. But perhaps her voice had reached him where he was wandering, for he quieted down after that, and the heavy regular breathing told her that his sleep was now deep and restful and she heaved a sigh of relief. He would be all right in the morning if he had a good sleep. A grey light was beginning to creep into the room, but Pat was so thoroughly cramped and chilled that she had hardly any sensation left in her, and she leant her head against the wall and dozed. Consequently she did not notice Pharmakos' awakening.

Gradually coming to his senses after his bout, Pharmako's found two lines of verse running in his head, and wondered what had suggested them.

> "O that 'twere possible, after long grief and pain,
> To find the arms of my true love around me once again."

It is a thought that comes to many prisoners and captives, especially such as Pharmakos, highly sensitive and affectionate and very dependent on those who are dear to them.

Every morning of his life, Pharmakos woke to wonder whether he were in prison or out of it. He had so often relieved the tedium of imprisonment by building castles in the air that he had always dreaded to open his eyes lest the beautiful room he had phantasied for himself should fade, and reveal the grey walls and narrow confines of his cell. He thought that someone was holding him and that his head rested against someone's side. He could feel the rhythmic movement of breathing. He knew without looking up that that someone was Pat. How he knew, he could not have said. But he knew all the same.

He kept perfectly still. Was this reality or phantasy? It was much more likely to be the latter than the former. Pat had taken up her bed and walked the previous night, and he had hated her going. His unstable mind was probably at its tricks again, like Freud's story of the little boy who dreamt he had eaten the cherries on which his mother had placed an embargo. There was nothing that would have been lovelier than to be cuddled by Pat, save that it was not fair to the kid to let her do it. Well, if his subconscious could provide him with as pleasant phantasies as this, more strength to its elbow. He was in no hurry to get up and face cold daylight, especially if the daylight came through a barred window. He lay still, listening for the heavy tread of warders on flagged passages and the rattle of the keys. But the first sound that came to his ears was the hooting of a tug on the river, and he knew that he had been a darned fool once again.

So it probably really was Pat he was lying up against. He wondered what in the world he had been up to the previous evening, and hoped to God he had not done the child any harm. The thought of what might have happened to Pat in his frenzy so startled him that he lifted his head and looked at her.

She was sitting, curled up on the pillow beside him, her head propped against the wall, her little face pinched and drawn with cold and fatigue, and nothing on her but a miserable little cotton nightgown like two handkerchiefs tacked together. Round himself was tucked the eiderdown. She was sound asleep. Her arms lay slackly about him. She had evidently sat up all night holding him, and then dropped asleep from exhaustion as he quieted down towards dawn.

"God bless you, Pat," he murmured, as he laid his head back again in her lap very gently, so as not to rouse her. What pluck the kid had! How many girls would have been found snoozing peacefully after the kind of night she must have had with him? Prison warders declined to sit up with him single-handed.

He wondered what had happened the previous evening. This was like waking up in solitary, wondering what in the world the row had been about, and knowing that he had probably smashed up somebody pretty thoroughly before they had got him there. He felt stiff and sore all over, so there must probably have been a shindy of some sort; and he wondered whether Pat had got the brunt of it, but thought it unlikely, or she would not have been curled up beside him so placidly.

Then he suddenly became aware of the rasped soreness of his throat and knew that he must have had one of his screaming fits, and a hot blush of utter shame went all over him. So Pat had heard that! He felt as if not one single rag of self-respect remained to him. What must she think of him? How could she help despising the utter cowardice of that exhibition? She probably pitied him, which was no doubt well meant, but there was nothing he hated and loathed so much as being pitied, and by Pat of all people, before whom he had struggled so desperately to keep his end up! But the last thing in the world he wanted was to lose Pat's esteem. And what vestige of esteem could she have for him after an exhibition like the one she must have been treated to? She would expect him to have some sort of manhood, whatever his troubles, and not give way like a frightened child and scream the place down, as his rasped throat told him he must have done. For a moment he felt as if he could have strangled Pat as she slept rather than face her contempt.

The utter degradation of the whole thing! He was better dead. It was no use living on if one could not have some sort of decent life. No use dragging on a merely animal existence, with everything human fallen into decay. Into the river and done with it! He lifted his head again and stared wildly around him, and realised that his shoulders were bare. Beside him on the pillow lay the filthy and ragged remains of what could only have been the coat of his best silk pyjamas, the pyjamas he had put on when Pat shared his sleeping apartment. Good Lord, what had been happening? Had he, or had he not, parted with the trousers as well?

It was at that moment that Pat woke up.

She looked down at him and smiled. "So you are awake?" she said.

He could not meet her eyes. "Yes, I'm awake," he muttered.

She saw that he was in the self-hating mood that Eric was always in after an outbreak, when he could look no one but his gollywog in the face. How alike they were, the grown man and the small boy, both so afraid of being thought unmanly. How much simpler it was to be a woman, and cry like a hydrant and have done with it. Well, she would have to see if she could get him to let her be his gollywog and put aside his pride with her. After Eric had told her what he had been dreaming about, he always felt better. Pharmakos had frankly admitted the same thing, and announced his intention of using her as a kitchen sink down which to pour his troubles.

But it was no use pressing him, Pat knew that. It would be, as he said, like pulling teeth, and he was too sore to be touched at the moment. Till something had restored to him his armour of male pride, without which the male is as a plucked chicken, nothing could be done with him. He would be on the defensive against the whole world, and his defence would be to play 'possum.

Pharmakos moved uneasily on the bed.

The silence had got to be broken, but she must walk warily, thought Pat.

"I wonder what time it is?" she said. Big Ben immediately answered her question by chiming the hour, and then booming five.

"Do you know what I'd like to do?" said Pat. "Let's go upstairs and brew a meal; we've both had a broken night." She felt that the happenings of the past hours must not be buried in oblivion, because then they would be a cause of festering embarrassment between them. Tacitly to ignore them was to admit their importance. The shrapnel in the wound had to be got out before it would heal. But it was more like a vet's job than a doctor's, thought Pat. Pharmakos would turn on her if she hurt him, even though she hurt to heal. She had got to look out for her patient's teeth and claws while she ministered to him.

But Pharmakos did not respond to her invitation. He merely burrowed deeper into the bedclothes till nothing but the back of his red head was visible. Pat looked at him in perplexity. He was simply letting himself go. Something had got to be done to make him pull himself together; but the spur must be applied very, very gently else he would kick and bolt. He was not a child like Eric; he was a man, with a man's pride.

She gently rubbed the rusty red stubble that just showed among the tumbled bedclothes at her side. She couldn't help thinking that it was exactly like the coat of an Irish terrier.

"What am I to do with you?" she said, meditatively.

Her words had their effect. Pharmakos was recalled to a sense of his responsibilities, and squirmed uneasily.

"I'm frightfully sorry," he muttered.

"You needn't be," said Pat, continuing to rub the rough

red head, as if it were a dog's. "It's just the same to me as if you came out in a rash. You know I do understand, Julian."

"I don't do it on purpose, Pat," came the muffled voice from the bedclothes.

"I know you don't, old man," said Pat, "I've got enough sense to see that. It's just the same as a nightmare."

Pharmakos sat up so suddenly that he nearly knocked Pat off the bed. He looked very exhausted, and very wild, and a great deal of the whites of his eyes was showing, like a frightened horse, giving him a queer and inhuman look. It was the face of a maniac, and Pat knew it instinctively.

"It's not the same as a nightmare. It's a great deal worse than that. I'm mad, Pat, mad as a March hare."

"And I'm illegitimate. What of it? You're not the only person with a past. I don't see that there's a great deal to choose between us."

The saving grace of Pharmakos was a sense of humour, and crazed as he was, Pat's remark tickled him. He suddenly laughed, but it was not the laugh of insanity, and his eyes became human.

Pat was so relieved by the success of that one quick slash of the scalpel, which she knew was all that would be allowed her that she began to tremble from sheer relaxation of tension, and hoped to God that Pharmakos would not notice it and get upset again. But instead he suddenly flopped back, right into her lap, and with such complete abandonment that he knocked the breath out of her.

"Ouch!" said Pat, involuntarily.

"Do you mind my doing that, Pat?" asked Pharmakos hastily raising his head again.

"Not a bit," said Pat, pushing the offending head back on to her knee. "You can lie there as much as you like; but you mustn't butt me in the bread-basket. It isn't sporting."

Pharmakos was shaking with laughter so much himself

that he could not feel Pat shaking from another cause.

"Pat, you are an owl!" he said, "You are the most unsentimental female I ever met."

"Well," said Pat, "At the very outset of our acquaintance you set before me the ideal of a marble wash-stand, and I've tried to live up to it. Besides, being brought up with a lot of brothers knocks all the sentiment out of you. I don't suppose I have got many illusions left. Legs ain't no treat to me, as the bus-conductor said."

Pharmakos put his arms round Pat's waist and gave her a hug.

"Pat, you're a darling," he said, "And you've been a perfect angel to me." How firm her waist was! Pat was no flopping odalisque. She was a muscular little thing. Her waist without her stays was a lot firmer than most women's when shored up with whalebone. The thing he especially liked about her was that she could be affectionate without being sentimental or emotional. He hated any display of emotion because it cracked up his self-control, and yet he craved for sympathy by the bucketful. Pat expressed her sympathy in such a queer way that she made him laugh, and thus saved his face. The sympathy was there all right, he could feel it in every move she made, but her endearments were those of a tough little urchin, not a moon-struck maiden. What fun Pat was and what a darling! How perfectly she knew how to take him, easing the pressure off all his sore spots. Was she doing it consciously, or was it just instinctive? He favoured the latter view. It was altogether too clever to be altogether conscious, especially on the part of such a youngster. There had been a very good doctor at the asylum, but he hadn't been as good as this. No, his nature and Pat's fitted into each other like the two ends of a dovetail.

Pharmakos was in no hurry to move. Lying up against Pat like this and having his head rubbed was balm of Gilead to his sore soul. This—this was the thing he wanted from Pat; she had absolutely touched the spot. He felt the years rolling off his shoulders and every taut nerve slackening off.

He would care nothing for prison bars now. He could breathe his fill at the bottom of a coal-mine. He had not realised what it was that he wanted from Pat before. He had known that it was not marriage; that marriage, in fact, was out of the question. It was this—this—this that he wanted, and it was heaven, peace, and healing. The dead weight of the Sealyham pup was reposed on Pat. Psycho-analysts say that cure proceeds via transference, and undoubtedly they are right. But how is one to find folk to accept—and keep—the oddly assorted transferences that neurotics have to dispose of?

Pharmakos was warm and comfortable, for Pat had pulled the eiderdown over him. But not so she, sitting in her thin cotton nightdress close to the open window. He felt her shiver and suddenly woke to the realisation that Pat must be having an uncommonly thin time of it. He lifted his head from her knee and looked at her. Her round childish face was pinched and grey with fatigue and cold, and her eyes looked as if she had been crying.

"Pat, my dear!" he exclaimed in consternation, "Have you been sitting up all night like this?"

"It's quite all right," said Pat, her voice jumping uncertainly from key to key despite her efforts to control it.

Pharmakos sat up and put an arm round her shoulders, "My dear—" he began, and then stuck fast, and Pat burst into tears. He drew her head down upon his shoulder, and she rested her nose on the crag of his collar-bone and wept unrestrainedly. Nineteen lacks staying power. Pharmakos found out for himself how chilly it is to sit in front of an open window at five o'clock in the morning with precious little on.

But all the same, the situation had its consolations. He

was mothering Pat now, instead of Pat mothering him, and he liked that. It equalised a situation that might have become too one-sided. He rested his cheek on Pat's red-gold fluff and was supremely content.

But he soon had enough of it. The habit of sitting up with teething nurslings is not innate in the male. The cold wind blowing on his bare shoulders made him feel that Pat needed pulling together.

"Sweetheart," he said, "What was it you said just now about going upstairs and having a meal?"

Pat gave a gulp and a snuffle and began rummaging under the pillow.

"What is it, my sweet?"

"Handkerchief," said Pat.

"Oh, Lor', I can't lend you one this time, darling."

Pat sat up and disentangled herself from his arms and pushed him firmly away.

"You lie down and go to sleep," she said, "while I get my dressing-gown."

Pharmakos shouted with laughter and put his head under the bedclothes. He knew Pat's wispy cotton kimono so well. She might just as well have worn nothing at all. Still, it was advisable to observe the conventions so far as was possible. There was all the difference in the world between the incidental and the deliberate.

"I say, Pat," came a voice from under the bedclothes.

"Yes?"

"How much did I keep on in the way of clothes?"

"Not a great deal, but sufficient. You kept your trousers. I suppose that is what you're really worried about."

"Well, now you mention it, Pat, it was. I am devoted to my trousers."

"You can get up now," said Pat.

Pharmakos sat up and swathed the eiderdown round

himself.

"Have a blanket, old dear," he said, handing her one, "You look darn chilly."

"I'm more than darn chilly, I'm damn chilly," said Pat, "Where are your bedroom slippers?"

"Haven't got 'em. Where are yours?"

"I don't own any at the present moment."

"Didn't Woolworth's stock them?"

"Oh, yes, they stocked them all right, sixpence a foot, but I forgot to get them."

The ridiculous procession moved off. A Red Indian chief and his squaw. Pat with her pen-wiper hair in her eyes, and both their feet as black as ink from the filthy stairs.

Pat put him into bed, got him a hot-water bottle, and gave him hot milk to drink. He stretched his neck and purred like a cat having its ears scratched. The shadowy bars still wavered on the ceiling, but he didn't give a hoot in Hell for them now. He noticed that Pat looked rather limp, but he was so filled to the brim with heavenly satisfaction that he could hardly concern himself even with his beloved Pat.

She sat cross-legged on the foot of the bed as before, pulled the eiderdown over her lap, and shared his glass of milk.

"Come on Pat," he said, "Tuck in under the eiderdown and share the hot-water bottle." He pulled a spare pillow from behind his back and threw it to her. She sighed, and did as she was bid. She was past caring. She was dead to the wide, and wanted to get warm. So it was that Skilly, looking in next morning in hopes of breakfast, saw them lying head and tail like peaceful sardines, grinned his blessing, and tactfully withdrew.

CHAPTER XVII

PAT was the first to wake in the morning, and she lifted her head with a start, wondering where in the world she was, and saw Pharmakos' head on the pillow at the other end of the bed, and one lean, sinewy arm flung out over the purple eiderdown, and the other resting limply across her feet. Recollection returned to her, and she wondered what time it was, and whether Skilly had yet put in an appearance and observed the two sleepers tucked up so comfortably under one eiderdown, and if he had, what he thought of the arrangement.

Oh, well, it was no use worrying. Skilly would certainly think the worst, but would equally certainly approve. Pharmakos might just as well have his sleep out. She dropped her head back on the pillow again and lay tranquil. It was the oddest imaginable arrangement; in fact the whole *ménage* at Quilp Cottage was the oddest imaginable arrangement. But there was not one single item in it which her conscience told her was wrong. She and Pharmakos were doing no wrong, and had not the slightest intention of doing any wrong. If he tried any antics, she would smack his head and walk out, and that was that. He was a bachelor and she was a spinster, and if they wanted to marry, they could; but as marriage obviously was not indicated, why should they, merely to propitiate a mythical Mrs. Grundy? Certainly not. They had a perfectly clear conscience, and that was all that mattered.

Pharmakos had made his position plain from the very start. He had not the slightest intention of getting on to sentimental terms with her and would never want any of the things from her that were implied in a love affair. He had specifically warned her of this, so that she might not go and get sentimental over him, and so make herself miserable. What he wanted was nursing, and if he did not get it he would probably go under. It was up to her to give him what he wanted, and no more than he wanted; and if she worked up any superfluous emotion, to keep it to herself. If she burnt her fingers over him, that was her look-out; she had been specifically warned.

A woman had probably played a part in his breakdown, and that was the only woman there would ever be for him. If he ever recovered sufficiently and that woman were available he would in all probability go to her. At any rate, he would want to go to her; and any other woman who tried to stand between him and that ideal was a fool, and would be inflicting a great wrong on him into the bargain; for even if, in a moment of weakness induced by his sickness, he were willing to accept a substitute, as soon as ever he was restored to his normal balance he would reject the injurious imitation that had been foisted upon him.

If Pharmakos were to be pulled through, it was necessary that he should be deliberately nursed, and not merely secretaried, and the nursing in which he stood in need involved a great deal more than mere tending; in fact, the proper word for it was not nursing, but mothering. Affection was the thing that got underneath Pharmakos' skin. The minute a little affection was shown him, there was an instant response, an instant slacking off of tensions and quieting down of the whole man. The way to handle him was to mother him, and love him, and pet him and cuddle him, like Eric to the nth degree. And to really love him, too, not just to ladle out endearments. If she waxed demonstrative, yet kept back a part of the price, it wouldn't work. She must give herself, her very innermost soul, to the task, and she must expect no return. Pharmakos would never give himself back to her. Love was not for him. She must love as a mother loves, expecting no reward save that the child of all her hopes and sacrifices shall go from her in the end, safely launched on the sea of life. She must love Pharmakos, launch him, and stand aside. She must literally give her life in exchange for his, for she saw that she would be sucked pretty dry by the time he had finished with her; and from him she must expect nothing vital in return, for all he had once had to give a woman was dead and gone, she knew not where.

It was a kind of vicarious atonement, she thought to herself as she lay at his feet through the long summer morning and listened to the tugs hooting on the river and the clack of the derricks working cargo in London Pool. "Greater love hath no man than this, that a man should lay down his life for his friend." She loved Pharmakos. She would not deny it. It was no good pretending she didn't, for her love for him was the secret of her power over him. Unconsciously he felt the love that was going out to him, and his sick soul absorbed it, and fed on it, and began to heal. When it was healed it would not need her love any longer, and her work would be done. She had given a soul back to life that was being dragged down into the Pit, and that must suffice for reward.

Pat did not blind herself to the fact that it would hurt to save Pharmakos and let him go, and to do it with her eyes open; but it would hurt more to hold back a part of the price that could have been his ransom, and see him break up and go under. So she made up her mind. Pharmakos should be nursed, and loved, and set free. She would not keep caged birds.

She sighed, and snuggled down under the eiderdown, and pressed a bare foot into the hand that lay flaccid beside it, and dropped off to sleep again. So it was that when Pharmakos awoke, he found that he was holding Pat's foot.

His fingers closed on the bare toes in his palm. It was immensely comforting to have hold of a bit of Pat. What a dear she was, to trust him, and curl up beside him like this, and give him just the comfort he needed. Then there suddenly struck through him like a knife the realisation of what hung over his head—Jurgens—arrest—confinement in a cell, and above all, separation from Pat. His hand closed over her toes so convulsively that he woke her up.

Up popped her pen-wiper head from under the eiderdown at the foot of the bed.

She saw by his strained expression and his silence that he was in distress. With an eel-like movement, she did a right about turn under the eiderdown, perched herself on the pillow beside his head, and gathered him into her arms.

"What is it that's bothering you?" she asked softly.

"Jurgens," said Pharmakos, and hid his face against her side.

For awhile he lay without stirring, and Pat held him to her with a firm, steady pressure. How wise she had been, she thought to herself. Nothing could have been conveyed by words, but everything could be conveyed by just holding him against her like this.

Her reward was not long in coming. Pharmakos raised his head, and his eyes were normal. He looked worried, but he no longer had the scared, dazed look that was so distressing to see on a man's face, and when she smiled at him, he smiled back.

"Pat, my dear," he said, "Do you realise that we are behaving most scandalously?"

"No," she said, "I don't realise anything of the kind. In fact the exact opposite. Mrs. Grundy is a dirty-minded old lady. Let her get on with it. We're doing nothing to be ashamed of, and I decline to be ashamed."

"Mrs. Grundy knows human nature, Patsie," said Pharmakos, though he made no move to put himself at a safe distance.

"I'm just the wash-stand," said Pat, airily, "Don't worry about me."

"That's all right for you, my innocent, but what about me?"

"Aren't you all right, too?" asked Pat anxiously, a sudden qualm assailing her lest she were dropping bricks without knowing it.

"I'm very much all right, Patsie. Much too all right, in fact. But Mrs. Grundy would say I was being a thorough cad to you, and she would be right."

"Rats!" said Pat.

There was silence between them for a space, Pharmakos' head resting against Pat's side, and rising and falling rhythmically as she breathed. Suddenly he broke the silence.

"Patsy," he said, "Would you like to marry me?"

Pat shot off the bed as if she had been stung.

"No!" she said, with furious emphasis, "I'd simply hate to!"

"Well, you needn't if you don't want to," said Pharmakos, not without a certain acerbity, "But there's no need to fly off the handle, I was only trying to do the polite."

He had never expected her to accept him. His proposal was only a sop to his conscience, which pricked him smartly from time to time concerning his treatment of Pat; for he saw that in her innocence she realised none of the implications of what she was doing, and that although he might be a burnt-out cinder incapable of any further emotional reactions, she was young, and presumably inflammable, being red-headed; and in cuddling and being cuddled by Pat, he was engaged in the salubrious occupation of throwing cigarette-ends into gorse.

Pat sat down at the foot of the bed, as far from him as possible, and scowled at him angrily, looking more like a pen-wiper than usual. He scowled back. He was not feeling particularly pleased with her at the moment. Her refusal of his offer of marriage had been quite unnecessarily emphatic.

"What did you ask me that for?" demanded Pat angrily.

"Ask you what?" snapped Pharmakos.

"Ask me to marry you, when you know you don't want to."

"Well, Pat, I thought it was only fair to give you the offer."

"You and your offers be damned."

"Thanks," said Pharmakos, "I know I'm no catch, but there's no need to rub it in."

Pat's face softened. "I didn't mean it that way," she said. "I meant, why did you suggest getting married when what you feel for me is brother and sister?"

"Well, Patsie, dear, it seemed to me that it was rather rough on you. I've got dashed little to offer you, Pat, but I can give you my name, if it's any use to you."

"Don't you think we're very well as we are?" she said, watching him.

"As far as I'm concerned we are. I've got all I need, just cuddling up to you like this. I've told you a dozen times, I'm a burnt-out cinder, and I should think that by now you believe me.

"You'll be dust and ashes if I don't give you some breakfast," said Pat, "That's Big Ben saying it's eleven."

She swathed her kimono round her and marched off to the kitchen, leaving Pharmakos alone. He lay back, his arm under his head, watching the door through which she had departed, wondering what to make of the recent exchange of views. One half of him said, "How perfectly heavenly. Pat has the same make-up as you have, and you can make the best of both worlds, with nothing to worry about!" The other half said, "Don't be a darn fool! "

Pat popped her head round the kitchen door. "I've put the kettle on, and I'm going downstairs to get dressed. Will you turn the gas down if it boils over?"

"Right you are," said Pharmakos, "I think I'll have a wash myself."

He watched her set out on her walk across the great room, and when she disappeared through the church door at the far end, he swung his legs out of bed. But he got no farther, and sat on the edge of the bed, staring into space.

What would be Jurgens' reaction to the refusal of extradition by the English police? His hands were freed. Would he act? Pharmakos asked himself what he would do if he were in Jurgens' position. There was no question what he would do if the positions were reversed. Mr. Jurgens would find himself under lock and key before he was much older. Was there any reason to doubt that Jurgens would do the same by him? None, that he could see.

And if Saunders or one of his pals turned up with a warrant? Conviction was practically certain. There was no question whatever about it. Jurgens had been burgled and beaten up, and there was a butler and a couple of footmen to swear to identity. Conviction was a certainty if the charge were made. And the sentence? It couldn't be less than two years for a job done by an ex-convict. Could he stand it? Apart from any question of the endurance of prison conditions, which for him, in his neurotic condition, were concentrated torture, would his mind hold together until the end of his sentence? Or would he be removed from the prison to the asylum? If his mind went permanently, he was better dead; but in both those places, prison or asylum, the opportunity to give himself the merciful release of death would be denied him. Consequently, if his mind were likely to give way if he were imprisoned again, he had better go while the going was good; in other words, he had better commit suicide while the means of suicide still lay to his hand.

Then a sudden pang shot through him. Pat! He would hate to leave Pat. The thought of separation from her tore at him. Then he reminded himself that he would be separated from Pat if he went to prison. But supposing she were waiting for him when he came out, could he endure his two years, and then settle down with her and be happy? But would she be waiting? What a fool he was to even think of it. She had just refused his offer of marriage, and in no uncertain terms; she was the very best pal a man could possibly have, but she obviously no more wanted the physical relationship of marriage with him than he wanted it with her. Very understandable. As soon expect her to want to marry something left over from the anatomy school after the students had finished with it.

Besides, what girl in her senses would want to marry a convict? He was a fool to have asked her at such a time, with Jurgens hanging over his head. It was only an idiotic attack of conscience that had made him do it, and Pat had sensed as much, and hadn't been any too pleased. Still more was it inadvisable to marry in his unstable mental condition. It was just possible that Pat, if she loved him, would have waited two years for him, but it would have been sheer wickedness to marry her if there were any likelihood of his going insane during his sentence, and leaving her permanently tied to a lunatic.

Pat was young. Twelve years younger than himself, apart from his premature ageing and ill health. The mothering instinct was strong in her. He could see that by the way she dealt with him. When she wanted to caress him, her instinct was not to kiss him, but to take his head on her shoulder. He was certain that it was only his size that prevented her from taking him bodily on her lap. The fulfilment of Pat's destiny would be to have an annual baby; and lovely kids they would be, too, given any sort of a father. And he? Well, there would be no babies if Pat married him. And if by any extraordinary miracle there were, they would probably be weak-minded, or have fits. Pharmakos had had the best classical education that England affords her favoured sons, but his scientific education had been the usual nil, and although he knew that there was such a thing as heredity, he had no idea how it worked, nor that it was unlikely that his offspring would share his nerves as they had not shared his prison experiences. Consequently he ruled a line across the page on which he was adding up the pros and cons of marriage to Pat, and wrote the whole idea off as a bad debt. It might be exceedingly nice for him to have a *"mariage blanc"* with Pat, at least for a time. But what would his feelings be when she began to find out how she had been misled, and her ignorance abused? And what would her feelings be as the womanhood in her woke up and demanded its rights, and there were no red-headed babies for her to cuddle?

No, he must strictly ration his use of Pat. She had evidently had the sense to see that there was no point in her marrying a man who did not love her; hence the tartness of her reply to his fool proposal. Then came the sudden shattering remembrance that he was simply sitting there waiting to be arrested, and that arrest would be the end of him, for he would probably be in a straight waistcoat before nightfall. It was a peculiarity of his damaged mind that whole sections of ideas could drop clean out of their frame and never be missed. Pat had observed his quick pick-up, but had not realised that it was a far worse symptom than a slower recovery would have been. It simply meant that Pharmakos had forgotten all about what it was that had upset him. She had only got to distract him and the thing was gone. Any ordinary distraction, of course, would not have sufficed, but the distraction of a caress from her did the trick. Though she did not know it, it was as unwholesome a sign as the flush on the cheek of a consumptive.

Equally, of course, when the painful idea had resumed its sway, every alleviation or possibility of compromise vanished also, and Pharmakos' dark hours were of unrelieved blackness, without one ray of hope. The worst, however, was when two ideas contended for mastery, as when he wanted Pat, but did not like to take her; for then the worn gears of his mind simply failed to engage, and he slid off into a dream-state wherein the perplexing problems of reality ceased to exist and the horrors assumed another form, but one in which he merely had to endure and was not called upon to do anything. His mind had played him these tricks so often that he knew perfectly well the tracks they left behind them, and yet he was never able to catch them at their tricks.

All the signs of one of his storms were gathering in Pharmakos, when suddenly there cut clean across them, like the sword on the Gordian knot, the brilliant idea of death. Pharmakos spent most of his time being more than half in love with easeful death, for which it was difficult to blame him, considering that he walked through life on the psychological equivalent of red-hot coals. It was only the unfailing vigilance of Skilly and Lamprey between them, with occasional moral suasion from Saunders, that had prevented Pharmakos from committing suicide dozens of times.

Supposing he made the most of Pat while he had her—which could only be for a day or two at most, and might only be a matter of hours if Jurgens had got off the mark promptly, and then, when arrested, make his exit? The scheme clicked home and solved all his problems, and his rising nervous tension instantly slacked off. He could let himself go in loving Pat in his own peculiar way, it couldn't hurt her for a day or two, and God knows, she would be no less of a virgin when he had had his will of her than when she started, and then one quick pang, and finish.

He sprang up from the bed, and head high in air, not dropped as was his wont, went striding across the room on his bare feet to a panelled corner; and there, manipulating a spring by pressure, swung back the panelling and revealed the green-painted door of a large safe. A twisting of the alphabetical lock released the bolts, and the heavy door swung back. Pharmakos pulled out a drawer and took from it a small leather case such as jewellers use, and opened it, disclosing a large gold ring of intricate design and antique workmanship. He shut the safe and took the ring over to the nearest window, where he examined it carefully.

It was a large and heavy ring, apparently a signet-ring, whereon two marvellously-chiselled scorpions held in their claws a bloodstone. But on closer examination it could be observed that the bloodstone was not the genuine article, but cleverly imitated in enamel.

Pharmakos pressed the bloodstone firmly with his forefinger, and then twisted it sideways and the enamelled surface slid round on a pin like a sliding-lid, and revealed a small cavity in which lay a pinch of sparkling white dust. Pharmakos looked at the dust long and intently. He hoped it was fresh enough to do the tick quickly, and not give him some minutes of agony before it got in its work. He felt confident that there would be no chance of reviving him after he had had the tip of his tongue in that white powder; but all the same, he did not want a lingering death. He had a suspicion that death by this means would be particularly unpleasant if it did not come quickly. He was not afraid of death, but he dreaded pain—he had had so much, poor fellow.

He closed the deadly little capsule carefully, giving its lid a twist or two to make sure that it worked freely on its pin and could be relied on for quick action when needed, and then slid the massive ring on to the little finger of his left hand. But although his hands were coarsened by manual labour, the great ring proved to be too large for the little finger, and he transferred it to the ring-finger, where it fitted well enough, though it was a struggle to get it over the enlarged knuckle, thickened and coarsened by swinging a pick.

He would wear that ring night and day, for there was no saying at what hour of the twenty-four the arrest might not be made. The C.I.D. do not work trade union hours. Then when the fellow was saying his piece, " Julian—alias Julian Pharmakos—" he must watch his chance, and get that ring to his mouth, and all would be over.

CHAPTER XVIII

PHARMAKOS had spent so long in meditating on his troubles, and then in messing about with his ring, that he was still standing by the window examining it when Pat reappeared.

"Well, you are a beauty!" she said. "Aren't you going to put any clothes on?"

He suddenly woke up to the fact that he was clad in nothing but his pyjama trousers.

"Pat," he said, "if you had not completely undermined my morals I should be feeling bashful, but as it is, I don't care a damn, and I don't believe you do either."

"I certainly don't," said Pat, "you needn't flatter yourself on that point. I haven't bathed three brothers a night for the last five years without completing all the researches in anatomy I've any taste for. I'll give you a bath any time you like, and it's no more trouble to me than washing up the milk-jug."

"I believe you, Pat," said Pharmakos, "you are the most unblushful female I ever met. And consequently, it wouldn't be any amusement to be given a bath by you. Besides I hate having my ears soaped, and no one else can ever get one really dry because they never know which bits are still damp."

"I can't be bothered with your susceptibilities at the present moment," said Pat, "I'm much too hungry. Come along and get some clothes on. You are quite big enough to dress yourself. I'm not going to shove you into your shirt."

Pharmakos seized her hand. "Come on, Pat, let's set out

on our walk. It is a good ten minutes from here to the bathroom. There was a poem I used to know which began: 'They wandered hand in hand—' "

"There was one I used to know," said Pat, which ended, 'All hollow, hollow, hollow!' and that's how I feel at the present moment; and it isn't going to take ten minutes to reach the bathroom from here at the pace I'm going."

When Pat appeared from the kitchen with the breakfast, Pharmakos was clad in white flannel trousers and a tennis-shirt.

"Aren't you going to do any work to-day?" she asked in surprise.

"No, Patsie," I'm going to stop at home and make love to you."

"Huh," said Pat, "we'll see about that. At any rate, you've got your letters to do first."

It was quite likely he did not feel himself in a fit state to keep his appointments after his bout of the previous night, although he looked all right; but all the same, it was a bad thing for him to be cutting appointments without notice, and she knew he had some important ones, for she kept his engagement-book for him. However, she would see what mood he was in after he had had his breakfast, for the appointments were not till the afternoon, and then, if necessary, she could do some telephoning for him.

As soon as they had passed the porridge stage, and arrived at the eggs, which required two hands for their manipulation, Pat observed Pharmakos' ring.

"Hullo," she said, "I haven't seen that before. Do let me look at the fascinating little lobsters."

Pharmakos jerked his head back after the manner of a startled horse, which was a trick he had when a tender spot had been touched upon, and put his hand under the table.

"It's only an old ring," he said sullenly. He suddenly felt

the greatest aversion to letting little Pat examine the deadly poison-ring.

Pat said nothing. The ring was on the third finger of his left hand, the ring-finger. Perhaps it was a ring that had been given him as an engagement ring by *The* woman. He obviously did not wish her to have anything to do with it.

But boiled eggs are not things that can-be managed with one hand, and Pat soon had an opportunity to take a further look at her little lobsters, otherwise, Benvenuto Cellini's scorpions, such apt supporters for the deadly poison-capsule. She noted the big red hand, broadened and coarsened and rendered high-coloured by the use of pick and shovel, and the jagged white scars on the wrist, that told of terrible scenes in handcuffs, and she resolutely banished from her heart all resentment against *The* woman and her ring, and tried to banish all pain too, in the perfection of love that seeketh not its own. So when Pharmakos recovered his wits sufficiently to want to talk to her, he found a serene and cheerful Pat, prepared to rag or sympathise as occasion required.

Pharmakos suddenly put a hand over hers, and she had a close-up of the ring, and saw that the stone was imitation.

"Pat, my dear," he said. "At the moment I happen to be a little madder than usual, though quite cheerful. You asked me if I were going out to business to-day, and I told you, no. And now I'll tell you why not. Because it would be waste of time, my darling. Also I am waiting in for a caller. If you ask me who he is, I should tell you that I didn't know, though I hope it will be Saunders. In fact, Patsie, to put it briefly, I am just sitting here waiting to be arrested because it is perfectly useless to make a bolt; and I intend to make the most of my time by making love to you, although you tell me you don't want to marry me. And I don't want to marry you, either, Pat, to be quite frank with you; but I'd love to make love to you, if you'll let me. And I swear I won't do you any harm.

And to-night I'll probably be safely under lock and key. So there you are, Pat. Shall we eat, drink, and be merry, for tomorrow we die?"

He laughed harshly, and gripped her hand so hard that it took all her self-control not to wince. His eyes, she saw, were unnaturally bright, and there was a dull flush on either cheek-bone, underneath the dry, sallow skin. She did not like the look of him at all. In fact, she liked it so little that she hardly took in the significance of his words, and was debating in her mind whether she really ought to get the help of a doctor in dealing with him, and decided to take counsel with SkiIly at the first possible moment.

"What do you say, Pat?" demanded Pharmakos, his mouth twitching oddly.

She pulled herself together with an effort, and forced herself to realise the significance of his words.

"You don't really mean we die to-morrow, do you?"

"Not you, my sweet, there's no reason why you should. But I don't expect to see the sun rise to-morrow morning. There are just two things I am going to ask of you, Pat. The first is to let me love you in my own queer way until the end comes, and it can't be long delayed, my sweet, or I wouldn't ask this of you. But it can't hurt you for a few hours, and my way, though queer, is harmless. It can't hurt you for a few hours, though it wouldn't do you any particular good if it were kept up, and I should enjoy it enormously. And the other thing I am going to ask of you, Pat, is to do the last offices of a friend for me after the good old Roman fashion. Do you know what that was? Well, a Roman soldier's pal was expected to polish him off if he were beaten and too badly wounded to finish himself off, and a very humane custom it was, in my opinion. I won't ask you to give me the actual *coup de grâce*, but I am going to ask you just to stand in front of me for a moment when the fellow comes to arrest me."

Pat's breath came sobbingly, but her eyes were dry and steady as she looked straight into his and nodded her head in agreement.

"Now the next thing," continued Pharmakos in a cheerful, nonchalant voice, "is to make my will. I am not going to start making love to you till I have done that, or I might get absorbed and forget to do it. I daresay you would be good enough to type it for me; you can do that without invalidating it, but you can't witness it, because you are going to be one of the legatees, and only persons who have no concern in a will can witness it. Skilly and Lamprey are legatees too, they have been faithful devils, so we must hunt up some totally disinterested persons. Go out into the highways and byways, in fact. Or the nearest pub, to be precise. Come on! let's get it over, and then to enjoy ourselves. Saunders might get here early, you know."

"Oh, Julian, don't!" cried Pat.

"Sorry, dear," said Pharmakos, patting her hand. "Do you really care, Pat?"

"I care awfully," said Pat, in a strangled voice.

That is something I hadn't counted on," said Pharmakos thoughtfully. "I am sorry to hear it, dear, for it means you may have an unpleasant time for a bit. However, we will have our single hour of glorious life, though frankly, I wish you didn't care, for I hate to see you get hurt, my darling; but you're young, so I expect you'll get over it. Now, come on, get out the typewriter, for I should be really annoyed if Saunders got here before we had finished."

So Pat sat down and typed his will, quietly dropping tears into the machine as she did it, and trying to keep them from being observed by Pharmakos. There was his gold watch for Saunders, and a tie-pin for the superintendent at the local police station, and a hundred pounds each for Skilly and Lamprey, "Though God knows what they'll do with it," said

Pharmakos, and Pat herself was residuary legatee, whatever that might mean; she herself had not the faintest idea. She thought how quaint it was that Pharmakos' legacies were equally divided between the criminal classes and the police. Were the police usually on such friendly terms with their-well-clients? As a matter of fact, a criminal who has any inclination at all for reform finds very good friends in the police.

"I'd like to leave Warder Mills something, Pat, as a slight return for his introduction to you. If it hadn't been for the way he put things, I don't believe I'd be enjoying the pleasure of your company now. What shall I leave him? A poke in the eye with a burnt stick, for choice, as the old saying has it. Shall I leave him my toothbrush? There's some wear still left in it for anyone who isn't particular."

"You might leave it to him," said Pat, trying to fall in with his mood, "But judging from appearances, I don't suppose he'd find much use for it."

It was curious the influence Pharmakos had over her. When he was phantasying himself in prison, she almost saw him in prison; and now that he was determined to throw off the black cloud that hung over him, and thanks to his unstable mind, succeeding to a very great extent, it faded and became unreal for her also.. When roused, and therefore temporarily normal, Pharmakos was a very dominating personality, and could impress his will and viewpomt on most people with whom he came in contact. What his career would have been had things fallen out otherwise for him, it was impossible to say, for there seemed to be little limit to what he could have achieved; for when first-class brains are combined with magnificent physique and a compelling personality, who is to say where it will end? As it was, Pharmakos, with all his handicaps, held a unique position and had an international reputation among private enquiry agents, for both his judgment and integrity were absolutely trusted. Pat was residuary legatee of a much larger estate than she realised, every penny of which Pharmakos had made by his unaided wits, with all the dice loaded against him.

Pat fair-copied the brief will and handed it to him.

"Now, my sweet," he said, "I will put on a jacket of some sort, and sally forth, and get this witnessed at the nearest pub. Care to come with me? I feel like Pippa with her one brief day. Did you ever read *Pippa Passes?* I don't suppose you did, for I only read it because I was in prison. There are some sorts of literature, Pat, that can only be read in prison. Browning's longer poems are among them. Also Swinburne's plays."

Pat felt that he was rambling on in this vein to hide emotion, and she gladly fell in with his mood for it spared her emotion too.

They went out together into the brilliant summer sunlight, both of their red heads hatless; Pharmakos with his hand tucked through Pat's arm, his will in his pocket, the poison ring on his finger, and a cigarette in his mouth.

He turned into the pub on the corner for a moment, and then rejoined Pat on the pavement.

"Now for the post office," he said, "and then I am finished and can give you my undivided attention."

They turned round the corner and entered the post office.

"Damn," said Pharmakos, "I forgot to bring any paper for the covering letter."

However, an obliging official supplied him with the form on which one applies for dog-licences, and he wrote on the back an admonition to look after Pat and to take his word for it that she had never been anything but his sister, and sent it off, together with his last will and testament, to the eminent solicitor who had given him his first professional case.

Then he took a telegraph-form, and after some cogitation, bent his head over it and wrote concentratedly for a brief second. Not many words, but they evidently required close attention to put together. Then he begged an envelope from the friendly official, who evidently knew him well, and liked and respected him, as everyone seemed to, sealed up the telegraph-form inside it, and handed it to Pat.

"Take charge of this, will you, Pat? And after I am—defunct, send it off? It's to my father. It may amuse you to know who he is. I shan't mind after I'm dead, and somehow, I'd like you to know what my real name was. It's not a blessing I'm afraid, Pat. It's a pretty hearty cursing, to be frank. My God, why shouldn't I quit life with a sting in my tail?"

His harsh laugh made the loungers outside the pub turn round and stare at him, and Pat hurried him back to Quilp Cottage as quickly as she could get him along, wondering what his idea of love-making might be, as he appeared to consider it entirely original; and determined to go through with anything and everything dry-eyed, even if it meant the loss of her virtue, and then to stand in front of him when the end came, and give him a chance to put himself out of his misery. What that misery was like, she knew, for she had heard him scream, and she would not stay his hand.

One ended the suffering of a hopelessly injured animal. Pharmakos should go if he wished, and she would be thankful to think that he was at peace. What was to become of her, she did not choose to think. She had no home behind her, and jobs were, as she well knew, hard to come by, and the reference of a criminal and a suicide would hardly help her in obtaining one.

So Pat set her teeth and determined to go through with it. Pharmakos should have his day, and it should be as perfect as she could make it. She would keep back no part of the price. Anyway, what there was of Pharmakos would be hers, and the other woman, *The* woman, could never deprive her of that, as she would always have been waiting to do had Pharmakos lived. She was startled to find herself already thinking of Pharmakos in the past tense, and pulled herself up hastily—and then decided that it was the best thing she could do, as she would feel so much freer with him and could make his one last day so much more perfect than if she were filled with inhibitions and shyness.

CHAPTER XIX

THEY re-entered Quilp Cottage. All was quiet. Skilly was out, as usual, and Lamprey had evidently been and gone, having done miracles during their brief absence. The day's provisions stood ready on the kitchen table. They had the place to themselves for their brief day of love.

Pharmakos put his arm round Pat and drew her across the big room to the divan, and lifted her up and put her among the heaped cushions.

"This is the only window that will open, thanks to Skilly's care for my miserable existence, so if we want to enjoy the air we must just sit on my bed, and rats to Mrs. Grundy."

They sat quietly for a time, Pat gazing out of the window at the river with eyes that saw nothing, and Pharmakos watching her. At length he reached out his hand and took hers gently. She jumped at his touch, despite his gentleness, and her eyes looked startled for a moment as she turned to face him. Then they softened, and her fingers closed round his.

He slid his hand up her bare arm till it came to the plain gold slave-bangle that she always wore above her elbow.

"Pat," he said, "Will you give me this?"

"Yes, dear, if you'd-like it," said Pat, "That is, if I can get it off. The only reason I've been allowed to keep it is that once I got it on, I couldn't get if off. At least, I couldn't if I held my arm out straight. It is fatter that way than if you bend it slightly, and Father did not know that."

"How did you come by it?" asked Pharmakos, wondering

whether his chosen love-token was doing duty for the second time.

"A pal of Helen's gave it to me. God knows why. To annoy her, I fancy. Anyway, it had that effect. I'll have to fetch the soap. I can't get it off unless I lather myself."

Pat went off to the bathroom. Pharmakos' eyes followed her as she went and came. She had a wet cake of soap in her hand, and after this was rubbed on her elbow, the bangle came off readily enough.

He commenced to roll up his shirt-sleeve.

"What are you going to do?" asked Pat, puzzled.

"Put on your bangle."

He pushed his big red hand through easily, for it was meant to be worn on the upper arm, but to get it over his big-boned elbow was another matter.

"It won't go over your elbow," said Pat.

"It's got to go over my elbow," said Pharmakos, setting his teeth and shoving at it ruthlessly.

"But why? It won't fall off if you push it firmly on to your arm."

"I want to be buried in it, Pat, and so it's got to go where it can't be got off."

"Oh, Julian, don't, I can't bear it!" cried Pat, her voice shrill with distress.

"I'm sorry, my darling. I won't speak of it again, and we will enjoy our perfect day. But I had to fix things up, hadn't I? Now forget it, and help me to get this darn thing over my elbow. Hand me the soap. Now shove. What fits you ought to fit me, for you're a plump little pigeon."

The bangle, lubricated by the soap, went on with a run, and settled itself on the lean, sinewy arm well enough, and Phalmakos surveyed it with satisfaction. Then he turned down his shirt-sleeve and hid it.

"We will forget about it now," he said, "and enjoy our

day."

At that moment the kitchen door opened and Inspector Saunders entered.

Pharmakos sprang to his feet, and the two men faced each other. Pat quietly rose from among the cushions, came round the corner of the big divan, and stood in front of Pharmakos.

"It's all right, it's all right," cried Saunders, waving his bowler hat cheerfully, "I haven't come for you. It's just a friendly call. I've got a bit of good news for you. Good Lord, what's the matter with the young lady?" For Pat had collapsed in a dead faint at Pharmakos' feet.

Saunders hastened forward to help to pick her up, but before he could do so, Pharmakos had gathered her into his arms as if she had been a child, and sat down on the edge of the divan with Pat in his lap.

"Get a sponge from the bathroom, will you, Saunders?" he said.

Saunders hurried off to do as he was bid, and made such good speed that he got back before he was expected, and was in time to see Pharmakos kiss Pat's hair.

Between them they soon revived her, for Saunders was an expert, having served his time in the uniformed force before he joined the plain-clothes branch. So Pat opened surprised eyes to find Pharmakos bending over her with Inspector Saunders hovering in the background, both looking very much concerned, and neither seeming in the least disposed to do anything desperate to the other.

She sat up on Pharmakos' knee, quite unembarrassed, her legs dangling, for his shin-bones were longer than hers.

"What was it?" she demanded of Saunders.

"What was what?" they both said together.

"What was the bit of good news you had for us?"

"Bless your heart," said Saunders, "We was so busy with

you we forgot all about it."

He sat down and dangled his bowler and smiled at them affably. Pat suddenly realised that she was sitting on Pharmakos' knee, and struggled to put her feet to the ground.

Pharmakos lifted her off his knee and set her beside him on the divan, still keeping an arm round her waist, however, as if expecting her at any minute to collapse again. There was something awfully comforting about the pressure of the big hand against her side, for one does not feel too well immediately after a thorough faint.

"Yes, Inspector, what was your bit of good news? We could do with some. We haven't been feeling too cheerful just lately."

"Well, it's this, sir. I've been talking to the feller that had to go into matters with Jurgens when the Dutch police asked us for him, and he says that Jurgens doesn't remember anything about the burglary because you gave him such a thorough concussing that he lost his memory for the whole thing. It takes you like that, you know, sir, if you're badly concussed. I've given evidence in compensation cases when the feller that had the accident couldn't remember a thing about it. Jurgens remembers Skilly, because he knew him before, but he doesn't remember you. Leastways, he knew Skilly had a pal with him, but he can't recall anything about the pal, though he might if he saw you. I wouldn't care to guarantee that his memory wouldn't come back to him then. But he don't associate J. Pharmakos with Skilly's pal what bashed him. He'd like to do J. Pharmakos down all right, because he hates him like poison, but he's got nothing to go on. And he'd like to give the chap what bashed him a charge, because he's had an uncommon sore head and it hasn't sweetened his temper, which was never of the best, from what we've been able to hear of him; but it has never occurred to him that they were one and the same chap. He thinks that Skilly sold the papers to you; it never occurred to him that you collected them yourself. So there you are, sir. As long as you can keep out of Jurgens' sight, he'll never spot you, and even if he saw you, there's even chances he mightn't remember you. You can't say for certain how a concussion will go. It just depends how badly he was concussed, and if you don't mind my mentioning it, sir, he was concussed just about as badly as a feller can be and still have the breath of life left in him. They trepanned a piece of his skull as big as the palm of your 'and at the horspital. Our fellers took the opportunity to have a look at it because that sort of thing comes in handy for identification, and that's how the whole story came out. I should have come along with it before, knowin' how anxious you and the young lady must be, but I just ran up to Hampstead police station to find out what they knew about the job, and found that they had got a description of you from the butler, but as your 'air was practically white then, sir, they put your age down as sixty, and now the young lady has fed you up a bit, and your 'air 'as come back to its natural colour, you don't fit that description particularly well, and I for one wouldn't take you on it. You've got a good deal more than a sporting chance of getting away with it, sir, providing Jurgens doesn't actually come face to face with you. And even if he did spot you and charge you, you've got a good many pals, you know, and although we should do our duty, we shouldn't do more than our duty, see? Knowin' you and Jurgens as we do."

"You mean you'd let me slip through your fingers, eh Saunders?"

"No, sir," said Saunders, " Certainly not. But we'd make him prove his case up to the hilt before we would apply for a warrant. And we wouldn't be easy satisfied as to what constituted proof, neither."

Pharmakos laughed. He could imagine the tremendous inertia of Inspector Saunders, sitting stolidly, all seventeen stone of him, with the red tape of Scotland Yard looped about him by the fathom, unable to see the points that were being put to him by an exasperated Jurgens.

Saunders tactfully declined an invitation to a meal. He knew the kind of strain they had been through, and that they would find visitors an infliction, and he could see from the way that Pharmakos was eyeing Pat that he was anxious about her. When Pharmakos returned from seeing him out, he found that Pat had laid herself flat on her back on the divan, still looking very white.

"How are you feeling, my darling?" he asked as he bent over her.

"A bit groggy," said Pat. "I don't think fainting agrees with me."

"Are you in the habit of doing it?"

"Not in the ordinary way. I fainted once when father overspanked me, and once when mother made me get up too soon after influenza. That's about all, I think." She reached out her hand and took his.

"Darling, do you think you could make me a cup of tea?" she said.

"I'll have a shot at it, Patsy. But I'm the world's worst parlour-maid. If I want a drink myself, and everyone's out, I take It in a tooth-glass from the tap. I didn't have a domesticated upbringing."

"You know when the water's boiling, I suppose?" asked Pat, wearily.

"When it spits all over the stove? Yes, I know that. Don't you worry. I'll see it boils all right and Lamprey can clean up after it to-morrow."

Pat still felt too giddy and breathless to do much thinking after Pharmakos had withdrawn to the kitchen. Would he, under the circumstances, carry on with his day of love. She did not know. She could only wait and see. Perhaps he wouldn't, she thought, and felt half relieved and half disappointed, for she was curious, so she told herself, to see what he would do.

Pharmakos returned with a tea-pot suitable for a Sunday school treat; a quart bottle of milk under his arm, two tea-cups, no spoons, and a canister of sugar. It had not occurred to him to make use of a tray, but his power of balancing was wonderful.

"The water boiled all right, sweetheart," he said. "It shot clean across the kitchen and hit the far wall."

Pat sat up shakily. He put the impedimenta on the floor.

"Let me get you back among the cushions," he said, and picked her up as easily as if she had been the tea-pot, to her great surprise, for she had always thought that because Pharmakos had such bad health he must be physically weak. Then, with the tea-things on the floor between his feet, he poured Pat's tea out for her, carefully and clumsily, like a man who has never in his life had to do such things for himself. They drank their tea in silence. Pharmakos attempted no endearments as he sat beside her, and there were no signs of the day of love. Pat felt vaguely disappointed and flat.

Pharmakos was doing some pretty hard thinking, however. Was it a pity or providential that Inspector Saunders had turned up when he did? Providential, was his considered judgment, though something in him felt defrauded and resentful. He and Pat had got to shake down together again quietly, as brother and sister. He only hoped the ice had not been broken to a point when it would no longer bear them.

Pat, the dear thing, although she might have been willing to give him his day of love before his exit from the stage of life, would certainly not be prepared to accept unlimited caresses from a man whom she had no intention of marrying. Not if he knew her. She was as straight as a die. He would get his head punched if he overstepped the mark. A change had come over his tune, however, though he did not notice it. Twenty-four hours ago he would have said that he had no right to caress Pat and rouse her emotions if he did not intend to marry her. Now he was saying to himself that as Pat was not willing to marry him, he must not attempt to caress her, or he would give offence and lose the friendship which was all she was prepared to afford him. It appeared to him conclusive that what Pat gave him was pity, and nothing more; and although he would have wrung anyone else's neck who had offered him pity, it was very sweet to have Pat's sympathy. After all, it was the most he could expect from a pretty girl twelve years younger than himself, and he was lucky to get it. He had better not start cuddling her again, but it was very nice to sit beside her like this, and he must be thankful for small mercies under the circumstances.

Neither of them spoke, except to make the small demands of the tea-table, which in this case was the floor, thanks to Pharmakos' lack of training in parlour-maiding. The bottom had dropped out of the day of love with a vengeance .

"I wonder what the time is," said Pat wearily.

"Getting on for six, I think," said Pharmakos, "I forgot to wind up my watch. We shall have to wait for Big Ben."

"Too early for supper," said Pat pettishly, "All the meals have gone wrong to-day."

"Do you want your supper, my sweetheart?"

"No, I only want to go to bed. I'm tired. And if I go to bed without my supper, I shall wake up hungry half-way through the night, and not be able to go to sleep again." .

"Would you like to go to bed now, darling, and I'll bring you some supper presently?"

"No, I wouldn't. I shouldn't sleep," said Pat, peevishly, moving restlessly among the cushions. "I'd like to go for a walk. I think the fresh air would do me good."

Pharmakos reached for her wrist and felt her pulse.

"I don't think you would like to go for a walk," he said. "Shall I read to you? I used to be rather a good reader, once upon a time."

Without waiting for an answer, he went over to the bookcase and selected a handful of books, returned to the divan, sat down beside her feet and began to read aloud. Pat, who expected to be bored, suddenly found her attention caught and held. Pharmakos had a most marvellous reading voice. Usually it was either flat and toneless or harsh with tension; but in reading poetry he was rapt away into another world. Pat had no idea that a speaking voice could have such a range of tone. It was not merely loud and soft, as they taught in the elocution class, but it rose and fell by semi-tones and almost sang the lyrical lines. Pat did not know it, but she was hearing the trained speaking-voice of a silver-tongued orator who, had the course of his life been different, would have spoken to nations. .

Neither had she ever heard such poetry. The Bowdlerised selections from standard authors that had been forced upon her at the high school bore no resemblance to this. True, she met one or two old acquaintances, they could hardly be called friends after the class had parsed them, but in a guise so new that it was several lines before she recognised them, even though she herself had once had to learn them by heart. The "Ode to the West Wind" for instance. The marvellous change from the flute-music of the spring visions to the deep organ-tones of the storm pictures—all were rendered within the compass of a few notes by the wonderfully flexible and resonant voice, not loud, but full of vibrant undertones. And then the last verse, with its personal touch and change of key from line to line. She wondered how he would render that. And presently she heard.

"Make me thy lyre, even as the forest is—!"
It was the trumpet-note of acclaim. Pharmakos was standing

in his hereditary place, speaking to the listening multitudes at his feet, and his voice rang out, filling the great room; and Pat, who always caught his visions intuitively, thought of the time the school had been taken to see over the Houses of Parliament.

"*What if my leaves are falling like its own—!*"

The voice sank to the flat tonelessness of the broken man who had done seven years in Portland.

"*The tumult of thy mighty harmonies
Will take from both a deep autumnal tone,
Sweet though in sadness—*"

Pharmakos' voice was gathering strength again.

"*Be thou, Spirit fierce,
My spirit! Be thou me, impetuous one—!*"

The clarions were beginning to call in the vibrant voice.

"*Drive my dead thoughts over the universe
Like withered leaves, to quicken a new birth;
And, by the incantation of this verse,
Scatter, as from an unextinguished hearth
Ashes and sparks, my words, among mankind!
Be through my lips to unawakened earth
The trumpet of a prophecy—!*"

The great organ-tones went rolling through the room like the organ in Westminster Abbey. Then suddenly the tone changed.

"*O wind,
If Winter comes, can Spring be far behind?*"

It was not again the flat, toneless voice of a broken man, but a cry of pain and appeal to the whole universe, and lifting his eyes from the book, Pharmakos looked at Pat.

Pat leant forward and put out her hand, unable to speak, and Pharmakos took it, and they sat, looking at each other speechlessly.

"I don't believe spring is very far behind," said Pat at last in a broken voice.

"Isn't it, Patsie? Well, it will have to come and look for me, for I don't know which way to look for it. Now listen to this." And still holding her hand, he picked up another book, and turned over its pages till he came to the poem he wanted and read her Kipling's strange, half-hinted poem-story of "Helen all Alone," which only those can understand who themselves have stolen out from Limbo Gate, looking for the Earth—the story of the two souls, haunted by night terrors, who met in their dreams.

"Hand in pulling hand amid
Fear no dreams have known,
Helen ran with ,me she did,
    Helen all alone!"

Pharmakos' hand tightened on Pat's.

"In the teeth of things forbid
And reason overthrown,
Helen stood by me, she did,
    Helen all alone!"

"We know that, don't we, darling?" said Pat softly.

"Yes, we do," said Pharmakos, "Now hear the end."

"When at last our souls were rid
Of what the night had shown,
Helen passed from me, she did,
    Helen all alone!"

"No!" cried Pat, "No!" twisting her fingers into his.

Pharmakos laughed his harsh, bitter laugh.

"Let her go and find a mate,
As I will find a bride
Knowing naught of Limbo Gate,
Or who are penned inside.
There is knowledge God forbid
More than one should own.
So Helen went from me she did!

Oh, my soul, be glad she did!
    Helen all alone!"

Pharmakos raised his head from the book and looked at Pat with hard eyes, having got himself well in hand.

"There you are, you see, Pat. Kipling knows our story all right. There must be no more talk of days of love. That was an emergency measure. We have got to settle down and live our everyday lives now. What do you say to some supper?"

"I don't want any supper!" cried Pat, and ran out of the room and slammed the door.

CHAPTER XX

PHARMAKOS never touched alcohol, and very seldom any form of drug, but the strain of the day had been so great that he treated himself to a sleeping-draught. Consequently, although he dreamt of Pat all night, he did not know that she came creeping into the room and stood beside him towards dawn.

She saw the drug-stained tumbler on the table beside his bed and picked it up anxiously, wondering what it had contained. Then she saw the box beside it, read the instructions, and was reassured.

She stood looking down at Pharmakos as he lay in his deep, drug-induced sleep. A low-power, heavily-shaded electric light burnt above his head, for Pharmakos would not sleep in the dark, and as he lay, completely relaxed by the opium in the sleeping-draught, the dim light softening his lined face. Pat saw an entirely new Pharmakos, and realised what he must once have been like before he was smashed beyond repair. His head was that of a Roman Emperor; the magnificent profile, clearly outlined against the white linen of the pillow, was cut like a cameo—high forehead, eagle nose, powerful jaw. With improving health his hair had lost its dry harshness, and he was able to let it grow and brush it back, abandoning the hideous convict crop with which she had first seen him.

His neck rose lean and muscular from the open collar of his unfastened pyjama jacket. He hadn't got a single button to his name, thought Pat. She must take his clothes in hand as soon as she had finished sorting his papers.

She stood looking down at him like a mother beside her child's crib. The window was wide open immediately over the bed, and a cold northerly wind which had sprung up during the night was blowing in on to the sleeper. Pat shut the window softly. Pharmakos did not stir. She put the eiderdown over the arm and shoulder that lay exposed on the coverlet. Still he did not move. Then she took a chance, and bent down and kissed him. After that she tiptoed off across the parquetry to the kitchen and helped herself to some biscuits.

Her original errand had ostensibly been to get something to eat, as she had gone to bed supperless and could not sleep, but in her secret heart she thought that Pharmakos too would be sleepless after such a hectic day, and hoped that she would have company and consolation at her midnight meal. She had not reckoned on sleeping-draughts. However, it had soothed her just to tuck him up and come away again.

She had run out of the room the previous evening because Pharmakos, after stirring her emotions with his poetry reading, had suddenly caught her absolutely on the raw when she was in no state to exercise self-control. "Helen all Alone" might have been written about the two of them. "Let her go and seek a mate, as I will find a bride!" That was telling her pretty plainly. Moreover, although he wanted to be buried in her bangle (he had still got it on his arm, by the by), he had also put a ring on his ring-finger like a wedding-ring— probably a ring that *The* woman had given him.

"So Helen went from me, she did.
Oh, my soul, be glad she did,
*   Helen all alone."*

Pat sat up in bed and munched her biscuits and washed them down with tap-water from a tooth-glass, and the words ran in her head. She thought to herself that she had been well and soundly snubbed and put in her place, and told what not to expect. And yet why had his hand tightened on hers at the opening lines of the poem? And why had he looked at her as he did when he cried out the last words of the great ode as if they had been wrung from him by sudden pain?

She was powerless to follow the twists and turns of his mind. First one thing and then another. First clinging to her desperately, and then repelling her, kindly enough, but quite firmly; and then suddenly turning to her again as if he couldn't keep away. Was it that she could not follow the twists and turns of his mind because it was a sick mind and therefore abnormal? Or was it that she didn't know enough of life to understand all that was going on between them?

It was probably a bit of both, if she had known, but she did not know, and had no one whom she could ask, so she sighed, and referred yet another item to her reference file of unsolved problems, and determined to adhere to her original resolution and love Pharmakos, nurse him, and leave him free. There could be no harm in that; she must just bide her time, and see how things shaped themselves, and act accordingly. But she must always bear in mind that in the end she would go from him and be Helen all Alone. Pat wiped away the tears that had been slowly trickling down her cheeks as she was eating her biscuits, turned out the light, and being young, fell asleep.

When she went upstairs the next morning, Pharmakos was still in bed. The drug-induced sleep had given place to the sleep of exhaustion, and he was making up for his night of brain-storms as well as his day of anxiety and emotional tension.

Pat went into the kitchen and found there Skilly eating his breakfast out of the frying-pan, and was too dispirited to rebuke him.

She dropped into a chair at the side of the kitchen table and rested her head on her hand.

"Oh, Skilly," she said, "We've had such a time of it."

"Wot's up, Coppernob?" asked Skilly, pausing with an entire rasher of bacon poised in mid-air on his fork.

Pat told him. Skilly whistled softly.

"Gor-blimey! You've 'ad your money's worth, Coppernob. Wish I'd known. I could 'ave lent yer a 'and. Not that I could 'ave done much. You can do more wiv 'im than I can. But it might 'ave been some 'elp to yer to 'ave 'ad me arahnd the corner. Next time you 'ave trouble, leave a note in me quarters, and I'll 'ang arahnd the premises till 'e settles dahn."

"What's going to be the end of it?" asked Pat drearily.

"There's only one end of it as I kin see."

"What's that?"

"Well, you got 'em on a string properly 'aven't yer, Coppernob? I suppose you'll be gettin' 'im to make an honest woman of yer next. That's what my girls always does with me."

"What do you mean?" asked Pat, not without a suspicion as to what he meant.

"Give yer yer marriage lines and strighten things aht. Why don't yer get 'im to, Cop? 'E'd do any think you arst 'im, 'e's that potty abart yer."

Skilly was the first rational human being Pat had talked to since she joined up with Pharmakos, for Pharmakos himself certainly could not be entertained in that class. Pat relaxed, and opened her heart to Skilly, oblivious of his appalling exterior and equally appalling outlook in her loneliness and need of counsel.

"We talked about that, you know," she said, "And decided not to."

"Whatever did yer do that for? You are a fool, Cop. Why don't yer pin the feller while yer can?"

"I don't want to pin anybody, Skilly; and anyway, marriage is not the thing we are either of us after. What's the use of getting married if you don't want to be married? "

Skilly looked at her curiously.

"Look 'ere, Cop, is there any truth in this yam about yer bein' the boss's sister, not actually, I mean, but reely?"

"It's perfectly true, Skilly, believe it or not, as the papers say."

"I've knowed fellers like that before," said Skilly. "But if it wasn't girls, it was generally some think else, and there's been no sign of any think during the two years I've bin wiv 'im. It beats me, Cop. I believe in 'uman nature, I does, and this ain't 'uman."

"Do you think he's fond of some woman?" Pat only just checked herself in time from saying "some other woman."

"Never 'eard of none. But then I mightn't. The boss was always one to keep 'isself to 'isself. But I should 'ave said 'e was fair dippy about you, Coppernob."

"Well, he isn't, Skilly."

"Then blowed if I know, and all the signs is wrong."

At that moment Lamprey stole in on cat's feet.

"Look 'ere, Lamp," said Skilly. "Wot do you make of old Pharm? I should 'ave said 'e was fair dippy on Cop, 'ere, wouldn't you? But she says 'e ain't, and she don't know where she is."

Lamprey did his usual wriggle before replying, and Pat's soul revolted against him. But as soon as he spoke she saw that here was a more useful counsellor than Skilly, because a more intelligent one.

"Very awkward for the young lady, I'm sure," said Lamprey cautiously. "Yes, Miss-madam, I 'ave watched the way things was going. I 'ave seen persons like that before, madam, after prison. In fact, I was like that myself for a time after my first sentence, but I got over it."

"Wish to Gawd I was," said Skilly, "I'd never try to get over it. Save me no end of money, it would. If I thought jug would cure me of wenchin', I'd give meself up to-morrer."

Lamprey cast a look of scandalised horror at Skilly, deploring such frankness, but Pat felt she was on the right track for illumination, and determined not to spare anybody's blushes in an effort to get at the truth.

"What really is the matter with him?" she demanded, looking from one to the other.

Lamprey looked down his nose. SkilIy whistled. "Ask your Ma," he said.

"Haven't got one," said Pat.

"Well, Miss-madam," said Lamprey with evident effort, "The position as I see it is this," (an evident quotation from Pharmakos, Pat had often typed these words), "Mr. Pharmakos, and a nicer gentleman never stepped, is undoubtedly very attached to you, in my opinion. You would agree with that, wouldn't you, Skilly?"

"Never seed anybody 'alf as dippy in all me puff. 'E's fair got it blind, I should 'ave said. You should 'ear the splutter if 'e gets 'ome fust when she's out! Shall I make yer a cup o' tea, Boss? 'ses I. 'Tea be damned, 'ses 'e! Where is she?' And there 'e is, walkin' up and down, and mooin' and wringin' 'is 'ands like a cow what's lost 'er calf till you come 'ome, an then you'd think butter wouldn't melt in 'is mouth."

"I 'ave observed the same thing myself," said Lamprey, "But in spite of that, Miss, the gentleman is in a difficult position, for I do not think that he feels himself capable of havin' a family. I can't put it plainer than that, can I, Miss?"

"You suttinly can't," said Skilly, and Pat felt that it was impossible to pursue the subject any further, though it' was still far from plain to her.

"Nice ole mix-up fer you, Cop," said Skilly. "I should go while the goin's good, if I was you."

"You won't do that, will you, Miss?" asked Lamprey anxiously. "It will be the end of him if you do."

"No," said Pat, "I'll stick to him. It's a queer mix-up, but I'll stick to him."

"They all say that," said Skilly with a snort. "I've 'ad it said to me 'undreds of times, but they never do."

"No, I daresay they don't and for good reasons, too," said Lamprey tartly. He and Skilly heartily disapproved of each other socially, but each had a great respect for the other professionally, for each possessed the qualities the other lacked. Skilly had physical courage and Lamprey had brains, and they united in adoring Pharmakos because both qualities were united in him in a high degree.

"Do you know what I think, Miss?" said Lamprey. Pat noticed that he had stopped calling her madam, evidently having accepted her alleged virginity as a fact. " 'E 'as now been out of prison somethink over two years, 'asn't 'e Skilly?"

"Two years last May the second," said Skilly. "I know because I earned the price of me fare to go dahn and meet 'im demonstratin' on Labour Day in 'Yde Park. And I demonstrated too much and nearly got meself run in."

"I was a year before I got right, after I come out of prison the first time," said Lamprey, "But I wasn't broken up any think like as much as 'e is. I never seed a chap so cracked up, did you, SkiIIy?"

"The 'igher you fall from, the 'arder you 'it," said Skilly.

"Yes," said Lamprey, "I expect that explains it. Well, Miss, as I was sayin' 'e 'as now been out of clink two years and a bit. Well," he wriggled uneasily, "I shouldn't give up 'ope, if I was you." And he departed precipitately with a broom in one hand and a duster in the other.

"Well, Cop," said Skilly, when they found themselves alone. "You've 'ad it straight from the 'orse's mouth. Lamp's quite right, though I 'adn't thought it out that way meself. You 'ang on to old Pharm and don't take no for an answer and you'll land 'im in the end."

"But suppose there is another woman? " said Pat.

"Oh, kipper the other woman!" snorted Skilly.

At that moment they heard Pharmakos' voice, speaking to Lamprey.

"Go on, Cop," said Skilly, giving her a push towards the door. "You'd better show yerself. 'E'll be on the look-out for yer."

Pat had crepe rubber soles to her sandals, and she crossed the parquetry silently and stood beside Pharmakos without his observing her. He was watching the door at the far end of the room with an anxious and rather grim expression. He reached out his hand towards his cigarette-box without taking his eyes off the door, failed to find it, and was obliged to turn round. Then he saw Pat, and his whole face lit up in such a way that even Pat, who feared to think the best lest she were deluding herself with vanity, knew that she must mean something to him.

"Hello, Patsie," he said, "You clothed and in your right mind? How are you feeling this morning, old thing?"

"First-rate," said Pat, " How's yourself?"

"None so dusty, considering the sort of time we've been having lately. What o'clock is it?"

"Goodness only knows. I suppose you have forgotten to wind up your watch again. Whatever should we do without Big Ben?"

"He's just struck the quarter," said Pharmakos, "Though he didn't say which, but it's a late quarter if my internal clock is anything to go by."

"I suppose that means you want your breakfast," said Pat.

"Pat, you must be psychic," said Pharmakos.

She retired to the kitchen, and found that Skilly was having the grace to wash up the frying-pan.

" 'Ow's the boss?" enquired Skilly in a husky whisper.

"He seems all right."

"You stick to 'im, Cop. 'E's a bee good chap."

Breakfast was rather an embarrassed meal. Neither Pat nor Pharmakos could forget the emotional unrestraint of the previous day, and neither of them wished to renew it, or for the matter of that, felt able to renew it now that the keyed up tension was over; yet at the same time, neither of them wished to lose touch with the other. Pllarmakos, being a neurotic, desired not to eat his cake, and yet to have it; and Pat, though normal enough in her mentality, was working in the dark .

Pharmakos smoked the after-meal cigarette, on which Pat insisted without speaking. His memory was apt to be a little hazy concerning moments of emotion, and he never knew for certain how much was real, how much he had imagined, or how much he had forgotten. Seeing Pat so placid and matter of fact and friendly, he concluded that there could not have been any very desperate emotional scenes between them, though he knew she had fainted, and girls as sturdy as Pat did not faint for nothing. But he comforted himself with the thought that she had probably fainted over the arrest business, and that owing to the providential arrival of Saunders he had not made a complete cad and fool of himself.

He was busy turning over in his mind just how far he might permit himself to go in his relationship with Pat, now that it looked as if, with any reasonable luck, he might expect immunity from Jurgens. He had got to begin again as he meant to go on, he saw that; and they were drifting into an intimacy and affection which, though exceedingly pleasant to his sore soul, was not particularly good for Pat, and might lead to embarrassments in the future if she got up steam and he had to call a halt.

On the other hand, he did not want suddenly to cool off and so hurt her feelings, and he felt pretty sure that all his attempts at explanation of his state of mind had gone off like water off a duck's back owing to her inexperience.

He felt that he might permit himself as much caressing of Pat as a normally affectionate brother might do, and demand as much of her as he might of a favourite sister. He did not think he could go far wrong if he did that. But in addition to his affection for Pat as a person, there was also his need of her as a drug. In her presence his troubles rolled away, in her absence he relapsed into a brooding melancholia. He literally could not bear to let Pat out of his sight. He had got into the way of ringing her up at mid-day to tell her what time to expect him back in the evening, a thing he could perfectly well have done before he went out, for he knew what his appointments were; but just a word with Pat on the phone was like the nip of alcohol the toper takes between meals. If interviews were going badly and he was getting depressed, he used to ring her up and ask if there had been a phone call for him, though he had no reason to expect there would be.

Pat was becoming an obsession; it could not be particularly good for him, he told himself, and it must certainly be exceedingly irritating to Pat. But on the other hand, his health had been improving hand over fist under her regime until the Jurgens upheave gave him a setback, and there was every reason to believe that if no further setbacks occurred, within measurable time he would be restored to normal. When that came about he would *(a)* cease to be so dependent on Pat, and *(b)* might possibly feel justified in offering her marriage in good earnest. Therefore it would be very foolish of him to cut himself off from the help she could give him when that very help might avail to straighten out all their problems. He would therefore maintain a reasonably affectionate and intimate, though brotherly relationship with Pat while his malady was in its chronic phase, and reserve more active endearments for the times when it assumed its acute form, or in the words of the old song, " Another little drop won't do us any harm." Pharmakos, having reached this highly satisfactory conclusion, which made the best of both worlds to the complete satisfaction of a neurotic conscience, was at peace, since he did not at the moment recall the melody aforesaid.

Consequently he suddenly threw off his silence. "Patsie, I'm going out on patrol to-day; care to come with me? You may as well learn the ropes, it might come in useful."

Pat was delighted. There was nothing she would love more than to go out with him about his thrilling work. She was beginning to get rather bored with undiluted Quilp Cottage, now that the interest of getting things ship-shape had worn off, and there was not enough to do during the long hours of Pharmakos' absences. She changed her overall for a neat blue serge costume made for her by a little Jew tailor in the Lower Marsh, who combined an admirable cut with an absurd price, for he charged Pat the same as he charged the West End firms whose fifteen-guinea costumes he made for them. She pressed down on the red-gold hair a little blue hat that she had obtained from a young Frenchwoman, who combined millinery with prostitution in the New Cut, and with a pair of patent leather shoes that she had picked up for five shillings on a barrow, but which had been priced at fifty shillings in the shop from which they had been stolen, and stockings from the same source, and at the same discount, Pat presented an appearance that was rather more than creditable to her escort, as he noted appreciatively; for hitherto, he had only seen Pat in the frock that Mrs. Stone had considered suitable for office wear, and her little cotton overalls.

CHAPTER XXI

"**I AM** afraid you are going to be disappointed, Pat, my work is not at all thrilling," said Pharmakos, as they made their way towards Waterloo station in order to pick up the Tube. "People seem to think that private detectives spend all their time sprinting round corners with revolvers in their hands, though what their boots, let alone their nerves, would be like after an eight-hour day at that sort of game, nobody bothers to enquire; nor what would be the aftermath of the revolver if they started loosing it off. Certain formalites have to be observed, Patsie, before the enemies of society can be shovelled underground. The unfortunate individuals who are appointed by the nation to cope with its criminals are targets, not marksmen. If that applies to the official police, how much more does it apply to us private enquiry agents, who are the half of nothing?"

"Do you never go for anybody, then, whatever they may do to you?" asked Pat.

"Oh, don't I just? Like to look at my stick, Patsie?"

Pat took it in her hand and found it unexpectedly heavy.

"What is it made of?" she asked.

"Malacca, with a steel core and a sharpened ferule. I can break a fellow's arm or collar-bone with it as easy as kiss hands, good old-fashioned single-stick method, and with the crooked handle I can fetch a chap on to his nose by hooking it round his ankle. It isn't all done by kindness in our trade, Patsie, though we make kindness in the form of a few quid go as far as possible. You can always intimidate a fellow after you've squared him, but you can't always square him after you've tried to intimidate him and failed. At any rate, his price goes up out of sight."

The noise of the Tube prevented any further conversation, and as Pat sat beside Pharmakos, who attracted attention because of his great height and extraordinary face, she wondered whether she would come across any of her friends and acquaintances in the Tube, for this was the line they used when they went shopping in the West End.

They got out at their appointed station and started down a long straight, sordid street and soon found themselves in a shabby-genteel residential district where the houses, with their innumerable door-bells and name-plates, only just escaped being tenements. They quitted the taxi and Pharmakos, who seemed to know every alley in London, took Pat by short cuts through mews instead of following the right-angled main streets.

"It is all right through here for the two of us," he said, "Especially as one or two of the residents have made acquaintance with my stick; but if ever you are round here by yourself, you must keep to the bus-routes."

Pat thought it was wonderful to be tucked under Pharmakos' wing and protected from all evil by the formidable swordstick.

"Now, Patsie, we will have a bit of fun in this district, and you shall have your share in it, as you've been such a good girl recently. Moreover, your feminine charms may accomplish what my particular type of fascination would certainly fail to do.

"There is a certain house I want you to call at and ask for Mrs. Duggan. You won't get Mrs. Duggan, for she doesn't exist; she is merely a password; but if you ask for Mrs. Duggan it shows you are in the know and you will have the entrée to the sort of place which I hope you have never visited before, and that you will not remain in long on the occasion of your call. In fact, don't go in, Pat, just parley with them on the doorstep."

"When the parlour-maid, if there is one, answers your ring, say you have a message for Mrs. Duggan, and it's private and urgent. That will produce somebody who is also in the know. You tell this someone that you want to get a message to Mr. Walter Simmons urgently, and would they be good enough to give you his address. They may give it to you; but they more probably mayn't. In that case, you ask them if they would be good enough to send a telegram to him for you. Impress on them that it must be a telegram as there have been leakages over the telephone. Give them a bob for the wire, and ask them to say that the securities are dropping and he had better sell out at once. Decline to sign it, or to give your name, but say he will understand and it is very important that he should get it at once. Then hop it, and come to me at the A.B.C. at the corner. I will then take up my part in the song and follow the person who sends that telegram, and if our luck holds, the address will show through on the form underneath the one he writes it out on, and we shall know where Mr. Waiter Simmons hangs out and be able to pay him a call, which for reasons of our own, which I will explain to you later, we are anxious to do. He, pending our arrival, can addle his brains over the meaning of our cryptic message. He'll know what it means all right after we've met him. You will see the house when you turn the corner, number 53, with a glass porch, set back a little bit from the road. Come back to me in the A.B.C., and don't you be too long, Patsie, or I shall begin to get agitated."

He patted her shoulder and started her off with a push, watched her until she was out of sight and then turned into the A.B.C. and ordered a meal as an excuse to sit down and await her return.

Pat went off in high feather, delighted with her commission and the excitement of it for red hair loves thrills and can stand anything better than monotony. She found the house with the glass porch, marched up the little path, and rang the door-bell. It was a neutral-looking house, neither smart nor shabby, clean nor dirty, and very adequately curtained. As she went in at the gate she felt the flagstone shift slightly under her feet, as some shop-mats do that operate a bell to summon the shopman. Involuntarily she felt thankful that Pharmakos and his sword-stick were just around the corner. There was something sinister about that house, though It was impossible to say what. Its spiritual smell was all wrong. Pat felt the short hairs on her neck beginning to stir.

The door was opened in answer to her ring, not by a parlourmaid, as Pharmakos had surmised, but by a man in a showy lounge suit, who might have been an edition de luxe of Skilly, for he was the same unmistakable bruiser type, further embellished by a squint. Pat, as instructed, nervously asked for Mrs. Duggan.

The unprepossessing face relaxed into a smile, which was by no means an improvement to it, and asked Pat to walk in.

Pat declined.

"You can't talk to Mrs. Duggan on the door-step, you know," said the man, grinning more widely.

"I don't want to talk to Mrs. Duggan," said Pat, "I want to leave a message, and it's private, and it's urgent, and I won't come in because I can't wait."

"All right," said the man, "You can give the message to me."

"It's for Mr. Walter Simmons," said Pat.

The man's face became expressionless.

"He doesn't live here," he said .

"I know he doesn't," said Pat, "But I want to get a message to him as quick as ever I can, and its very urgent, and I think he'll be very glad to get it."

"I don't know anything about any Mr. Walter Simmons," said the man. "But Mrs. Duggan may. She's out at the moment, but if you like to leave the message with me, I'll give it to her when she comes in."

"All right," said Pat, "It's this. Would she be good enough to send him a wire. She mustn't phone, because the phone's been leaking lately."

"You don't need to tell me that," said the man, "I shouldn't have used the phone in any case."

"And would you please say in the wire that the securities are going down, and he had better sell out immediately."

"Right," said the man, "I'll see it goes at once. Who shall I say it's from?"

"No need to say it's from anybody. He'll know all right. He's been expecting it. Here's a shilling for the wire. Do you think it will be enough?"

"Ought to be," said the man, " But a penny one way or the other don't matter to Mr. Simmons. I'll put it down in the petty cash.

"Thank you very much," said Pat, " Good afternoon."

"Oh, come on," said the man, "don't run away like that. Come in and have a chat and a cocktail, won't you?"

"No, thank you very much," said Pat, "I'm in no end of a hurry."

"Well, I'm not," said the man, "and I'd like to have a word with you. I'm always glad to have a word with nice little girls, and so's Mrs. Duggan," he added with a wink. "You may find it worth your while."

"I know all about Mrs. Duggan," said Pat tartly, "and I'll thank her to mind her own business."

The man looked over Pat's shoulder. He could only see straight across the road, for the glass porch limited his vision like the blinkers on a horse. Equally, the glass porch limited the vision of anyone passing up and down the road. They could only see what was happening on that doorstep when they were exactly opposite. There was nobody passing down the road.

"Look where you've put your foot!" exclaimed the man, suddenly. Pat did so involuntarily, and he caught her by the shoulders and with a sudden jerk pulled her inside the hall, and kicked the door shut before she knew what had happened. He let go of her and laughed.

"Well, what about that cocktail now, girlie?"

Pat tried the door and found it locked.

Now Pat had a flaming red head, as has already been noted, and she had been brought up in the contentious atmosphere of a tribe of Stones, and when she found herself locked in, she did not so much fear the danger as resent the insult.

"You open that door!" she cried, her face scarlet, to the great surprise of the bully, who was accustomed to see girls turn white in such circumstances. "You open that door or I'll smash your windows."

"They'll take some smashing, dearie," he grinned, "they're Triplex, same as wind-screens."

Pat turned on him angrily. "What are you playing at?" she demanded.

"Pleasure of your company, dearie."

"Pleasure of my company!" snorted Pat, "You'll get the pleasure of somebody else's company as well as mine before you're much older if you aren't careful, and someone who'll put the fear of God into you as it's never been put before, you cock-eyed cad!"

"Better let her go, George," came a woman's voice from the inner hall. "We don't want complications with someone else's girl."

George sulkily stretched out his hand behind a curtain, released a catch, and the door swung open. He was reluctant to let such an attractive, and consequently profitable girl as Pat escape him, and he had resented her reference to the cast in his eye. He looked at her closely. If ever he came across her again he meant to remember her.

Pat turned on her heel and stalked off down the garden path, not deigning to look behind her. If she had done so she would have seen the woman come out and have a good look at her too.

As she came out of the gate she was amazed to see Pharmakos pausing to light a cigarette just outside. He paid no attention to her and her quick wits caught the hint. She passed him without recognition and went down the road, and into the tea-shop, and there sat down to await his arrival.

She saw a half-eaten meal on the table and a waitress and manageress surveying it dubiously, and concluded that Pharmakos had bolted without paying his bill. She seated herself at the table.

"It's quite all right," she said to them with a smile. "The gentleman's coming back. I'm expecting him to meet me."

They looked relieved, especially the waitress, who would have had to pay for that meal herself if Pharmakos had not returned.

Pat ordered a pot of tea for herself, and settled down to await Pharmakos' advent. She guessed that he had gone on to the post office trailing the person who was sending the bogus telegram. She had not long to wait. Her tea had only just arrived when she saw Pharmakos come striding in at the door in seven-leagued boots.

"My God, Pat," he exclaimed, dropping into a chair, "I was never so glad in all my life to see anybody as I was to see you coming out of that house. Why did you go in when I told you not to?"

"I didn't go in," said Pat, "I was pulled in forcibly."

"Good Lord; what is this you're telling me?"

Pat gave the history of her adventures.

Pharmakos heard her silently. At the end he said: "When you found yourself trapped, did you think of me?"

"Yes," said Pat, "I did. I jolly well wished you were there."

"Well, I saw you," said Pharmakos.

"Saw me?" exclaimed Pat in surprise.

"Yes, saw you as plain as a pikestaff. I was sitting here dawdling and thinking of nothing in particular, when something suddenly made me look up, and I saw you standing right in front of me. I said, 'Hullo, Pat,' and the next minute you weren't there, and I had an awful feeling that something was wrong. I simply shot out of the shop. The waitress gave a yell, but that made no difference to me. I tore down the road after you, and stood outside that beastly house, wondering if I would come and bang on the door, or get a policeman with me first, when the door opened and you came out. Then I had to justify my existence outside their gate, so I lit a cigarette, and you, my dear, had the wits to cut me dead, bless you."

"Did you get the address all right?" asked Pat anxiously.

"Yes, I've got it here. It's perfectly legible. A place down at Maidenhead. A burly-looking bruiser came out almost on your heels and overtook me, going for all he was worth. You must have told the tale convincingly."

"I certainly put my heart into it," said Pat. "I got the wind up as soon as ever I got through their beastly gate."

"What scared you, kiddy?"

"There was something funny about the first paving-stone. It sort of gave under you. I think it rang an alarm or something. The bruiser person was awfully slick on the front door."

"I think we'll tell Saunders about this little crib," said Pharmakos. "He mayn't be interested himself; consider it beneath his notice, in fact, but some of his pals may; it's a beastly shame to let them go on trapping girls in the way they trapped you."

"Were they trapping them for the White Slave Trade?" asked Pat, feeling a little embarrassed at referring to such a subject.

"Well, not *for* the trade. The girls they would bag would be already in the trade. Decent girls don't get kidnapped forcibly against their will, they kick up too much of a shindy. At any rate, I've never heard of a case, and I know the underworld pretty thoroughly. That's the yarn they keep for the rescue workers, But there's a lot of kidnapping goes on within the trade. Girls getting into houses like that and having a difficulty in getting out again. They are not fond of appealing to the police because magistrates have a knack of shoving them into rescue homes, and precious few of them want to be rescued as long as their health holds out. When you kicked up a shindy, did you invoke the police?"

"No," said Pat, " I said I'd got a friend who would put the fear of God into them."

"Well, there you are. That was the correct reply. Naturally he took you at your word over the telegram. I've been called a good many things in my time, but I've never been called that before."

"Called what?" asked Pat.

"Never mind," said Pharmakos, thinking that Pat's mentality reminded him more and more of the west coast of Scotland—full of the most unexpected projections and indentations.

"I can promise you one thing, Pat," said Pharmakos. "You shall never be let in for anything like this again."

"Why not," asked Pat, "It was no end of a lark, I loved it."

"I didn't," said Pharmakos, "I had the worst quarter of an hour of my life till I saw you coming out of the beastly place."

Pat looked at him in perplexity. If he had had the worst quarter of an hour in his life waiting for her, what sort of a time would he have when she came to find a mate and he to find a bride? His backings. and shiftings left her utterly bewildered. As Skilly had said, she did not know where she was with him. There were times when she found it very difficult to be entirely impersonal and selfless and just nurse him, always bearing in mind that when he recovered he would no longer need her.

Without thinking, she said, "I wonder if you will miss me when the time comes for me to leave you."

The result was startling. Pharmakos' face, which had been looking happy and fairly human in his relief at the safe return of his beloved Pat, suddenly changed into a Tibetan devil-mask. Pat gazed at this horror speechlessly. It was like nothing on earth that she had ever seen. This must be how he looked when he had done his murder, she thought, and she was probably right. Pharmakos had hazel eyes, lightish, with flecks of brown in them. Under the stress of his insane emotion the pupils dilated till they were jet black. The effect of the dilation was extraordinary. Pharmakos' whole personality changed from man to devil. For the first time Pat saw the murderer in him.

She sat petrified and speechless, staring at him. Fortunately for them both, Pat's face told him what he must be looking like, and with a superhuman effort he recovered a measure of control. He rose from the table.

"If you've finished, we'll go," he said curtly, and threw a handful of loose change on the counter and walked out bareheaded without waiting for his bill. Pat seized his hat and stick and followed him.

He went tearing down the road with his long raking strides, Pat running after him for her life, for she did not know what part of London she was in and had no money on her. She was terribly distressed at the effect her thoughtless words had had on him, and did not know what to do, save to follow after him until the storm had spent its violence, and then try to undo the disastrous result of her words, if that were at all possible. The stormy figure ahead of her suggested that it might not be.

A taxi-rank was at the corner of the road and Pharmakos strode towards it. It was only with his hand on the door of a taxi that he remembered Pat, and looked round angrily for her. He held the door of the taxi open, and gestured for her to enter.

She sprang in thankfully.

"Where to, sir?" asked the driver.

Pharmakos looked at him, and then at Pat, helplessly. He did not know where in the world he wanted to go to. He had not the faintest idea where he was, nor what his address was, or for the matter of that, what his name was. All he knew was that Pat was there, and he turned to her instinctively for help, despite the bomb that had exploded between them.

"Waterloo Station," said Pat to the cabby, and taking Pharmakos by the hand, she drew him into the cab. As he dropped into the seat beside her, she felt that he was trembling violently.

His face had lost its devilish look, and was an expressionless mask, tense and rigid in its immobility; and he stared straight ahead as fixedly as if he were driving a racing-car. Pat gazed at him, wondering how in the world to straighten out the painful misunderstanding between them.

"Oh, Julian, I didn't mean it. Not the way you took it."

"Then why did you say it?" said the man, without looking at her.

Pat looked steadily at him. Nothing but the truth would serve. Pharmakos would instantly detect the false note in any equivocation. She hated to show her heart on her sleeve, but it had to be done.

"I'll tell you why I said it," she answered, "and then perhaps you will understand that you've been hurting me just as much as I've hurt you."

Pharmakos looked round at her out of the corners of his eyes, without turning his head. He looked terribly insane, and Pat was thankful for the broad back of the taxi-driver just in front of her.

"You remember that poem, 'Helen all Alone'?"

"Yes?"

"You remember it said:

"When at last our souls were rid
Of what the night had shown,
Helen went from me, she did!
    Helen all alone."

"Well?"

"Well—" said Pat, " That hurt."

"Why?"

"Who wants to be sucked dry and chucked out?" flamed Pat suddenly, her red-headed temper getting the better of her.

Pharmakos did not answer, but sat as rigidly immobile as a wooden image, and Pat had almost despaired of ever seeing him move again when he suddenly spoke, still without looking at her.

"Pat," he said.

"Yes?"

There was another long pause, and then he spoke again.

"Pat, my mind's completely conked out. I don't know where I am, or what I'm doing. Forget everything, will you? and just take me home."

"Of course I will," said Pat, tucking her arm through his. Explanations mattered nothing now that Pharmakos had come back to her; and he slumped down on the seat of the taxi and put his head on her shoulder, regardless of any view of him that passers-by might obtain.

As they neared the approach to Waterloo Station, she said to him:

"Shall we get out here, or drive home?"

"Drive home, Pat," he said without stirring, "I'm all in."

Pat explored his pockets and collected some loose change with which to pay the taxi, for she knew he was quite incapable of doing so.

She did not relish the task of steering a very shaky Pharmakos, who did not seem to see where he was going, along the narrow path between the wall and the water, so she guided him into Skilly's abode, intending to take him to his own quarters by way of Sister Ann's passage, and there came unexpectedly upon Skilly, very deshabille.

Skilly whistled when he saw the state Pharmakos was in, and took him by the arm to guide him up the stairs. Pharmakos, without looking at him, and apparently quite oblivious of his presence, drove his elbow into his ribs with such violence that Skilly went flying, with all the breath knocked out of him. Pat and Skilly looked at each other in consternation, and then at Pharmakos, who had come to a standstill in the middle of the room, still staring grimly into space.

Then, with much trepidation, Pat crept forward, wondering whether she was going to receive the same treatment as Skilly, and whether, if she did, her ribs would stand it, and took Pharmakos by the arm in her turn. He yielded instantly to the pressure of her hand, and she steered him as if he were a blind man up the stairs and along the passage.

"Good for you, Cop!" whispered Skilly, following behind in his shirt-tails, trousers over his arm, awaiting a suitable opportunity to put them on.

CHAPTER XXII

PAT put Pharmakos into his big chair, and he went down with the simultaneous collapse of all his joints like a rag doll in the same way that he had done when Inspector Saunders had brought him home on the first memorable occasion. Pat heaved a sigh of relief. That was a familiar symptom, anyway. She had found a landmark she knew.

Skilly signalled to her that he would stop in the kitchen, within call in case of need, and disappeared, drawing the door nearly shut behind him, but leaving a crack for observation.

Pat was thankful he was there, though she hated to have to tackle Phannakos in front of him, for there was only one way in which Pharmakos could be tackled. However, it had to be done.

She sat down on the arm of his chair and put her arm round him. He was utterly limp and unresponsive. Then she began to talk in a quiet monotone, which she hoped that Skilly would not overhear.

It was very difficult to make a start in cold blood, trying to lay bare her heart to that unresponsive figure, but Pat had a curious feeling that her words had power over him in proportion to the effort it cost her to utter them. She had exorcised his devil effectually after his last outbreak by referring in plain terms to the fact that she was illegitimate. By doing so, she felt, in some queer way, that she had won admission to the strange hell of the insane where he was wrestling with his devils, and had been able to find him and bring him back.

They had swopped incubi.

Now she was going to do the same thing again. In proportion as she sacrificed her own feelings would he be helped. She took a good grip on herself and began, praying that Skilly couldn't overhear. That really would have been the last straw.

" Julian," she whispered, "Julian!" using once again the magic of the name to summon his wandering attention. She had no means of knowing whether she had succeeded or not, and went on, trusting to luck. She half hoped he was not hearing anything she was saying. It would be much less embarrassing if she could get warmed up in private, as it were.

"Julian," she began again, "It's me. It's Pat. And I'm coming after you. I am not going to let you go away and leave me. I am just going to hang on to you because I want you, and I don't care whether you want me or not.

"You're the only living soul I've ever cared for, and I care for you a tremendous lot. More than you will ever know. I never had any sort of peace or happiness till you brought me here and looked after me. I simply adore this place. I've never known it was possible to have such happiness as I've had here. I've nowhere to go if you send me away from here, and I'm just awfully fond of you."

Pat paused for breath, she was warming up now. Skilly was forgotten. It was unlikely he would hear, even if she raised her voice, the distances in Quilp Cottage were so vast. It was a warehouse, not a dwelling-house.

"Oh, Julian, darling, come back to me, come back to me! I can't bear to see you like this. You shan't be hurt any more, darling."

Still there was no sign from the figure lying slackly in her arms. But Pat had accepted the fact of his unresponsiveness. It did not seem to matter. She could say what she liked and he would never know, and somehow, now she had started, she couldn't stop.

She clutched him to her.

"Oh, my dear, what does it matter to anybody if we love each other? Why shouldn't we if we want to? We do, you know. We do love each other. I don't care what you say. Oh, Julian, Julian, why can't we care for each other? It is tearing me to bits like this. I know you care for me. You couldn't go on the way you do if you didn't. Why won't you let yourself care for me? What is there to prevent it?"

Uncontrollable weeping seized Pat, and she hung on to the limp form in her arms in her anguish as if her whole world were slipping away from her.

When the storm had spent itself she felt better. The cumulative nervous strain of the last two days was relieved, and she settled down to tackle Pharmakos in good earnest, and fetch him back from the hell of the insane where his wits were astray. Over and over again, speaking softly so that Skilly might not hear, she told him how much she loved him; how much it meant to her to have him to take care of her; how much she loved Quilp Cottage, and how he had given her the first happiness she had ever known.

She went over it, and over it, and over it, and was finally pausing for breath in despair, when the rag doll in her arms suddenly said: "Pat, you are a brick!" and tucked its nose into her breast and became human again.

Pat held him for a little while to let him settle down, and then said in a matter of fact voice: "Now for some refreshments."

"That's what you always say," came the muffled voice of Pharmakos, and then they both laughed.

"Go on, Pat. Go and kill the fatted calf. I'm all right again now," said Pharmakos, and Pat heaved a sigh of relief, laid him back on the cushions, and went into the kitchen. There she found Skilly sitting on the table armed with the rolling-pin, round which he had twisted a dish-cloth, evidently all ready to apply his favourite remedy of knocking Pharmakos out if all else failed. She was relieved to see that he had got his trousers on at last. Bright blue socks, pale mauve suspenders, gooseberry shanks, and fly-away shirt-tails had been a combination so mirth-provoking that Pat feared that she would have been reduced to hysterical laughter had she looked upon them again.

"He's all right now," she whispered.

"Gawd, Cop, you're a wonder!" Skilly whispered back, and laying the rolling-pin in its drawer, he faded softly away through the concealed door in the direction whence he had come.

When Pat returned with the tray, she found Pharmakos smoking a cigarette and looking rather self-conscious.

"Come here, Pat," he said. She went to him. He held out his hand. Pat ledged the tray on her hip and put hers in it. He lifted her hand to his lips and kissed her fingers gently.

"Patsie," he said, "I haven't the remotest notion what I've been up to, but I know I've been making a nuisance of myself. Can you forget it, dear?"

"Of course I can," said Pat, smiling down at him. And then the salad began to slide, and she had to snatch her hand away from his and grab it.

Pat sincerely hoped that his forgetfulness extended to the confession of love which she had poured steadily into his ears for the last twenty minutes. But it hadn't. Nor to the incident which had precipitated all the trouble. Everything in between, however, was a grey nightmare, and he wondered how much he had scared his beloved Pat, though he had not the slightest recollection of having knocked the stuffing out of Skilly. The first thing that had broken in upon his miserable dream was Pat's voice, telling him how much she loved him, and how happy she was with him, and he had returned down an enchanted pathway, hand in hand with his beloved, the grey dream turning to gold; and he had, most perfidiously, kept quiet long after he had really wakened for the pleasure of hearing Pat telling it to him all over again, and of leaning up against her.

Although he had returned to his normal senses, he was not in a state to do much thinking, and he just delivered himself passively into Pat's hands, to do what she liked with him. Which was an excellent arrangement for a gentleman with a tender conscience, for Pat's one idea was to find out what he wanted, and do it.

The following morning at breakfast Pharmakos announced that the day should be a holiday. They both needed rest and recuperation.

"I was a bit of a fool to go traipsing around yesterday like I did," he said, "but I thought that getting a move on would take the taste of Jurgens out of my mouth."

"Is that how you spend your days when you are away from here?" asked Pat.

"Yes, more or less. I do a lot of interviewing at solicitors' offices too. It's safer for me to interview clients there, because then there can be no question of my blackmailing them, for you never know which way some of these beauties are going to turn. Especially if I don't fancy their cases after I've heard their tale. It's only a certain type of enquiries that Skilly and Lamprey can make, though they are simply invaluable for that. I wish to goodness I could find the right sort of partner. This business is too big for one person to handle comfortably, and it is still growing."

"Can't I help you more?" asked Pat.

"You are simply invaluable, Pat. How I ever existed without you is beyond my comprehension."

"But can't I help you with the detective end of the work?"

Pharmakos suddenly clutched her.

"Not on your life!" he said, "I am never going to let you out of my sight again as long as I live!"

He let go of her with a self-conscious laugh.

"Come along, Patsie," he said, "Come over to the window and give the gulls their crumbs."

They gathered up the broken bread from the table and knelt on the divan and put their heads out of the only window that would open. As soon as the gulls saw the splash of the bread falling in the water, they were round the window in crowds, wheeling and circling and uttering their shrill cries, and swooping to take the bread from Pharmakos' hand. Finally when the bread was all gone they took a disconsolate departure, and the two remained with their heads out of the window, enjoying the morning freshness. To Pat's amazement, she felt Pharmakos put his arm round her. He had never done such a thing in cold blood before. This was a great step for him.

"Patsie," he said, "are you happy here with me?"

"Yes, awfully happy," said Pat.

"Well, I love having you here, darling, and I'm most awfully grateful to you for all you have done for me. I hope I'm not putting too much strain on you. Do you feel you can put up with me? You aren't scared of me, are you, Pat? I'd never hurt you wilfully, you know, darling. As long as you don't let yourself get trodden on when I'm having one of my turns, you'll be perfectly all right. You don't take my antics too seriously, do you? It's just nightmares as you yourself said."

Pat laid her hand on his where it rested against her waist.

"Julian," she said, "can you realise what it is like, when you have always had everybody against you, and been bully-ragged from pillar to post and back again, to be with someone who likes you?"

"I more than like you, Pat," said Pharmakos softly, "and if I get better, I shall talk to you seriously on the subject. But I am a sick man at present, even if I am walking about on my two feet. I am not in a fit state to talk seriously to anybody, or even to think seriously, for that matter, but if you can put up with me as I am for the present, I think I shall get better, providing Jurgens leaves me alone.

"Now listen, Patsie, you said some awfully sweet things to me yesterday. I couldn't say much in return, because I was too thoroughly and completely busted, but I appreciated them all the same, and if I started to return the compliment, God knows where we'd end, and I'm not in a state to end anywhere at present. We don't want the lid flying off till I'm fit to deal with it; therefore I suggest that we both sit tight on that lid for the present, see, Patsie? You're my sister, my very dear little sister "—he gave her a squeeze—" for the present. If I get upheaved and wax affectionate, I am not to be encouraged, do you see, dear?"

She didn't see in the least, but she acquiesced. It was enough for her to have his arm around her.

"Pat, did I ever tell you my back history? My life story, I mean? I don't believe I ever have, and you ought to know it. I didn't keep it from you because I didn't want you to know it, but because—well—bits of it are rather sore and one tends to evade talking of them if one can. But I'm not nearly as sore as I was, thanks to you, darling." He gave her a squeeze that nearly toppled her out of the window. "And I am going to tell you about it; or at least enough of it to show you how I came to be what I am, as there is no point in boring you with three-volume novels."

Pat acquiesced. She would not have been bored with him if he had been in encyclopaedia form!

Pharmakos lit a cigarette and began.

"If you want to reform a man you ought to begin with

his grandfather, they say, so I had better begin with mine. He was a fierce old bird. I am supposed to be rather like him. I have got his beak and his hair, anyway. Red hair is funny stuff. Sometimes it's black, if you know what I mean. That's to say; red-haired parents will have some red and some black offspring. I don't pretend to understand it. The Mendelian law or something. Anyway, they do. And our family throws red and black like a pack of cards. My grandfather was the red kind, and so am I, as there's no need to tell you. You can see my beacon burning a mile off on a foggy night. My father and elder brother were black." He paused. That explains a good deal."

"I know it does," said Pat, "I've been the red-haired one in a mud-coloured family, and I know what it means."

"My position was nearly as invidious as yours, Pat, for my father's first wife had been the daughter of the local vicar, whom he married for love in the face of family opposition; and my father's second wife, my mother, he married for money under family pressure.

"My stepmother, I suppose you'd call her, had one kid, a son; and being T.B. she died soon after he was born, poor soul. This kid, a blue-eyed angel, taking after her and not after us red and black devils, is the absolute apple of my father's eye. I call him a kid although he's five years my senior, because he's always seemed a kid to me. I could slog him all round the nursery by the time I was three. My earliest recollection is being pulled off my elder brother by the slack of my little petticoats after there'd been a hell of a row in the nursery.

"Well, as I say, Aneurin, my brother, was the pater's pet, but I was my old granddad's pet, and he shoved my claims for all he was worth, in opposition to Aneurin's because poor old Ann is tubercular, like his mother, and grand dad had made up his mind that he would never make old bones. That was chiefly why he shoved my pater into a second marriage. He wanted to make sure of an heir. Well, he got me, God help him. Fortunately he was gathered to his fathers before I started my troubles. Fortunately for him, but unfortunately for me. It was having not a single soul to turn to in my trouble that capsized me, for I was only a youngster and old Aunt Julia had gone too. When my father came to see me in prison while I was awaiting my trial, the only thing he did was to blow me up for upsetting Aneurin's wedding festivities, and he never showed up in court once during the case. That sort of thing takes the heart out of a youngster you know, Pat.

"He left me to the biggest old fool of a family solicitor you ever set eyes on, who had never handled a criminal case in his life and hated 'em like poison. It was the judge conducted my defence. Well, I'll tell you about that presently, when I come to it in this strange eventful history .

"Anyway, there we were, the family rivals. Poor little sickly Aneurin, and my buxom, bouncing self. I was all right as long as my grandfather was alive because he and Aunt Julia jolly well saw to it that I was. But as soon as they died, and they died within a year of each other, I was all wrong.

"You see, Pat, my mother started drinking. I don't blame her, poor soul, I expect she had a lot to put up with, and if her nerves were anything like mine she certainly stood in need of consolation.

"Anyway, as soon as my grandfather's hand on the reins was removed, the pater and mater separated. Now this is the thing for which I blame my father—although he knew she was drinking like a fish, he let her keep me.

"She used to turn up at my school on speech-days and such like, reeling, rolling, roaring tight and kick up no end of a hullaballoo. Well, you can imagine what that was like for a boy. I was an absolute pariah. I was very good at all sports, but when it came to the show-day and she was there, for she never missed anything like that, I was completely off my stroke, for I never knew when they would have to throw her out. She capsized my school life for me completely, and when I went to college she did the same there, though. It wasn't quite so bad then, for I was older and could cope with it better. Still, it was quite bad enough.

"Well, you can understand how that sort of thing addles a lad, can't you, Pat? I also have to thank her for my vile temper. She nagged the life out of me. Red-haired tempers are hot tempers, Pat, as you probably know to your cost, but they are not bad tempers unless they are mishandled. Well, mine was mishandled as thoroughly as any kid's temper could be mishandled. When I got in a tantrum she used first to whack me till she was tired, and then refuse to forgive me till I said I was sorry. And I never would say I was sorry. Half the time she had simply got in a temper with me on her own account, and I had nothing to be sorry for, except having been born at all, and I was exceedingly sorry for that, believe me. She'd keep up her disfavour for weeks on end. Well, a day is a long time for a small kid to be in disgrace. Keep him in disgrace for weeks and something goes wrong inside him.

"Anyway, it's no good labouring that point now, but I wasn't a pleasant child by the time she had finished with my upbringing.

"Then she died, just as I left college. My father intended me for the Bar. He didn't want me at home, fighting with Aneurin, so he shoved me into digs, and didn't spend too much on 'em, either, although he had got all my mother's money. He shoved me into digs with a soapy old Sam who was one of the clerks of our precious family lawyer. So you can imagine the kind of defence his boss put up for me after I had disorganised the office by killing him.

"Soapy Sam coached me for my exams, and I will say this for him, what he didn't know about the practical end of the law wasn't worth knowing. I've found the tips he gave me simply invaluable in my present line of business, and I should never have got 'em from a better man. What he didn't know about fraudulent bankruptcies, evading liabilities, wriggling round the law of libel, and disposing of unwanted spouses, would have lain on a three-penny-bit.

"Well, this old beauty had a daughter, and she was a bit of a bird. But I should about as soon have thought of carrying on with her as you would of carrying on with Skilly. Moreover I had other fish to fry at the time, for I was very much in love with the daughter of a pal of my grandfather's. It was a very suitable match. Her people were quite pleased, only they said we were too young for a formal engagement. Only the pater was displeased because he had wanted this girl for Aneurin, but he daren't be displeased openly because he could hardly give that reason.

"Well, Soapy's daughter—Gerty was her name, of all names to saddle a girl with. Well Gerty got in the family way by God knows whom. I certainly didn't have anything to do with it. I'd as soon have connubulated with a sack of potatoes. And her blessed father started to plant the business on me! I naturally swore I hadn't, and swore a good deal more on top of it, but I daren't go to my father because I knew he would be only too pleased to queer my pitch with this girl I told you about; and anyway, he was always very ready to believe the worst of me. So as a youngster of twenty-two I had to handle the situation as best I could.

"Well, old Soapy sighed like a furnace over his sorrow, and finally said he'd accept my word as a gentleman that Gerty's ghastly offspring wasn't anything to do with me. But as he was desperately hard up at the moment, would I lend him something to see her through her trouble? Well, I had a fairly decent allowance, and was working too hard to have time to spend much of it, so it had accumulated at the bank, and I gave him fifty out of pure good nature; paid it by cheque, too, being a fool. I didn't know what it cost for creatures like Gerty to hatch out. She ought to have been shoved in a box of hay in the back yard and left to get on with it. I don't believe now that she ever was going to have a baby. I believe he had played this trick on generations of law students. She was simply putting on weight because she ate too many chocolates.

"Well, the next move was that poor Gerty was complicated and had to see a specialist, and his fee was three guineas. Then she had to have an operation, and that was another fifty guineas. Then her brat had to have an outfit and that was twenty guineas. I was beginning to get a bit dry by this time, and pretty sick of Gerty and her pup, so I called a halt and said I had done all I was going to do for Gerty, and if she had any more pups they must drown them.

"Soapy had also begun to get a bit sick of me, I fancy, because I had no capital to dip into, and my allowance did not go very far with foaling Gerties. So he hit on a new wheeze. He had always known that Aneurin was sickly, but that did not cut much ice with him. He wanted more solid benefits than that. But suddenly he discovered that the money was my mother's, that the pater only had a life interest in it, and that it would come to me, not Aneurin, in the end. Then he changed his tune. He reverted to his original proposition that I was responsible for Gerty's condition. Pat, I assure you that it was a physical impossibility. That girl was an emetic. Oh, well, I won't trouble you with these details, you're too young. Anyway, Soapy Sam tackled me with a view to my becoming his son-in-law, and said he'd raise hell if I didn't. Looking back, I think that he was simply using this proposition as bargaining power: Nobody in his senses would want me for a son-in-law with my temper. But I didn't realise it at the time, and took him literally, and you know what followed. I thought he was going to queer my pitch with this girl I was fond of, and I saw red and banged his head on the mantlepiece, and that was the end of both of us.

"Well I might have survived even that, Patsie, for they let me down very lightly at the trial; but I was fool enough to write to this girl I was fond of and ask her to believe that I was absolutely innocent where that wretched Gerty was concerned, for it all came out in the cross-examination. I did not ask her to wait for me, I only asked her to believe that I was innocent of the filthy part of the charge. Well, she never answered, and I just turned my face to the wall and that was the end of me.

"So you see how it was with me, Pat, when you came along. I've been pretty thoroughly let down by my women-folk, and I wasn't having any more, not if I knew it. I'd even cut females out of my day-dreams, and when a fellow does that, he's pretty far gone. But when I found a woman—" he drew Pat very close to him, "Whom I could classify with my old Aunt Julia, and old Maggie, my nurse, it began to put a different complexion on life. Though frankly, Pat, every now and again I find myself wondering when you are going to rat on me."

"Never!" said Pat quietly.

"Well, be that as it may. I must be grateful for small mercies, my dear, and you have simply done wonders for me. So that is my story, Pat, and the end of it, and the thing that put the lid on the lot, was that my pater has cut me off without a shilling from my own mother's money, for he has a life interest in it though he can't leave it away from me, and God knows he would if he could. Whenever there was a question of doing anything for me, it was always No, he couldn't afford It. He had to save for Aneurin.

"When I came out of prison I hadn't a bean except what the Prisoner's Aid Society gave me, and I was only just out of bed after pneumonia, which I got from sweating during one of my turns and having no dry clothes to change into. The only person who did anything for me was Skilly, and I stand by the people who stand by me, Pat, whoever they may be. Handsome is as handsome does.

"That was why I gave you that telegram to my father to send off if anything happened to me. And I still expect you to, if anything does. They say a father's curse is an effectual weapon. I wonder what a son's curse is like under such circumstances? I guess the one I compounded will blight him pretty thoroughly if anything can."

CHAPTER XXIII

ALTHOUGH Pharmakos had said he was not to be encouraged if he waxed affectionate, he had not given any instructions that he was to be repulsed, so though he showed no signs of removing his arm from Pat's waist, she let it stop there, and they knelt on the divan with their elbows on the window-sill, watching the river in silence for over an hour, each busy with their own thoughts; each deeply conscious of the other; of the bodily warmth, the rhythm of the breathing, the touch of skin on skin. A deep peace enveloped them; all barriers seemed down between them, and the man's quick, nervous breathing gradually slowed to the girl's tranquil rhythm.

At length he heaved a deep sigh and straightened himself.

"Patsie, I was nearly asleep," he said.

Pat smiled and looked up at him, and was amazed at the change in his face. The skull-like look was all gone. The skin no longer seemed to be stretched tight across the cheekbones. The mouth was no longer a narrow, lipless slit. The retracted lids no longer showed the whites of the eyes, making him look like a vicious horse. All the tension had gone out of the man, and for the first time she saw him looking normal and within not much more than five years of his real age.

The change startled Pat. She had got so used to the skull-like, abnormal Pharmakos, who was not really to be reckoned as a human being at all, but rather as some special creation, to whom none of the ordinary expectations could be applied, that the sudden appearance of a normal man, youngish, rather fine-looking, completely upset her calculations. This was a stranger and she felt shy with him. She had always been shy with men because her father never let her have anything to do with them, believing that since she was the child of sin her inclinations must naturally be sinful. She had never been shy with Pharmakos because he had not seemed to her like a man. But this was very much a man, and a young man too, Pat began to blush and dropped her eyes.

Pharmakos laughed softly. "Pat, you're coy," he said, and there was a curiously vibrant note in his usually flat, toneless voice.

Pat tossed her head and snorted. "I'm nothing of the sort!" she exclaimed. "And even if I were, I've no time for it. It's twelve o'clock and you haven't looked at your letters, and the breakfast is still on the table."

"That's right, Pat," said Pharmakos, "You keep me in order. I'm going to need it."

While Pat was clearing up the breakfast she heard Pharmakos phoning, and gathered from his conversation that he was cancelling appointments. What in the world was he up to now, she wondered.

She was soon to learn. He came prancing into the kitchen, seized her by the strings of her overall, which tied behind and swung her round. Pat howled and clutched her garments. For she had no frock on underneath her overall and was afraid she was going to fall bodily out of it.

"Go and put your bonnet on, Patsie!" chanted Pharmakos. "I have arranged for a week's holiday, and I am getting the old car out, and we are going junketting off in it, and you have got to learn to drive it."

Pharmakos shot out of the kitchen as precipitately as he had shot into it. Pat left her domesticities for Lamprey to attend to, and ran off to her own quarters to change her frock.

It is of the essence of an expedition of that kind that one flies off forthwith, without a lot of fussing and preparation. If Pharmakos had to cool his heels while she tidied up, half the joy would have gone out of it for him.

So quick was she that he was half in and half out of a very baggy pair of plus fours when she returned.

"Hi, Pat, you immodest young woman, why don't you knock?" he demanded.

"Good God," said Pat, " I was brought up on shirt-tails. They're no treat to me. Here are your braces. Now I suppose you've lost your collar-studs?"

They went swinging off, hand in hand, as gay as two birds. Just round the corner was a garage, and the proprietor, very surprised to see Pharmakos, helped him to get the dusty car out of its lock-up and attend to its needs; informing him *(a)* that he had given him up for dead, and *(b)* that he had taken him for his own younger brother as he came into the yard. The entire garage ran round with rags polishing the car and in an incredibly short space of time they were out on the road, with Pharmakos cutting in and out of the traffic and dodging round the near side of trams in a way that sent Pat's heart into her mouth, for her motoring had hitherto been confined to charabancs. His nerves might be all to pieces in the ordinary sense of the words, but his nerve left nothing to be desired.

The car at first sight was nothing much to look at, for it was painted the neutral drab of a Morris Cowley which does not show if you do not clean it. It was painted, moreover, with a dull paint, not a glossy one, and there were no bright metal parts. Neither was it pronouncedly stream-lined. It was, in fact, as meek and inconspicuous as a car well could be. But it had a very long bonnet and very big headlights, and was very low in the body, and a soft, mellow purr came from its engine; and these things told the expert that it was a thoroughbred; but those who judge a car by its coachwork would just have thought it another road-louse. It was, in fact, the proper kind of car for police work; inconspicuous, but effectual; and there was nothing on the road that could have got away from it when Pharmakos was at the wheel.

Pharmakos was like a child with a new toy, so delighted was he at the return of his nerve to drive his beloved car. He had told Pat that they would drive up to Ashdown Forest and then leave the car and go for a tramp; but when they got up on top of the first ridge, he was enjoying himself so much that he decided to go on to the next ridge; and when they got up there, they saw the sea in the distance, and Pharmakos exclaimed: "Come on, Pat, let's have a bathe," and sent the car flying down the long steep hill before she had time to express an opinion. She wondered anxiously how a bathe would affect him. She had seen him have one attack of cramp, and had no wish to see him have another. But she had been brought up with a pack of brothers, and knew better than to try and check a male when in full career on a hobby-horse.

They soon found themselves among the far-flung suburbs of Brighton, that metropolis by the sea-side; Pharmakos, who seemed intimately acquainted with its geography, drove up to a large female emporium, and marched in, with Pat in tow, and equipped her with a very exiguous emerald-green backless bathing-dress, which folded up into a parcel which went into her under-arm bag.

When he came to equip himself at a gentleman's outfitters, however, it did not prove to be so simple a matter. He wanted a bathing-dress that came high at the back, and in these nudist days it proved hard to find. Both Pat and the shopman wondered why he insisted on such extreme modesty. Then suddenly she remembered that scarred back she had seen by moonlight on the night of his terrible outburst and screaming, and it seemed as if something had hit her and half-stunned her. All the spontaneous joy was gone out of the expedition for the moment. But she pulled herself together, for she did not want to spoil his enjoyment.

All the same, it was a somewhat subdued pair that finally departed with a bulky parcel containing a black woollen affair left over from before the War, when it was still customary to cover a good deal of the body in public. Pharmakos was asking himself whether he was ever going to get to the end of his punishment. Was it always going to bob up and hit him at every turn? And in what unexpected places it hit him! Who could have imagined that he would have difficulty in getting a bathing-dress because he had been in prison?

All the joy seemed gone out of the expedition for him, too. His feet felt leaden as he walked with Pat towards the bathing place. He wondered what she would say if she knew he was marked for life as a criminal. He looked down at her, and as he did so, she looked up at him, and he saw by her eyes that she knew what was passing in his mind, and remembered the torn pyjama coat on the night of his outburst. Unnoticed in the crowded street she slipped her hand into his, and immediately peace came back to him. He gave Pat's hand a squeeze, and then pulled it through his arm, and away they went, happy again, and parted with laughter at the pay-box after sorting out their respective towels and tickets.

Pharmakos was out on the beach first. Males always are—! and he sat down on the pebbles to sun himself at a point where he could see the females of the species issue from their coop and go down the long matting path to the water. The beach was crowded at this spot, for watching the females of the species in a state that is practically that of nature was a popular occupation.

Presently out came Pat in her green bathing-dress.

"Shades of my maiden aunt!" murmured Pharmakos.

He had known that bathing-dress was going to be scanty, but he had not known it was going to be quite as scanty as all this. But Pat seemed quite unperturbed, and came stalking down the matting path over the pebbles with her little nose even more in the air than nature had made it, ignoring the greasy-eyed starers, and looking round for him.

She was looking right over his head towards the men's bathing enclosure, and it never occurred to her to look down at her feet among the crowd of odious oglers. Not seeing him, she wisely continued on her way to the water, for it was no place for a girl to loiter by herself. Pharmakos was half-enraged, half-flattered by the muttered comments that were going on all round him. Pat's milk-white, satiny limbs with the dimples in them were in striking contrast to those of the rest of the fair ones who had achieved the fashionable boyish figure and sun-tanned hide. She was evidently being regarded as the belle of the beach; Pharmakos saw cameras being got out and when first one, and then another, and then a third of the half-naked men around him arose from the pebbles in a leisurely fashion and began to stroll towards the water in Pat's wake, Pharmakos thought it was time to rise too.

"Oh, there you are!" said Pat as he came wading towards her through the shallow water. "Give me a hand, will you? I'm skidding on these pebbles."

Pat was an excellent bath swimmer, but she was not accustomed to breaking water, and Pharmakos had great fun teaching her the art of surf-bathing and all troubles were forgotten. Again and again they came out of the water and sunned themselves in the scorching sun, and again and again they returned to their play in the sea.

"Oh Lor', look at that!" exclaimed Pat, holding out towards him an arm with which he could see nothing wrong, though Pat appeared to be regarding it with the greatest concern. He examined It closely, and discovered that the white skin looked as if it had been sprayed with a fine golden powder. Pat had begun to freckle already.

Threatened by her *bête noir*, Pat entirely forgot the onlookers, and began to search herself all over like a puppy hunting fleas, calling on Phamlakos to examine her back and see if it were likewise afflicted. He reported all clear save for a party of seven, arranged after the manner of the Great Bear, upon a spot that is usually sat on.

Pat was relieved, for Pharmakos assured her that it would not show when she wore evening dress.

Pat rose up and demanded one more dip, but Pharmakos shook his head.

"I am getting a bit chilly, old thing. My vitals are not as well covered as yours. I think we had better pack up now."

"All right, you go and get dressed," said Pat, "And I'll have just one more swim."

"I shouldn't, if I were you, Pat. You'll find it pretty rough out there without me, and I don't want to hang about any longer and get chilled, You'll have every lounger on the beach eyeing you."

"Let 'em eye till their eyes drop out," said Pat. "Who cares two hoots?"

"I care several hoots. I hate having you stared at like this. We'll go to a quieter place next time."

Now Pat had thought that being admired was half the fun, and she cocked her head on one side and looked at Pharmakos quizzically. But she saw he was really serious, and although a bathing-dress does not lend itself to earnestness, she knew he had got to be taken seriously or his feelings would be hurt. Whether a woman cares more for her fun or his feelings is a very good test of her affection for a man, as he generally knows instinctively. Pat passed the test. She turned good-humouredly towards the dressing-enclosure with a farewell wave of her freckled hand to Pharmakos, to show that there was no ill-feeling.

He watched her go, noting her complete indifference to all the staring eyes and realised with a sudden shock that her viewpoint differed from his by a generation. He went striding off across the beach to the men's enclosure, stepping over recumbent families with his long legs as if they were not there, and no one remonstrated, for the expression of his face was not that of a man with whom it would be well to remonstrate.

He stood staring out over the brilliant blueness of the sea as he waited for Pat, and his face was not pleasant to look at; for it seemed to him that life was like a Rugger match with a bad referee. As soon as ever he got going, the whistle blew and pulled him up. While he had been hunting for Pat's freckles he had been doing mental arithmetic. If he had no nerve-storms for six months, would he be justified in marrying Pat, or ought he to wait the twelve months he had first determined on? And now, at the first hint of a check, he felt the old surging and whirling rising up within him, and it seemed to him that marriage with dear, lovely Pat was a thing he ought in common decency to put out of his head for ever. She was so innocent, so unsuspicious and carefree, that he had got to be worldly-wise for both. He had to be a mother to Pat as well as a lover, and it was a damned difficult undertaking now that the lover was beginning to get up speed. He had told himself once that Pat was as safe with him as with a dead man, but the dead man was sitting up in his coffin and taking notice. He would have to be going round to the registrar's and getting a special licence to make an honest woman of her if he weren't careful; and then Pat might find herself tied for life to a lunatic. He had got to be damned careful or he might inflict far worse injuries on his beloved than her bitterest enemy could contrive to do.

When Pat joined him, she found him rather glum; but she was so used to his moods by now that they did not disturb her. It was, as she had once told him, as if he had come out in a rash. She loved the real man underneath the come-and-go of the surface moods. When he was moody and irritable, she merely cast about in her mind for some artifice to exorcise his blue devil. She had soon discovered that the easiest way to exorcise Pharmakos was to flirt with him. When she did this, he succumbed without a struggle and danced to whatever tune she piped.

He was perfectly well aware of her manoeuvres being exceedingly shrewd and observant; but that made no difference to his surrender. He was as putty in Pat's hands, and knew it. It was odd that a man with an eagle nose and a pugnacious jaw should not have resented being putty in anybody's hands; but when between that nose and chin there is a sensitive, mobile mouth, that man is preordained to be putty in the hands of some woman or other, and God help him if it is not the right woman, for his masterful jaw will avail him nothing. The enemy is within the camp.

It amused Pharmakos to realise that if Pat had been a designing minx instead of what she was, she could have taken fur coats and diamond rings out of him till his pockets were empty, and he would have given with both hands and his eyes shut. He could never have resisted her wiles. But as it was, he had to steel himself against Pat's deliberate blandishments in order to prevent the child from flinging away her future and her happiness upon his unworthy self with a complete disregard of anything except his welfare. If anything could have made him struggle against Pat's wiles, it was that; in fact, it enabled him to hang on to his sulks for nearly an hour, while Pat alternately coaxed and tossed her head. But in the end she got the better of him and grew radiant as his good resolutions melted like snow in summer and he yielded himself up to her innocent luring and began to fondle her.

They had dinner on a terrace overlooking a sea silvered by Pharmakos' old enemy, the moon, for which at the moment he cared not even Pat's two hoots, for he was engaged in rubbing ankles with her under cover of the table, and stroking her hand under cover of the menu, and generally misconducting himself.

Pat was in the seventh heaven, and when he pulled up the car on top of a ridge and kissed her, she felt that God was in His heaven and all was right in the best of all possible worlds. She had no chance to do any thinking, for Pharmakos drove like a man inspired, handling the big, powerful car as if it were a bicycle; but she was too exhilarated with happiness to feel any nervousness, moreover she had such complete confidence in him, that if he had proposed to drive it across Niagara on a plank, she would have acquiesced serenely.

However, his mood had changed by the time they had arrived back at Quilp Cottage, and when she put up her face serenely to receive a good night kiss, for she considered that they were as good as engaged, she received a peck on the scalp that nearly cracked her skull, and Pharmakos wished her a hasty and rather cross good night, thrust her into her own quarters with a push, and slammed the door after her. But even that did not prevent her from sitting up in bed and hugging her knees after she had put out the light, and singing softly to herself in an ecstasy of happiness, "I love him, I love him, I love him!"

Pharmakos, for his part, was doing exactly the same thing, only the burden of his song was, "You bloody fool! You bloody fool!"

CHAPTER XXIV

LONG before that week's holiday was over, Pharmakos was praying for the end of it. Pat was so overflowing with love and happiness, so serenely certain that any attempt on his part to keep her at arm's length was merely one of his sick moods, out of which he needed to be beguiled, that he was at his wit's end to know how to comport himself as a decent man should. There were times when he was on the verge of yielding to temptation and going round to the registrar's office and putting down a couple of pounds for a special licence and taking his beloved to his arms forthwith. Then his better self prevailed and he angrily cursed himself; at least let him see another full moon out before he did anything. He had still got Jurgens hanging over his head; any untoward incident might capsize his precarious mental balance, and while in one of his crazy states he might do something that would place him permanently behind asylum bars. Then Pat might find herself tied for life to a lunatic, and penniless, for he would not be able to earn anything if his mind gave way. He had no savings invested. His income depended on his health.

When his better self prevailed he treated poor Pat to bouts of bad temper that Skilly described to Lamprey as fair eye-openers. But nothing made any difference to Pat; at worst, she retired to her own quarters for half an hour, to reappear serene and unruffled but with a heavily powdered face. Pharmakos knew perfectly well why the powder had been plastered on to Pat's usually clear skin, and cursed himself savagely, and when one day Skilly ventured on a protest, "Here, go easy, governor!" he suddenly went for him, and it was only the quickness of the ex-pug that saved Pharmakos from doing another murder. After these outbreaks, which day by day increased in severity, Pharmakos, in utter despair, would go to Pat, and kneel down beside her and put his head in her lap without a word and let her soothe him.

Finally, he could bear no more. He must have something to do to occupy his mind and work off his energies, or he would not be responsible for what would happen.

"Pat" he said on Saturday morning, "Do you remember your friend Mr. Walter Simmons? Shall we go and look him up?"

"What do you want to look him up for?" asked Pat, disgusted at having her pseudo-honeymoon interrupted.

"I don't particularly want to, but I think it is my duty to a rather pathetic client to do so. You see, the amiable Mr. Simmons is wanting to divorce his lady wife. Personally, I should have thought she was well rid of him at any price, but he proposes to bag the kids, and she, being a mother, considers that price too high even for the pleasures of his absence."

"Has he got a case against her?" asked Pat, trying to take an interest.

"Unfortunately, yes. Having been a negligent husband for years, he suddenly became concerned for her health and packed her off to the seaside for a change of air. At the shady hotel to which he consigned her, an exceedingly dashing gentleman became enamoured with her rather faded charms and seduced the poor lady, being caught in the act by a chambermaid. Said dashing gent vanishes into space forthwith and cannot be traced. At least, I have failed to trace him and anyone has got to do a pretty slick get-away to get away from me. One would have expected everything to have settled down after that, but not a bit of it. This rather shady hotel gets a sudden attack of virtue, and chucks poor Mrs. Walter into the street, bag and baggage. Mr. Walter arrives down on a surprise visit to his wife and finds her in process of being chucked out. All most unfortunate and unlucky. In fact, so unfortunate and unlucky that the solicitor who was preparing her defence came to the conclusion that the whole thing was a put-up job and sent for me."

"Do you think the hotel belonged to him?" asked Pat.

"Well, I don't know about belonging to him, but he has certainly got his foot in there all right."

"I believe that beastly house belonged to him," said Pat.

"What makes you think that, Patsie?"

"Because the bruiser person said that if the telegram came to more than the shilling I gave him, he could put it down in the petty cash."

"I expect you're right. It probably does belong to him, but we would never be able to prove it. There is always some dummy between the man higher up and the actual business in places like that. He probably owns a whole chain of places, and the hotel is one of them. Shrewd little puss, aren't you? That is a line which might be worth following up, though it is sure to be well defended. We shall probably find that some wretched Mrs. Smith, who couldn't push a pram, owns the one place; and a miserable Mr. Jones, who couldn't run a whelk stall, owns the other, and neither of them have ever heard of Mr. Walter Simmons. I've played this game so often, Pat, I know the moves before they make 'em.

"No, our most promising line of advance is to follow up the address we got via the telegram. Walter obviously wants to get rid of his wife. Consequently, he probably wants to legalise a relationship with someone else. He is away from home on business a great deal, including week-ends; and nobody knows where he goes at the week-ends, though he is easy enough to trace during the week-middles. My guess therefore is that he visits his fair intended, and is jolly careful to cover his tracks.

"He is interested in theatrical matters, and when he proposes to do a getaway, he simply drops in at one of the theatres he is connected with, and you know how many exits there are to a theatre, Pat, I can't surround the place with a squad of police as Saunders could if he wanted to take him. Walter simply disappears into thin air and turns up again on Monday morning.

"My guess is that as he only visits his inamorata at weekends, she too is working, for he is his own boss, and could take time off whenever he had a mind to. As he is interested in the stage, my guess is that she is an actress; a mighty change from the poor little woman whom I am trying to fish out of the soup.

"Now, if we can catch him red-handed with this donah, his case against Mrs. Walter goes down the drain. Moreover, if We can by hook or by crook follow up your idea, which I begin to like the more, the more I think of it, and prove that he is in any way connected with that blinking hotel where the poor lady was done brown, we have him on toast, and she could probably get the court to exercise its discretion in her favour, and bag the kids and the cash and get shut of Walter.

"Now, my dear, I propose to employ your noted charms to land the poor fellow. For if I walk up to the front door of their little love-nest at Maidenhead and ring the bell, they will not be at home; but if you in your best hat, and me in my best suit stroll up about tea-time, we may get a glimpse of them, and a glimpse is all we need, just enough to enable me to swear to Mr. Walter S. for two tweaks in the witness box, and the job is done and the poor lady gets her kids and cash. Are you game, Patsie?"

Was she game? Need he ask? Need anyone ask?

"Well, now, my sweetheart, since we are going to call upon theatricals, we must give a theatrical touch to ourselves or we shall not be welcome. I propose to sally forth with you in the direction of the West End, my Patsie, and procure for you garments that shall strike the right note."

Pat was immensely amused at Pharmakos' procedure in the shop to which he took her. So were the shop assistants. It was not the first time they had seen a gentleman purchase intimate garments for a lady, but never before had they seen a gentleman who did the job so grimly. If he had been ordering Pat's coffin he could not have been more unbending in his demeanour. In the end Pat sallied forth into the sunshine clad in a pale yellow organdie frock that stood out like a crinoline, and a wide-brimmed hat to match (which soon had to be taken off and put in the dickey, wrapped in a newspaper which Pharmakos purchased especially from a grinning vendor); all topped off with a loose white foxaline wrap about her shoulders, which made her look as if she were off to Ascot. Pharmakos himself was looking exceedingly doggy in a suit of shepherd's plaid checks. Between them, they appeared as if about to do a turn at a music hall.

Arriving at Maidenhead, they had no difficulty in locating "The Willows," whose name had been faintly indented on the blank telegraph form to which Pharmakos had helped himself at the Maida Vale post office. It proved to be the abode of a Mr. and Mrs. Forrest. Mr. Forrest was in poor health, and was ordered by his doctor to have a complete rest at week-ends and see no one. Pharmakos winked at Pat when this information was obtained from a local tobacconist.

They drove a little way out of Maidenhead, and then turned as instructed into an unmade road, little more than a cart-track through a wood, and found it was a blind alley leading to a mock Tudor cottage surrounded by an unkempt garden.

They walked boldly up to the front door and rang the bell. Pat heard faint sounds from within, and judged that someone on tiptoe was crossing the hall to inspect them. As instructed by Pharmakos, she had turned her back to the house after ringing the bell, and the drooping organdie hat hid her face; therefore all that the observer from behind the curtain could see was that there was a showily dressed girl accompanied by a loudly dressed man who wore his hat at a rakish angle. Mrs. Forrest had no means of knowing that the girl was not one of her own theatrical pals, whom it would be unwise to offend, even if the man were a stranger, so she opened the door, and when the girl in the big hat turned round and presented an unfamiliar face, it was too late to draw back.

"Mrs. Forrest?" said Pat as instructed, with her sweetest smile, "May I introduce myself? My name is Miss Stone, and this is my brother. We are your next-door neighbours through the wood, though it is a long way round by the road, and we have come to call on you. Are you at home?"

Mrs. Forrest could not very well say she wasn't, so she put the best face she could on it, and asked them in.

They found themselves in an untidy, undusted drawing-room, which looked as if Mrs. Forrest dispensed with the ministrations of servants over the week-end and had a grand clean-up on a Monday.

Pat having finished the usual opening nothings of new acquaintances concerning the weather and the locality, Pharmakos chipped in.

"Is your husband in, Mrs. Forrest? We are really combining business with pleasure in this visit. I want to see him about a matter that is of mutual importance to us as neighbours."

Mrs. Forrest looked uncommunicative.

"My husband is very overworked at present," she said. "The doctor has ordered him complete rest at the week-ends.

Perhaps you could tell me what it is that you want to see him about, and I will talk it over with him."

"Well Mrs. Forrest, I am going up to London to-morrow morning early, and I shall have to give a yes or no answer to the people I am in negotiation with. I am sorry I cannot give you time in which to make up your minds, but to tell you the honest truth, it never occurred to, me to give you the offer until my sister mentioned It. I hadn't realised that your house stood where it did, you are so effectually hidden in this wood. But my sister said it would make your house almost uninhabitable if I sold that plot to these sportive policemen—"

"These what—?" exclaimed Mrs. Forrest, suddenly on the alert.

"The Metropolitan Police Sports Association, to give them their full title. They want the bit of ground between you and the river to put up a boat-club, and they will have to use the same road as you to get to it. My sister thought you might find them rather noisy neighbours, and suggested that I should give you the first refusal of the plot at the same price I am asking them, which is eighty pounds." .

"When do you want to know by?" said Mrs. Forrest.

"Well, I had hoped to be able to take an answer away with me now. In fact, if it is to be yes, it must be now, because I have an appointment with their surveyor chap to-morrow morning, and I have got to tell him yes or no myself."

"I'll speak to my husband," said Mrs. Forrest, and vanished so precipitately that Pharmakos knew that the cottage must be something more than a love-nest. They obviously did not want policemen, not even policemen off duty and sportive, to be wandering around in the neighbourhood of their premises. In laying his plans, Pharmakos had been at considerable pains to think out what they would dislike most, and had wavered between a sewage farm and a children's convalescent home but he judged that in choosing the M.P.S.A. he had really touched the spot. There was everything against it that there possibly could be. It was noisy; it was numerous; and it was sharp-eyed.

They heard the sound of voices in anxious discussion, for the cottage was mock-old, not the genuine article and the walls were of the usual flimsy riverside bungalow construction. Pharmakos winked at Pat and she giggled. Then they heard heavy footsteps in the little hall, and Mrs. Forrest reappeared, followed by a big, heavily-built man with a pale, square face and high cheek-bones. His eyes were of that pale, steely blue that is not seen among Anglo-Saxons.

Pat heard a sudden, gasping sound from Pharmakos, and the bulky stranger came to an abrupt standstill in the doorway. With a quick instinct of danger, Pat rose to her feet; but she was sharp-witted in an emergency, and kept her head. This was an emergency; she felt sure. She had heard Pharmakos gasp, and guessed that they had come out shooting rabbits and put up a tiger. She did not know what Phannakos' nerves were going to be like in an emergency, and she felt it was up to her to pull the situation out of the fire if it were possible to do so; or at any rate to create a diversion and give him a chance to pull himself together.

"Mr. Forrest?" she said, with her pleasantest smile, stepping in front of Pharmakos as she held out her hand to greet him. He took it in a large, leathery fist, that felt as if it would have a grip of steel if it closed on her. He looked at her closely and unsmilingly, and then turned his pale, cold eyes on Pharmakos.

"I think I have seen you before," he said.

"I was just thinking the same thing," said Pharmakos affably, and Pat heaved a sigh of relief and she realised that he had got himself in hand.

"And I know where I have seen you before, too," said Mr.

Forrest.

"You have the advantage of me there," said Pharmakos.

"You came to my house in Hampstead two years ago, in the company of a man called, Skilly, and there is a warrant out for your arrest."

" I beg your pardon?"

"There is a warrant out for your arrest," said the man steadily. "And it is no good denying identity because there were finger-marks."

"I have not got a notion what you are talking about, but I don't allow people to talk to me like that. The offer of the plot is withdrawn, Mr. Forrest, and I hope the police give a party every night of the week. Come along, Pat."

He held the door open for her, and she sailed out, her organdie skirts billowing all around her, her nose in the air, not deigning to give a glance at the glowering Forrests.

They went down the garden path without a word and Pharmakos started up the car, still in silence. It was not until they were back in the main road that he spoke.

"Know who that was, Pat?"

"Jurgens," said Pat.

"Yes" said Pharmakos. "The thing which I greatly feared has come upon me. I believe it always does. You sort of hook it to you by being scared of it. Keep a lookout behind, will you, Pat, and see if we are being followed."

But nothing save aeroplanes could have followed Pharmakos.

Eventually they stopped their mad career at a riverside hotel and went into the tea-garden.

"Tea for you, I suppose, Pat?" said Pharmakos, "But I am going to break my usual rule and have something stronger. I have got to get you back to town to-night somehow, and I am missing on half my cylinders. I was a damn fool not to teach you to drive while I had the chance."

As they sat waiting for her tea and his brandy and soda, he held out his long, lean hand with the scarred wrist at arm's length toward her. It was perfectly steady.

"Not much the matter with that, is there, Pat?" he said. "I can face up to the thing that is actually happening all right, but if I get imagining the possible consequences I shall go all loopy, and then God help us."

Pat noticed that he drove back to town steadily and tentatively, like a novice, in marked contrast to his usual style of driving, which was almost criminally bold. He heaved a sigh of relief when he had got the car safely into the garage.

"Thank God for that," he said, "There was a drop-scene in front of my eyes all the time I was driving, and I never knew when it was going to come down with a run and blot everything out, and then I should have driven into the first thing that came handy."

When they got back to Quilp Cottage, Pat suggested supper, but Pharmakos declined.

"No good offering anything to my tummy at the present moment, I've had a shake-up, Pat. But I tell you what I wish you would do, get a fire going, there's a good lass. I'm cold."

Pat was perspiring in her thin organdie frock after the walk from the garage, but she got the lire going for him without protest, and he sat huddled over it in the gathering dusk, staring into the flames.

"This won't do," he said at length, heaving himself out of his chair. "I shall get the wind up if I sit and think. Let's dance, Pat, I'll get the gramophone out."

So they danced in the big room, lit here and there by the gorgeous lamps, its far corners full of shadows. They danced till Pat was footsore and weary, striving to keep the devils of panic fear at bay.

CHAPTER XXV

THE days that followed were difficult ones in Quilp Cottage. There were no more tantrums, it is true, but there was something that Pat liked a great deal less-a kind of remoteness about Pharmakos, as if he were living in another world. From time to time he returned as if with an effort, and in a sudden burst of fiery energy tackled things that had to be tackled; but his energy was short-lived, and his memory for details dangerously uncertain, and his confusion of names laid all sorts of pitfalls for unwary solicitors.

He paid no attention to anybody except Pat, and to her he was no longer a lover but a fretful child. Saunders came and looked at him and shook his head, and when told of the finger-prints, whistled and made no reply.

Pharmakos would not go out for fear of being seen and recognised by Jurgens: emissaries, who were certain to be making a search for him; and he would not be left alone, consequently Pat could not go out either. Such fresh air and exercise as they got was obtained by pacing up and down the path between the warehouse and the water; and as this path was narrow, the person next to the water was walking on a space no wider than a kerb. As Pharmakos never looked where he was going, Pat saw to it that she had the outside edge. She did not mind this when the tide was up, and the dock full to the brim, but the twenty-foot drop to the foul Thames mud was a most unpleasant neighbour when the tide was out.

Indoors, Pharmakos paced the great room from end to

end in a moody silence. He wore a path with his feet on the polish of the parquetry which in the end not even Lamprey's elbow-grease could efface.

No letters would have been attended to if Pat had not extracted instructions from him by means of cross-examination, and when the typed letters were put before him for signature, he wrote his name upon one after the other without even looking at them. Fortunately for him, business was slack at the moment, for all London was away on holiday in the summer heats and the law courts were in vacation.

It was now that Skilly and Lamprey showed the mettle of their pasture. When it was suggested to Skilly that he should disappear into the underworld till the trouble was over and so avoid being involved in Jurgens vengeance, he had sworn so long and so viciously that even Pharmakos had been roused from his apathy and burst out laughing.

Pat was very grateful to the bigamous burglar for his fidelity, for he and Lamprey stood watch and watch, never leaving her to contend with Pharmakos single-handed.

But though Skilly was as faithful as a dog, he was little more than that, for he had not the intelligence. It was here that Lamprey rose to the occasion, showing a very pretty turn of shrewdness, and he and Pat ran Pharmakos' enquiry agency between them. But though they could get the routine work done all right, they could not do the necessary interviewing. It was here that, as Pharmakos had foreseen, he badly needed the right sort of partner.

Pharmakos spoke seldom, paying less and less attention even to Pat as the days went by. Once he said suddenly, pacing at dusk in the shadowy room: "Now you see why I wouldn't marry you, don't you, Pat? Where would you be if you were tied to me now?"

Pat found her wiles wasted on him during these dark days.

Once, and once only did he show a trace of his old affection for her, when suddenly pausing in his pacing, he took her in his arms, apropos of nothing, and said:

"Oh, Pat, it would be so easy if it weren't for you!" and then let go of her, and turned away without waiting for a reply and resumed the ceaseless back and forth.

When Pat told Skilly of this he scratched his head, and as usual referred the problem to Lamprey.

Lamprey seemed to regard it as a good sign, however. "It is 'opeful as long as 'e 'as difficulty in going hout, miss, for previous we 'ave always 'ad great difficulty in keeping 'im 'ere at all!"

"Where does he propose to go to?" asked Pat in perplexity.

"Some would say 'Ell," said Skilly, "but I should say 'Eaven meself, even if 'e does commit susan-side, for 'e's 'ad 'Ell enough 'ere."

"But-but-how will he do it, Skilly?" asked Pat aghast.

"You seen that ring 'e wears? 'Is big Booja ring?"

"The ring with the little lobsters on it?"

"Yus. That's a Booja ring, that is."

"What's a Booja ring?"

"It used to belong to a feller called Booja, an Ey-talian. 'E was a Pope's pup, 'e was, and they're allus the worst sort. Look 'ow a parson's kids allus turns out! Wot d'yer expect of a Pope's kids? It don't do to bring kids up too strict, I sez."

"Oh, never mind the Pope. What about Mr. Pharmakos' ring?"

"Well, I'm telling you. It' s a Booja pizon-ring. They was all pizoners, they wuz, them Boojas, Pope and all. Same as Armstrong and Seddons and them fellers. It ran in the family."

"But what about the ring?"

"It's full o' pizon, Cop. That stone's a fake, and slides back, and there's pizon inside it. When 'e's arrested, 'e'll lick it, and whiz-bang, 'e's gone, same as Whittaker Wright."

Pat felt her knees giving way under her, but she pulled herself together with an effort, and managed to sit down safely in a kitchen chair.

Lamprey saw her distress and hastily made amends.

"Don't you fret too much, miss. If 'e 'ad meant to commit suicide over this, 'e would 'ave done it by now. 'E wouldn't 'ave waited. It's you 'e's 'anging on to, miss. You 'ang on to 'im, and 'e won't do it unless 'e's druv to it."

Pat returned to the great room and went up to Phannakos where he was pacing, and put her hands on his shoulders.

"Julian," she said, "will you do something for me?"

There was something in her voice that roused him. "What is it, Pat?" he said.

"Will you give me your Borgia ring to keep for you?"

He turned his face away and looked out of the window for a long time without speaking.

"Don't ask me that, Patsie," he said at length. "I must have some way out as a last resource. I cannot face a lifetime in an asylum."

"Then will you remember, Julian, that I have no one except you, and nowhere to go if you leave me?"

His face was suddenly convulsed. "Oh, Patsie, aren't I remembering it every minute?"

At that moment the telephone bell rang, and Pharmakos, with an oath, picked up the instrument. Pat took advantage of his preoccupation to vanish to her own quarters and have the relief of a good cry.

"Is that you, Pharmakos? This is Otway speaking. How are you?"

"A bit rocky. I am not taking on any fresh cases at the moment."

"This isn't a case. It's a young fellow making enquiries about your typist. He says he's a friend of the family, and I rather suspect he's an old flame of hers. I think he's genuine, myself. I have cross-examined him pretty rigorously. He's a lad in quite a good position, if what he says is true, and I don't suppose it isn't, because it could be so easily verified. That is the girl that is mentioned in your will, isn't it? What would you like us to do in the matter? Shall we put him on to you?"

Pharmakos thought so long over his answer, that Sir Charles Otway came to the conclusion that they had been cut off, and demanded angrily of Exchange what it was up to.

At length, Pharmakos spoke. "Where is this chap? Is he with you at the moment?"

"He is in the outer office. Would you like to come round and see him?"

"Yes, Otway, I would if I may. I feel that I am practically this girl's guardian, and I should like to have a look at the fellow before I let him loose on her. I say, Otway? How did he come to turn up at your place?"

"He went to your old office and the porter put him on to us. He naturally would as your letters come here."

"Do you know whether the porter told him anything about my record?"

"No, I don't think so for a moment. We put the fear of God into that porter for you, believe me. But this young Matthews knows who you are. He has an enormous respect for you, too."

"How did he come to know who I am, and how in God's name does he come to have any respect for me?"

"My dear chap, you are as well known over here as Pinkerton in America. You can't hide your light under a bushel."

"All right, Otway, I'll be round in about twenty minutes, if you'll be good enough to tell the chap to wait."

Pharmakos took his hat and went out without telling Pat.

He felt at that moment, with the resolution that was in his mind taking shape and form, that he could not bear to see her. Neither did he arrive at Sir Charles Otway's offices in the promised twenty minutes, for he walked all the way instead of picking up a taxi, for he felt he had need to get his poor addled brains to work as best they would.

One thing was perfectly clear, if this young fellow turned out to be all that Otway had led him to believe, the best thing Pat could do was to marry him, as she probably would have done if he, Pharmakos, had not come upon the scene and swept her off her feet.

The best thing for Pat, and the best thing for him; for then the rending, tearing conflict would be over, and he could give himself up to the peace and relief of death by his own hand, painlessly. As Pharmakos walked, the resolution grew on him. It merely required the determination to endure whatever laceration of his feelings there might be during the process of the handing over of Pat, and then—peace, and the ending of all his problems—his prison record, Jurgens, his hopeless love for Pat—everything—. And then peace, silence, sleep. Pharmakos had not had much sleep lately, and the more he thought of the idea, the more it appealed to him.

It almost seemed to him that in this sleep of death he might possess Pat in dream, without all the perplexing problems that beset the possession of Pat in reality. If he sacrificed Pat in the wake-world, he would possess her in the dream-world.

The idea grew on him almost to obsession. He was not giving Pat away to this young fellow. He was simply translating her to another plane of existence. As soon as her physical life was safely off his hands, he would cross the Great Divide and there she would be waiting him.

His only problems were to persuade Pat to accept this young fellow in spite of her affection for himself and to sidetrack her with regard to his intention to commit suicide.

Pharmakos' mind was clear enough now, or so he thought, for it was working with a lunatic cunning and facility now that he saw a way to settle all his problems at once.

He arrived at the shabby old building where Sir Charles Otway had his offices, and leapt up the liftless stairs three at a time, an utterly different man to the one Pat had been wrestling with for the last ten days.

Young Leonard Matthews, waiting in the dingy little cupboard called a waiting-room, suddenly looked up to see a very tall, very lean, Red Indian-looking man standing over him and frowning down at him. He rose to his feet as if jerked by a string, he knew not why; this was evidently no clerk with a message.

"My name is Julian Pharmakos. I am told you wish to see me about a typist in my employment. Will you be good enough to state your business?"

Now, Leonard Matthews was in actual age only seven years younger than Pharmakos, but so strongly did he receive the impression of being in the presence of seniority and authority that he involuntarily addressed the older man as sir; a mode of address he had not used since he left school. Moreover, he stuttered and lost the thread of his words under the gaze of those steely, grey-green eyes, deep-set under their heavy thatch of rust-coloured brows. He had never in his life met a man like this before at close quarters. His usually cocksure self was simply flattened out by the other's mere presence.

Pharmakos stood silent, waiting for an answer, and the young fellow in front of him pulled himself together with an effort.

"My—my name is Matthews, Leonard Matthews, and I happen to—to know Miss Stone, and I—I should like to get in touch with her again since she has left home."

"Are you known to her family, Mr. Matthews?"

"Oh, yes, yes, I know them well. We were practically brought up together."

"Was it Mr. Stone who gave you the address of my office?"

"Er—no, it wasn't exactly. It was one of the youngsters. I didn't like to ask him. You see, there's been a bit of a mix-up. He always thought I was after Helen, the eldest; but as a matter of fact, I was after Pat. So I didn't dare ask him for Pat's address after she cleared out—."

"Was turned out, you mean," said Pharmakos dryly.

"No? By Jove, was she really? Old man Stone told me she had run away from home."

"If Mr. Stone told you that he is a liar. He turned her out of the house without notice and without money, and I have made it my business ever since to see that she came to no harm. I look upon myself as her guardian as well as her employer, under the circumstances, and I am therefore going to take the liberty of satisfying myself as to your bona-fides before I agree to put you in touch with her. What is your purpose in seeking out Miss Stone, Mr. Matthews? I expect you to answer me as you would her father if he asked you that question."

Leonard Matthews was more than relieved to find that the formidable Pharmakos was taking this fatherly attitude. He had been led by Mr. Stone to believe that he had stolen Pat away from her home and made her his mistress. At first sight he had thought from his alert bearing that Pat's employer was a comparatively young man, and therefore a potential rival; but now he had had a good look at him, he judged by his lined face that he was getting on for sixty.

Nothing could have been more ideal from his point of view. If this employer fellow were disposed to be favourable, and Leonard could imagine no possible reason why he should not be, he had a far better chance of getting hold of Pat than he had in the midst of the odious Stone family, whose one idea was to make a Cinderella of her and push the heavy and featureless Helen on to him.

"Well, Mr. Pharmakos, I will tell you exactly what my position is. Er—may we sit down?"

"Certainly," said Pharmakos, seating himself and motioning Leonard to do likewise. Leonard was beginning to feel as if he were in the presence of royalty. Oddly enough, he did not resent the feelmg as he normally would have done, but found himself solely concerned with the impression he was making on this dignified stranger who had impressed him so profoundly.

Pharmakos looked at him expectantly, and he felt as if he were standing up to say his piece in front of an audience.

"Er—it's this way, Mr. Pharmakos. I should like to marry Miss Stone. Miss Pat Stone, that is," he added hastily, as if the terror of having Helen thrust upon him still overshadowed his mind.

"May I ask what your position is, Mr. Matthews? Are you in a position to provide for her adequately?"

"Er—yes. Yes, I think I may say I am. My father was the senior partner in Matthews and Elton, the brokers. He died recently. I am the only son. The only child, in fact. Our business is, of course, a fluctuating business, as are all Stock Exchange concerns, but much less fluctuating than the firm Mr. Stone is in. We carry a big reserve, and the partners average what they take out year by year. My share comes to between eight and ten thousand a year on the average, out of which I have to pay two thousand to my mother during her lifetime."

"Who runs the business?" asked Pharmakos, wondering how long the young man's share would come to between eight and ten thousand now that the father's steadying hand was withdrawn.

"My uncle runs it. For all practical purposes I am a sleeping partner. I suppose I could take the reins if I chose, but I don't understand the business, have no head for it in fact, so I leave it to my uncle. He can't make money for himself without making it for me, as we are partners."

"Can't he, though!" thought Pharmakos to himself. "You don't know the world, my young cub. No one is going to make money for long out of a business he doesn't take the trouble to understand."

"If you marry Miss Stone," he said aloud, "I presume you would be willing to make an adequate settlement on her? I consider this essential in view of the speculative nature of your business. I myself have left her something in my will, but not a great deal. I have other claims on me."

"Yes, rather;" said young Matthews, delighted at the turn events were taking. He felt he had a strong ally in Pat's employer. This death's head of a chap was no rival for Pat's affections. Very decent of him to remember Pat in his will. Pat might drop in for that legacy before very long, too. The fellow looked as If he had one foot in the grave.

"Very good, then. I will instruct Sir Charles Otway to make the necessary arrangements with regard to settlements with you, when the time comes. Meanwhile, the decision must rest with Miss Stone, I will tell her I have seen you, and she can write you if she has a mind to. If not, that is her affair. She has your address, I presume?"

"Yes, she has my address, but—er—I think it would be better if she did not write there just at first. You see, it might upset my mother. Tell her to write me care of the tobacconist at the corner of the road. She'll know."

"Now look here, Mr. Matthews, I don't like this business of an accommodation address. You have got to treat Miss Stone properly. Make up your mind what you mean to do, and stand up to it like a man. Don't play about like this. Does your mother open your letters?"

"No, she doesn't exactly open my letters, but if she sees an unfamiliar handwriting, she always asks who it is from. I don't want to upset her, you see, until Pat and I get things definitely settled. She'll be quite all right then."

"Well, Mr. Matthews, whether she is, or whether she isn't, I won't have Miss Stone played about with. So you had better make up your mind what you mean to do before you start. For if there is any nonsense, I shall have something to say on the subject, and I shall say it to your uncle."

"Yes, Mr. Pharmakos," said young Matthews miserably. He had no intention whatever of playing about with Pat. He was much too scared of Pat's red-headed temper, anyway; there was no need for this brute to bully him.

"Very well, I will have a talk with Miss Stone, and you will hear from either her or myself in due course, and I have no doubt your mother will ask her to come to see her in the near future."

"Yes, Mr. Pharmakos," said young Matthews again, even more miserably, wondering anxiously how his mother would be induced to receive even a putative Stone civilly. For receive her she must; Leonard had for once met someone he was more scared of than he was of his mother.

CHAPTER XXVI

PHARMAKOS did not walk back to Quilp Cottage, but took a taxi. He felt as if he were up for the first time after a long illness. The fire that had flared up in his mind during the interview with Leonard Matthews was beginning to die down; but he must keep it alive until he had had a talk with Pat and put everything in train. How would Pat take it? She would probably upheave at first, but she was young, and once married to Leonard, and with himself out of the way, she would get over it and settle down. This Leonard Matthews looked a decent enough young fellow, and he would certainly be easy to manage. Pat would be able to put him around her little finger.

Arrived back at Quilp Cottage, he went straight up the winding stone stairs to his big room. Pat, if she were in her own quarters, always gave him a call as she heard his footsteps passing her window. Therefore, not hearing any call, he presumed she was upstairs.

But she was not, and when he looked in kitchen and bathroom and failed to find her, a sudden misery welled up in him. Where was she? Why had she gone out and left him just when he needed her so much? And then there came the agonising realisation that he was making all arrangements to cut himself off from Pat for ever, and his brain whirled as if he were on a spinning disc and the room disappeared from his sight in spiral streaks of mist.

When his sight cleared again, he found Pat standing before him looking at him enquiringly. She had evidently been speaking to him, and obtaining no answer. He must strike now while the iron was hot; for if he once let himself cool down, he would never be able to do it. And it was so much best done; and once done, he would be at peace.

"I want to talk to you, Pat," he said, "about a matter of importance."

Pat's heart sank. Something drastic had happened, she could see that by his face. She had never seen him look quite like this before. All his lethargy was gone, and there was an odd kind of excited exaltation about him that she did not understand, and mistrusted.

He dropped into his big arm-chair and signed to her to seat herself in the other, on the opposite side of the fire-place. There was to be no curling up together on the big divan this time. Pat seated herself as she was bidden and looked at him anxiously.

"Do you know a man called Leonard Matthews?" he began abruptly.

So this is it! thought Pat. An attack of jealousy.

"Yes, know him well. He's one of Helen's flames. Her bright particular, in fact."

"On the contrary, he says he's one of yours."

"Then he's a dying flame if that's the case. I've no particular use for him."

Pharmakos was prepared for opposition, and had made up his mind to butt straight through it. The sooner this thing was over, and he could seek the mercy of oblivion, the better, for he could not stand much more. He might be handling Pat roughly at the moment, but it was the most merciful thing in the long run.

"Now, look here, Pat. This young fellow has been to see me, and he wants to marry you. He seems to be a decent, well-set-up young chap, and quite well off, and in my opinion the best thing you could do would be to marry him."

Pat went as white as a sheet and stared at him wordlessly.

He continued:

"Pat, we've just got to make up our minds that there can never be anything doing between you and me. Therefore the sooner we make the clean break the better. If I have you safely off my hands and provided for, it gives me a chance to do a getaway from Jurgens. With you on my hands, I can't."

"That's all right," said Pat quietly. "I'll get some sort of a job right away. Domestic work or something. One can always get that. There is no need for me to marry Leonard in order to get me off your hands."

"I should be much happier if I left you safely married to Matthews," said Phannakos irritably. "Jobs are not so easy to get nowadays, and pretty hard work when you get them."

Pat knew that.

"And you've got no home behind you now, in case you are out of a job or ill. I shan't be here because I—am going away —abroad."

"Do you think it would be fair to marry one man while caring for another?" asked Pat in the same low voice.

Pharmakos was relieved. The only fault he had ever found with Pat was that she was a weeper, which he hated because it unmanned him. But there were evidently not going to be any tears over this transaction.

But although he was relieved, he was also more than a little hurt. Pat ought not to have taken the proposed transfer of her affection quite so philosophically. It was not very complimentary.

"Don't talk nonsense, Pat," he said crossly, to cover his emotion. "You will soon get over me when once I am out of your sight. You are too young for anything to have gone deeply. What you have got is a crush on me, not a love affair."

"You can call it what you like," said Pat, still with the same unemotional quiet. "But I feel as if it had gone pretty deeply. No, I won't marry Leonard, but I won't be a burden to you. I will get busy to-morrow and unload myself as soon as ever I can."

And with that Pharmakos had to be satisfied for the moment. Though he, told himself he would return to the attack again, and probably with more success when Pat found for herself how difficult it was to get a job in these hard times. One thing was quite certain, he could not possibly do away with himself until he had seen Pat safely provided for. What he could leave her was not enough to provide for her. He cursed himself that he had spent so freely and not saved more. No, she had got to be safely married to Leonard Matthews before he took his departure. She might not like it at the moment, but later on she would realise the wisdom of what he had done, and be thankful that she had not been allowed to follow her own childish inclinations to her undoing. To leave little Pat to battle with the world alone was a thing not to be thought of. No, she must be married to Leonard Matthews forthwith, and then he would be free to enter his rest.

Pat white-faced and silent, prepared the evening meal, and sat down to it with him. But she soon found out why he would never eat when he was upset. Her mouth was too dry for mastication, and she could not swallow. Pharmakos, on the contrary, helped himself liberally to the cold salmon and began to eat with apparent gusto. Then, equally abruptly, he rose from the table without a word, went over to one of the windows and lit a cigarette, and stood with his back to Pat and his hands in his pockets, watching the sunset over the river. Pat silently cleared away the uneaten meal and then curled up in a huddled heap in the corner of the big sofa, watching him.

He stood motionless, save for the slight movements of cigarette-smoking, lighting one cigarette from the butt of the last in an endless chain, till Pat had seen five fag-ends sent in a curving line of fire out of the window in the gathering dusk. Finally he lit no more, and became as immobile as a statue; either he had run out of cigarettes or considered he had smoked enough.

Suddenly he turned towards her. It was too dark to see his face, but she felt instinctively that his mood had changed.

"Pat," he said, "I feel uncommon queer. I think I am going to be sick," and he vanished precipitately into the bathroom.

Pat shot after him to put her foot in the door before he had time to lock her out. But she need not have troubled. Pharmakos was past caring for appearances.

Then she saw on a large scale what she had seen several times with Eric on a small scale—uncontrollable, long-distance vomiting. Pharmakos was sick of life—literally.

But a grown man's vomiting is a very different matter to a small boy's. and it seemed as if any moment Pharmakos' body and soul would be torn apart. Pat rang the bell for Skilly and fortunately caught him just as he was departing for his nightly promenade among the belles of the Borough. Skilly took off his coat and gripped Pharmakos round the waist, giving him what support he could, but in a short time Pharmakos ended up in a heap on the floor, and they had to let him lie there.

"You better phone for a doctor, Cop," said Skilly, " 'e can't go on like this."

"You'll do nothing of the sort," gasped Pharmakos, between his spasms. "I won't have anything to do with a doctor. He can't do anything for me."

" 'E can dope yer, Boss. You'll rupture yerself if you go on like this."

"I won't have one," gasped Pharmakos, half under the bath.

Skilly dragged him clear of the bath, lest he injure himself in his struggles.

"If 'e won't, 'e won't," he said, "I've tried gettin' a doctor to 'im before when 'e didn't want one, and it was no use."

"Get a blanket and a pillow off the divan, will you, Skilly?" said Pat. "We can at least keep him off the cold tiles."

Skilly departed as bidden, and Pat knelt down beside Pharmakos and began to loosen his clothes.

"Pat," he whispered huskily. "I'll have a doctor if you'll promise me you'll marry Matthews."

Pat gasped. Pharmakos was torn by a fresh bout of retching and rolled under the bath again.

The storm spent itself, and he rolled clear of the bath on to his back and she saw his ghastly, contorted face for the first time.

"I can't go on like this, Pat," he muttered, "For God's sake marry him and let me go."

"All right," said Pat, "I promise."

When Skilly returned with the blankets, he found Pharmakos quiet, and Pat, looking very queer, greeted him with the news that his boss had agreed to see a doctor.

The doctor who Skilly produced appeared to have had dealings with Pharmakos before, and knew his ways. He helped Skilly to carry the semi-conscious man to the divan and gave him an injection of morphia.

Pat and Skilly between them got Pharmakos out of his clothes and into his pyjamas, and so to bed. As they turned him over to get his pyjama coat on to him, Skilly pointed to his back and made a wry mouth at Pat, and Pat suddenly dropped him and ran out of the room.

Later on, after the morphia had taken effect and Pharmakos was in a dead sleep, she crept back again, and sat beside him, erect and dry-eyed, listening to the voice of Big Ben as hour by hour he told the time.

At nine o'clock in the morning, Pharmakos not yet being awake, she switched the telephone through on its extension to Skilly's quarters, and speaking from there, secure from overhearing, she rang up Leonard Matthews.

"This is Pat Stone speaking," she said in a calm, level voice, as soon as he arrived at the phone. She heard a whoop of joy from the other end of the line.

"Mr. Pharmakos told me he saw you yesterday, and that you want to marry me. Is that so?"

"You bet it is," said Leonard, somewhat taken aback at the rapid progress things were making.

"Well, look here, I think I ought to tell you that I've been in love with someone else, but it went wrong. Do you want to have me under the circumstances?"

"That's all right Pat. That won't make any difference to me. You give me half a chance, and I'll swear we'll be as happy as two birds."

"Very good," said Pat, "If it's all right for you, it's all right for me. I'll do it."

"Do what, Pat?"

"Marry you."

"Oh, er—yes, right you are. That's splendid. When can I see you?"

"I'm not sure. Mr. Pharmakos was taken ill last night. I'm rather tied just at the moment."

"I say, I'm awfully sorry. What's the matter with him?"

"Some sort of stomach trouble. The doctor didn't say what."

"I thought he looked pretty rotten when I saw him yesterday. Tell him how sorry I am, will you, Pat?"

"All right. Good-bye, I must go now, I expect he will be wanting me."

"Right you are. Good-bye, Pat. I say, Pat—?"

But the silence on the line told him that she had hung up and gone away.

He was a little startled, poor lad, as he had every reason to be, at the pace his affairs had marched. He also felt a little defrauded out of his wooing by Pat's sudden capitulation. But he knew better than to take chances with the gifts the gods had sent him, for she was a notoriously difficult young woman; with the temper of a fiend, despite her fascination, as both his and her family had often warned him.

Pharmakos awoke with his nerves quieted by the morphia. Memory returned to him slowly, but when it did, he marvelled how he could have made such an egregious fool of himself as he had in the affair of Pat and young Matthews. Of course he couldn't force the child into a loveless marriage against her will. He must apologise to Pat and tell her to try and forget it. It was just another of his antics, and she must take no notice of it. He felt very exhausted, and as stiff and sore as if he had played a strenuous game of Rugger while out of training, but he did not feel in the least suicidal or confused any longer, thanks to the merciful morphia.

He saw Pat in her green overall crossing the great room towards him. She came and stood beside him silently, her hands in her overall pockets. What a dear she was, and how sweet she looked in the green overall.

"Hullo, Pat!" he said, and smiled up at her from among his pillows.

She did not smile back at him, but stood looking down at him with a white, strained face without speaking. Finally she said: "I've been through on the phone to Leonard and fixed things up with him. I'm definitely engaged to him now, so that's that."

Pharmakos stared back at her, unable for a moment to take in the significance of her words. Then everything came back to him with a rush.

"All right; Pat," he said, and turned over with his face to the wall.

When the doctor came to see him an hour later, he gave him another heavy dose of morphia.

CHAPTER XXVII

AS soon as Pharmakos was able to be up again, in a couple of days' time, he rang up Leonard Matthews on the phone, and invited him to visit Quilp Cottage.

Leonard arrived in his best suit and in high feather. Having got over the shock of Pat's announcement of her intentions, he was disposed to feel highly gratified at the way life was treating him. His fear of Pharmakos had caused him to beard his mother boldly, and she, being handled firmly for once in her life, had proved unexpectedly mild. Leonard was particularly pleased with life because his engagement to Pat had suddenly put manhood into him, and he no longer felt like a small boy, whom his mother and uncle were in the habit of relegating to the nursery when they wished to talk business.

He was as fascinated by Quilp Cottage as Pat had been. He had heard of the mystery man, whose real name no one knew, who appeared from nowhere, got aristocratic clients out of every imaginable scrape, and vanished as mysteriously as he had come, and now he was to see the secret lair of the famous detective, and it was infinitely more exciting than he had ever imagined it could possibly be. He had thought that Pat, when she mysteriously disappeared, had been spirited away to some house remote from all other human habitation. But this warehouse overlooking the water to which access was gained through underground tunnels and slums far exceeded his wildest expectations.

He had been met at Waterloo by the most villainous looking individual it had ever been his ill-fortune to set eyes on, but a cheery, "Come on, Guv'ner," had reassured him, and he had followed on the heels of the thug over a long and winding trail, for Skilly had no intention of letting him know too much about the whereabouts of Quilp Cottage, and took him thither via Lambeth Palace, Bedlam Lunatic Asylum and Guy's Hospital, which is not the most direct route.

The gigantic and glorious room, with its great windows looking out over the sunlit river, simply took his breath away. It seemed the only appropriate setting for the tall, dignified, strange-looking man, who had so dominated his imagination at the interview in the dingy little cupboard of a solicitor's waiting-room.

Pharmakos, he thought, looked deadly ill. Cancer was his guess. Pat looked peaked and sullen, as if overworked and bullied. It did not appear to be a genial *ménage*. It was a jolly good job that he had come along to take Pat out of it.

She would soon get all right when they got going to dances and theatres and all the festivities that his ample funds laid open to them. He wasn't going to worry about that, though she looked decidedly off colour at the moment, and had greeted him without any trace of enthusiasm. He saw himself as a rescuer of damsels in distress. This Pharmakos was obviously a bully. One could see that from the way Pat looked at him. He must be a nigger-driver, too, for Pat looked as if she had been run off her feet.

Pharmakos received him with the frigid dignity of the old school of aristocrats. The fellow had the manners of an ambassador, thought Leonard. He did not mind his attitude towards himself; was rather fascinated by it, in fact; but he very much resented the authority with which her employer turned to Pat and bid her withdraw out of earshot. She went silently and without a word, evidently well broken in to bullying, and took her perch with her back to them in the seat of the far window, half a day's march away. This Pharmakos chap followed her with his eyes without speaking till she had settled herself, as if he expected to see her try to do a break-away, and only then did he turn his attention to his visitor, who was still standing in the middle of the vast hearthrug, clutching hat and stick.

Pharmakos did not trouble about his hat and stick. If he had got himself into the room still clutching them, that was his look-out.

"Won't you sit down?" he said, indicating a vast armchair with a curt gesture. Leonard put his hat and stick on the floor and sat down. In a fold of the cushions he saw a skein of bright embroidery silk in Pat's favourite green, and the sight affected him peculiarly. He did not know whether to be thrilled by it, or to resent it as evidence that she was altogether too much at home in her employer's bachelor quarters.

"Pat tells me that everything is fixed up between you, Mr. Matthews?" said Pharmakos.

Leonard squirmed at Pharmakos' use of Pat's Christian name, but was too much in awe of the formidable man in front of him to dare to allow any sign of resentment to appear outwardly. But, Lord, didn't the beggar look ill? Was he going to collapse on the mat? Leonard hoped not. He hated scenes. Pharmakos' looks effectually distracted his attention from the affront to his dignity as a future husband.

"Yes," he said. "Oh yes. We've got everything fixed up except dates and such like."

"It is dates I want to talk to you about, Mr. Matthews. Now, Pat doesn't know this, and you must regard it as confidential, but I am not likely to live long, and I am very anxious to get her off my hands before anything happens to me."

"Oh, I say, I'm awfully sorry to hear that," said Leonard. He wasn't. He was anything but sorry, for it had seemed to him that Pharmakos might be inclined to make himself a darned nuisance with his dictatorial ways, and he certainly was not going to allow any fellow who wasn't a relative to interfere between man and wife. He was the best judge of Pat's interests, he considered.

"Never mind about condolences," said Pharmakos impatiently. "There is nothing to regret, I assure you. The thing is this. I want you to marry Pat as soon as possible."

"I'll see what I can do," said Leonard. "I'll have a talk with my mother this evening."

"You'll have a talk with me now," said Pharmakos grimly. "It is nothing to do with your mother. You're of age, aren't you? I suppose you are not thinking of taking Pat to live with your mother?"

"Oh no," said Leonard. "Certainly not. I had thought of leaving my mother the house and taking a flat in town for Pat and myself."

Pharmakos need have no anxiety on that score. One of the great advantages of marriage for him was that his mother would now have to agree to his living apart from her. To live apart from her without her consent was an idea that had never entered his head.

"Now look here, my boy," said Pharmakos. "I don't want to die on Pat's hands and scare the child to death. You have got to take her over. And I'll tell you another thing, too. If you don't marry Pat while I'm alive, you'll never marry her at all. I gather she has told you she has had a bit of a disappointment, luckily for her. She would have had a bad bargain on her hands if she had gone on with that affair. She thinks she will never love again; but I tell her that is all nonsense. Once she makes a start she will be all right. Especially when she has all the interest of her own home. Besides, what is the girl to do if she doesn't? She has got nobody to look after her when I am gone, thanks to the amiable Mr. Stone's method of disposing of his daughters.

"If you risk waiting till I am no longer there to give Pat a push behind, she may get an attack of sentimentality and back out. Don't you risk it, my boy. Go while the going's good and break it to your mother afterwards."

"Right, sir, I will," said Leonard heartily, not at all sorry to have his mind made up for him and so be able to present his mother with the accomplished fact and avoid argument.

"You can get a special licence and be married at the local registry office in three day's time," continued Pharmakos, "I'll be delighted to give you a send-off from here, and I would like to give Pat her trousseau, If you've no objection, though she will have to buy it after she is married. You and Pat can trot off and have your honeymoon and all that, and then you can put up at an hotel and go house-hunting at your leisure. That's my advice to you, Matthews, and I've seen more of the world than you have."

Leonard was so delighted at Pharmakos' increasing cordiality that he instantly agreed, and returned thanks heartily. Pharmakos smiled grimly to himself, wondering what the young man would say if he suspected the truth, and making up his mind to stage his departure really effectually so that his complicity in his own end might not transpire. He would walk over the edge of the wharf into the Thames in a heavy overcoat on the first dark night that warranted it. It would be very hard to bring that in as *felo de se*.

"Don't say anything to Pat at the moment," said Pharmakos. "You leave her to me. She'll take it better from me than from you."

Leonard's hackle rose again at Pharmakos' calm assumption as to the priority of his position with Pat over that of her chosen husband.

"I expect you would like to have a word with her before you leave. I am going to ask you to excuse me as I am far from well. Perhaps you will take her downstairs to her own quarters."

"Does she live here?" asked Leonard, every feather of his hackle standing straight up on end.

"She lives downstairs in the caretaker's quarters with a front door of her own," said Pharmakos tartly. "I had to make the best arrangement I could for her when Mr. Stone suddenly cast her on my hands; but I do not think you will have any reason to complain of the condition in which she is handed over to you. Now perhaps you will be good enough to collect her and take her downstairs. I wish to be alone."

Leonard set off on the half day's journey across the enormous room. Pat did not hear him approach, as the latter part of his walk lay across one of Pharmakos' inch-thick rugs, and Leonard had dropped down on the window-seat beside her and had his arms round her before she knew he was there. Her startled exclamation brought Pharmakos to his feet involuntarily, but he controlled himself with a supreme effort, though the short hairs in his neck rose like a dog's while Leonard did a thing which a man of his generation would never have dreamed of doing—he kissed Pat openly and publicly.

Leonard was used to necking parties, and a kiss or two, whether public or private, meant nothing to him.

Then a thing happened which, if Pharmakos had not seen it he would never have believed. Pat turned to Leonard and returned his kiss, and in another moment the two were locked in an embrace which seemed likely to continue indefinitely.

Pharmakos turned and walked unsteadily across the rug-strewn space to the bathroom, where he locked himself in, and sat down on the edge of the bath to wait till they had finished. This was the end of all things for him. He would slip out of life now as easily as a boat putting out to sea on a full tide. He had always half expected Pat to rat on him, and now she had done it. They were all alike. Pat was no better than his first love. If 'each man kills the thing he loves,' what about women? How many men have died at a woman's hands to everything that makes life worth living?

He heard the far door of the great room close noisily; and let himself out of the bathroom and went and lay down on the divan, feeling deadly ill. When Leonard returned for his forgotten hat and stick, he found him there, and thought he was dead already, so ghastly was his appearance. But Pharmakos suddenly sat up when he heard a step on the parquetry, and Leonard saw the blazing eyes of a lunatic looking at him, and bolted like a rabbit.

Pat crept back like a whipped dog after Leonard's departure, but Pharmakos had turned his face to the wall and would not look at her, and presently she crept away again disconsolately.

Pharmakos lay motionless in his clothes all night. How was he to know that when poor, heartbroken Pat had surrendered herself to Leonard she had closed her eyes and phantasied that it was he himself to whom she was yielding?

CHAPTER XXVIII

PHARMAKOS had recovered his self-control by next morning, and it was a quiet and self-possessed, but very remote man, very much her employer, who summoned Pat to his desk next morning and bade her be seated in the stenographer's chair.

"Now look here, Pat, I had a good talk with Matthews yesterday afternoon, and he agrees with me that an immediate marriage is the best thing for all concerned. You know how I am placed. Every hour I delay my departure increases my risk of arrest. Since you have made up your mind, and Matthews is willing, what do you say to a special licence and get the thing over?"

"I don't mind," said Pat apathetically. She too felt that the sooner it was over the better, quite apart from any question of Pharmakos' getaway; and she would never have forgiven herself if he had delayed his flight on account of her, and then been caught and driven to suicide.

"Very well, then, Pat. Here is a couple of quid. I don't know exactly what a special licence costs, but it's somewhere in that neighbourhood. It may be guineas, I don't know. If it is, take the odd change out of the housekeeping money. Go round to the registrar's before twelve. You know where it is, don't you? It is only a step from here. Skilly can tell you where it is if you don't know, he's been there dozens of times, under a different name every time. They'll get to know his face soon, I should think. Fix this thing up for Saturday morning if you can. You ought to be able to if you go before twelve, and let's get it over and done with. Run along, child. I know you feel as if you were going to the dentist, but believe me, it is the best thing for you, and after I am gone you will soon settle down and begin to enjoy it."

He did the best he could in the way of a smile, and Pat smiled back at him drearily, took the money and departed without speaking.

Left alone at his desk, he began to calculate how long it would take a swimmer as strong as himself to drown if he dropped into the water at the turn of the tide in a heavy overcoat, and whether he dared risk a book or two in the pockets to hurry matters up.

Pat put on her Woolworth beret and set out for the registrar's, feeling as if she were arranging her own funeral. It was only the thought that Pharmakos would be able to make his getaway when once she were off his hands that kept her to her resolution. She had come to the conclusion that this time Pharmakos really meant what he said when he announced it as final that he could never marry her, for he did not deny now that he loved her, but simply declared that the difficulties in the way of their marriage were insurmountable. This might well be the truth, for she had often thought that the difference between their respective social positions was considerable, and when Pharmakos put on his dignity and assumed formal manners, as he had when dealing with Leonard, the gulf between them was so unmistakable that no one could be blind to it. Before he became outcast Pharmakos most distinctly must have been somebody.

Arrived at the registrar's, Pat found herself faced by the indignity of taking her place in a queue and giving the particulars of her marriage in public. She herself had to wait patiently while other folk told the registrar all about themselves and their intendeds, and knew that the people who were now queueing up behind her would do likewise. It was a sickening experience.

The day was hot and close; the office stuffy, the local residents none too thorough in their ablutions. Pat felt within measurable distance of fainting. If only it had been Pharmakos whose name she had to give to the registrar—if only—if only!

Suddenly she was recalled by a peremptory voice addressing her and saying: "The gentleman's name, please, miss?" and before she knew what she had done, she had said: "Julian Pharmakos," and in paralysed horror had seen the registrar's clerk writing it down in his book.

Heavens above, what had she done! To retract before the gaping crowd around her was impossible. To explain was impossible. One does not give the name of a man as one's future husband, and then suddenly say: "I have made a mistake, that's not the one; it's someone else." Imagine the gapes! Imagine the indignation of the irascible clerk, demanding explanations! No, the best thing was to let it stand for the moment, get quietly out of the office, and get Skilly to come round and straighten things out afterwards. She simply couldn't face an explanation at the moment. Flesh and blood had their limits.

So she gave the rest of the particulars that were required of her, adding a year to her age to save complications, as Skilly had advised when instructing her as to the procedure in which practice had made him perfect.

Finally she received the requisite form, paid over her money, and staggered rather than walked out of the stuffy office and gaol-like building.

She fled back to Quilp Cottage and knocked on the door of Skilly's apartments, and was admitted after a slight delay, for Skilly invariably seemed to be minus his trousers whenever she particularly wanted him.

She dropped down on the neatly made bed, that Lamprey

dusted occasionally, for it was for ornament rather than use so far as Skilly was concerned, and silently held out towards him the form she had received at the registrar's.

"What's the matter, Cop?" demanded Skilly, taking the form between his fingers gingerly, as if expecting it to explode.

"Read it," panted Pat, who had run most of the way home.

"Can't. Never had no schoolin'," said Skilly, sulkily, handing her back the form.

"Do you know what I've done, Skilly? I've done something simply awful. You know I'm going to marry Mr. Matthews, don't you?"

"Yus, the boss told me. Bloody silly, I calls it."

"Well, I went round to the registrar's to see about a special licence, because Mr. Pharmakos wants us to be married at once and I went and gave his name instead of Mr. Matthews by mistake!"

"Good for you, Cop!" exclaimed Skilly, slapping his thigh with delight. "You stick to it, old dear! That's the stuff to give the troops."

"Oh, Skilly, Skilly, I can't!" wailed Pat, almost in tears. "I can't. He wouldn't like it. He's told me quite definitely it's all off, and I know he means it. I can tell that from the way he said it. Please, Skilly, would you go round and straighten things out for me? I simply can't face it myself. I can't, I can't!" and Pat began to have hysterics.

"Lor', yus," said Skilly, hastily, terrified at Pat's gulps and gaspings, "I'll go right away," and he seized his coat without troubling about waistcoat or braces, and fled, holding up his trousers with one hand.

However, he did not go right away; and by the time he had dropped in at the Prince of Wales's Feathers and had one with himself and then one with a pal, and then the pal had had another with him, and then he had had another with himself, time had elapsed, and when he arrived at the registrar's he found Pat's particulars were up on the notice-board for all the world to see.

Skilly whistled and stared at them. He could read sufficiently well to spell out the names, although he would not venture on an attempt to decipher in public the closely printed form with which Pat had confronted him.

"Now you know, that looks all right to me, whatever they may say," he murmured to himself. "Bloody silly, the way they goes on, I thinks. Wot's the matter with Pharm is Cop, and wot's the matter with Cop is Pharm; and then they goes on like this! Fair makes me heave, it does. Wot's the use of 'avin' a conscience if it's allus gettin' in yer wy? A few guts is wot they wants, and a bit less of this yer bloody conscience, that never did anybody any good as I could 'ear of."

He stood in front of the offending notice-board and swore at it steadily and softly for several minutes on end. Finally he shook his head with abysmal melancholy. Then suddenly he brightened up. He had seen in the distance his particular pal, the famous local gang-leader, Mr. Joe Hannan. The six beers he had had were working cheerfully inside Skilly, and he felt capable of moving mountains at that moment. He set off at his ungainly, crab-like sprawl across the road after the disappearing Mr. Hannan, and hailed him into the Prince of Wales's Feathers, an invitation not to be refused in that district.

There, having bound Joe to secrecy, he unfurled a tale embellished with as many B's as would have stocked a hive. Philologists tell us that 'E' is the commonest letter in the English language; which may be the case in the West End, but the Borough is faithful to its own initial and theoretical considerations do not apply there.

Joe Hannan was divided between ungodly mirth at the

antics of the conscience-ridden Pharmakos and sympathy at the sad plight of poor neglected, unappreciated Pat, who was being shoved onto a Tiddlypush like the **BBBBBBBBBBBB** that Skilly had tramped 'is bleedin' feet sore toddlin' rahnd the previous dy.

Mr. Hannan was entirely in agreement with Skilly's view re matters of conscience, and added a few B's of his own as his contribution to the argument. Finally a plan was outlined, and an arrangement made, after more beer, and they parted company, each firmly believing himself to be Cupid in person. They had one point in common with the God of Love, however beside their present interest in matters matrimonial, for they were both by now practically blind.

Consequently, when Pat slipped down to Skilly's apartments, having heard his musical entry later in the evening, she could get no more information out of him when she demanded if all were now well with her wedding, save that everythingsh in the gardensh wash shlovely, and had to be content with that, and variations on the well-worn theme of dear little Rowshy-Powshy, syncopated by hiccoughs.

CHAPTER XXIX

FOR the first time since she had come to live at Quilp Cottage, Pat found herself debarred from Pharmakos' big room, for he told her curtly he desired to be alone, and relegated her to her own quarters, which she had used so little that her personality never seemed to have struck root there. She miserably occupied herself with sorting her meagre belongings, and then, unable to bear the solitude and inaction any longer, took some of the money Pharmakos had forced upon her for her trousseau, and set out for Waterloo and the West End to get a few essential items.

Meanwhile Pharmakos was sitting huddled in his big chair, brooding wretchedly. Since his attack of vomiting he had been too weakened and pulled down to pace the big room any longer, and most of the time he lay on the divan, generally with his face to the wall.

The thing that had cut him to the heart was Pat's willing, nay, enthusiastic, surrender to Matthews. Despite the fact that he was deliberately forcing her into the marriage, and that he honestly wished her to settle down and be happy in it, the sight of his Pat putting her arms round the fellow's neck and hugging him had been something utterly outside his reckoning, and had upset all his calculations. He felt now that even in the sleep of death he would not have Pat for his dream. She had utterly gone from him and broken all links between them by that one voluntary act, and all he had to hope for now was the mercy of oblivion when once the agony of drowning was over. For a good swimmer cannot commit suicide either easily or painlessly by drowning, but he had perforce chosen that way because it was the only way that could be made to look accidental. Anyone could walk over that dock-edge in the dark. In fact, Skilly had actually done it, and his evidence would be available at the inquest. If possible, Pat must not be allowed to suspect that he had committed suicide; at any rate she must never suspect that his suicide had anything to do with her.

Pat's faithlessness had shattered Pharmakos in a manner that nothing else had ever done. In some strange way it had shaken his self-respect, which even his imprisonment had left intact. He felt he had been such a complete fool to trust a woman again—to give his happiness and pride into feminine hands for safe keeping and get them dropped in the mud and trodden on heedlessly. Alone in his big room he asked himself what he had ever seen in Pat, that bit of pink and white flesh with a mop of red-gold hair on top of it. It was his imagination that had cast a glamour over her. There was nothing in the girl herself. He thanked God that he was rid of that ridiculous obsession, and told himself that but for the gnawing anxiety of Jurgens for ever hanging over his head, he would not have troubled to commit suicide over Pat. Then Pat would come into the room, and immediately he found himself thinking how sweet she looked, what a dear she was, and all his old torment returned a hundredfold, and he knew that there was nothing for it but to put an end to it. His problems were insoluble and he could bear no more, and the less he saw of Pat the better.

All the time, day and night, there hung before his eyes a picture of Pat kissing Leonard, and he suddenly wondered whether he was going to have that dream in his sleep of death for all eternity, and even the mercy of extinction would be denied him.

The doctor looked at him askance, and said something

to Skilly about a private mental home, but got sworn at so savagely for his pains, and Skilly looked so formidable and pugilistic, with Lamprey snarling like a vicious mongrel in the background, that he decided it was not his responsibility what became of the patient, and as it would obviously require a squad of police to extract him from his barricaded dwelling, he had better wait till Pharmakos had done something that would produce the necessary squad before he tried to remove him to safe keeping.

Meanwhile, Pat shopped drearily in the West End, picking up any old rag that was offered to her, and eventually got on the Tube at Oxford Circus en route for Waterloo and Quilp Cottage, realising miserably that the next time she left Quilp Cottage she would not be returning to it.

So absorbed was she in her miserable thoughts that for a while she did not realise that she was being stared at by the woman opposite whom she had sat down on entering the train. This woman, though little more than middle-aged, looked as if she had worn badly. Though heavily made up, she had the air and bearing of an ancient parrot that had led an evil life. She was of a peculiar type that Pat could not quite place, for she combined the hard-featured ruthless alertness of a seaside landlady with the showiness of a theatrical.

She was a complete stranger to Pat, however, and Pat wondered why she had caught her staring so hard when she looked up unexpectedly, and wondered whether her face bore signs of what she was going through.

At Waterloo Pat got out, and so did the woman. But in the lift there was a hitch. The woman had travelled beyond the station to which she had taken her ticket. As she debated the matter with the lift attendant, it suddenly struck Pat that though the woman's face was strange to her, her voice was not. Somewhere she had heard that metallic voice before, but she could not place it. Then she heard the lift-man mention the station at which the woman had entered the Tube—Warwick Avenue—and she knew where she had heard that voice, for they had used Warwick Avenue Tube station, she and Pharmakos, in their trip to that house of ill-repute in Maida Vale where all the trouble had started. The voice was the voice which had come from behind the curtains of the inner hall, telling George to let her alone as they did not want trouble with someone else's girl. She also knew that the woman had recognised her, and realised that the longest way round might be the safest way home, and that she must take care that she was not followed when she came out of the station, for it was evident that the woman had changed her plans since entering the train, for she had only booked to Piccadilly.

Pat edged near the lift gates, and saw out of the corner of her eye that the woman was doing the same thing. As soon as the gates rolled back, Pat shot out of the lift, and scurried across the great station, circled round through the booking offices, dived in at one entrance to a cloakroom and out at the other, and generally ran in circles.

Then satisfied that she had thoroughly confused the trail, she set off on her homeward journey through the underground roads. Now it is a peculiarity of these roads that they carry and magnify sound like a speaking-tube, and Pat had not gone very far before she heard the sharp click-clack of highheeled shoes hurrying along behind her.

She turned on her heel, and began to walk back the way she had come, but she took the precaution to walk in the middle of the road, not on the pavement, for she knew that she in her crepe-rubber soles would have the advantage over those high heels on the irregular granite setts.

Round the first turn she came face to face with the woman who was following her, and obeying a sudden impulse, which

Mr. Stone would certainly have denied came from his side of the family, stuck out her tongue and then ran.

Pat dashed up to Pharmakos' big room with her news, but found the outer door barred against her and no notice taken of her knockings. But her news was too important to permit of standing on ceremony, and she dashed down again, and round through the yard, and in at Skilly's quarters, and along Sister Ann's passage, and in at the kitchen door which, as she had expected, Pharmakos had forgotten to lock, for he could not keep two ideas in his head at a time these days.

He was lying face downwards on the divan, and Pat with a sudden terror at her heart, seized him by the shoulder and tried to turn him over, dreading to find him stiff and cold. But to her relief her efforts met with a very decided resistance.

"What is it?" he asked sullenly, without raising his head.

"Julian, I've been followed."

"Who followed you?"

"The woman who was in charge of that house in Maida Vale."

Pharmakos turned over wearily, and his eyes looked like the eyes of a dead man. "Good job we pushed your wedding on wasn't it, Pat?"

"Oh, Julian, Julian, what can we do?" cried poor Pat in anguish.

"Can't do anything," said Pharmakos; and rolled over on to his face again. "I wish you'd go. I want to be alone."

Pat crept down to her own rooms feeling utterly spent. Pharmakos was gone from her for ever. He no longer cared. She could feel that. There was no contact with him for her, save the surface contacts of casual associations. To speak to him now was like speaking on the telephone after you have been cut off. There was no response to be got out of him.

She wrote a note telling Skilly to come and see her immediately on his return, printing the words in large capitals so that he might be able to spell it out, and ran along to his quarters to put it there for him. As she came out of the slovenly room she heard a knocking on the great gate, and ran up the corkscrew stairs to Sister Ann's window to see who was there before she risked opening.

Below her stood Leonard Matthews, applying his beautiful Malacca cane to the stout wooden gates in a manner that was not calculated to do it any good.

Pharmakos had evidently been ignoring his ringings of the bell.

She ran down and opened to him.

"I say, Pat, I've got a couple of tickets for a show. Would you care to come out and have a bit of dinner with me, and then go on and do a dance and night-club afterwards? Or have you to be in by ten to tuck the old boy up?"

As Pat in the ordinary way would have tucked Pharmakos up, Leonard's innocent attempt at humour exasperated her. But she was just as cross at the moment with Pharmakos as she was with him; moreover, she was completely at the end of her tether, and felt that she would go off in screaming hysterics if left alone and unoccupied any longer. So she agreed to Leonard's plan with a readiness that somewhat surprised him, for he had judged from her face when she opened the gate to him that she was in an exceedingly bad temper.

She deposited him in her little sitting-room while she changed into the yellow organdie frock that Pharmakos had bought for her, shedding a tear or two in memory of the happy start of that expedition as she got into it.

"I say, the old boy hasn't wasted much cash on furnishing your quarters, has he?" said Leonard when she rejoined him, glancing round superciliously at her New Cut bargains.

"Mind your own business!" snarled Pat viciously, only just checking her tongue in time for quoting Skilly and telling him to mind his own bloody business, for there is nothing like bad language for slipping out at the wrong moment if one becomes habituated to it. But even as it was, they set off in a somewhat constrained silence for the evening's pleasure.

But meanwhile things had been happening at Quilp Cottage that Pat was unaware of. Pharmakos had heard the ringing of the bell the first time that Leonard had rung, and had gone along Sister Ann's passage to the look-out, poison-ring on hand, to see whether it was a Scotland Yard man with a warrant for his arrest. He had heard Pat's quick light footsteps on the corkscrew stair, and guessing that she was on the same errand, and dreading to meet her, stood behind the passage door till she had descended again, and heard every word she said as she greeted Leonard and readily agreed to go out with him for an evening's enjoyment.

The reference to the tucking-up had stung him even more than it had Pat, for it made him feel a complete fool when he realised how Pat's motherings of him, in which he had so delighted, would have struck the average male.

He returned to his own quarters more than ever confirmed in his belief in Pat's perfidiousness. Fancy going out and leaving him when he was simply lying there feeling deadly ill, waiting to be arrested! She could surely have kept him company till the end. He had completely forgotten that he had turned Pat out of the room and locked the door against her, and he was too absorbed in his own misery to realise the state to which he had managed to reduce the poor child.

Even though he had avoided seeing her, the sound of her voice had upheaved him again. He dropped on his knees beside the big divan and buried his head in its voluminous pillows. For the first time since he had passed out of old Maggie's hands, he formulated a prayer. He hardly knew it was a prayer. It was a kind of speechless crying-out to anything there might be in the universe that could have mercy on his misery and torment. He did not know what he wanted. He merely knew what his torments were. His terror of Jurgens. His dread of prison. The insanity that threatened him. His broken body and mind. And finally, his hopeless love for Pat, who had betrayed him, and yet he could not stop loving her.

The sun sank behind the towers of Westminster, and the dusk began to steal into the great room. It came earlier than it did on the day when he had bidden Pat to light the lamps because he was weary, and she had taken him in hand and mothered him and brought him hope and peace. All his life with Pat unrolled like a cinematograph film before his eyes. All her little ways, the toss of her head when she was indignant, as she frequently was; her firm, square-fingered little hand slipped into his when he was distressed; the way she gathered him into her arms as if he were a child to comfort him; her unfailing staunchness and understanding. And now Pat had ratted on him. He could hardly realise it was possible. It seemed so utterly unlike her. If there was one thing in the world he could have pinned his faith to, it was Pat's fidelity. He had traded on her love for him to push her into the security of marriage with Leonard, but he had never imagined that Pat would throw her love for himself over her shoulder all in a minute and kiss Leonard as if she meant it. The bottom had dropped out of Pharmakos' universe, and he hardly had sufficient energy left to do away with himself.

CHAPTER XXX

IT was while he half-knelt and half-crouched at the side of the divan among the heaped-up cushions that Pharmakos heard a step which he knew instinctively to be that of a stranger. He raised his head cautiously and saw Jurgens standing in the middle of the floor with a revolver in his hand, looking all round the room as if seeking for something.

Now Pharmakos was wearing the same dark blue suit in which Pat had first seen him, and he was right up against a dark blue curtain, and the room was getting dusk; consequently Jurgens, who had never thought to look for his enemy on his knees in a corner, did not see him.

Pharmakos looked at the revolver in Jurgens' hand, and a sudden exaltation flowed into him. He would die fighting. He would go for that armed man with his bare hands till Jurgens had to shoot him in self-defence. Then he remembered that his heavy, steel-cored stick was close beside him, in its hiding-place at the bed-head behind the curtain. Cautiously he put out his hand to it, grasped it and rose to his feet with a quick, pantherish motion.

The movement caught Jurgens' eye, and he turned swiftly, covering Pharmakos with his revolver.

Then his mouth opened in amazement as he stared at his enemy speechlessly.

"So it's you, is it?" he managed to stammer at length, his foreign accent very much in evidence. "So you're Pharmakos, and Pharmakos is you!"

Pharmakos laughed.

"So you've grasped that at length, have you?"

"Yes, I have. Put your hands up."

Pharmakos laughed again, and responded by putting his thumb to his nose.

Jurgens snarled like an angry animal at this insult, which was what Pharmakos intended, for he wanted to make him lose control of his temper and disregard consequences. Pharmakos wished to be shot dead, not merely winged.

"You put your hands up, or it will be the worse for you," snarled Jurgens.

Pharmakos responded by twirling the heavy stick after the manner of a drum-major with his staff.

"You move, and I'll shoot you dead," asserted Jurgens.

Pharmakos raised the stick threateningly above his head and began to advance towards him. It is a poor plan to threaten to shoot a man who is exceedingly anxious to die at your hands in order to save himself the odium of dying by his own. But it is also a poor plan to invite Death to come and take you, for that scares Death off. Death suspects a catch somewhere, and nothing can persuade him to come near a man who really wishes to die. And not only would Pharmakos meet his death in an eminently respectable and unsuspicious fashion if he could goad Jurgens into shooting him, but he would in all probability revenge himself most effectually on his enemy, for Scotland Yard, under the guidance of Saunders, would know where to look for the man who had murdered Phalmakos.

But Pharmakos' eagerness to meet death was his undoing, for Jurgens, ruthless and hardened as he was, found it physically impossible to pull the trigger on this absolutely fearless man. Consequently, the armed man gave ground before the unarmed, and Jurgens began backing towards the door under the threat of that lifted stick.

This annoyed Pharmakos, who saw his plans going astray

in consequence, and Jurgens, who was a polyglot like himself, heard a stream of abuse in three Continental languages and underworld English so vivid and venomous that even he was taken aback for a moment at the blended stream of vitriol and sewage which swept over him.

It was at this moment that the kitchen door opened and Pat, whose dinner had made her feel sick and who had struck at further entertainment, entered in her yellow dress, followed by Matthews, and shrieked as she recognised Jurgens. Jurgens recognised her. And having no desire to do a murder in front of witnesses, and especially in front of witnesses who knew him, took to his heels and made for the door in the carved partition at the far end of the room, with Pharmakos after him. There was a moment's delay, as Jurgens discovered the door to be locked and got it open, which enabled Pharmakos almost to catch up with him, and then the pair of them had gone pelting down the stone stairs, three steps at a time, all Pharmakos' illness and weakness forgotten in the exhilaration of the scrap, to the great astonishment of Leonard Matthews, who had believed Pharmakos to be in a practically moribund condition.

Not knowing Jurgens to be armed, for why should he have fled before Pharmakos' stick if he had been? Leonard raced after them to see the fun, and Pat raced after him in terror for her beloved, for she had seen the revolver in Jurgen's hand, and knew him to be a bold and desperate criminal, who would shoot as soon as look at you, provided he was sure of his getaway.

When they arrived at the bottom of the stairs, they found Pharmakos standing under the naked electric light, gazing into the dark depths below.

"Where is he?" they both cried simultaneously.

"Gone to earth," said Pharmakos. "He went down a flight too many and missed the door, so we've got him cornered. I say, Matthews, put your head out and see if any of his pals are outside, will you?"

Leonard protruded a nose and half an eye cautiously; he had been brought up at a school with ideals, where rough games were not played, and he had no mind to have that nose punched, for he wasn't used to such things, and they are an acquired taste.

"I say," he whispered," There's a boat with some chaps in it pulled up alongside your wharf!"

Suddenly there was a roar like the bull of Bashan on the war-path, and a terrible pounding of hoofs on the flagged path along the dock-side, and Skilly, nothing daunted by the odds charged past brandishing an iron bar taken from the gate.

"Look out, Skilly, don't do a murder," shouted Pharmakos for one tap with that bar would have cracked the hardest skull, and Skilly was brandishing it as if it were a fly-swatter.

But the boatload of thugs did not wait for his arrival but cast off and pushed out hastily, and the current caught them and spun them round, and they had their hands full to avoid being swamped as a six-knot tide swept them down towards the treacherous arches of Blackfriars Bridge. They would not be returning that way in the near future, that was quite certain.

Skilly joined the party at the foot of the stairs.

"Gor blimey, Guv'ner, 'oo's been callin' on yer?" he exclaimed.

"Jurgens," said Pharmakos briefly.

Skilly invoked the wrath of God upon his internal arrangements, regardless of Pat's presence, to the great scandal of Leonard. But Pat was no more concerned for Skilly's tripes than she was for those she stewed in milk for Pharmakos.

"Where's the blankety-blankety-blank now?" demanded the stout ex-burglar, itching to use his trusty iron bar.

Leonard wished he had the courage to tell him to modify his language in the presence of ladies, but found it was lacking. The New Education does not teach one how to deal with rough customers.

Pharmakos jerked his head in the direction of the cellars.

"Below-stairs," he said.

"Gor blimey, Bill! We got 'im properly cornered, ain't we? But 'ow are we goin' to bag 'im, Guv'nor? 'E'll take some baggin' dahn there in the dark. 'E's certain to 'ave a gun, and yer got the light be'ind yer as yer go dahn."

"He's got a gun all right, but whether he will use it is another matter."

" 'E'll use it orl right. 'E's got ter. It's 'im or us and 'e knows it. Besides, 'e's a killer anyway. I knows of three 'e's 'ad to my certain knowledge. Wodjer goin' ter do? Barrakide the stairs and starve 'im aht?"

"No. Can't spare the time. Rout him out."

"Damme, Pharm, yer can't rout 'im aht wiv a stick! 'E ain't a rat!"

"Can't I, Skilly? You watch me do it."

" 'Ere, Pharm, this is bloody sooicide!"

"Well, and what if it is?" said Pharmakos, giving Skilly a queer look.

There was silence for a moment at the foot of the stairs, as the three stood, each in their different way trying to take in the significance of Pharmakos' words.

Pat was the first to do so, and flung herself at him shrieking "Julian, Julian!" and trying to get her arms round his neck. He picked her up with one hand as if she had been a puppy and thrust her into Leonard's arms.

"Here, look after her," he said, and went down the cellar stairs as tranquilly as if he were after the beer instead of an armed desperado who meant to murder him.

"You cowards!" shrieked Pat, "You aren't going to let him go alone, are you? Julian, Julian!"

"Why don't you telephone for the police?" demanded Leonard, who was beginning to have had quite enough of the affair, with all these underworld thugs flying about with revolvers and iron bars, and looking as if they meant business.

"No 'urry. Let 'em get finished dahn below fust."

"But, good Lord, why wait till they've finished down below? They're probably murdering each other. Why not give the fellow in charge and be done with it?"

"Because if I give 'im in charge, 'e'll give Pharm in charge, see? You're in the bleedin' underworld, young feller me lad, see? An' you must ply the glme the wy we plys it."

"I say, Skilly, is it true that Mr. Pharmakos has been in prison for murdering a fellow?"

"Yus, an' you'd better look aht, for 'e'll murder you, too, as soon as look at yer."

Leonard believed him. He had not liked the way he had caught Pharmakos looking at him once or twice.

A shot rang out from the darkness of the cellar, and a hurricane of shrieks came from Pat. Leonard hung on to her. He was decidedly annoyed at the way she fussed over Pharmakos under his very nose. Not at all the thing for an engaged girl.

"Now they're gettin' goin'," said Skilly, philosophically. He might be courageous enough charging about in the open with an iron bar, but his was not the two o'clock in the morning kind of courage that goes down cellar stairs in the dark in pursuit of armed desperadoes.

Now Leonard, being a male, was naturally stronger than Pat, but he was an only child, and had never had a party of brothers to scrap with; consequently, when Pat made up her mind to break away from him, he was powerless to hold her.

She stamped on his toes, drove her elbow into his stomach, and away she went. But to his relief she charged upstairs instead of down.

Pharmakos heard the patter of her feet flying upstairs as he listened in the silence of the cellar for Jurgens' breathing, and smiled grimly to himself. Pat was running true to form. She was making for safety as soon as the first shot was fired. He had rather thought Skilly would have joined him. The shivering, dithering Lamprey he knew would have done so.

A chorus of expostulations from upstairs smote on his ears, and then the noise of a scuffle, an oath from Skilly, a squeal from Leonard, followed by the sound of sneezing.

Then all was quiet, save for the slapping of the water among the timbers supporting the warehouse, which was rendering it impossible for him to hear his enemy's breathing. He would have to wait for a movement or a shot and then try and rush him.

Suddenly he heard a faint rustle immediately behind him, and turning cautiously, began to move towards it, stick raised, ready to strike. Then there came to his nostrils a faint waft of scent—the scent that he had bought for Pat when they had gone shopping together, and that she had put on her yellow organdie frock.

Was it Jurgens who had worked round and got behind him—or could it possibly be Pat, come down here to stand beside him in his extremity? It would have been just like the original Pat to have done this, but would the Pat who had kissed Leonard do anything of the sort? He could not tell, he could only wait and see. Rats scuffled and squeaked in the darkness. The timbers groaned as the tide thrust at them; the hurrying water slapped and gurgled all along the outer wall, and the dank, frowsy air of the cellar weighed upon him like fold upon fold of thick wet black cloth.

Suddenly another shot rang out, and by the light of the

flash, Pharmakos caught sight of Pat's yellow organdie skirts upon his left a couple of yards away, and Jurgens crouching behind a baulk of timber almost beside her. He sprang for the flash, but before he could reach it there was a yell of pain, followed by such a choking, snorting, sneezing, spitting and swearing, punctuated by groans of agony that it seemed as if all the cats in creation had gone mad together. Then some heavy body, certainly not Pat, charged past him like a mad buffalo, nearly knocking him over, and vanished up the cellar stairs, to be received with yells at the top by the valiant rearguard, who had never expected to be called upon to go into action.

Pharmakos blundered forward in the darkness and felt Pat's organdie frills under his hand. His arms went round her before he knew what he was doing, and they clung together in the darkness, Pharmakos weeping just as freely as Pat.

Leonard, advancing boldly down the cellar stairs now that the danger was over, threw the beam of a small electric torch on them, and was struck speechless by the sight.

"What do you make of that? " he said at length, turning to the villainous Skilly, who stood watching him, grinning from ear to ear. "How's that for a man who's going to be married to-morrow?"

"Orl right as long as yer don't mind 'avin' other folks' cast-offs," said Skilly, bent on doing everything in his power to make bad as worse as possible.

"I mind them very much indeed," said Leonard, switching off his electric torch, and turning on his heel and disappearing.

Suddenly Skilly smelt a spicy odour wafting up from the cellar, and gave half a dozen explosive sneezes one after the other, this recalling Pharmakos to his senses.

Still unable to speak, he took Pat's hand and drew her towards the stairs, and as they stumbled up the slimy stone steps towards the light that shone at the top, they, too, smelt a spicy odour and began to sneeze, Pat with delicate atishoos like a kitten and Pharmakos with a brazen clangour through his mighty beak.

"Good Lord, Pat, what in the world's the matter with us?" he gasped between explosions.

"Pepper, atishoo!" gasped Pat.

"Where from?" demanded Pharmakos, protecting his nose from fresh invasions with a handkerchief. Pat as usual, was handkerchiefless, and went on sneezing.

"Kitchen. Me. I threw it. 'Shoo, 'Shoo, 'Shoo!" gasped Pat.

Pharmakos remembered his casually spoken words that Pat would have to rely on throwing pepper to defend herself if she got into unpleasantness, and realised that her dart upstairs had not been in search of safety, but in search of the big kitchen pepper-pot, and that Jurgens, to judge from the noises he had made, must have received the contents of it fairly in the face. That ought to have put him out of action and rendered him innocuous, but what had become of him?

Pharmakos thrust Pat behind him and pushed on up the stairs hastily. The light shining out through the door revealed the broad back of Skilly, who appeared to be contemplating the dark water of the dock dreamily.

"Where did Jurgens go to?" demanded Pharmakos of his meditating henchman.

Skilly pointed silently to the water.

"Do you mean he took to the water? I thought the boat had cleared out."

"Took to the water? 'E come chargin' out of the door, runnin' blind like a mad dorg, and plopped strite in."

"Did you make any attempt to rescue him?"

"Rescue 'im? Rescue that—? Not 'arf didn't I rescue 'im!

John's AmbIance and the Royal 'Umane wasn't in it wiv me. I fetched 'im one bleeding good kick in the fice as 'e come up and ain't seen 'im since. Wot didjer do to 'im, Cop? You fair took the 'ide off 'im. I never seen a feller in such a mess. 'Is eyes was bunged right up an' 'e couldn't open 'em."

Pat held out the large empty tin in her hand, decorated with a neat label, announcing in Lamprey's laborious handwriting that it had once contained pepper.

Skilly folded up in a gale of laughter. "Lor' love a duck, ain't our Cop a fair knock-out! Wot's it feel like to do a murder, Cop? Tip us the wrinkle, old dear!"

Skilly's words brought to Pat for the first time a realisation of what had happened to Jurgens, and of the part that she herself had played in it, and a sickly sense of horror came over her as she looked at the dark, oily waters of the dock eddying with the tide, and realised what they had sucked down and carried away. She turned to Pharmakos.

"Can't anything be done?" she said huskily.

" 'Oo wants ter do anything?" said Skilly dryly.

Their voices roused Pharmakos from his reverie as he stood gazing at the dark water, trying to realise that the burden of Jurgens had rolled from his shoulders and disappeared beneath its oily surface for ever. He turned and looked at Pat, and saw by her white, horrified face that something was amiss with her.

"What is it? What's the matter, Pat?" he asked, alarmed by her appearance.

"Are you-are you going to let Jurgens drown and do nothing?" she asked.

"Can't do anything, Pat, it's too late, tide's taken him. If Skilly had been a good Samaritan when he first came up—"

"I don't think—" retorted Skilly.

"You're not as used to battle, murder and sudden death

as we are, child. You're in the underworld now, you know. We fight for our own hands here, we don't call in the police to protect us. Jurgens took a gun to me when he thought I was unarmed. I reckon that Skilly did no more than equalise things when he booted him in the face as he came up. A fellow who gets an unarmed man against the light and pots at him can't expect much mercy when the tables are turned. Come along upstairs and I'll give you a cocktail with a drop of brandy in it. I could do with one myself, too. I'm not as fond of this sort of thing as Skilly. Come along upstairs and have a reviver too, Skilly? Not that I think you need it, but just to be matey."

"Never refuse a good offer, Boss," replied the grinning Skilly.

"Come on, then, and we'll have one each all round, and then we must pull ourselves together and go into mourning before the police arrive. It won't do to look too cheerful, or two lugubrious either, or they may think we have had something to do with Jurgens' unhappy end. Skilly, you put a couple of brick-ends in those boots of yours and drop 'em in the river, in case there's hair or blood or something on them where you kicked Jurgens."

The police arrived while cocktails were being partaken of, and were offered their share, but declined, being of different ranks. They had brought their surgeon along with them, hearing there might be a corpse to deal with, and he happened also to be Pharmakos' doctor, and stared in amazement at the change wrought in his patient by the attempt to murder him.

Pat was interested to hear that the name of Jurgens was never mentioned in Pharmakos' account of the tragedy. He identified his assailant as a Mr. Walter Simmons, alias Forrest, whose wife had employed him, via Messrs. Willis and Plunket, the solicitors, of Grays Inn, to knock the bottom out of a bit of perjury he was putting up in her divorce case, thus satisfactorily explaining Jurgen's presence with a revolver on his premises. Two revolver bullets found in the cellar, and the tickling noses of the police officers, confirmed the rest of Pharmakos' story.

They fetched grappling-irons and dragged Pharmakos' private dock, but fished up nothing save a quantity of dead cats and a very dead pig. The tide had taken Jurgens.

CHAPTER XXXI

PAT crept away to her room and went to bed while all the fussing with the police was going on. She was not used to cocktails, and a cocktail to a stomach that has already rejected its supper mayor may not be acceptable. Moreover the cheerful assumption by Skilly that she was the person responsible for Jurgens' horrible death, had been a terrible shock to her, even though his attitude had been congratulatory. He and Pharmakos were used to the underworld, where life is cheap, but she was not, and the kicking in the face of a blinded and drowning man as he struggled to drag himself out of the water, had made an impression on her imagination that could not readily be effaced. The only concern Pharmakos had shown in the matter had been for Skilly's boots.

Skilly was a professional and avowed thug; but Pharmakos himself was only one degree removed from a thug, and only that because he was clever enough to keep out of the reach of the law as a matter of policy. She guessed that it had been touch and go as to which side of the law Pharmakos had found himself when he started in life again after coming out of prison. He must have known he was being introduced to something shady when he had agreed to accompany the ex-burglar to the secluded house hear Hampstead Heath. It was only because the particular type of shadiness that was offered him had happened to catch him on his tender spot that he had declined it.

Pat was completely at the end of her tether, worn out with emotional strain and lack of sleep. She had reached the point when she agreed with Pharmakos that the best thing for her to do was to give up the hopeless struggle and drop into Leonard's arms and let him deposit her in the softly-upholstered cage awaiting her.

She had had just about enough of Pharmakos and his upheavals. He had worn her out. She no longer felt any emotion over him. That was over and dead and done with, and she was thankful. It had been a too disturbing joy while it lasted. The jolly, good-natured, amusing Leonard was better value for the money and would make an infinitely better husband. After all, one had to live with a husband as well as love him, and Pharmakos was not an easy person to live with, as she had found to her cost. The wedding was fixed for ten o'clock to-morrow morning, or, more exactly, that morning, for it had just struck one, and she was prepared to go through with it. She did not realise, any more than Pharmakos had, that a person who is exhausted is incapable of the more strenuous forms of emotion. As we all know, when the Devil was sick, he inclined towards sainthood and sublimation. There had been a brief moment of emotion in Pharmakos' arms in the cellar, dispelled all too quickly by the drifting clouds of pepper, for sneezes and kisses are mutually exclusive. But even so, she never knew where she was with him for two minutes together. He had worn her out, and she had better stick to the steady-going Leonard for the future. Moreover, the casualness of his manner towards her in the presence of the police, when he was very much the employer and she the typist, had hurt her. She did not realise that the more a man cares, the more will he try to cover his tracks, and that her presence in her showy frock in his bachelor abode at that hour of the evening required some explanation. Pharmakos had not attempted to pass her off as his sister to the police. The death of Jurgens on his premises, practically at Pat's hands, was too serious a matter to be played about with. He could have as many mistresses as he liked for all the police cared, but he must not have any pseudo-sisters.

Pat would be thankful when it was all over and she and Leonard had got away. He was taking her to Cromer for the honeymoon, where it would be cool. These sweltering nights when the low tide laid bare the cats in Pharmakos' private dock were hard to bear.

Meanwhile, Pharmakos, having got rid of the police, looked round for Pat. She must have slipped away to her own quarters. Was she all nght? He went quietly down the stone stairs, and Pharmakos could move very quietly when he wished and put his head out of that low, sinister doorway giving on to the wharf to see if there was a light in her room. He was just in time to see the bedroom light switched off, and knew that Pat had retired for the night. And without saying good night to him, either.

Pharmakos was hurt. Surely, after all they had gone through together that evening, she could have said a word to him? Could have given him a chance to thank her for standing by him in the cellar. He owed his life to Pat's courage. Pharmakos had forgotten all about his suicide at the moment, and was very pleased to have his life.

Then there came back to him the memory of Pat in Leonard's arms, or rather, to be precise, Leonard in Pat's arms. That, of course, was the key to Pat's behaviour. She, like himself earlier in the evening, had felt that the less they saw of each other the better, in view of what had been between them. And she was right. And for her sake he was glad; though he himself felt as if he had been dropped back again into an acid-bath that was eating the flesh off his bones.

Now that Jurgens was out of the way there might have been something doing between himself and Pat. But he had seen that kiss she had given Leonard. He was no fool and he had seen something of the world. That was a passionate woman's surrender to the full tide of her passion, if he knew anything of life.

The most probable explanation of the whole situation was that though he had gained Pat's affections, it was the younger man who had roused her instincts. He had better leave it at that. He himself had only got just about enough virility to make him quarrelsome. Pharmakos mixed himself a sleeping draught, switched the light off, and laid his head on the pillow.

SkiIly was astir betimes, which was contrary to his nature, but he expected to have a busy morning. He was to be one of the witnesses at Pat's wedding, and Pharmakos was to be the other, or so he fondly believed. Lamprey was to stop at home and prepare the wedding feast of cake and champagne to which they would return after the ceremony, if that is the right name for the sketchy formalities at the registry office.

Skilly stood looking down at the huddled heap on the bed, and judged that what he had foreseen had duly come to pass, and that Pharmakos' mind was slipping its clutch when it came to the point of seeing Pat married. Old Pharm wouldn't know whether he was standing on his head or his heels, and you could do anything you liked with him.

Skilly made him a cup of tea as a start. Breakfast, he knew, was out of the question. Pharmakos would only start being sick if given anything to eat. Skilly shook his head sorrowfully as he watered the tea. What it was to have innards like that! His own innards consisted of a combination of gizzard and tank and took what was given them and offered no comments. But he had always noticed that fellers with good heads had poor insides. However, Pharmakos could be trusted to sit up in his grave and drink a cup of tea.

Skilly practically had to dress him, keeping a wary eye open all the time for the sudden blow that was liable to come when anything irritated Pharmakos when he was in this state. Skilly had wanted him to be in a fairly dazed condition, but he had not bargained for him being quite as dazed as all this. If he weren't careful, he would never get Pharmakos as far as the registry office.

Presently Pat appeared in her organdie frock, not quite as fresh as it had been since its adventure in the cellar, and with her face heavily plastered with powder in an endeavour to hide the ravages of tears and a sleepless night.

Although Pharmakos was too dazed to take any notice of her, which was perhaps just as well, or there might have been an explosion, he was sufficiently alive to be got on his feet and started off with a push down Sister Anne's passage, for Skilly had no mind to risk his lurching into the dock.

Skilly took hold of Pharmakos by the arm and marched him through the streets as if he were under arrest, which was what Pharmakos probably thought he was, for he went along with a hang-dog air and stubbed his toes on all the irregularities in the pavement because he would not pick up his feet. It galled Pat inexpressibly to see Pharmakos handled like this, with all the manhood gone out of him but what else could one do with him?

Fortunately, they passed no one until they were in the crowded main street, save one solitary telegraph-boy wending his way God knows where.

They were ahead of their time at the registry office, and so Pat was not surprised that Leonard was not there to meet them, and they sat down in the waiting-room and watched the other wedding parties in their finery and buttonholes. The only person who had a buttonhole in their party was Skilly, who owing to his extreme smartness and the look of pleasurable anticipation on his face, was taken by everyone for the bridegroom. Pharmakos had been thrust into his old blue suit by Skilly because it was the first thing that came handy, and did not look at all like a wedding guest. Pat's housewifely eye noted that he had got on a very dirty shirt and a tie like a bootlace, which showed to what depths the natty Pharmakos had fallen.

Skilly sat between Pat and Pharmakos on a long, horse-hair-seated mahogany bench with a wooden back, directly facing the door. He had been at some pains to get that perch, even risking a brawl with a costermongerly gentleman who had also fancied it for himself and his intended. Pharmakos was leaning forward with his elbows on his knees and his head down, contemplating, if anything, his shoes, which Skilly had neglected to clean when preparing him for the wedding, though his own second-best pair shone like an advertisement, his best pair being at the bottom of the Thames. Pat was leaning back with her head against the wall and the organdie hat in her lap, feeling as if she might faint at any moment. Only Skilly was on the alert, looking like an evil but amiable gargoyle.

Presently he rose and thrust his head out of the window which was wide open for ventilation on that sweltering day. On the opposite corner before the ever-open door of the Prince of Wales's Feathers was a little knot of loungers, and not very pleasant-looking loungers either. A shabby old Morris with the hood up stood by the kerb, its engine just ticking over. Anyone coming from the direction of Waterloo and going to the registry office would have to pass right through that knot of loungers. All was quiet at the moment, however, and the loungers were paying no attention to anybody, till one of them, glancing up and seeing Skilly at the window, gave him a wave of the hand; and then all the others looked up and began to laugh, and the man sitting at the wheel of the softly purring car put his head out of the sidescreens that were almost opaque with age and dirt, and laughed too. Although a very unsavoury and dangerous-looking lot, they were apparently in a highly hilarious mood, as if contemplating a practical joke instead of crime for a change.

Skilly returned and took his place on the far side of Pat, and bent over towards her ear.

"Say, Cop," he murmured in a husky whisper, "You ain't nervius, are yer?"

"I don't know, Skilly," said Pat wearily, "I'm feeling beastly faint. Is there any chance of getting a glass of water?"

"Naow, none," said Skilly, hastily. To have Pharmakos muzzy and Pat feeling faint just suited his book nicely.

"Now look 'ere, Cop, don't you worry; just you do as I tell yer, an' I'll pull yer through orl right. I knows all the ropes 'ere. I bin twice to this very registry office meeself, let alone the others."

Pat murmured something that Skilly took for acquiescence, and at that moment the registrar's clerk put his head out of the inner office, recognised Pat, and beckoned the party in. Skilly hauled Pharmakos to his feet, and Pharmakos, accustomed to being pushed about by warders, submitted limply.

"Is your name Patricia Stone?" asked the registrar curtly. He was polishing off couples on that Saturday before August Bank holiday at the rate of one pair every four minutes. It took a smart clerk to keep pace with him.

"Yes," said Pat.

"Is your name Julian Pharmakos?" said the registrar, turning to the gorgeous Skilly, resplendent in his buttonhole.

"Naow," said Skilly contemptuously, "This is 'im," and thrust the hang-dog Pharmakos forward into the centre of the room. The registrar was accustomed to hang-dog bridegrooms and paid no attention to his ghastly appearance. Bridegrooms often looked like that after an eve-of-the-wedding party.

"Sit here, please," said the registrar, indicating two chairs side by side opposite a substantial table. Pat sat down as she was bid, and Skilly dropped Pharmakos into the other chair, all his joints collapsing simultaneously, in the way that Pat now knew-so well. Even the registrar, who had seen all manner of strange symptoms displayed by nervous or reluctant bridegrooms, opened his eyes at the flop with which Pharmakos went down into that chair, and Pat herself was startled out of her misery by his manner of seating himself.

"It's orl right," said Skilly to the registrar in a loud stage whisper, " 'E's just been drinkin' a bit."

The registrar nodded. They were used to that in his district. Bridegrooms frequently disguised the flavour of their brides with alcohol when engaged in making honest women of them. All the registrar wanted was to keep pace with the ever lengthening queue and run the weddings on something like time so that people who had trains to catch could do so, for this was the most popular wedding-day of the year.

He proceeded with his business. The bride answered readily enough, though in so low a voice that he had to keep on asking her to repeat what she said, which was very irritating on that hot day; moreover she was spoiling his average and keeping other couples waiting. Consequently his manner became more and more abrupt and peremptory, and he bustled his clients along regardless of whether they were following the proceedings intelligently or not.

Suddenly he woke up to the fact that there was only one person present beside the happy couple, his clerk and himself.

"Where's your other witness?" he demanded angrily.

" 'E ain't turned up," said the villainous-looking brute who seemed to be acting as best man and prodding the answers out of the drunken wretch of a bridegroom. What a bargain for the girl, who looked miserable enough, in all conscience. He supposed it was one of those compulsory weddings, soon to be followed by a christening.

"You've got to have another witness. Go into the waiting-room, and see if you can get someone to act for you."

Skilly shot through the door and returned in a flash with someone else's bridegroom, bewildered at being separated from his bride, but believing this to be part of the ceremony. Skilly dared not delay for explanations in case either Pat or Pharmakos woke up to what was happening and got out of hand.

The registrar, very angry, started off all over again at a redoubled pace. Suddenly Pat roused and looked round.

"Where's Leonard?" she said.

" 'E ain't turned up," said Skilly, "It's orl right. Pharm's doin' 'is job for 'im."

"Skilly, what do you mean?" exclaimed Pat, half rising to her feet. She had never seen a registry office wedding, and believed that Pharmakos was sitting beside her at the table in order to give her away when the bridegroom appeared, as her father would have done had she been married in a church.

"Come, come my dear young lady, don't get hysterical," snapped the registrar, "You are keeping everybody waiting."

But Pat ignored him and faced Skilly.

"Did you do that thing I asked you to?" she demanded of him.

"Naow," said Skilly, "I left it as you fixed it, cos I thought it was best that wy."

They glared at one another as if they meant to fly at each other's throats, and then the girl suddenly burst out laughing and subsided into her chair.

"Look here, miss, I can't have hysterics here!" rapped out the registrar.

"It's quite all right," said the girl, "I won't treat you to hysterics. Oh, Skilly, you are a devil!"

They got through the ceremony somehow. The bridegroom was so tight that he had forgotten the ring, and a large ornate brass affair had to be got off his own finger to put on the bride's, for whom it was much too large. Pat nearly went off into helpless laughing hysterics when she realised that she was being married to Pharmakos with the Borgia poison-ring.

The registrar, however, did not know what was inside that capsule, nor that Benvenuto Cellini's special alloy, which he worked with his inspired chisel, was not brass off a cheap-jack's barrow. Such rings as that are not often seen on the south bank of the Thames.

Of all the disgraceful weddings he had ever seen, in all his wide experience, this was the most disgraceful, thought the disgusted registrar. The bridegroom was so tight that he could hardly be got to answer to his own name, and when the time came when they had to stand up and announce their intention of taking each other as man and wife, although the bride answered up manfully enough, with, in fact, an emphasis that sounded as if she meant to keep the bridegroom in un-common good order when once he was safely and irrevocably hers, the bridegroom had to be prompted at every word, and if the villainous best man had not suddenly bawled at him to do as he was told and not answer the governor back, at the same time hitting him hard between the shoulders with his clenched fist in a manner that must have hurt him considerably, to judge by his face, though he made no protest, they would never have got through with the wedding. As it was, they took more than treble their fair share of time, and spoilt his record, concerning which he had a bet on with the registrar of another district adjacent to his own. Altogether he was very glad to see the last of them, what with the girl in giggling hysterics and the man blind drunk. Quite the most disgraceful wedding he had ever seen in all his wide experience, thought the registrar.

Skilly shepherded his newly-married pair out of the

gloomy building to be greeted open-eyed and open-mouthed by the little crowd of toughs on the corner, with their car still softly purring beside the kerb. Skilly made the gesture of placing a ring on the third finger of his left hand, and then blew them kisses, and they burst into uproarious mirth, and gave three cheers and waved their hats in the direction of the oblivious Pharmakos, who was heading for home at five miles an hour, with Pat, running to keep up with him.

"Oh, Skilly, Skilly," she gasped, as he caught up with her. "We've been and gone and done it! Whatever will he say?"

" 'E'll sy Gawd bless yer,' orl right, Cop, don't yer worry abart that."

"It was very naughty of you to tell the coroner he was drunk."

"Well, wouldn't you sy 'e was tiddley, to look at 'im?" Skilly pointed to the broad, angular back of Pharmakos, who was gaining on them at every stride and stumbling up and down kerbs without looking where he was going.

"An' it wasn't the coroner I told neither, Cop. Shows wot yore mind's runnin' on."

"But supposing the—the shock of all this makes him ill again?" panted Pat, hurrying for all she was worth to keep Pharmakos in sight.

"It won't, Cop. Don't you bother abart that. It was the worry of not bein' married to yer wot was doin' 'im in. When the doctor kime, 'e sez to me, 'Wot's the matter wiv 'im? 'e sez. Wot's upset the feller?'

" 'Ow do I know wot's the matter wiv 'im? sez I, for I warn't givin' awy nothin', That's wot we sent for you to arst.'

" 'There ain't nothin' the matter wiv' im as fer as I kin see sez' 'e. But all the sime, I think the feller's goin' ter die,' sez 'e.

"Well," sez I, "If there ain't nothin' the matter wiv 'im, I only 'opes I never 'as the 'alf of nothin' the matter wiv me," I sez.

" 'I'm wiv you there,' sez 'e. 'There's a lot o' wyes I'd sooner die 'n 'is wy,' 'e sez, and shot 'im chock full o' morphia, which they don't give awy for nothink nowadyes."

As they approached the great gate of Quilp Cottage, something shadowy moved behind the dirty window-panes of Sister Anne's look-out. Skilly blew it an eloquent kiss, and it vanished.

When they reached Pharmakos' big room, Lamprey, in a very chic white steward's pea-jacket, stood before a gaily decorated table with a freshly opened bottle of champagne in his hand.

"May I congratulate you, sir, madam?" he said politely.

Pharmakos took not the remotest notice of him, but made straight for his usual arm-chair, flung his hat on the floor, and slumped down among the cushions in a heap.

Skilly went after him with a glass of champagne in his hand.

"Come on, guv'ner, yer can't go on like this. Yer got to pull yerself together an' do the perlite."

Pharmakos lifted his head. There was Pat in her organdie dress, and the wedding cake and the flowers and the champagne on the table as he had ordered. He must pull himself together and give the child a decent send-off. He took a firm grip on himself, rose from his chair, took the glass of champagne from Skilly's hand, and came towards the table, his eyes on Pat.

"We must drink the health of the bride and bridegroom," he said in a flat, toneless voice. "But where's the bridegroom? We can't drink his health in his absence," and he looked round for Leonard. .

"This came for you after you 'ad left, sir," said Lamprey, producing an orange envelope that looked slightly sodden, as if it had been subjected to the influences of steam. Pharmakos set down his glass and tore it open, easily distracted as he always was when under the weather.

"What's all this about?" he demanded of Pat, as if she ought to know. " 'Sorry cannot, proceed with marriage. Kindly tell Miss Stone. Matthews.' What's all this about? Has old Mrs. Matthews cut up rusty? And if so, what's it got to do with her?"

"Now this is where we makes a tackful exit," said Skilly. "Come on, Lamp." And off he marched, a glass of champagne in one hand and a large wedge of wedding cake in the other with Lamprey trailing meekly behind him, quietly clutching a newly opened bottle of champagne to his bosom. Which was typical of the way they went through life; Skilly swaggering along with a half-filled glass provocatively displayed, and Lamprey skulking behind with a full bottle tucked under his coat.

"What's all this about, Pat?" demanded Pharmakos again, leaning unsteadily against the table, champagne glass in one hand and the telegraph form in the other.

"Come and sit down," said Pat, "I want to talk to you," and taking him by the elbow, she guided him across the wide floor to his big chair once more. He dropped into it, spilling half the champagne, and stared at the glass in his hand as if he had never seen it before. Then seemed to realise what it was meant for, and tossed down the rest at one gulp as if it were medicine. Champagne acts quickly on the empty stomach of an abstemious man, and Pharmakos' face showed its effects almost immediately. He looked sharply at Pat, and saw that she was shaking like a leaf.

"What's the matter, Pat?" he demanded, "And where's Leonard?"

Pat felt her knees giving way under her, and dropped down in a little heap on the floor beside him and put her head on his knee.

He laid his hand gently on the bright, soft hair.

"What is it, Patsie? What has upset you?"

He could feel her shaking violently. He bent down and put his arm round her. Even if she were now another man's wife, he could not have this. Through the thin organdie he could feel Pat's heart going like a captured bird's. He waited a little, to see if she would quiet down, but instead her heart began to miss beats, and he knew she would be fainting soon if she were not tactfully handled.

"Can't you tell me what the trouble is, darling, and let me help you? You know I'll stand by you through any mortal thing, don't you, Pat?"

Leonard was completely forgotten now, and Pharmakos held her very close to him with one hand and caressed her bright hair with the other.

A muffled voice came from underneath his coat.

"I've got something to tell you, which I think will be all right in the end, but which is very difficult to say."

He waited without speaking, knowing that it was the best way to get her going.

"I think I had better tell you how it came about, and then maybe you'll understand a little better, and it doesn't sound quite so awful."

Pat buried her nose in his waistcoat pocket, and her voice became even more muffled.

Pharmakos wondered what on earth was coming.

"You remember when you sent me round to get the special licence?"

Pharmakos took his hand off her head as if it had burnt him. He had remembered Leonard.

"Yes?" he said curtly.

"Well, I made an awful mistake. I gave the wrong name. I gave yours in mistake for Leonard's. And then I asked Skilly to go round and put things right, and he muddled it up worse than ever, and—and then Leonard wasn't there, I don't know why. And—and oh, Julian, I did an awful thing. I simply couldn't help it. I let the registrar marry me to you, and you never noticed it because you were feeling so rotten."

Pharmakos heard this amazing confession with such complete bewilderment that his hand dropped limply back on to Pat's head and lay there. He could feel her panting against his knee as if she had been running. What could he say? Before his eyes there was the picture of Pat kissing Leonard.

"I'm sorry you've been let down, Pat," he managed to say at length.

Pat did not answer, but got up and walked away, and stood at the window with her back to him.

Pharmakos walked over to the table and poured himself out another glass of champagne and tossed it down, and the devil entered into him along with the champagne. After all, he had always wanted Pat. Why should he refuse the good things the gods offered him?

He walked across the big room to where Pat was standing, stared blindly at the river, put his arm round her waist, and kissed her roughly.

"I'm sorry I'm not Leonard," he said, "But I'll do the best I can."

Pat twisted round in his arms and gazed up at his face. He looked very evil at that moment.

With the making of her confession Pat's nerve returned to her, and she saw that she had got her crazy child on her hands again, and that she must handle him very carefully if their life together was not to be wrecked at the outset.

But there was something in Pharmakos' action that had given her a clue to the trouble. He had taken hold of her in exactly the same way that Leonard had done that evening, and he had exactly repeated Leonard's action.

His big hands were gripping her soft-fleshed upper arms, the hands that had been strengthened and coarsened by pick and shovel, and his finger-nails were cutting into her, and he was looking at her as if he hated her. She must keep her head, or there would be trouble, and bad trouble.

"Shall we sit down?" she said, striving to steady her voice.

He dropped down on the window-seat without waiting for her to seat herself, and glared at her savagely. It amused him to see that his finger-marks were showing up scarlet on Pat's soft, bare arms. He supposed they would be showing up black by the next morning, and that amused him still more. The idea suddenly occurred to him that he might pitch Pat head first through the glass into the river. Then she spoke, standing up before him with her hands behind her as if she were saying her piece at a Sunday-school treat.

"There are lots of things you don't understand Julian, and I'm one of them."

"That's quite likely," said Pharmakos, "Mind if I smoke?" and he got out a cigarette, furious to find his hands were trembling so that he could hardly light it.

"You don't understand why it was that I gave your name instead of Leonard's at the registrar's, do you?"

"I certainly don't, but I have no doubt you had an excellent reason," said Pharmakos.

Things were going to be even worse than she expected, thought poor Pat, and God knows she had expected them to be bad enough.

She struggled on, looking him straight in the eyes.

"I gave your name accidentally, because—because I happened to be thinking of you just then, and—wishing it wasn't Leonard I was getting the licence for."

Pharmakos sat motionless, cigarette in one hand and lighted match in the other, till it burnt his fingers, and he threw it away with an oath.

"Can you understand why I did that?"

"Not quite, Pat."

"Well, you see, I had made up my mind that you really meant it when you said you didn't want me—"

"I never said that. I said I couldn't marry you."

"And—and I had made up my mind that I must go through with it with Leonard in order to leave you free to get away from Jurgens. But, oh, Julian, I didn't want to! And when I went to the registrar's, I was thinking about you, and thinking and thinking about you, and your name slipped out without my meaning it to, not because I meant to give it, for honestly, Julian, I meant to go through with Leonard, but because—because—Oh, I don't know—because I just couldn't help it."

Still Pharmakos did not speak, but sat looking at her under level brows.

"And then I asked Skilly to go round and put things right, and he just laughed at me. And—Oh, Skilly is a devil! He said he would, but he never did. And I didn't know how they did things at a registry wedding, and Skilly put you into the proper chair, and—the registrar went and married us."

"And at what point in the proceedings did you tumble to what was happening, Pat?"

"Oh, about half-way through."

"And what did you do when you realised?"

"Went through with it," said Pat, sticking out her chin defiantly.

Pharmakos struck another match, and laboriously lit his cigarette.

"Well, Pat," he said, "You have paid me a very great compliment. No one would kidnap me in the way you have done who did not really desire my company, and I am much obliged to you, but I can't get it out of my head that you would have preferred Leonard if you could have got him."

"You are wrong," said Pat, scowling at him.

Pharmakos suddenly lunged forward and caught her by the wrist, his powerful fingers nearly breaking the bones. "I saw you kiss him, Pat! No one would have kissed a man like that who did not love him."

"You bloody fool!" said Pat, "I was trying to imagine he was you!"

Pharmakos looked at her dazedly. "What do you mean?"

Pat flung herself into his arms; drew two or three gasping breaths, squeezed her eyes tight, and succeeded in bursting into floods of tears.

Pharmakos' battered mind worked slowly, trying to take in the meaning of Pat's words. Slowly the real significance of the scene he had witnessed dawned on him, and the even deeper significance of Pat's slip of the tongue; and the picture of Pat embracing Leonard, that had seemed seared on his brain, was replaced by the picture of Pat standing at his side in the dark cellar, facing Jurgens' gun for his sake.

His arms tightened about her. A faint squeak came from Pat and she snuggled up to him.

He bent over her until his cheek rested upon her hair.

"Pat, my darling, I would never have married you of my own free will, because I care too much for you to want to hurt you. But you have gone and done it, my dear. You know what sort of chap I am, and you know how I am placed—Oh, my dear, what is the use of talking? We couldn't help it, either of us, could we?"

Skilly strolled into the big room between ten and eleven the following morning to see if there were any signs of breakfast. Pat and Pharmakos were still sound asleep. He noticed the bruises on Pat's bare arms, and grinned happily.

"Blessed little love-birds!" he murmured beaming down on them for a black eye is as good as a wedding ring in the

Borough. Then he went over to the flower-decorated table and finished off the remains of the flat champagne with gusto, for he was one of those who judge a wine by its effect on the head not the palate, and esteem it in proportion to the manner in which it makes the former swim without actually corroding the latter.

CHAPTER XXXII

THERE was a certain doctor who practiced in the insalubrious districts to the south side of the Thames who had read sufficiently widely to have heard of the couvade—that curious practice whereby certain primitive peoples put the husband to bed and tend him while the wife is giving birth. When he was called up to a certain red-headed young woman, who was unexpectedly brought to bed of her first, having miscalculated her dates, as women will with their first, he saw the couvade for himself, and heartily wished she had had the expensive specialist who had arranged to attend her.

Fortunately for all concerned, the young woman could fend for herself, so he left her and the charwoman to get on with it, and attended to the husband, with the help of an ex-bruiser, who needed all his ring-craft before he had finished.

Luckily for all concerned, the lady was expeditious, and took her labour philosophically, which was not surprising considering the kind of husband she had got; even her first confinement would be taken in her stride by a girl who was used to that kind of husband. After the baby was born, father and mother rested together on the enormous divan in the enormous room, and the little mother was the fresher of the two.

Pat flatly declined to have a professional nurse resident in Quilp Cottage; she felt certain it would not be a success. Pharmakos had got thoroughly upheaved over the birth. It was a blessed mercy it had come off unexpectedly, when he still thought he had got a month ahead of him. Pharmakos had got all his eggs in one basket, and any risk to that basket he took hard. Pat was quite content with Mrs. Mullins, who had been handy woman to innumerable neighbours, and was blessed with "God's own common sense, which is more than knowledge!"—a thing that the best of trainings cannot inculcate if it is not there. Lamprey also was exceedingly handy with a baby. Skilly, however, had no ideas on the subject, save that an infant could be entertained by pulling faces at it. Fortunately, Pat's infant was as yet too young to notice.

The thing that surprised Pat about her baby was that although she and Pharrnakos were both red-headed, it was born with a thick thatch of black hair, comparatively coarse. She supposed it must owe this to her unknown father. At present its eyes were the indefinite baby blue that told nothing of its future complexion.

It was not until the baby was thirty-six hours old that Pharmakos suddenly demanded of her, "Patsie, is it a boy or a girl? I believe they told me, but I did not take it in."

He had been so concerned over Pat that he neither knew or cared anything about the baby. Pat was slightly indignant. After all the effort she had made to bring it into the world, she thought it merited more attention than it had received from a father who had forgotten its sex and would have forgotten its very existence, so concerned was he with its mother, if it had not been well equipped in the matter of a voice. Pharmakos had had many doubts of himself as a father, but its first yell had dispelled them.

"He's a little son, Julian, and I wish you wouldn't call him it, because I don't like it."

"That's odd," said Pharmakos, staring at the baby's black head thoughtfully. Pat did not think it was particularly odd; in fact it was a fifty-fifty chance.

"What's odd?" she demanded indignantly. Her baby was not in the least odd. Both the doctor and Mrs. Mullins had said they had never seen a finer.

"I think I shall go out for a bit of fresh air," said Pharmakos, rising and stretching his long legs, "You ought to be having a snooze. Mrs. Mullins will wring my neck if I hang about any longer. And I may as well get the baby registered while I am about it. Have you quite made up your mind about the name? Is it to be Julian John?"

"Yes," said Pat, "I don't think we shall do better than that, do you?"

"That's what I should like for him, Pat. The Julian perpetuates my old aunt to another generation, and the John after old Saunders. I stick by the people who stick by me, Pat, and to Hell with the rest of 'em."

If Pharmakos had gone straight to his destination at the registrar's he would not have had far to go; but instead he crossed the river to the Embankment, and strolled slowly along, deep in thought. He found it difficult to understand the effect on him of the realisation that Pat's child was a son. He had enrolled under the banner of Ishmael wholeheartedly, and never looked behind him once he had got over the shock of his penniless and friendless return to freedom. If he ever thought of his father and elder brother at all, it was with a smouldering bitterness; he had no wish whatever to return to the big house in Berkeley Square; the only thing that ever pulled at his heart was the old castle on the banks of the Severn where his forbears had been reared for so many generations. The only kin he had ever felt a care for were the old grandfather and the little maiden aunt, now sleeping in the churchyard under the castle walls.

He wondered what his grandfather would have had to say about the birth of Pat's black-haired boy. It would have been little better than a bomb in the family party, he thought, for he felt pretty certain his grandfather's sympathies would have been with his child, not with Aneurin's offspring, and jealousies would have blazed fiercely, as ever. The old man had had a fine strain of the unregenerate Adam in him, and would have delighted in annoying the unpopular party by a blatant display of partiality.

Pharmakos wondered what kids Aneurin's wife had had by now. He called to mind his grandfather's prophecy that Aneurin would never make old bones. Well, as long as he had managed to produce a son, that wouldn't matter very much, only he hoped to God a sickly strain had not been introduced into the stock.

But what was he bothering his head about that for? What did it matter to him whether the stock degenerated or not? Let Aneurin marry a mulatto if he wanted to, and have black and tan kids. It was no concern of his. He had done with the lot of them as completely as they had done with him.

But somehow, now his family had come into his mind, he could not get it out again, and he crossed the river once more, and made his way to Lambeth Public Library, and there surprised the librarian by demanding a Debrett.

Debretts are not much in demand on that side of the river. However, they knocked the dust off it, and gave it to him, watching him as he flicked the pages over with a cynical smile on his face, for he was wondering how many pups his brother had had by now, and out of idle curiosity was looking to see.

But they saw a sudden change of expression come over the tall, lean man, with the indefinable thoroughbred look about him, for he had discovered that the Christian name of a certain viscount was given as Julian and not Aneurin, and that he was the last of his line. Pharmakos closed the Debrett and handed it back to the librarian and went away without a word.

This discovery put an extraordinarily different complexion on matters to that which they had worn that morning. The realisation that Pat's child was a boy had sent his mind back over old memories. Race is a very strong thing, and dies hard, and Pharmakos discovered to his surprise that it was by no means as dead in him as he believed it to be.

Since Aneurin's name did not appear in Debrett, and as he himself was listed as his father's heir, then his brother must have died without issue, and his grandfather's prophecy had come true; the tuberculous Aneurin had made neither old bones or new blood. And there was that mite curled up in Pat's arms, throwing as true to type as a prize pig. Race was a very strong thing.

His father Pharmakos hated as only the unloved child can hate the parent who has been unfair to him; but his fierce old red-headed grandfather had been his hero and ideal. And how his grandfather had loved the old name and the old home! It would have broken the old boy's heart if he had thought his favourite grandson had proved faithless to them. The old boy would have loved his spirited, peppery Pat, too, he was sure of that. Just the sort he would have admired just as he had despised his son's die-away, ash-blonde, tubercular bride. His own mother, too, whom his grandfather had always been fond of, even after her weakness began to show itself, must have been the same sort of warm-hearted, spirited girl as Pat was, before an unhappy marriage had started her drinking. Pharmakos wondered how Pat would have turned out had she gone through with her marriage to Leonard. He did not think that Pat would have taken to drink; she was too sound stuff for that; but Leonard might have!

Now what was he going to do about his little son? An odd thought, that. He couldn't get used to it—that he had a son. That he was a link in the endless chain of race, and that this black-haired mite in Pat's arms connected through his red-haired self, and his black-haired father, with his red-haired old grandfather, and a black-haired great-grandfather. It was odd how they threw alternately red and black, like a pack of cards. Odder still, his grandfather was so convinced of this regularity of the alternate red and black that he had based upon it his prophecy that Aneurin would never succeed to the title, and had had a terrible row with his son for christening his first born Aneurin at all, for the old Welsh name was a heritage received from the first holder of the title, who had been a Lord of the Marches and solved the problem of keeping the king's peace in his particular district by marrying the local chieftain's daughter and calling his first born after him. The eldest son of the eldest son was always called Aneurin to perpetuate the memory of the famous Welsh ancestor who played so important a part in founding the family fortunes, and as the stock was a very tough one, the black and red Aneurins had come down in an almost unbroken line save when war or pestilence had intervened and spoilt the record for a generation; and it was maintained that they held the record for direct descent of a title from father to son or grandson, without having to fall back on collateral branches. The Welsh ancestor must have been a virile old gentleman.

All this Pharmakos turned over in his mind as he leant on the parapet of London Bridge, watching the shipping in the Pool, when he heard a voice behind him saying:

"Might I be permitted to enquire after the health of my daughter, Mr. Pharmakos?"

Pharmakos turned round and beheld the narrow, sallow face of Pat's putative father.

"My wife is as well as can be expected, considering that she gave birth to a son the night before last, and it won't be called after you, either, Mr. Stone. Good afternoon." And he turned back to the contemplation of the river, which, muddy as it was at the turn of the ebb, was much less muddy than Mr. Stone's complexion.

For some odd reason, the encounter with Mr. Stone crystalised the resolution that not even his loyalty to his grandfather had been able to enforce. His beloved Pat should have the pleasure of using her small snub nose to cock snooks at the despicable Stones, who should find that in despising and rejecting her they had backed the wrong horse. He turned on his heel and went off to the town hall; but Pat's little son was not registered as Julian John, as arranged, but as Aneurin John; neither was his surname given as Pharmakos.

This formality concluded, Pharmakos boarded a bus that would take him down the Strand, only to find that in the excitement of the arrival of his son and heir he had forgotten to change over the contents of his pockets from the suit that Skilly had torn to rags on the night of the birth. Consequently he was ignominiously put off the bus by the conductor. But so set was he on the idea that was in his head, that he started out to walk to his destination, which was the office of a firm of solicitors that was so dingy, be-lumbered, and generally unsuitable for the transaction of business that it could only have belonged to a firm of the highest repute, with a clientele of the bluest blood.

When he walked into the office as if he knew his way, he was received with indignant coolness by a generation of young clerks that knew not Joseph; but a certain old, white-haired managing clerk rose up and stared at him, speechless and open-mouthed, looking as if about to bolt, for Pharmakos reputation in that office was sinister.

Pharmakos demanded the senior partner in a voice that would have caused the old clerk to fetch him the Devil from Hell. The senior partner was interrupted, though busy with a client, and came out of-his private office into the outer one rather than run the risk of keeping such a visitor waiting.

"This is an unexpected pleasure," he exclaimed with a nervous, forced cordiality. It is not easy to meet a client after he has heard you being informed by a Lord Chief Justice that you have messed up his case about as thoroughly as a case could be messed up, and that it is no thanks to you that he isn't going to be hanged.

"It is a pleasure you could hardly expect to enjoy very frequently," said Pharmakos grimly, "I like efficiency."

A most offensive remark to make in front of the clerks; but the fellow was as big as a grenadier, and no doubt had, the temper of all the rest of the red-headed portion of his family, and was actually leaning up against the very desk that had been used by the poor old chap—but it was better not to think about that. The best thing to do was to get him out of the office as quietly as possible, even if it did mean letting him have a little money, and then to warn his father that he was about again.

"I have come for my grandmother's jewellery," said Pharmakos, looking down from his great height on the tubby, pompous little man as if he were having his boots blacked by him.

"You know the terms of your grandfather's will, Mr. Julian? that the jewels are for the viscountess after she has born an heir?"

"Yes, I do, and I'll thank you to call me by my proper name."

"You have a son, born in lawful wedlock?"

"Yes, damn your eyes," said Pharmakos, and the office gasped, and it suddenly dawned upon the older clerks that this must be the man who—but nobody dared actually to voice it, but only to exchange significant glances.

"Have you got the birth certificate?" said Mr. Hallett frostily, determined to have his pound of flesh anyway, and as much blood as would come with it. He was not used to being sworn at.

Pharmakos opened his pocket-book and took out the all important little slip of paper and handed it to him.

"And your marriage certificate?"

Pharmakos handed it to him also. They like to see that in the Borough before they will register a child as legitimate, and he had still got it on him.

"It docsn't say who her father is," said Mr. Hallett triumphantly.

Pharmakos told him who his own father was, and what; and something also of the habits of his mother and female ancestors for several generations; and what his own matrimonial tastes were like, and where he would go in the afterlife, and why. The office listened aghast. They expected to see their Mr. Hallett go up in flames. Pharmakos was not a good person to try and score off because he had no scruples.

Mr. Hallett turned sullenly to the old clerk who was wilting at his elbow.

"Get them, will you?" he said, handing him a bunch of keys.

The old clerk disappeared into an inner chamber and returned in a few minutes with a black morocco case like a young portmanteau.

"Will you kindly sign a receipt for it?" said Mr. Hallett severely.

Pharmakos did so, but marked it "Unexamined" as if it had been a package from Carter Paterson.

"I should be glad if you would wrap it in brown paper," he said, when the formalities of handing over were concluded.

The office were nonplussed. They hadn't got any brown paper. So Pharmakos had to be content with newspaper, held together with pink tape.

Once out of the office, he made his way towards the Law Courts. He did not want to carry the heavy steel-lined case all the way back to Quilp Cottage on foot. He wanted to find a pal, and borrow the price of a bus-fare. He put his head inside a certain door, and there found the expected pal, and with thirty thousand pounds' worth of heirlooms under his arm, borrowed tuppence off a policeman.

Pat had had a good sleep and was very wide awake, and so was the baby, for the moment, though being very young, he did not remain wide awake long. As soon as he had settled down to his slumbers again, Pharmakos opened the black morocco case and revealed its contents to Pat.

"Oh, I say, aren't they lovely! " she exclaimed, "Did you get these on appro? Am I to choose something?"

"You can have the lot if you like, Pat," said Pharmakos, watching her and noting that she was pleased but unimpressed. "Where do you suppose they came from?"

"The Burma? Or possibly Ciro's?" she breathed the latter name with awe. Helen had had a string of pearls from them that had cost two guineas. It never entered her head that this profusion of enormous stones could be real.

"The pearls are Ciro's, aren't they, Julian?"

"I am afraid not, Pat. They are only oyster's, and secondhand at that."

"Well, they are very pretty, anyway," said Pat, trying the set of a royal gift around her neck.

CHAPTER XXXIII

NOW Pharmakos had known that things would begin to move after he had visited the solicitors', but he had not thought they would move as quickly as they did. Mr. Hallett, being thoroughly upset by the treatment he had received and the language that had been used to him in front of his clerks, sought to soothe himself with such revenge as might be obtained by being vindictive over the telephone. So he had rung up a certain number in Berkeley Square, and adopting that tone of sorrow rather than anger which is much more effective when you want to damage someone than out-and-out resentment, had passed on the news that the black sheep had turned up and was out for mischief, advising that the butler be warned not to admit him. He made the mistake however, of passing on the address he had seen on the birth certificate.

But he had misjudged his man. To the weary old man in the big, book-lined room in Berkeley Square, race was a stronger thing than considerations of personal convenience or dignity, and the news that an heir had been born to his heir overbore all other considerations, and he rose from his desk, where he had been listening to the mixture of vitriol and soft soap that was coming out of the telephone, and unlocked a safe, and took out a morocco leather case. Then he rang for the butler and gave instructions that the contents of the case should be cleaned and the car ordered.

The butler was nearly as old as his master, and had served the family man and boy since he was fastened into his first suit of buttons, and he knew that bowl and its significance.

"Might I ask, my lord," he enquired, "Whether this means there has been a happy event in the family?"

"Yes, Watkins, Mr. Julian has a son."

"Mr.-er-Julian, my lord?" said the old man uncomfortably. This was not the way the heir should be referred to, but the old earl found it hard to transfer the familiar name from the apple of his eye to the black sheep.

Pat was still playing with the family jewels when Skilly put his head in at the kitchen door.

"There's an old guy with a Dymler art side, and 'e wants ter see yer."

Pharmakos had a shrewd notion who the old guy would prove to be, though he had not expected a personal call, but rather formal communications through their mutual solicitors. This somewhat complicated matters, especially as Pat's baby had arrived so recently, and he did not want her to be excited or upset, well though she was. But there was a perverse demon in Pharmakos, and he could not resist the pleasure of watching his father's face when he saw his grandson for the first time, the grandson who was defrauding Aneurin's unborn sons of their heritage.

"Bring him along," he said grimly.

"Where will you see him?" asked Pat anxiously. It was hardly fitting to interview clients alongside her bed.

"In here. It's all right. Bring him along," said Pharmakos, not vouchsafing any other explanation.

So the old man was led along Sister Anne's dusty passage and into the big room via the kitchen, Skilly thinking that anyone who arrived in a Daimler would be the better for a back-door entry.

Pat had guessed that the visitor must be someone Pharmakos knew well since he was-being received so unceremoniously, but she had not expected Pharmakos to stand with his feet apart and his hands behind his back, grimly surveying the newcomer without uttering a word.

He was obviously receiving an enemy. But the old man did not behave as if he were an enemy, but stood looking at Pharmakos rather pathetically clutching a black morocco case under his arm as if he had brought a present. Fortunately the baby had the social sense to wake up and begin to squeal.

"I suppose this is what you have come to see?" said Pharmakos, indicating his son with a wave of his big navvy's hand.

"Yes," said the old man, "I have, and I have brought him this."

He opened the morocco case he was carrying, and laid upon Pat's lap a small silver bowl of antique, almost primitive workmanship.

"Oh, how lovely!" exclaimed Pat, who had an instinctive appreciation of beautiful things. "Why, it is two bowls, one inside the other. How curious!"

"Yes, my dear," said the old man, "The inner bowl, the original one, had grown so thin that it had to be placed inside a kind of framework to hold it together. For you see, my child, this is not a museum specimen, but something that has been in daily use for a great many years."

"What is it used for?" demanded Pat.

"It is a child's porringer, my dear. It has always been used by the eldest son of the eldest son in our family. I used it, and my father used it, and my eldest boy used it; and now, my dear, it is the turn of your boy."

Pat looked questioningly at Pharmakos, but he would not open his mouth, though she could see that he was deeply moved as he gazed at the bowl. Half the nursery rows had taken place because he was never allowed to touch the sacred silver porringer, reserved for the bread and milk of the heir.

And now it was being offered for the use of his own son by the father who had disliked and neglected him. The wheel had indeed swung full circle.

Pat was racking her brains to imagine who the old man could be. She did not think he could be a relative, because there was no family likeness between him and Pharmakos. Then she noticed a curious thing, a little fluted convolution in the lobe of his ear, the exact twin of one that had puzzled her in the lobe of her baby's ear, and she guessed the solution to the riddle. Pharmakos had said that they threw red and black alternately in his family, like a pack of cards. It was this old man's grandson she was holding in her arms.

She was torn two ways. She knew the story of his treatment of Pharmakos, and bitterly resented it for his sake. But the old man was looking at her so pathetically, as if silently begging her to turn aside his son's wrath and help make things right, that she could not resist him.

She held out the little bundle in her arms towards him.

"Will you please bless my baby?" she said.

The old man took the child in his arms, and the tears began to overflow on to his wrinkled cheeks. He pushed back the wrappings and examined the ear.

"You can say what you like, Julian," he said triumphantly, "but he is a black de Claire."

Julian did not choose to say anything, but turned away to the window with his hands in his pockets.

The old man looked helplessly at Pat, and she smiled at him to encourage him. Julian really ought not to be treating his father like this, whatever he had done, and especially if he were disposed to take an interest in the baby.

He sat down on the edge of the bed. There was nowhere else for him to sit, for Pharmakos had neglected to offer him a chair.

"So you are amusing yourself with these, my child? " he

said, turning over the scattered jewellery with his forefinger. "Has your husband told you their history?"

"No," said Pat, "He did not say where they came from. We have only got them on appro."

"No, my dear," said the old man, smiling, "These are not on appro. These are family jewels, and one of these days you will be handing them over to this little fellow's wife."

He looked at his daughter-in-law curiously, and it suddenly occurred to him that she only knew an assumed name.

"You know who I am, my dear? " he said.

"You are Julian's father, aren't you?"

"Yes. Do you know what my name is?"

"No, he has never told me what his real name is."

"Our family name is de Claire. This little fellow's name is de Claire and he ought to be christened Aneurin. You must try and get Julian to have him christened Aneurin. The name has been in the family so long that it would be a thousand pities if the record were broken. My eldest son, the boy I lost, was called Aneurin. And now that he is gone, your child is in the direct line."

"I will see what I can do," said Pat, mystified but thrilled.

"And what was your name before your marriage?" continued the old man.

"1 don't know. I am illegitimate."

Her father-in-law looked at her curiously for a moment, and then his face suddenly wrinkled into a smile that made him look just like Julian in one of his mischievous moods.

"It is better to be illegitimate than commonplace, my dear," he said.

He bent down and picked up a cabochon emerald off the floor. "Don't lose these baubles, my child, they did not come from Woolworth's."

He pulled upon a drawer in the base of the jewel-case.

"Here is a pretty toy for you," he said, and drew out a miniature diamond crown, a countess's coronet.

"It is very pretty indeed," said Pat, politely, "But I do not think I shall choose that one. It would be no use to me. You see, we don't go to dances much."

The old man seemed very much amused, and Pat concluded uncomfortably that she had dropped a brick of some sort, and looked anxiously at Julian's broad back in the window and wished he would turn round and take his part in the conversation.

"Do you know your own name, my dear?" continued the old man, making Pat feel as if she were expected to know her catechism.

"Julian always calls himself Pharmakos."

"Pharmakos? Whatever made him call himself that? It means a drug, doesn't it? They didn't teach me much at school, but they taught me enough to know that. Whatever does Julian call himself a drug for?"

"It is not a drug. That is pharmakon. It means a scapegoat. Someone who was taken outside the city gate and sacrificed so that the city might be saved."

There was a very strange expression on the old man's face, and he looked up and saw that Julian was standing over him.

"A very suitable name, don't you think?" his son was saying.

"We have all done things we have regretted, Julian," said the old man.

"Unquestionably," said Pharmakos, "But only fools give a person the opportunity to do something he may regret twice."

The old man rose. "Perhaps I had better be going," he said. He turned to Pat, "Good-bye, my dear. You will be very welcome any time you care to come to Caerleon." He bent down and kissed the baby, and Pat put her arm round his neck and kissed him.

"You oughtn't to have treated him like that, Julian," she said, as soon as the door had closed behind the old man, "He wanted to make things right, and it was a beastly shame to refuse to make friends."

"Can't help it, Pat," said Pharmakos, "My immortal soul is addled within me where he is concerned."

The old man had hardly departed when another visitor appeared unannounced. Pharmakos was rather annoyed. He thought Pat had had enough excitement for one afternoon, but Inspector Saunders was not a visitor to whom he could very well deny himself. He soon discovered, however, that the visit was not an official one, nor yet one of congratulation on the arrival of an heir, whom he was very surprised to see, having entirely forgotten that one was expected, to Pat's great disgust, who thought that the whole universe centred round her baby.

The old detective looked strangely deflated; all his air of bland but overwhelming authority had gone from him. He was in need of consolation, and soon made his need known.

"Well, sir," he said, "It's come at last. I've got to go."

"Why, what's up, Saunders?" asked Pharmakos, "Where have you got to go?"

"I've not got to go anywhere," said the detective mournfully.

"I've got to go from the Yard. Time's up. Got to take my pension."

"Hard luck, old chap," said Pharmakos, "But you'll soon find some new interests. Take up golf, or gardening."

The plain-clothes man shook his head sadly.

"Thirty years I've been at the Yard," he said, "And I don't know no other life. I'd take to crime myself, for two twos, the way I feel at the moment."

Pharmakos changed the conversation, and the melancholy policeman made an effort to pull himself together.

"I seen your Pa as I come along here," he said. "He been calling?"

"What do you know about my father?" demanded Pharmakos, cocking his head indignantly.

"You don't suppose we got you listed at the Yard as J. Pharmakos, do you, sir?" said Saunders. "I suppose it's the baby brought him. But you got a brother, ain't you?"

"Had one, but he conked out," said Pharmakos curtly.

"Lor!" said Saunders, "Then you come in for the coronet?"

"I suppose so," said Pharmakos sulkily, "But it's no use to me. You can have it second-hand if you like."

"No use to me either," said Saunders, "I wear a bowler."

Silence fell between them for a period as they both meditated on their unwanted promotions, and Pat tried to picture herself in a coronet.

Finally Saunders broke the silence. "Now I'd made sure you'd retire," he said.

"I don't want to retire any more than you do," said Pharmakos, "Everything else would seem damned flat after hunting your fellow-man. All the same, I'm darned bothered what to do, on account of the little chap," and he indicated Pat's baby with a wave of his cigarette. Pat pricked up her ears. Perhaps she would wear that coronet after all. She was sure it would suit her. After all, why have a coronet and not wear it?

"Well, sir, if you ask me, I should say there is a better future in high-class, scientific detection than in bein' an earl," said Saunders. "But I suppose it's only natural to hanker after the flesh-pots of Egypt when you've once had your snout in them."

"I don't hanker after them for myself," said Pharmakos.

"But what about the kid? Aren't I taking the silver spoon out of his mouth, so to speak? "

"There's that to be thought of," said Saunders, "And what does the young lady say about it?"

He winked at Pat, who winked back shamelessly and nodded at him to use his influence in favour of coronets.

"What you ought to do," said Saunders, "Is to make the best of both worlds. What you want is the right sort of manager. A good, sound, experienced chap, not too young so as to be flighty, what you could trust to look after your interests while you was at the Derby." He winked at Pat again. It was her turn now. If he helped her to a coronet, she ought to help him to a job.

"Oh, Julian!" exclaimed Pat, "Wouldn't that be wonderful! Isn't that just what you have often said you needed?"

Pharmakos looked at the detective thoughtfully.

"Saunders," he said, "Did you square my father, or did my father square you?"

Saunders grinned nervously. "Neither the one nor the other, sir. It's just providential, that's all."

"Then in that case," said Pharmakos, "We had better not fly in the face of providence. There's only one man in the world I have ever thought of for the job, but I thought you had another ten years to go. You don't look anything like retiring age. But what do you say to a partnership, Saunders?"

"Well, reely, sir, I'd never thought of that. Me in partnership with the likes of you? Would it work?"

"You ought to know, Saunders; you've had me as a case."

"I ain't never had to run you in, sir. You never know what a feller's reely like until you do that."

"I don't wear a coronet in private life any more than you wear a helmet," said Pharmakos. "We've always met man to man so far, and I don't see why we shouldn't go on doing so. You never rubbed it in when you had the upper hand, so why should I?"

"Well" sir," said Saunders, "If that's how you look at it, I'd like fine to join up with you." And the old detective looked so absolutely blissful at the prospect of hunting his fellowman once more that Pat got the giggles and woke the baby.

THE END

Printed in Great Britain
by Amazon